DEAD IN
THE WATER

Also by Aline Templeton

ALINE TEMPLETON

DEAD IN THE WATER

To Aga
Thank you so much for
your help with this book.
I hope I haven't made any
mistakes!
With best wishes,
Aline Templeton.

HODDER &
STOUGHTON

First published in Great Britain in 2009 by Hodder & Stoughton
An Hachette UK company

1

A CIP catalogue record for this title is available from the British Library

Hardback ISBN 978 0 340 976944

Typeset in Plantin Light by Hewer Text UK Ltd, Edinburgh
Printed and bound in the UK by CPI Mackays, Chatham ME5 8TD

Hodder & Stoughton policy is to use papers that are natural, renewable
and recyclable products and made from wood grown in sustainable
forests. The logging and manufacturing processes are expected to
conform to the environmental regulations of the country of origin.

Hodder & Stoughton Ltd
338 Euston Road
London NW1 3BH

www.hodder.co.uk

For Eloise with fondest love

ACKNOWLEDGEMENTS

My thanks go to Colin McCredie, Blythe Duff, Morag Fullerton and all the *Taggart* team for their generous help when I was with them on location, to Aga Phillips for her kindness and patience in providing Polish translations, and to Robin and Gillie Johnston-Stewart for fresh insight into farming in Galloway. I am grateful, as always, to my agent Teresa Chris, my copy-editor Helen Campbell and my editors Carolyn Mays, Alex Bonham and Kate Howard.

PROLOGUE

October 1985

The north-easter came tearing through the night across the Irish Sea. Thundering waves lashed the cliffs, launching themselves as walls of water thirty, forty feet high round the Mull of Galloway, the exposed southernmost tip of Scotland. In this hell of howling wind and roaring water, the air was thick with salt spray and blinding squalls of rain.

High above on the headland, from the solid bulk of the great white lighthouse, the lantern's beams stabbed at the encompassing darkness as it revolved, revolved, revolved slowly and steadily through the night.

And far below, in the boiling waves, something tumbled over and over as the breakers rolled it towards the cliffs.

As the light of an uneasy dawn lit the sky with streaks of fiery gold and dull, angry red, the man in the lightroom below the lantern switched off the huge light, yawned and stretched.

It had been a wild, wild night, but with it being near enough November now you had to expect it. The lighthouse had stood against many a worse storm than that in its hundred and fifty years, and John Fairlie never minded the solitary night shift. He was a quiet, dreamy man, fond of his own company, happy to watch the dramas played out by the elements from his crow's-nest position, making the records and checks in his own unhurried time, reading a bit. Poetry – that was his favourite. You could think about poetry, after.

The wind had dropped to an unnatural calm though there was still an angry sea, with a greasy sheen to the surface and a heavy swell. John opened the little door giving access to the platform around the base of the lantern, white trellis-work cast-iron, and climbed out.

It had been hot and stuffy in the cramped office below the light. The shock of the chilly air made him gasp, but he welcomed its freshness, taking deep, hungry breaths. There was nothing better than this: high up in the clear air, the world to yourself apart from the seabirds wheeling below you with their raucous cries. Kittiwakes they were mostly, this morning, as well as the usual herring gulls. He liked watching the birds, particularly the gannets, when they were doing their death drops with wings folded, but they wouldn't be fishing in a sea like this. There were no puffins this morning either, to whirr on their busy way like so many clockwork toys.

John looked down through the mesh of the platform – you couldn't afford to suffer from vertigo in this trade – and saw smoke beginning to curl from the chimney of one of the assistant keepers' cottages across the courtyard. He'd be relieved shortly.

He had turned to go back inside when it caught his eye. Just to the north of the lighthouse, a small stack of rock reared up, needles of sand-coloured stone, with a half-submerged flat surface between its base and the face of the cliff. There was something lying on it, some dark mass, but with gold strands that rippled in the waves that were washing over it. John stared, shading his eyes.

> *'Oh is it weed, or fish, or floating hair –*
> *A tress o' golden hair, o'drownèd maiden's hair . . .'*

The words came to his mind and his stomach lurched. Fumbling the catch on the door, he went back in to fetch the powerful binoculars kept in the office. His hands were shaking as he came back out and focused them.

He left without even shutting the door, half-falling down the ladders before he reached the spiral staircase, then taking the hundred-odd steps at breakneck speed, even though he knew that there was no need to hurry for the sake of the girl who lay dead on the rocks below.

'Well, I think we could confidently state this has been a complete disaster, DI Fleming.'

Standing under the impressive portico of the Glasgow High Court of the Justiciary, the woman who spoke was wearing a fake fur coat, wrapped tightly about her against the keen March wind. She was tall and bulky, with the thick pale skin, full red lips and dark blonde tresses of a Tamara de Tempicka model, but at the moment those lips were pursed in disapproval and her pencilled brows were drawn together above slightly protuberant blue eyes.

The woman coming out behind her through the revolving doors was tall too, but with a long-legged, athletic build. In contrast to the other woman's exotic pallor, she had a fresh complexion and she was not pretty, nor even handsome, but she had an interesting, intelligent face, clear hazel eyes and a humorous mouth. Today, though, her expression was grim.

DS MacNee, a small man wearing a black leather jacket, white T-shirt, jeans and trainers, emerged to line up beside her in a pose suggesting this was not the first street fight he'd found himself engaged in. Both officers wore identical expressions of angry humiliation.

'I can only apologize, Ms Milne,' Fleming forced through her gritted teeth. 'I should have checked.'

'Yes, you should.' The acting Procurator Fiscal's tone was

icy. 'That colossal waste of time and money will have to be explained.'

'I understand that.' Fleming did, too, and she wasn't looking forward to the process.

'I shall be talking to Superintendent Bailey about an enquiry. I am extremely—'

She broke off. The door was revolving again and the sound of laughter and loud, cheerful voices assailed them. A couple of photographers, sitting on a broad low wall beside some unhappy-looking shrubs, suddenly moved forward, raising their cameras.

'Here's them coming now,' MacNee said unnecessarily, and without discussion the three of them headed for the car park opposite, to avoid the exultant villain who, after months of intensive police work and meticulously assembled evidence, had been told there was no case to answer and was even now emerging triumphant, immune from prosecution on these charges at least, and ready to go back to his interrupted life of crime.

'See lawyers?' MacNee said bitterly in his strong Glasgow accent. 'Of all the sleekit sods—'

'Only doing his job,' Fleming said, driving through the city traffic. 'Being smooth and cunning's what they're paid for.'

'And who does the paying?' MacNee returned to a long-held grievance. 'You and me, that's who, and all the decent folk who'd rather not have their houses broken into and their cars nicked. Just so some bugger can come up with a daft technical objection that gets the man off.

'Anyway, his lordship had only to look at that bastard's brief to know he was guilty, no need for a trial. The day that one's defending an innocent man'll be the day the Rangers and Celtic get together to form a social club.'

'It was my fault, though, Tam – I can't get away from it.' In a gesture of frustration, Fleming ran her hand through her crisp chestnut crop, greying a little at the sides now. 'I was fair away with having got the man to make that unguarded admission – last piece in the jigsaw! Never occurred to me to check Hatton's procedure.'

'He'll be sick as a parrot too. He's a decent lad, even if he is English.'

'Well, there's a compliment, coming from you!' Fleming said. DS Hatton was indeed a decent lad, and the collaboration between the Galloway and Cumbria police, nailing a criminal with an extensive stolen cars practice on both sides of the Solway, had been a triumph. They'd picked him up on the Galloway Constabulary's patch, but somehow no one noticed that Hatton, as the arresting officer, had used the English caution on Scottish territory, which invalidated any evidence procured in later questioning. No one, that is, except MacNee's 'sleekit sod' who had, with a smirk of triumph, produced the objection in court this morning and got the case dismissed.

'It's bad enough losing this one, but the kicker is that Sheila Milne's been waiting like a cat at a mouse hole for me to get it wrong. Now . . .' Fleming groaned. 'The woman wants to jerk us around, that's the problem. Always quoting Statute 17 (3) to point out that the Procurator Fiscal is the investigator, while the police are nothing more than her agents, and now she can claim I'm not fit to operate except under close direction.'

'Today she'd a face like a dropped meat pie when it didn't go her way. They're saying she's like that about everything – the depute PFs are all muttering. And there's rumours about her taking a strange interest in some of the minor cases that wouldn't usually come her way. Like prominent citizens' speeding tickets, for instance . . .'

Fleming looked at him sharply. 'Tam, what are you saying?'

'Me? I'm saying nothing. Only that it's the Fiscal's decision whether to prosecute or not. And she's had a big extension put on to her house.'

'Are they suggesting she's doing favours? That's serious stuff.'

'Oh, no one's daft enough to come right out and say anything. Just mutterings, like I said. They're all hoping Duncan Mackay recovers and comes back.'

'He's not far off retirement. I think we're stuck with her. And of course the Super will go doolally about the headlines.'

MacNee nodded in sympathy, then opened his mouth to speak.

'Tam,' Fleming cut in, 'if you're going to quote Burns at me, or tell me I never died a winter yet, I swear I'll do you a mischief.'

Wisely, he shut his mouth again and in gloomy silence they took the long road south to Kirkluce.

It was no surprise, when DI Fleming reached her fourth-floor office in the Galloway Constabulary Headquarters in the market town of Kirkluce, to find a message waiting for her from Superintendent Donald Bailey, requesting an urgent meeting.

She grimaced. Sheila Milne had obviously got to him already. Mobile phones had their uses, but all too often it only meant trouble came your way faster.

Fleming had never relished deskwork, but it looked positively tempting compared to having her head pulled off by Bailey. She might as well get it over with – do the penitent bit, suffer his recriminations and hope the storm would blow itself out before there was significant damage to life or property – but it wasn't a fun way to spend quarter of an hour. When she reached his office and heard a crisp 'Come!' her stomach gave a nervous lurch.

To Fleming's surprise, she was greeted with, 'There you are, Marjory! Good. Now, what are we going to do about all this?'

She could read the signs of displeasure – furrows in his brow going right up into his bald head, plump cheeks flushed, down-turned mouth – but apparently she wasn't the target. She had barely sat down before he began his tirade.

'That woman is simply, totally and utterly impossible! I have never heard such impertinence in my life. She spoke to me in a tone that – that – what's that phrase? "Would be offensive if the Almighty God used it to a black beetle!" Who does she think she is? Oh, I'll have to see the Chief Constable about *this* – though of course he's in the States for a fortnight.

'She had the gall to suggest this was an incompetent Force – and on what grounds, pray? That an advocate who specializes in finding loopholes had found one – as if cases didn't go off because of technical failures by the PF's office every week! Then she'd the nerve to rant about a waste of money, and demand an investigation! I pointed out this would only waste more money and I certainly wouldn't authorize it, since the reason was plain as a pikestaff – an unfortunate mistake.'

'I'm very sorry, Donald. There's no excuse. An elementary error.'

'I won't deny it's most unfortunate, but these things happen,' he said with uncharacteristic magnanimity, explained as he continued heatedly, 'To be honest, what concerns me more is the Fiscal's general attitude. Naturally we must comply with all lawful instructions, but Mackay always had the grace to acknowledge expertise. I haven't directly crossed swords with her until now, but you have had unwarranted interference, haven't you?'

As she agreed that working with the Fiscal was no bed of roses, Fleming breathed a grateful prayer for the Law of Unintended Consequences. Sheila Milne losing it today had given Fleming useful protection against the woman's hostility, dating back to a murder case over which they'd disagreed, when Milne had been proved wrong.

'So,' Bailey was saying, 'what can we do about it, Marjory?'

'Tam MacNee's got suggestions, but I don't think any of them are legal, or even in some cases physically possible. Short of that, I'm not sure that there's much. Comply with definite instructions, but keep reports as general as possible, while we do what's needed, I suppose.'

'Good, good. That's what we need – a strategy.' He sat back in his chair, propping his fingers together in a pyramid over his paunch. 'In a sense, she's even threatening the position of the CC and I can tell you now that he won't like it at all. Questions may have to be asked at a higher level, with the Lord Advocate, perhaps. Though of course, today's problems weaken our position. She's been trying to get her foot in the door – this gives her a chance.'

'Yes. And the headlines tomorrow may not be exactly friendly,' Fleming warned. Bailey was inclined to panic about adverse press coverage.

His frown returned. 'I have to say that worries me. A bad press can do us a lot of harm.'

'Perhaps you could issue a statement regretting that a mere technicality should ruin months of painstaking police work, pointing out that despite this setback we will vigorously pursue further investigations to ensure justice is done in the end. The press always like that – how the courts are too soft and more interested in the rights of the criminal than the rights of ordinary decent working families.'

Bailey was impressed. 'Excellent, Marjory! I'll get the press officer to draft it right away.'

'Fingers crossed. And I can only apologize again.' She got up. 'I'd better go and tackle my desk—'

Bailey shifted in his seat. 'Actually, there's something else I have to talk to you about.'

'Oh – fine.' She sat down again, then realized Bailey was looking distinctly uncomfortable.

'Ms Milne's parting shot was to remind me of government policy on cold cases, and she'd obviously been trawling the records. There is only one unsolved murder on our books and she wants it reviewed. Nineteen eighty-five – before you joined the Force, Marjory. A girl found in the sea, down at the Mull of Galloway.'

'Yes,' Fleming said slowly. 'I remember something about that, but only very vaguely.'

'I am hoping you will take this on. I've called the CC and he agrees we should check it out ourselves. We don't want to wait until there's a demand for an external review – reflects badly on our efficiency.

'The thing is, I was in charge and your late father was involved. I'm afraid his behaviour led to a formal reprimand, and it may make difficult reading for you.'

'I see.' She was taken aback. Her relationship with Sergeant Angus Laird had never been easy, but she had always believed he had an unblemished record as a straightforward, if distinctly old-fashioned policeman. Nineteen eighty-five – she would have been twenty-four, still living at home, doing a series of unsatisfying jobs. But she'd never heard of a problem at work; she wondered if even Janet, her mother, knew. She realized Bailey was waiting for her to speak.

'Sorry,' she said. 'I was just – surprised. Yes, of course, if you want me to review it I'll treat it like any other professional commitment.'

He relaxed a little. 'I knew I could count on you. This way, we're seen to be running our own ship and – well, it's in the family, isn't it?'

Thinking about her father, Fleming hadn't considered how embarrassing this was for Bailey too. An unsolved murder case is a professional failure for the Senior Investigating Officer, and to have someone else check on you, trying to pinpoint mistakes you might have made, perhaps even finding the answer you hadn't found, must be an uncomfortable thought.

It wouldn't be comfortable for her either. She'd have to put him on the spot, quite possibly find fault . . . Not exactly the best position to be in with your boss. A nasty suspicion took hold of her. '*In the family?*' Was he, and was the CC, expecting her merely to rubberstamp his decisions?

As delicately as she could, she suggested someone from outside. 'They would find it easier to see things clearly. I might find it hard to be totally objective—'

'No, no!' he cried. 'I have confidence in you as the best officer I know. And we want the best possible job.'

She hadn't thought it would work. 'Thank you for the compliment,' she said with a sickly smile.

Bailey beamed. 'Well deserved. And naturally, you must *grill* me on what I did. I don't expect any favours. And if you succeed where I failed, I shall be delighted.'

Perhaps he even thought he meant it, but human nature being what it is, he wouldn't be delighted in the least. He had to be hoping she too would find the case insoluble. Fleming's heart sank further. 'I can only do my best,' she said hollowly.

'Good enough for me. I'll arrange for the material to be

sent to you, and you can have whatever back-up you need, of course.'

Fleming left with a sense of foreboding. The classic no-win situation: success would mean her superintendent being humiliated; failure would give Sheila Milne ammunition for the vendetta she seemed determined to pursue.

The connection with her father, too: the more she thought about it, the more uncomfortable she felt, as if she were being drawn into disloyalty. And she had, too, an uneasy, superstitious feeling about digging up events from long ago. You never knew what ghosts would emerge from the grave of the past.

Marjory Fleming headed out of Kirkluce on her way home to the farm owned by her husband Bill, and his parents and grandparents before him. Farming wasn't an easy life these days – if it ever had been – and the catastrophe of foot-and-mouth, scare stories about BSE in sheep and the flood of ever-changing European directives had made the last few years particularly stressful, but even so her heart always lifted when she turned up the farm track.

Mains of Craigie was looking particularly appealing today. It sat on rising ground, looking out to soft green Galloway hills, and with the brisk March wind the daffodils that straggled up by the farm track were dancing with an enthusiasm to inspire Wordsworth to a positive frenzy of poetic rapture. The sky was clear, with fluffy clouds whipping past, and on the hill opposite were half-grown lambs, still at the playful stage, playing King of the Castle on a tussock. As Marjory parked the car in the yard and got out she could hear loud triumphant cackling coming from the old orchard below the house, where one of her hens had obviously laid an egg.

Smiling, she went to look down at them, the cares of a bruising day slipping away. Just watching them, plump and confident, strutting and scratching around in the rough grass, and hearing their comfortable sounds always put things into perspective.

She hadn't worked late tonight, so Bill would probably still be out around the farm. The kids should be home, unless Cammie had one of his rugby training sessions. It would be nice if they could all have supper together – it didn't happen as often as it should.

Supper was something to look forward to these days. Karolina Cisek, whose husband Rafael worked for Bill on the farm, had transformed Marjory's life, not only by helping with laundry and cleaning. She also provided delicious meals from the small catering company she had managed to set up, despite three-year-old Janek whose mission in life seemed to be to run his mother ragged. With her quiet, even shy appearance – soft fair hair, blue-grey eyes and dimples in her pink cheeks – you could never guess she would be so dynamic. She was fluent in English now, though her husband still struggled and they always spoke Polish at home. Marjory suspected Rafael wasn't altogether happy with his wife's new career, but no doubt the money was welcome.

Her mother's little car was parked in the yard, she was pleased to see. She was worried about Janet Laird, who had coped well with her husband's distressing decline, but since his death eighteen months ago had been . . . It was hard to define exactly what, since Janet was still her gentle, cheerful self, and her face was rounded and plump once more. But she was, Marjory sensed, diminished in some way, as if in losing Angus she had lost part of herself too.

It was hard to know what to do, since enquiries invariably met with a smiling 'Och, I'm fine,' to which you could hardly say, 'No, you're not,' without evidence to back it up. All Marjory could do was hold a watching brief and keep her mother involved in family life, without letting her do too much and wear herself out. She'd always felt guilty about taking advantage of Janet's uncomplaining readiness to provide childcare and supplement Marjory's own lack of culinary skills. Now the children were older and Karolina was doing most of the housekeeping, Marjory could make sure Janet was free to enjoy her friends and her garden instead of servicing the demands of the Flemings.

Taking off her shoes in the mud room, she could hear Cat chattering away in the kitchen. She sounded cheerful and excited and Marjory smiled. At sixteen, Cat had suddenly shaken off the worst of her teenage rebellion; she'd got very good marks in her Standard Grades last year and was working hard towards Highers, hoping to become a vet. She was even stepping out with a nice lad with ambitions to be a doctor, and Bill and Marjory were beginning tentatively to hope that, allowing for occasional lapses, the worst was probably over.

Cammie, at fourteen almost as tall as his father, had reached the spotty, hairy, grunting stage. He had dark hair and eyes like his mother's, but his looks weren't improved by bruises and the occasional black eye, and his nose was no longer the shape God had intended. Not that he cared; rugby and his training were still the most important things in his life, ruling out the drink-drugs-girls problems most parents with teenage boys worried about. He seemed set for a professional playing career with the farm to come back to later, and since he couldn't actually have forgotten how to talk, communication would no doubt be re-established in a year or two. He was good around the farm anyway, and conversation wasn't a necessity when you were heaving bales or dipping sheep.

Cat and Janet were alone in the kitchen, mugs of tea and a plate of flapjacks in front of them. The Tin, a family institution, was open on the table, with a chocolate cake, shortbread, a fruit loaf and some more of the flapjacks inside. It was battered now by years of service, but Janet still regularly filled it up to bring to the farm and take back empty.

Marjory came in and bent to give Janet a hug. Was it just her imagination, or had her mother got smaller this last year or two?

'Had a good day, pet?' Janet asked, as she had done since her daughter was coming home from Primary One. 'I'll just make you a cup of tea.'

'No, no, Mum,' Marjory protested. 'You sit down. I'll get it myself.'

Cat, unfolding her long legs, stood up. 'Stop bickering, you two. Mum, sit down and *I*'ll make some tea. You want another cup, Gran?'

Marjory and Janet exchanged smiles, doing as they were told. As Cat lifted the lid of the Aga and pulled across the kettle, she said over her shoulder, 'Did you hear about the filming, Mum?'

'Filming? No.'

'I was just telling Gran. You know *Playfair's Patch*?'

'Know it, yes,' Marjory said, 'but don't ask me to watch it. Playfair's a superintendent, allegedly, and does house-to-house enquiries. Try asking Donald Bailey to go out knocking on doors and see what answer you get!'

Cat brought back the teapot and put it on the table. 'Oh, Mum, get with it! It's a crime series, OK? It's not a documentary. Bet if they filmed what you do all day it'd be so boring no one would watch it.'

'You have a point there. Sometimes I can hardly bear to watch it myself.' Marjory took a flapjack.

'The thing is, they're coming to shoot an episode over in the South Rhins next week. Isn't that totally wicked?' Cat's eyes were sparkling.

'I thought *Playfair's Patch* was in Glasgow,' Marjory objected.

'Well – yeah. So? It'll look good and you could kind of think it might be somewhere in Strathclyde. *Anyway*,' Cat went on as her mother seemed ready to argue, 'the thing is, Karolina's going to ask you for a few days off – she's got a Polish friend in catering in Glasgow and heard they needed extra help in the canteen. They're wanting school kids as extras too, so I said how cool it would be if I could get in on it, and she goes, "Well, my friend knows the director – he'll mention you." Wouldn't that be fantastic? I phoned Anna and we could go together – it would be, like, amazing!'

Cat and Anna seemed to do most things together these days, but that was fine. Anna was a great improvement on some of Cat's earlier chums – pretty, clever and nice too.

'Sounds fun. But what's Karolina going to do with Janek?'

'I could baby-sit for her—' Janet began, but her daughter interrupted, shaking her head.

'It's so like you to offer, and granted, Janek's an engaging little scamp, but you've no idea what a handful a lively three-year-old can be.'

'Calling Janek lively is like saying it's a bit blowy during a hurricane,' Cat put in. 'I'm always wiped out after baby-sitting, even though he's mostly asleep. No, she's parking him in a nursery – worth the money, she said, because it could really boost her catering company. That'll be brilliant, won't it?'

Marjory agreed, as enthusiastically as she could. It wasn't impressive that her first thought had been to wonder about its effect on her domestic life, when this would indeed be a wonderful opportunity for Karolina.

Cat didn't notice, but Janet was quick to pick up reservation in her tone. 'Don't worry about the house, dearie. I can easily come up and keep things running for you, now I've no one to think of but myself.'

'Of course not!' Marjory exclaimed. 'I wouldn't take advantage of you like that. You do enough – visiting at the old people's home, all the baking for those constant coffee mornings and church fairs. You were exhausted after the Lifeboat fundraiser last week when I came to see you.'

'Well, I'd been on my feet the whole day,' Janet protested, but her daughter went on.

'Anyway, Karolina's doing fine at the moment and it may take some time to get major clients. But Cat – next week, did you say? You've got school.'

'Yeah, but it's a complete doss just now. It's only a week till the end of term, it's just revision and we've covered the syllabus already. I'll work in the evenings, I swear.'

Marjory looked at her daughter doubtfully. She was quite eye-catching, blonde and slim with long legs and pretty blue eyes, and if they needed an attractive teenager she would certainly fit the profile. 'You'll have to ask the Head. If he agrees, I won't object.'

Cat came over to fling her arms round her mother's neck. 'Thanks, Mum. I'm sure the Heidie will say it's OK. He's almost human – says it's good to broaden our experience.'

'Who's the star, anyway?' Marjory asked idly. 'I remember seeing him – quite good-looking, fortyish.'

'Marcus Lindsay. And his sidekick's Jaki Johnston. He's meant to be sort of posh, and she's not. It said in *Heat* they're an item.'

'Marcus Lindsay!' Janet said. 'Now, I know something about him – what is it, now? Give me a wee minute . . .' She frowned, then her brow cleared. 'That's right! It's not his real name – not the Lindsay bit. He's Marcus Lazansky – Lindsay was his mother's name, and I suppose he'd need something easier for folk to remember. His father was a Czech, Ladislav Lazansky – he was a fighter pilot. Stayed on after the war.'

Janet gave a little sigh. 'Laddie Lazansky! My, he was handsome – a charmer, too! We'd coffee mornings then too, raising funds for poor folks in Middle Europe, and he'd always be there. So dashing – I mind him wearing a blue cravat, just the colour of his eyes . . .'

'Gran! You've gone quite pink!' Cat teased.

Janet laughed softly. 'Oh, I was young once! And I'd an eye for a braw lad – I chose your grandfather, after all, and a fine-looking man he always was.'

Her eyes had misted, and Marjory said hastily, 'Was Laddie a suitor too, Mum?'

'Oh dearie me, no!' Janet seemed shocked at the suggestion. 'I was only a wee smout then, younger than you, Cat. Anyway, he'd a wife in Czechoslovakia, though I doubt he ever went back there. Got a divorce and married that Flora Lindsay – county family, with an estate up near Dumfries, but then he was meant to be the same kind back where he came from. They'd a grand house over Ardhill way.

'They're both dead now – I mind his mother died last year – but Marcus still has the house, though I doubt he's ever there. He'd be about your age, Marjory, I would jalouse, but they sent him away to school in the south so you'd never have met him.'

'Is there anyone in Galloway you *don't* know about?' Marjory said, amused. 'You put our official records to shame.'

She considered asking Janet about the unsolved murder, but she was reluctant to spoil this pleasant family time. Anyway, she could hear the roar of quad bikes arriving, then Bill talking to Cammie and the boy's familiar grunt in reply.

They'd be wanting their supper soon.

'You'll stay for supper, Mum, won't you?' she said to Janet.

'That would be nice, pet. Now, what can I do? Peel potatoes—'

'No, no need. I've a wonderful casserole with some unpronounceable Polish name in the freezer, and it only needs rice. You can talk to your son-in-law while I go up and change.'

'That'll be lovely,' Janet said, but, Marjory thought, her voice sounded a bit flat again. Talking about Angus must have brought it all back.

2

The fire in the basket grate of the Adams-style fireplace was burning low and it was a cold night. In spite of the central heating, the room felt suddenly chilly, and with an anxious glance at his companion Marcus Lindsay went to fetch logs from a huge wicker basket.

Even here in his own house there was an air of theatricality about him, as if he were following a stage direction: '*Cross to stage left, fetch logs and place on fire.*' He was above medium height, though not tall; he was slim and well-built, with a face marked by strong eyebrows and a square chin. It was too irregular for classical good looks, but his very blue eyes, in contrast to his dark hair, were striking. They had an attractive way of crinkling at the corners, too, when he smiled as he did now, picking out a couple of peat sods to add to the flames beginning to lick round the logs.

'I'm probably committing an eco-crime by burning peat, but I just love the smell, don't you?'

'*Après nous le déluge*, darling,' the woman said in the husky voice with a slight break in it which had made her famous. She held up the crystal brandy balloon she was holding in a toast and finished what was left in it. A moonstone ring on the third finger of her left hand sparkled in the light from the Chinese lamp on a side table.

Sylvia Lascelles was much older than Marcus, well into her seventies, and she was no longer the beauty she once had been. But good bones age well: she still had fine grey-violet eyes, and her thick white hair was swept up in a loose knot on her head. She was wearing black jersey Jean Muir, but the hand holding the glass was gnarled, and though she was sitting in a high-backed Jacobean armchair, a wheelchair stood waiting and she had a black cane with a heavy silver knob at her side.

'Another one?' Marcus suggested, going to the butler's tray where the drinks were, carrying his own glass.

She shook her head. 'Shouldn't even have had this one. Quarrels with my medication but I couldn't resist. Find me some bloody sparkling water, darling, and I can pretend it's champagne.'

Pulling a sympathetic face, he brought it to her. 'Here's to old loves,' she said, in her usual toast, then added with a touch of bitterness, 'and to charity.'

'Sylvia! If that means what I think it does—'

'Oh, sweetheart, forgive?' She held out her hand in what was still a graceful movement. She had great power to charm; he took it and kissed it.

'I'm such a self-pitying old bag,' she went on. 'I keep opening *Vogue* and seeing women my age like sodding Jane Fonda, all air-brushed and cut to shape, talking about being seventy years young.

'It's a real bitch, I tell you, when your body lets you down. Oh, there's no gratitude – the money I lavished on it, boring mud-wraps, massages, spas, hours on the beastly tread-mill . . .' She turned it into a joke, aware perhaps that old people talking about their ailments is the ultimate turn-off.

He smiled with her, then said seriously, 'Look, let's knock the charity thing on the head, right now. This part's made for you. Asking you to do it was a no-brainer. When I said I thought I could persuade you, the director went crazy. It'll probably double our audience – a rare appearance by the fabulous Sylvia Lascelles.'

'Flatterer! But it's dear of you to have thought of me. And to have a few days down here with you, in this heavenly place, with all its memories of darling Laddie—'

She turned the ring on her finger, her eyes going to the photograph on the mantelpiece, a photograph of a man with the romantic looks of a Thirties film star. His son's looks were much less striking, but there was a strong resemblance.

Marcus shifted uncomfortably in his chair. He had adored his father's mistress since the day when, aged sixteen, he had met her at lunch at the Ritz. She was sophisticated, glamorous and at the height of her fame, with a couple of wildly successful films and some acclaimed stage roles to her credit. The *coup de foudre* when Laddie had met her through a Czech director friend was by then a permanent relationship; childless herself, Sylvia had given Marcus the maternal warmth and open affection his awkward mother never showed.

Flora Lazansky had more in common with her dogs and horses than with her only son. Marcus made a dinner-party anecdote out of her kissing her black Labrador more often than him, but it had hurt nonetheless. His memories of home were fairly bleak, and since his father probably felt he took second place to his wife's favourite hunter, Marcus couldn't blame him for his infidelity.

Laddie was a passionate man. He adored Sylvia, but there could never be a divorce, because when he married Flora he had fallen in love – with the house she was given when they married, a dower house for the Kendallon estate.

Tulach House had an unexpected style in this exposed area where low, solid houses huddled against cruel winds from the Irish Sea. Built just outside the village of Ardhill at the same time as Edinburgh's New Town, Tulach had an aristocratic disdain for the elements: the view from its huge sash windows was incomparable, though the draughts, too, were in a class of their own. But the perfectly proportioned rooms almost compensated for having to wear thick sweaters for ten months of the year, given a good summer, or more, if not.

Flora took it for granted, but Laddie was impassioned about it. He was a displaced person; Tulach gave him the dignity he had lost.

The 'memories' Sylvia mentioned could only be of times when Flora was away judging horse trials or visiting a friend. Marcus could understand his father wanting to bring Sylvia to this house which so perfectly matched her in elegance, but he still felt uncomfortable about it.

Now Sylvia was looking round the drawing room, which probably hadn't changed for a hundred years. Perhaps the glazed cotton loose covers and interlined curtains had been replaced, if not recently, but the worn Persian rugs and the antique furniture, showing the patina of age through a fine layer of dust, certainly hadn't.

'It's not entirely *you*, sweetie, is it? How long since poor Flora died? More than a year? You can't feel obliged to keep it like this. Proper heating would make such a difference – and there's a divine man does the most brilliant modern country house interiors—'

Marcus was shaking his head. 'Sylvia, do you have the faintest idea what the upkeep costs are? TV actors aren't paid like movie stars, you know, and anyway I'm hardly here, except for the odd weekend. The fee for filming this episode here will keep me going meantime, but I'd sell it tomorrow if it wasn't that Papa loved it so much.'

'Oh, no! You couldn't, you couldn't!' Sylvia protested.

'There must be some money – what happened about Laddie's ancestral acres in Czechoslovakia? He was always talking about reclaiming them one day.'

Marcus pulled a face. 'To be honest, I'm not sure how extensive they were, except in his mind, and anyway, talking was as far as it got. I wouldn't fancy the hassle and the aggro. And even if I had the money, I'm not sure I'd want to change this room. I rather like it.'

Sylvia had been a little too obvious in her desire to expunge the influence of her old rival. That would be victory of a sort, and Marcus felt a strangely stubborn loyalty to his dead mother. He got to his feet. 'Time we all got our beauty sleep. Will you be – all right?'

He looked at her a little anxiously, imagining embarrassing personal needs, but she was quick to reassure him. 'Darling, the room was converted for Laddie when the stairs got too much for him, so it's perfect. And I'll have such sweet dreams. Be an angel and help me into my chair, then open doors, if you would, and I'll be fine.'

Marcus saw her to her room. 'You'll smell coffee brewing at around eight-thirty, but don't hurry. Jaki's going to come down later.'

'Super! I'm absolutely longing to meet her,' she said, with such dramatic enthusiasm that he knew she was disappointed at not having him to herself.

He bent to kiss her goodnight. 'Sleep well,' he said, then went back to the drawing room to put a guard on the fire. He switched the lights off, drew back the fraying curtains and opened the French windows which gave on to the terrace at the back. There were weeds growing through the stones and it was slippery with moss. He stepped out cautiously.

The night seemed to close around him. It was cool and clear: the sky was velvety black but studded with millions of stars, very close and very bright. You barely saw the stars in the cities, but here the only light pollution was from the stabbing beam of the lighthouse down on the Mull. He felt dizzy with the miracle of those wheeling galaxies.

He stood for a few moments, then sighed and went back inside. Locking up, he thought about Sylvia and Jaki and he found himself wondering if this weekend visit, before the rest of the team arrived, had been quite such a good idea after all.

As Tam MacNee and the other Warlocks from the Cutty Sark repaired to the bar of the Cross Keys in Ardhill to celebrate their darts victory over the local side, Tam thought how strange it was not to have the air thick with the familiar smell of smoke. He wasn't sure he liked this new ruling by the Holyrood Samizdat; his wife Bunty had made him give up the weed a while back, but somehow clean air and a bar seemed sort of unnatural.

The Cross Keys was full and there was a kind of edgy atmosphere, with Norrie the barman watching nervously to see whether he'd be called on to enforce the ban. When Tam had arrived with the team, Norrie had greeted him with special enthusiasm, but Tam's response was brief: 'I'm off duty, pal. You're on your own.'

Of course, you were never quite off duty. Even as Tam joined in the crack, he was looking across the bar at a group of men who'd come in together and weren't speaking English.

The Polish invasion had reached Kirkluce and the general reaction locally was favourable. These were skilled men, not afraid of hard work, who turned up when expected, didn't take tea-breaks every half-hour and didn't pad their bills.

There was resentment in some quarters, though. It threatened the local tradesmen – oh, indeed it did! Used to saying, 'I could maybe fit you in at the end of next month,

Mr MacNee, and I can make it six hundred quid if you pay cash,' it was natural enough they'd take exception to having their nice little racket spoiled.

It was harder to see why the native layabouts should resent jobs they weren't prepared to do being done by someone else, but they did. Tam could see a ripple of reaction from some local youths, bunched around the bar, as the Poles arrived.

There was one older man among them, but the others were in their twenties and compared to the home-grown variety mainly looked clean-cut and wholesome. One had an earring and slightly long hair, but as far as Tam could see none of them had tattoos – one of his particular bugbears. Ardhill's own neds – well, the less said about how they looked, the better.

There were four or five of them and up till now they'd been leaving the bar to smoke meekly enough, forming a raucous group outside, but the noise level was rising and from experience Tam reckoned one or other of them would try it on before long. It was cold out there, they were out to enjoy their Friday night and they were getting lairy.

Tam took a closer look as they all trooped back inside again. There was only one he knew: Kevin Docherty, skinny, in his early twenties, with a shaven head and a dotted linc tattooed round his throat – a joke, presumably, though the man was tempting fate. He was bad news, Docherty, convicted of assault and only recently out on early release – something else Tam didn't approve of.

He'd said he was off duty, but it didn't work like that. DS MacNee was replacing Tam already. He wouldn't trust Docherty as far as the bowl of peanuts at the end of the bar. The assault had involved a knife; he'd be surprised if the man wasn't carrying one, and from the way they were all nudging one another and laughing, trouble was brewing.

As one of the Poles picked up his pint from the bar, Docherty gave him a dunt so that it slopped on his jeans. MacNee saw anger in the man's face, then he tightened his lips, shrugged and moved away.

There was a burst of laughter. Docherty said something to his mates, then to cries of 'Go for it, Kev!' he ostentatiously got out a pack of cigarettes, took one out and lit up.

The barman saw him immediately. With a pleading glance at MacNee, he said, 'Come on, Kev. You know it's against the law now. Put it out, like a good lad.'

Docherty's unpleasant grin bared a snaggle of uneven teeth. 'Gonnae make me, then? You and whose army? Come on, lads, get out the fags. If we're all at it, what does he do?'

Emboldened, several more lit up. A hush fell as the drinkers watched the confrontation, and Docherty raised his voice. 'It's a daft law – we can get it changed. Come on, they can't arrest us all. What's wrong with you – feart?'

The reaction was unpromising. There was a mutter of disapproval, a few bolder spirits grinned, but the call to the barricades fell flat.

Disappointed, Docherty pushed forward to confront the Poles. 'Come on! You smoke – I've seen you!' Confronted by a wall of stony faces, he began swearing at them, then, getting no reaction, deliberately blew smoke directly into the face of a tall young man with dark hair and fierce eyes that were almost black.

'Enough,' he said. 'Outside.'

A gratified smile crossed Docherty's face. 'Oh aye,' he said. 'Outside.' With a jerk of his head he summoned his henchmen. 'Come on, fellas.'

With great reluctance, MacNee came round from the farther side of the bar. 'That's enough. Cool it, lads.'

Docherty looked at him in disgust. 'Oh, God – MacNee. What the hell are you doing here?'

'Never you mind. I'm here, that's all. And if you're asking about armies, it's me and the whole majesty of the law, the same that locked you up last time. You'll maybe remember what happens if you get it wrong, Kev – you're back inside before you can say, "I'm sorry, DS MacNee, it was just my wee joke."'

'Norrie, I'm sure you've still got an ashtray somewhere. Mr Docherty and his friends had briefly forgotten, and they're just going to put their cigarettes out, like the law-abiding gentlemen they are.' MacNee smiled his menacing gap-tooth grin.

Norrie, looking terrified, obliged. No one else moved until the young Pole stepped forward. He had clearly failed to follow this: he was high on adrenalin and righteous wrath, and all he saw was someone stopping him getting his revenge. Taking MacNee by the shoulders – he was more than six inches taller – he swung him out of the way.

'You – no! Me and him.' He gestured at Docherty.

There had been a sharp intake of breath around the pub. Startled himself, MacNee turned belligerently.

'Watch it, laddie. I'm the polis.' Then, as it didn't seem to register, he added a foreign word he thought he'd heard used in films, 'Politzie.'

The young man went white. '*Policje?* Sorry, so sorry. Not know . . .' He backed away.

MacNee nodded. 'OK. You weren't to know. Just relax, all right?'

'Sure, sure. OK, OK.' He tried to disappear among his friends, who were by now visibly uneasy. One after another, they put their glasses down and left. A ragged cheer went up from Docherty and his mates.

MacNee turned sharply. 'Now, Kev, let's talk about you. Threatening behaviour with racial overtones? Let me tell you this. I was chatting to one of the fiscals the other day, and he was saying he could drop a complaint of rape easier than racial harassment. Did you enjoy the jail, Kev? One foot out of line, you're back there.

'Oh, look, here's Norrie with an ashtray. What do we do when we see an ashtray? Oh, well done, Kev.'

With her coat buttoned up against the wind, the tall, gaunt woman, a basket over her arm, walked through Ardhill on Saturday morning. The village was little more than ribbon development: small houses huddled on either side, a guest house at one end, a pub at the other, a couple of small shops, a general store and a bakery. There weren't many bakers around now, and it always did a good trade.

She had been to the store already, but she still had to go to the bakery: Jean Grant always came up here from the farm to shop because she liked real bread, not the rubbish in plastic bags, and her son liked their Scotch pies for his dinner.

There were two women ahead of her, an older woman she knew and a younger one, in her forties perhaps, with blonde hair. Jean eyed her disapprovingly. The blonde hair had come out of a bottle, no doubt about that, and she was wearing those jeans they all wore nowadays, showing up her middle-aged bulges. She'd have been better wearing a decent skirt, at her age.

'Hi, Mrs Grant,' the girl behind the counter greeted her, and the older woman being served turned. 'Hello, Jean! Wee bit chilly today, isn't it?'

Jean inclined her head. 'Morning,' she said. She never indulged in idle conversation, but she wasn't above listening to it, and the girl's voice was excited as she went on with what she'd been saying.

'They'll be filming round here four days next week. And Marcus Lindsay came in himself, buying bread.'

'Marcus Lindsay!' the blonde woman chipped in. 'Goodness – haven't seen him for ages. Does he come often?'

'Don't think so,' the girl said. 'I've seen him a couple of times before, but I think he stays in Glasgow. He's at the big house for a week anyway, he said. And there's some film star staying with him, someone said – she's old, can't remember her name . . .'

'Sylvia Lascelles,' the older woman supplied. 'I heard that along the street. I mind her fine. She was in *For Ever* – my hankie was soaking wet when I came out after. Haven't heard of her for years.'

The blonde woman had seen the film too. They embarked on an enjoyable gossip.

Jean Grant was frowning, a light of calculation in her eyes. She listened a little longer, but as the conversation centred on the film star, she moved forward. '*If* you wouldn't mind. Some of us have work to do.'

The assistant flushed. 'Sorry, Mrs Grant. What was it you were wanting?'

Her bread and pies added to her basket, Jean Grant returned to the elderly Vauxhall parked further down the street and drove off, through Port Logan and Kirkmaiden and along the single-track road signposted to the Mull of Galloway, then over a cattle grid. A little further on, she turned up the track to Balnakenny.

She looked around for her son, but there was no sign of him in his tractor or out among the cattle grazing on either side of the track. He wasn't around the yard either; she looked at her watch, pursing her lips as she got out of the car, and went into the farmhouse.

Stuart Grant was lounging in a wooden chair by the kitchen fire. He'd been reading a magazine; she could see it inadequately hidden behind a cushion.

'What are you doing, in at this time?' Jean challenged him.

'Just taking my break,' he said, a defensive whine in his voice. 'Took it later than usual.'

'Well, you've no time to waste, sitting here. I've told you the dykes that are needing attention, and you've never got round to it.'

'All right, all right.' Stuart got to his feet and went towards the door.

'Listen,' she said. 'That Marcus Lazansky – Lindsay, he's calling himself now – he's back here. Staying for a week.'

Stuart stopped. Without turning round, he said, 'Is he?'

'Yes. What are you going to do?'

'Who said I was going to do anything?'

His mother glared at him. 'Your sister—' she began.

'Don't start!' His voice was ragged with anger. He gestured towards a table where a large photograph of a girl with long blonde hair stood, flanked by two candles that were never lit. 'You didn't help, at the time.'

'How dare you!' Jean's eyes flashed fury. 'Your sister's death ruined my life, and I've never forgotten who was to blame, even if you have.'

He looked as if he might reply, then shrugged. 'We know what we know,' he said. 'And I heard what you said.'

He went out, leaving her glaring after him. Then she got out a duster and a can of pine-scented Pledge to polish the table. She picked up the picture, rubbed the glass, and stood looking at it for a long time.

Jaki Johnston was in a bad mood by the time she reached Tulach House. She'd got up at an hour she'd barely known existed on a Saturday morning, driven for what seemed like years, and even so she was late for lunch. She should have called Marcus, but she was so pissed off she'd decided he could sweat it out and switched off her phone.

The way Marcus talked, she'd thought this was something really special, and she'd even got some cool stuff to wear. She'd seen country-house weekends in films, and actually meeting Sylvia Lascelles – well, that was special in itself for a girl who'd grown up in social housing in Wishaw.

Jaki was feeling quite nervous. The woman was a legend, after all. The whole team was excited about her being in this episode, but only Jaki would have the chance to get to know her properly before filming started.

But this – this plain, boring house, no turrets or anything, out in the sticks with an overgrown garden and windows needing painted? What a let-down! She'd thought there'd be a town – well, not exactly a town, she wasn't stupid, but a cute village with craft shops and a decent restaurant for eating out. Marcus had told her he hadn't any proper help and she couldn't see him cooking. But this Ardhill place was the ass-end of space. What did they do round here? Eat grass?

Her pretty, glossy lips were dropping at the corners as she parked her bright red Ka. She was small and slight, with neat, pert features, big brown eyes and a creamy complexion; her dark hair, cut in a feathery gamine style, had a henna shine. The wind ruffled it and she shivered. The outfit that had looked great in Zara wasn't suited to this climate and her stiletto-heeled ankle boots would be ruined by the time she'd crossed the weedy gravel to the front door.

Where was Marcus, anyway? She scowled, dragging her cases from the boot. He should be looking out for her, worrying in case she was lying in a ditch somewhere.

It wasn't a good sign. Just lately she'd sensed a slight cooling-off, which gave her a little flutter of panic. She wasn't absolutely sure she was still in love with him, but he was her security in the cut-throat game which was her profession.

Jaki was remarkably realistic. She was talented, but so were plenty of other pretty girls, and she hadn't yet won the viewers' hearts to the point where she was fireproof. While she was Marcus's squeeze, she could be pretty sure she wouldn't be written out.

That made her sound a hard, calculating bitch – well, perhaps she was, in a way, but she genuinely had fancied Marcus rotten. He was the dream answer to an internet WLTM ad: BHM, GSOH, NM – and who wouldn't like to meet a not married, big handsome male with a good sense of humour, and a bit of fame chucked in for extras? And he didn't fancy himself even more than you did and play the big star. He was a honey, and she'd had a crush on him right from the start, never thinking he'd look at her twice. But in the long intervals between takes they'd talked a lot, and she made him laugh, then one thing led to another.

For someone over forty, he was pretty cool, but she had to admit they hadn't much in common. His idea of a great night out was something heavy at the theatre, then a restaurant where the waiters winced if you clinked a glass accidentally, and the only time she'd taken him clubbing had been a disaster. 'How can you stand the *smell?*' he'd demanded, wrinkling his nose. 'All these sweaty bodies! And the noise . . .'

So she hadn't tried again. Jaki did her clubbing when he was otherwise engaged, but she was always careful. Marcus was showbiz news, in Scotland at least, and no rotten stringer was going to catch her draped around some other guy and write an item he'd see sooner or later. She'd no illusions about 'for ever' – and she knew he didn't either – but she was in no hurry to move on.

Though as she rang the bell and crossed the cavernous vestibule to open the front door, the thought crossed her mind that if spending much time in this dump was a condition of the relationship, she might be ready to move on sooner rather than later.

'Darling, could I possibly have some more Badoit?' Sylvia Lascelles was being saintly about the delay to lunch, but subtly so that it was hardly noticeable how saintly she was being.

Marcus, who had refilled his own glass with wine more than once, leaped to oblige. 'I'm sorry, Sylvia. I can't think what's keeping Jaki. I tried ringing, but she's switched off.'

'Very sensible, when she's driving,' Sylvia said sweetly. 'Don't worry. I'm happy just sitting here and looking out at that divine view.'

The conservatory at the back of Tulach House had an elevated position, making it possible to look out on one side to the Irish Sea and on the other to Luce Bay. The sun was shining but a strong wind was seeking out the gaps around the window panes where the putty had perished.

Sylvia, a veteran of Tulach weekends, had come armed with a soft blue-grey cashmere throw – by some happy coincidence, almost exactly the colour of her eyes. Marcus was wearing a thick-knit navy Guernsey sweater and even so his hands were red with cold. He was further away from the radiator than she was.

The sound of a clanging bell brought him to his feet, relief showing in his face, though Sylvia judged, clinically, that this had more to do with the delay to lunch than with loving anxiety.

'Great! That'll be Jaki. I'll introduce her, and check that the food – *not just food, M & S food –*' he parodied the advertisement, 'hasn't been reduced to a crisp.'

Sylvia sighed as he left. This tedious girl, butting in on her idyllic weekend in Laddie's glorious house with her darling Marcus! She didn't think the relationship sounded serious, though, and she'd just caught the faintest hint that he regretted asking Jaki down early. She'd seen the girl on the box and she wasn't Marcus's type at all – a common little floozie, Laddie would have called her. His son might well find his impression of her changed now she was here at Tulach, still so much infused with Laddie's personality.

She could hear their voices now, the girl's high-pitched and querulous. Marcus wouldn't like that, especially since she should be apologetic about keeping them waiting. Sylvia swivelled in her chair, prepared her high-wattage smile and beamed it at the girl who came in.

'Jaki, darling! Come and say hello.' She held out her hand, heavy with rings. 'Have you had an absolutely *ghastly* journey? Poor love!'

The girl did indeed look a little dazzled. 'Miss – Miss Lascelles,' she stammered, and came to take the bejewelled, twisted hand. She was wearing skinny jeans, green suede ankle boots and a short-sleeved, low-necked smock in olive, burnt-orange and brown, and she was shivering.

However much it might be 'in' this year, it wasn't a good look – muddy colours with that slightly sallow complexion and goose-flesh on her bare arms.

'But you're freezing!' Sylvia exclaimed. 'Come and huddle by the radiator, and Marcus shall run and get you one of his huge cosy sweaters. Quick, Marcus darling, before she dies of hypothermia!' Marcus departed.

'Now, what you need is a dram. Over there – the decanter.' She indicated a tray with a silver-topped crystal decanter, tumblers and a bottle of Badoit.

Obediently, Jaki went over to it. 'Is there any vodka and tonic?'

'Goodness, sweetie, here you have to drink the *vin du pays*! It's the only thing that keeps out the cold. That's Bladnoch, the local malt.'

Dubiously, Jaki poured some into a tumbler and came to sit as close to the panel heater as she could, sipping it uncertainly.

Marcus reappeared, holding a huge, very thick, scratchy-looking oatmeal sweater. 'It'll look a bit odd, I'm afraid, but it's the warmest thing I could find.'

He pulled it over her head and surveyed the result. 'Oh dear,' he laughed. 'It docs rather swamp you. But Sylvia understands all about the draughts here and I think you're gorgeous anyway.' He kissed her on the tip of her nose.

Amused, Sylvia noticed that the smile Jaki gave him as she thanked him and wrapped it more closely round her suggested that she had murder in her heart.

Marcus was peering doubtfully at the cottage pie – it seemed to have sort of black bits round the edges – when the phone rang. It was the landline, not his mobile, which was surprising. Being here so seldom, he never gave anyone this number.

It must be someone local, a family friend, perhaps. 'Hello?' he said tentatively.

'Marcus! A voice from your past! You'll never guess who it is!'

It was a loud, over-confident voice, and he did, in fact, recognize it. It belonged to Diane Hodge, and he almost groaned aloud. She was the spoiled only daughter of a Glasgow businessman who had come for years to holiday in Sandhead, over on Luce Bay, and she had horrified her family by marrying the barman from a local hotel. They'd lived there for a few years in the Eighties, but before long Gavin Hodge joined his father-in-law's building firm and they'd gone off to Glasgow.

The local grapevine must be working overtime. Before, no one knew if he was popping down for a weekend and he'd been spared this sort of call.

'Diane!' Marcus said without enthusiasm. 'This is a surprise.'

'You guessed!' She sounded disappointed. 'Well, once seen, never forgotten, as they say! I heard in the baker's you're back for a bit – to be honest, the whole place is talking about the great man!'

Diane laughed. Marcus held the phone away from his ear.

'We retired down here two years ago,' she went on. 'Dad died, and we thought, why not sell up and have a good time while we're young enough to enjoy it? Gav has a yacht to play with, and I'm afraid we're serial cruisers too – never at home! Still, we got back from the Galapagos a fortnight ago and we're here at Miramar all week, so you must come over – no excuses! Bring Sylvia Lascelles too, naturally. I hear she's staying with you.'

The last thing he wanted was an old pals' reunion, least of all with Diane and the boorish Gavin, who'd taunted young Marcus Lazansky about his foreign name and called him stuck-up because he'd gone to boarding school. He had no wish to revisit all the unpleasant memories of the time before Marcus Lindsay, actor, was born. He'd shut them off, padlocked away in some dingy attic of his mind, and now Diane was coming, crowbar in hand.

He spoke firmly. 'Terribly kind, but I'm going to have to say no. Sylvia's not awfully mobile so we're saving her strength for filming next week.'

He should have known that wouldn't work. Diane's attitude to obstacles in her path had always been to stomp them flat.

'What a shame! I'd have loved to show you Miramar – we designed it ourselves, you know. But we'll pop over instead, cheer you both up. Can't have you just sitting staring at each other all weekend!' She laughed again. 'Anyway, I'm dying to meet Sylvia. I'm her biggest fan! Tonight? Tomorrow?'

Tomorrow was at least further away. Outmanoeuvred, Marcus agreed to that.

'Brilliant! Sixish?'

'Sixish,' he agreed gloomily, and set down the phone. He should have said no, flatly, but he wasn't very good at that. He could only hope the price for his weakness wouldn't be too high.

3

No body. No crime scene. No SOCOs to send out to do a detailed search. No sophisticated forensic analysis to provide answers. No computer summary of reports. No eyewitnesses to question. No adrenalin rush.

Just dusty papers and reports, a box of personal effects and a few photographs of Ailsa Grant, alive and dead, yellowed with the passage of time. Cold case was a good description, though perhaps dead case was better. It would be no more than dry bones that lay in these boxes.

Fleming had only a hazy memory of the news story concerning a murdered young woman thrown into the sea at the Mull of Galloway and some sort of scandal, the detail of which eluded her. It wasn't like a case where the body was there in front of her. And yet, and yet . . . those photos.

The photos were on the top of the first, catalogued box. There was one of Ailsa Grant, alive: a studio portrait of the type then fashionable, showing a face broad across the cheekbones, with strongly marked brows and a wide mouth. The hair was long and blonde, though dark eyebrows suggested this was not its natural colour. She had slightly hooded, grey-blue eyes and a tiny mole to the left of her mouth. Her nose and chin were a touch too prominent and she had, Fleming suspected, the sort of looks that wouldn't wear well. Here, though, with the blush of youth and her lips parted in a studied smile, she looked pretty enough.

The post-mortem photographs showed wide-open, glassy eyes and a water-bloated face, battered with gashes and what looked like a smashed cheekbone, but she was perfectly recognizable.

As Fleming looked at her, the dead case came to life. This wasn't just a murder statistic, this was a girl who would have been her own age, if she had lived. She had worn the same fashions, danced to the same music, dreamed dreams and had visions of her future too. The gross injuries had been suffered by flesh and blood, and Fleming heard the cry for justice as if the images themselves had given voice. With new enthusiasm she turned to her dusty task.

She had come in reluctantly this morning. She was feeling edgy, and though she was technically off duty she wasn't relaxing. When Bill, exasperated by her fidgeting, suggested she'd feel better if she went in to work, she had groaned and agreed.

There were practical difficulties to deal with, but she knew in her heart that it was the link with her father here that was bothering her most. She didn't want to be a witness to the humiliation he had suffered in being reprimanded. Snooping on something he had chosen to keep a secret from her was distasteful enough, and the thought that she was reviewing his work as a superior officer was even worse. He'd minded that he'd never made rank as an inspector; she had only realized how much when she told him of her promotion with pride, then had responded to his bitter reaction with a certain bitterness of her own.

There had always been respect, though, and after his death she had even come to admire the way he had upheld the standards he believed in. If he had been arrogantly unprofessional, as it sounded as if he might have been, it would hurt to find her respect and admiration misplaced.

The investigation, though, wasn't about her domestic hang-ups. It was about this girl, whose case deserved the exhaustive investigation it would be getting if this had happened yesterday, and it merited urgency, too. After all, Ailsa had waited long enough for justice.

Fleming focused first on the post-mortem shots, and frowned. Ailsa's hair seemed to have been neatly combed back from her face – that was odd, surely, given what the other photos showed of extensive injury to the back of the skull. They were interior shots, not taken in situ when the body had been brought ashore.

How, Fleming wondered, had foul play been established? She could see no signs on the clothed body which weren't consonant with a violent sea. Many suspicious features can have an innocent explanation and there are no universal lab tests for murder by drowning.

Turning next to the box of personal effects, Fleming ripped off the sealing tape and lifted the flaps. On top, neatly folded, was a pale blue tweed coat, ragged and stained and bleached by sea-water. It still had two elaborate flower-shaped buttons, one hanging by a thread. There was a shapeless green dress and some underwear. That was all. Fleming closed the box on the pathetic collection, then hesitated.

She was tempted to go straight to the pathologist's report. On the other hand, working steadily through would reflect the ordinary course of an investigation. She went to Box 1.

The first item was Sergeant Angus Laird's police notebook. She hadn't quite prepared herself for the sight of her father's familiar handwriting. He had the fine, old-fashioned copperplate style taught in those days, very strong and confident. She could hear his voice as she read, and she felt her throat constrict.

He had been first on the scene, and on his own. A helicopter had been scrambled by the coastguard after a lighthouse keeper spotted a body, washed up on a spur of rock below the cliffs to the north-west of the lighthouse. The keeper had identified the body as Ailsa Grant from Balnakenny, a farm half a mile away.

There had been a firm presumption of suicide, and there was a tell-tale entry explaining Laird's conviction. 'Deceased was visibly pregnant.' His moral standards had always been uncompromising and there was a hint in his tone that, given the girl's condition, this was only to be expected.

Of course! Fleming remembered now. That was the scandal! The ultimate shame at that time, every parent's fear – and she had to admit that even today she wouldn't be overjoyed if Cat bounced in and announced she was pregnant, with no father around for the baby. She certainly knew her father had fretted that she, Marjory, with her independence and even a certain wildness at one time before she met Bill, might get herself 'in trouble' as it was always described.

Bailey's report came next. He too had believed it was suicide so, as she had guessed from the photographs, there had been no obviously suspicious signs. There was a cryptic passage about a 'major breakdown in procedure' before the body was moved to the mortuary and the word 'recalcitrant' was used to describe Sergeant Laird's refusal to accept that the presumption of suicide had led to serious error.

Fleming re-read it, puzzled. She had no problem with recalcitrant – being recalcitrant was her father's favourite hobby – and never admitting he was wrong was standard practice. But *breakdown in procedure*. The Procedure Manual was Angus Laird's bible: he'd always ranted against any form of policing which did not comply with it, boringly when she was a child and annoyingly when she was a serving officer herself. Yet he seemed to have let them take the young woman's body away to her home to wait for the ambulance. He had even taken identification from Ailsa's father and brother on the spot, which certainly now would be formally done in the mortuary.

It was a small, personal mystery; she couldn't afford to waste professional time on it, yet inconsistencies were sometimes like a swirl in the water which spoke of a fish below. She filed it mentally and went on.

Fleming flicked through the statements from lighthouse keepers and their wives. None had seen or heard anything, but then it had been a savage night; with their shutters latched against the elements they probably wouldn't have heard a brass band outside playing Sousa marches, let alone the sound of a car arriving, or the screams of a girl – muffled, probably, in any case.

She speed-read the notebooks of officers who had arrived later and the coastguard report, then paused over the statements from Ailsa's parents and her brother. It might be better to see the evidence of murder first. Hindsight might indicate questions not asked at the time.

The autopsy report must be here somewhere. This was it – in a format style, typed a little unevenly in blue. It had been conducted in the mortuary of the local hospital and she ran her eye down dates, times, list of officials present. She smiled at the name DI Bailey – he'd have loved that – and turned to the report's findings.

It was a serious disappointment, short and inexplicit. She hadn't expected the detail and the battery of test results that were standard now, but even so, she sensed it hadn't been a meticulous process – something to check with Bailey. A pre-death injury to the back of the skull from contact with a stone was recorded, but with no indication of size or shape.

Lungs: no water present, again baldly presented, but Fleming knew this didn't necessarily indicate murder. In a substantial minority of cases the shock contact with water produced vagal inhibition and stopped the heart.

It was only when she reached 'External Signs: Marks of friction on both wrists indicative of rope burn' that she understood. Ailsa's hands had been tied together; she had struggled, and ultimately the ligature, perhaps loosened too by the waves, had fallen off. A horrid picture came to Fleming's mind: the raging storm, the figure falling from the cliff into the boiling sea below, screaming, perhaps, as she fought to free herself. As if that would have made any difference! Poor, poor Ailsa.

There had been no recent intercourse and the presence of the foetus, approximately twenty-eight weeks, had been recorded, but this was pre-DNA. Was there the smallest chance that somewhere in a path lab samples still existed? And if they had, where were they to look? The local hospital, with its mortuary, had closed long ago. She glanced at the catalogue, but there was no mention of it.

As she turned to fetch the next set of reports, Fleming suddenly caught sight of the time. Ten to one! She was due at her mother's for Sunday lunch. Where on earth had the morning gone?

The compelling narrative of the crime had caught her imagination and now she was reluctant to leave. She shuffled the papers she had been working with into a rough pile to one side of her desk – never exactly tidy anyway – and hurried out.

Jaki Johnston sat gloomily in the chair nearest the fire, swilling round ice in her third vodka and tonic. The only person who'd paid any attention to her was Diane's husband Gavin

– like she wanted him to! Loose, damp mouth – yuk! – and a blotchy complexion, from the drink, probably; he downed whiskies like alcopops. He was a right letch too, sitting beside her, pawing her arm when he brought her a drink. Then he'd started on suggestive remarks, until he said, 'We'll have to get you over to Miramar for a bit of fun – we could mix it up together, you and me, couldn't we?' and she'd given him a look of such obvious horror that he flushed, turned away and was now, thankfully, ignoring her.

All the attention was focused on Sylvia. Somehow she attracted it without doing anything, just sitting there in silver-grey cashmere which screamed not only money but class. Diane was pretty much drooling over her and Marcus was watching her with soppy affection. She was on about her Hollywood days and admittedly she was being very funny.

'And darling Michael was so pleased with this new fact he'd dug out from somewhere that no one liked to tell him that really *quite* a lot of people *did* know it, actually!'

Her stories all showed signs of having been told before, but Sylvia had worked them up well and Marcus seemed happy to hear them again, even encouraging her indulgently to tell some she hadn't thought of.

Jaki could tell funny stories too about socializing with her chums, but it wasn't quite the same as when the chums' names were Michael, as in Caine, and Frank, as in Sinatra, and a score of others. They were all old now or dead, but even Jaki had heard of them.

It had been a totally crap weekend. She'd been bored, cold, and permanently slightly hungry, since Marcus hadn't a clue about catering and there wasn't a takeaway within miles. She'd have sold her grandmother for a curry right now.

The only entertainment offered was walking – she didn't have the shoes for it, or the inclination – and this afternoon as a special treat they'd all driven to see the lighthouse on the Mull of Galloway. OK, it was dramatic, and Sylvia was in ecstasies, but it was all right for her – she got to stay in the car and hadn't been dragged out in the cold to admire the view.

Jaki couldn't wait for the team to arrive tomorrow. There'd be decent food, and the guys would suss out the best pub in minutes. That was where she planned to spend her evenings, and if Marcus wanted to stay home and talk about old times with Sylvia, then good luck to him.

Diane had got on to old times now – the farmers' dances and ceilidhs in village halls. Marcus, and Diane herself, of course, starred in most of the anecdotes. Jaki listened from her corner, her jaws aching with stifled yawns.

Gavin, too, wasn't appreciating his wife's ramble down memory lane. He'd been sinking Scotches and his interjections became more and more aggressive.

'God, this is boring!' he exploded at last. 'Face it – our social life was boring at the time and it's even more boring now.' He turned to Jaki. 'Marcus was a spotty youth in those days – the glamour, if that's what you call it, only came later.' The look he gave his host was one of naked dislike.

Marcus did his best to change the subject, but Diane just kept banging on and making eyes at Marcus while her husband glowered.

Then she said, 'Oh, Marcus, do you remember that night down at the pier, when Gav got absolutely stotious and fell in the sea? Marcus did the hero bit, Sylvia – went in after him, then dragged him ashore. Gav was so out of it, he barely knew what had happened, staggering round soaking wet! We were killing ourselves laughing – God, it was funny!' She chuckled at the recollection.

No one else laughed. Gavin's face turned a dark crimson. 'Bit of an exaggeration,' he said defensively. 'I'd have got ashore myself perfectly well.'

'Nonsense!' Diane cried. 'You might as well admit it – Marcus saved your life!'

Marcus looked rigid with embarrassment. 'It was all a very long time ago. I don't remember much about it.' As Diane seemed prepared to jog his memory, he went on hastily, 'But when did you actually leave Glasgow to come back here?'

It said a lot for his acting skills that he managed to sound as if he cared. Gavin, not looking at his wife in a way that suggested there'd be bloodshed on the way home, started on about their wonderful Miramar, with its integrated sound system, swimming pool with underwater lighting and hot tub. By the end of the recital Jaki felt she could have written out the particulars for an estate agent. The walk-in wardrobes, his and hers, apparently had a light that came on when you opened the door – fascinating, that.

'We've got this great team of Polish builders adding a steam room,' Gavin was boasting now. 'These fellows really do know how to work. Of course, I've offered a serious bonus if they crack on with it.

'You should get them along here, Marcus. This old heap could certainly use a bit of work. And you could jabber at them in their own lingo – might get a better deal.'

'Sadly not – my father was Czech, not Polish.' Marcus's lips tightened, but he went on calmly enough, 'Actually, they came here when I was away – put a card through the letter-box and asked in the bakery if the owner was around. They haven't appeared again – you were obviously a better bet. At least, I suppose it was the same men. The shop girl said it was an older guy who did the talking—'

'That's him! Stefan,' Diane interrupted. 'Quite attractive, in a rough sort of way.'

'That would suit you anyway – a bit of rough trade,' Gavin said coarsely. 'But seriously, Marcus, should we be talking in whispers? This old heap looks to me as if it could crumble on top of us any moment, if we raised our voices or laughed too loud. But maybe that's just one of the natural hazards in a toff's life?'

The chip on his shoulder was becoming uncomfortably obvious. His attempt at provocation didn't succeed but the atmosphere was poisonous and Jaki, with an actor's training in sensitivity to emotions, felt uneasily that Gavin's feelings about Marcus came close to hatred.

At last the Hodges left, offering invitations to Miramar to the accompaniment of three sets of non-committal noises.

When they were safely out of the room, Sylvia, with a naughtily conspiratorial look, said, 'Oh dear!' and for the first time Jaki felt the full force of her charm.

'Don't you *want* to see how the wardrobes light up as you open the door?' she asked, wide-eyed, and the two women were laughing as Marcus, looking frazzled, came back from seeing them out.

'Are you sure they've gone?' Sylvia asked. 'I'm amazed you don't have stab-marks all over from the looks he was giving you.'

'I can't think why. He'd have drowned if I hadn't pulled the silly bugger out. He should be grateful.'

'Stupid boy!' Sylvia scolded him. 'You never forgive someone for playing hero, especially if it made you look foolish at the same time. And Diane didn't help, suggesting you were an old flame.'

'Never!' Marcus actually shuddered, and as both women laughed, went on, 'I claim I always had good taste.'

Discussing the departed guests provided good entertainment, but when that petered out there was still a whole evening yawning ahead. Jaki was resigned to staying in, but if it was Scrabble again, like last night – with much laughter and cheating from Sylvia – she'd have a headache and go to bed.

It was worse.

'Now, Sylvia,' Marcus said, 'guess what I've got. I found a DVD of *For Ever* – I know Jaki hasn't seen it, so that's our entertainment sorted out.'

Sylvia made token protests, but without being ruder than she cared to be, Jaki couldn't show anything other than enthusiasm.

'That's so sweet of you,' Sylvia purred. 'But if you're *too* bored, you absolutely must say.'

'She won't be.' Marcus spoke for Jaki. 'Now, I'll just bring supper through. No, it's all right, Jaki, I'm totally organized. I only have to take it out of the oven and everything else is on a tray.'

When he brought it, it was fish pie. With mussels. Jaki hated mussels.

Marcus finished stacking the dishwasher and collected up the food packaging to go in the bin. This weekend might be the stupidest idea he had ever had.

Jaki and Sylvia, for a start, were a lethal mix: Sylvia came over all feline and Jaki went silent. It was a pity, because Jaki was warm and funny on her own territory, with a young, appealing freshness. Perhaps it was that which had so attracted him: he was probably reaching a midlife crisis.

He still thought of himself as not quite ready to settle to serious maturity. But the '*You make me feel so young*' effect promised by Sylvia's old mate Frank hadn't actually worked. This weekend was spelling that out in capital letters.

The relationship wouldn't last, probably not past this week. They were still good in bed, but he'd found himself wishing she wasn't sharing his room. It had a deep bay window giving views of the sea in both directions and he liked the curtains open, going to sleep in moonlight or starlight and half-waking with the dawn. Jaki wanted the curtains shut, and he felt claustrophobic; she wasn't tidy by nature either.

Tonight after the film – which Marcus had to admit had dated, rather – she'd pled a headache and gone to bed early. He'd kissed her goodnight, saying he'd sleep in the spare room, and she hadn't demurred.

He'd been thoughtless, bringing her here. It wasn't her sort of place, and it was all too clear what Sylvia thought.

And somehow, with Sylvia here, the house felt full of ghosts. Perhaps she had summoned up his father's presence in the conservatory, so that Marcus felt awkward about sitting in the wicker chair where Laddie had always sat, immaculate in well-cut trousers and a hand-made shirt with the cravat he affected at its open neck, talking languidly in his not-quite-perfect English. Sometimes Marcus could almost smell the lethal little black cheroots he always smoked. Here in the kitchen where the dogs' beds still lay – he'd never got round to throwing them out – he almost expected to hear his mother's voice, with its cut-crystal, upper-class vowels, calling them for a walk.

How had Flora felt about her husband's mistress? Had they ever discussed the situation? Marcus doubted that; his mother preferred to ignore inconvenient facts if at all possible. Though Marcus had never had an intimate conversation with his mother, he believed she had loved her husband deeply, and Tulach House, unchanged since his death, spoke of the way she treasured his memory. Perhaps she had accepted deliberate ignorance as the price for Laddie staying. Was the unspoken bargain tolerance for his mistress if Flora was spared humiliation among her friends?

If so, bringing Sylvia here in his wife's absence was reneging on the deal. Laddie was an intensely charismatic and lovable man, but he was in many ways a total bastard, and it would be small wonder if Flora's gawky, awkward shade were restless tonight.

Marcus had hero-worshipped his father, but it wasn't easy being his son. What could you ever do to match being one of the Few who had done so much? To be fair, Laddie had never demanded that he achieve; he adored Marcus and simply assumed he would, which was almost worse. Any small triumph was inflated, any failure brushed aside and instantly forgotten. Such unquestioning admiration should have made his son supremely confident, but somehow it made him more aware of his own inadequacies and ineffectiveness. Even tonight, he had experienced the bizarre feeling of guilt he'd always suffered from, when he didn't take Gavin Hodge on instead of submitting to being bullied.

Anyway, Laddie had lived to see his son a successful actor, and Marcus still saw that success as a filial duty. Like his duty to Laddie's beautiful house, and to his beautiful mistress too.

Marcus had been distressed lately to see how frail and sad Sylvia was becoming: her fame forgotten, her activities restricted and her old friends dying or becoming frail themselves. This weekend had seen her confidence restored, her personality sparkling once more. His intentions had been good, but in proverbial style it looked as if they were paving the way to a week of absolute hell.

Jaki hadn't gone to bed. It was only half past ten, for God's sake, and if she took a blanket and wrapped it round her the cold was bearable. And the view from the window was amazing, even now it was dark. There were lots of stars and every so often she could see the flash of light from the lighthouse, making the darkness blacker than ever after it passed.

She was grateful Marcus had suggested sleeping in the spare room. It felt all wrong to come to bed to make love when they'd hardly spoken together all day, with Sylvia dominating every conversation.

There seemed to be a power struggle going on, one that she was losing. Sylvia and Marcus had a funny relationship; he'd told Jaki she'd been his father's mistress, very matter-of-factly – but surely it was kind of weird to bring her here to his mother's home?

Sure, Jaki had modern attitudes and all that, but she felt a gut distaste for this sort of decadence. Sylvia was almost flirting with Marcus – sort of like he was his father over again, in a kind of jokey, possessive way that cut Jaki out.

This was going to be one tough week, and it looked like they'd be history by the end of it. Fun while it lasted, but now it was only about the best way to get from here to there.

They wouldn't quarrel. They still liked each other, and Marcus was famously courteous. And perhaps she'd be so great in this series she'd fix her place on her own merits – and even if she didn't, quite, it had been good experience.

Jaki yawned, then shivered. The wind was rising: she could hear it rattling the windows and whistling through the gaps, penetrating even her woolly swathes. She wasn't going to decide anything tonight; she'd sleep on it, and see how things looked in the morning. She got up to close the curtains.

There were still lights on downstairs, throwing patches of gold on to the overgrown garden below. It was a spooky sort of place even in daylight, and tonight the waving branches of trees and shrubs cast dancing shadows. There were still shadows too, cast by the angle of the house, but there was another shadow, one Jaki couldn't quite work out. She stared down at it, frowning.

It was still too. You could almost imagine it was a man there in among the trees and bushes of the shrubbery, standing motionless, watching. It gave her a creepy feeling.

Don't be daft, she told herself. Watching what? And what on earth would anyone be doing away out here in the middle of the night, apart from freezing to death? The atmosphere in this house was getting to her, that was all.

It still hadn't moved. It was a shrub, of course it was. She'd only make a fool of herself if she went downstairs and wittered to Marcus about men lurking in the shrubbery. She drew the curtains firmly and got into bed.

In the centre of Kirkluce, it was a normal Saturday night. The pubs and takeaways were doing good business; it was a bit noisy, with groups of young people milling about and a few staggering a bit, but when the police patrol car drove through on one of its usual rounds there was nothing to demand attention.

The men who emerged from the Horseshoe Tavern weren't noisy. In almost total silence they split left and right, into two groups of perhaps ten or twelve, locals and Polish incomers, then crossed the road separately, heading for the square opposite. As they confronted one another at the foot of the War Memorial scuffles broke out, punches were thrown and the shouting started.

The skinny young man who was moving round the edge of the fray, eyes narrowed, spotted his quarry at last. Slipping through, quick as an eel, he confronted the tall, dark young Pole. He was holding a knife in one hand, the other extended for balance.

'Here, you and me – we've stuff to settle. Remember?'

The Pole's reaction was immediate. As he turned, the streetlamp glinted on the blade which had appeared in his own hand. Eyes locked, the two men performed their almost balletic movements, circling each other, feinting, gaining ground, retreating.

But the Pole was gradually, inexorably, being driven back. The other man's teeth were bared in a grin of savage delight and the lightning slashes of his knife, first to one side then the other, were becoming more difficult to dodge.

At last, the Pole found himself with his back to the plinth of the War Memorial, and with no room to retreat. The blade flickering in front of his eyes seemed almost to be mesmerizing him. His own thrusts had become wild and there were beads of sweat appearing on his face.

In a movement as swift and deadly as a snake striking, the other's blade came in under his guard and ripped up his right arm from wrist to elbow.

With a cry of pain the Pole dropped his knife. His assailant gave an animal snarl of satisfaction, then menacingly closed in. He raised his knife again—

'Polis! Polis!' The warning cry froze his hand. The patrol car was coming back along the High Street and seeing the gathering of men, turned into the square.

A moment later, the square was empty.

Karolina Cisek looked at the clock, frowning. It was almost eleven, and Rafael with his early start was usually in bed at half past ten. He had gone to the pub in disgust when she told him she must spend the evening preparing the Flemings' evening meals for the days when she would be working in the film canteen.

It was quarter past eleven when she heard their elderly Honda returning, and Rafael came in. He was a big, solidly built man, square-jawed and brown-haired.

'You are very late.' Karolina greeted him in the Polish they always used at home, trying not to sound accusing, but knowing she had failed.

'I expect you managed to fill in the time.' Rafael had the sort of excited aggression about him she'd seen in people on the way to being drunk, but he wasn't a drinking man and he was entirely sober.

'Cup of tea?' she said, trying to defuse the situation. 'I finished what I needed to do and I made some apple cake.'

'Fine.' He sat down by the dying fire, looking into it as his wife switched on the kettle. He didn't seem inclined to talk.

'Was the pub busy tonight?' she asked.

'Yes. A lot of us gathered there – and there were some strangers.'

'Strangers?' Karolina frowned. 'What do you mean?'

'They were looking for us. They had come into Kirkluce from different places.'

'Oh, Rafael! There wasn't – there wasn't trouble, was there?'

'Not of our making. But they challenge us – so . . .' He shrugged.

'What happened? Was there a fight?'

He shrugged again. 'Sort of. It turned nasty.' He mimed someone slashing with a knife. 'We had to protect ourselves.'

Karolina was dismayed. 'Were the police involved? It won't do us Poles any good—'

'No, no police. Someone was a little hurt, that's all. Kasper, in fact.' He turned to look at her coldly. 'You didn't tell me Kasper had come here. But you knew, didn't you?'

Karolina's face flamed. 'I – I forgot. It wasn't important. I saw him when I went to Mass this morning.'

'Why here?' Rafael said, a dangerous edge to his voice. 'He knew we were here – has he come all the way from Poland to find you?'

'No, Rafael, no!' She came over to kneel on the hearthrug in front of him. 'That isn't true! He has just come to make a new life, after he was in so much trouble. And you remember – I turned him down. I chose you!'

'But you could change your mind. He showed he could make money – what can I offer you? So little that I cannot support my wife and son, that you have to work—'

Tears came into Karolina's eyes. 'It isn't like that! You make enough for a good life, but I like to do this. It could be even better for us, that's all. Here in Britain it is right for women to work. Bill has this farm and the lovely house, so Marjory does not need to work. She works because it is important to her.'

'She has to have you to do a wife's job for her. And Bill has to do things a wife should do.' Rafael sounded stubborn, but what his wife heard was hurt pride. He took his responsibilities as the breadwinner very seriously.

She said gently, 'Everyone respects Bill. No one thinks he can't support his family because she has an important job. It is good for them both.

'Anyway,' she said, a dimple just showing at the corner of her mouth though her eyes were still wet, 'cooking good Polish food for more people than my husband and son isn't a big important job. I'll be back in plenty of time for Janek's bedtime and your supper. That's what I want – to be here with you.'

He looked almost ready to be convinced. She leaned forward and kissed him and felt him respond. Then she said, 'And Kasper? Pooh! He is a—' She added an extremely rude word.

It persuaded him to laugh. He got up, pulling her to her feet. 'Never mind the apple cake. Come to bed.'

The nurse unwrapped the blood-stained towel from the young man's arm and looked at the deep, ugly wound from his elbow to his wrist.

'What happened?' she said.

He was tall and dark, with very dark brown eyes which did not meet hers. He shrugged. '*Nie mówie po angielsku.*'

There was a name on the form he had brought in with him from reception, and an address in Ardhill; he had communicated to that extent, anyway.

'Kasper Franzik. Polish?' she asked, and he nodded. 'Is anyone with you? Someone who speaks English?'

He seemed to understand, pointing back to the waiting room, and she went to see.

It had been quiet in the small medical treatment unit in Newton Stewart and there was only one person there, a man in his sixties, perhaps, with longish, badly cut grey hair. He was a little above medium height, with the lean fitness of a much younger man; from the look of his heavy boots and his hands he did the sort of physical work that would mean you were unlikely to run to fat.

'Do you speak English?' the nurse asked hopefully, smiling.

'Yes.' He didn't smile back.

'Could you help me talk to your friend? He doesn't understand what I'm asking him.'

He got up without response and followed her through to the treatment room where he said something gruffly to Kasper which the nurse didn't understand.

She prepared a steel bowl with water and disinfectant, and brought a handful of swabs to begin cleaning the wound. 'What happened?' she asked again.

'An accident.' The man didn't consult her patient. 'He was working on some stone and the – the – I do not know the word,' he mimed a tool, 'it slipped.' That was his only hesitation; he had a strong accent, but his English was good.

'Working on stone with a knife, was he, on a Sunday night? Look, I know a knife wound when I see one. Why not tell me who did that, and we can inform the police?'

The older man's face went blank and his language skills seemed to desert him. 'Don't understand. Accident.'

'If that's how you want it, there's nothing I can do. But tell him to keep out of trouble. Whoever did that wasn't playing games.'

She cleaned the wound thoroughly. Kasper, biting his lip, didn't flinch.

'I'll put adhesive strips on and bind it up meantime. But it needs proper attention and you'll need to go to Dumfries. I'll give you a note – do you understand?'

Kasper nodded, and she guessed he understood more than he was admitting. Not speaking English could be a way of avoiding awkward questions.

'Do you have transport?' she asked. 'There's a bus service, but it's not great—'

'We have a van,' the older man said. 'I can drive him there.'

She finished off. 'There you are. No serious damage, but it needs to be checked and properly stitched. Is it very painful?'

Again, Kasper nodded, unprompted.

She fetched painkillers and gave them to him in a paper cup, with a glass of water. He swallowed them, then said a heavily accented thank you.

She smiled. 'That'll keep you going till you get it seen to.'

His smile made him very attractive, in a brooding sort of way. The older man's face had relaxed and she thought he too was quite good-looking, with nice blue eyes. She'd noticed before that a lot of Polish men seemed to be, and they usually had nice manners too.

This wasn't the first time she'd seen young Poles showing signs of conflict. It was the first time for a knife wound, though, and it worried her.

The nurse was just about to go off duty when Sergeant Christie from Newton Stewart police station brought in an early-morning cyclist who had come off his bike. She directed him into a treatment room, then spoke to Christie.

'Just thought you should know – I'd a young Pole in here last night with a knife slash on his forearm. He claimed it was an accident, but it looked as if he'd put up his arm to ward off a knife attack. Nasty.'

Sergeant Christie was a neat man with a little moustache, very punctilious and a little pompous. 'A sad reflection on today's society. Have you the address? We'll chase it up.'

4

'You're early this morning, ma'am!' the Force Civilian Assistant said as DI Fleming came in on Monday morning.

Fleming smiled at the woman on the front desk. 'Lot to do today,' she said as she passed. She didn't stop. FCAs had replaced desk sergeants, 'for efficiency', they claimed, though a chat with Jock Naismith had always seemed quite an efficient way of catching up with what had happened overnight. Now she got a report on her desk instead: more paperwork, less real information.

Fleming sighed. She was getting more like her father all the time. And thinking of her father . . . The case had been on her mind ever since she'd been forced to leave it yesterday and she was in a hurry to get back to it.

She had left the papers ready on her desk, with the second set of interviews with the Grants on top. She switched off her phone, paired them with the earlier ones, and settled down to read.

Robert Grant, Ailsa's father, had accepted her suicide unquestioningly and even after the pathologist's findings seemed unconvinced. The words 'some mistake' featured – had he special reason to block an enquiry? The son mentioned family rows, but then clammed up.

Jean Grant, like her husband and son, had said the three of them were together all evening and Ailsa was the only one who went out. But she had from the first flatly refused to accept her daughter had killed herself, and talked of a phone call to Ailsa that afternoon, and then of her putting on make-up before she left.

With a pang, Fleming thought of the young woman preparing to go out: her skin with that pregnant glow, eyes carefully shaded, mouth reddened before she put on the pretty blue coat, straining against the bump perhaps. Had she gone to meet her lover eagerly, hopeful that he would take her away, or offer marriage, even? Had she taken luggage with her? No one seemed to have checked.

The Grants had been asked separately if they knew who the father of the child was. Both men said no, but Jean had hinted at knowledge, while admitting her daughter had not actually told her.

It was only on hearing the report of murder that she made an astonishingly direct accusation. With a fiercely vindictive tone which came through the formal phrases, she claimed her daughter had been killed by Marcus Lazansky, a former boyfriend who had rejected Ailsa, then gone to Glasgow. Later, despite her mother's dark warnings, Ailsa had followed him there, with this result. Jean offered no evidence; she 'just knew'.

Marcus Lazansky – the man Janet had been talking about only yesterday, now Marcus Lindsay. How strange he should be here, just now! Though of course, since the man owned a house in the area, it wasn't really that surprising.

It took some time to work through intervening reports, most of them detailing enquiries which had led nowhere, then at last she came to the follow-up on Lazansky.

Donald Bailey had interviewed his parents, Ladislav and Flora. They had stated categorically that their son was in the United States and had been there all year, which, Bailey accepted, let Marcus off the hook.

Fleming sat back to consider it, looked at her watch and was astonished to discover it was almost eleven o'clock. She'd better check there were no urgent messages on the answer machine.

There were several, all routine stuff until the last one. The acting Procurator Fiscal's voice said crisply, 'Inspector Fleming, I understand you have been tasked with reviewing the Ailsa Grant case. I shall want a report from you on your progress as soon as possible. Perhaps you can call me – when you decide to return to your office.'

Fleming slammed down the receiver and swore, loudly, just as a knock came on the door and DC Kerr opened it, then stopped on the threshold. 'Sorry, boss! Is this a bad time?'

Fleming controlled herself. 'No, no, Tansy. Come in. It's as well you interrupted me before I strangled the phone, since I can't reach the Fiscal's neck. And you never heard me say that.'

Kerr grinned. 'Sorry – what was that? Sudden attack of deafness. Must see the doctor.'

'Nasty, deafness. Still, I'm glad you didn't catch what I said. An innocent young woman like you shouldn't hear language like that.'

'Wouldn't have understood it if I had, boss.'

Tansy was looking good these days, Fleming thought. Since the unfortunate business with a fellow officer last year, she'd become a lot less wacky. Her taste in hair colour, previously unusual to say the least, was rather more subtle – ash-blonde today – and her jeans didn't now look as if she'd gone wild with the scissors.

'What can I do for you, Tansy?' she asked.

Kerr looked surprised. 'We have an appointment. You wanted to see me.'

'Did I?' Fleming gestured at the boxes around her. 'I'm afraid I got caught up in this.

'Now, what did I want you for? Oh yes. Your appraisal's coming up shortly, Tansy, and I wanted to know how you saw your career before it reached me.'

Kerr looked alarmed. 'Um – not sure what you mean.'

'You're an able officer with almost the same years of service as Andy Mac, and he made sergeant eighteen months ago. Have you started working for your sergeant's exams?'

Kerr started pleating her fingers. 'Er – not exactly.'

'Not exactly?'

'Well – not at all, really.'

Fleming sat back in her chair. 'I'm not an aggressive feminist. Positive discrimination's insulting – in today's world if we want it, we can get it. I don't feel victimized because the lads describe us as lads as well, or are less than politically correct. I'm as tough as any man and I don't find people patronize me because I'm a woman.' She smiled. 'Well, not twice.

'But I still want more promoted women in the CID. Women have different skills to bring to the table.'

'Mmm.'

Fleming looked at her quizzically.

'You see, the thing is—' Kerr broke off, then started again. 'I know that's right. We need an all-round perspective. But I don't really want responsibility – not yet, anyway. Happiest day of my life was when I finished school exams and I want to have a good time while I'm young!'

Fleming looked at her with just a touch of exasperation. 'What age are you, Tansy – thirty?'

'Thirty-two,' Kerr admitted reluctantly.

'Not very young, thirty-two, really. Remember how old that was when you were twenty-one?' Kerr winced, but Fleming didn't spare her. 'Take it from me, your thirties whizz by, and suddenly you're forty.

'Still, it's your decision. But don't just drift, will you? Thanks, Tansy.'

Kerr rose, with some relief. Even cosy chats with Big Marge, as she was known to her officers, had a tendency to turn uncomfortable. She was just leaving when Fleming asked, 'Quiet day? Nothing's come my way, anyway.'

'Not bad. But Sergeant Naismith was saying a report's come in about trouble between the locals and some Poles – a knife involved. He's going to have a word with you.'

Fleming frowned. 'That's been brewing – vague reports of small incidents. All the gutter press talk about the "Polish invasion" is stirring it.'

'Part of the problem is they all get together and come in a bunch, not just ones and twos. I've seen a dozen of them coming out of the Horseshoe Tavern at weekends – wouldn't be my choice, I have to say.' Kerr wrinkled her nose. 'Spit and sawdust, but they say the beer's cheap.'

'The clientele's pretty rough as well. Faults on both sides, no doubt. And it's human nature – young men like fighting.

'Anyway, I'd better get on. Tell Tam I'll speak to him later.'

Kerr hesitated. 'Er – boss, you might want to know you've got dusty marks all over your face.'

'Oh,' Fleming said blankly, then looked at her hands and held them up. 'Not really surprising. I feel as if I've got dusty marks all over my brain as well, just at the moment.'

She watched Kerr go out of the door, then shook her head. She recognized that lack of direction, that restlessness, from her own youth. But she had been ten years younger at the time, and she had found her direction the day she joined the Force. She wasn't sure it was working out that way for Tansy.

★   ★   ★

'Miss Lascelles! Homage!' Barrie Craig, director of *Playfair's Patch*, came into the drawing room and bent low over the actress's hand.

Absurd little man! He looked, Sylvia thought, like a tennis ball – very round, very bouncy and with a fuzz of razor-cut grey hair round his spreading bald patch. Still, she murmured, 'Too kind,' with a gracious inclination of the head.

'Are you happy with the script, Miss Lascelles? Any problems, we can fix them.'

'Oh, Sylvia, please! No, it seems perfectly straightforward. I'm sure we can make any adjustments necessary as we go along. And of course I'm always happy to take direction.'

'Of course, of course – Sylvia,' he gulped. He gestured round the room. 'I've just been checking out the house – they told me it was perfect and it certainly is. That wonderful decayed splendour, the curtains frayed, the carpets threadbare, everything starting to fall apart, and you—'

With a certain sardonic amusement, Sylvia saw him realize suddenly where that sentence was leading and collapse into crimson confusion.

Marcus took pity on him. 'It shows the money and prestige Sylvia's character once had, and emphasizes the tragic disintegration of her life after her husband's murder years before.'

Barrie picked up the lifeline with the desperate enthusiasm of a drowning man. 'And, of course, with lighting we can make it very creepy indeed when she realizes the murderer is now coming for her too, and here she is – helpless! Those French doors there – perfect!'

Then he looked round. 'And where's the gorgeous Jaki? She's staying here, isn't she?'

'Oh yes,' Marcus said. 'Still in bed, is my guess – hasn't

emerged yet. Great to be young – I've somehow lost the talent for sleeping in.'

Sylvia saw the director give him a curious look. She was interested, too, in what this revealed about the Marcus–Jaki situation, but neither of them said anything. In their world you learned that happy coexistence depended on bland acceptance when it came to relationships.

'I'll get Mrs Boyter to bring some coffee. I've managed to lure her away from her usual clients to look after us this week,' Marcus said, with some pride. 'I hooked her with the promise of meeting Sylvia – she's always been one of her biggest fans. Of course Sylvia was wonderful and Mrs B's purring like a kitten – can't do enough!'

'Darling, I'd have done anything to avoid more of your suppers – I didn't know it was possible to ruin a ready meal just by putting it in the oven! Barrie, you wouldn't believe!'

She turned to the director, her intimate smile inviting him to join in the teasing, and pink with pleasure, he laughed.

'Shocking!' he agreed, as Marcus, hurling, 'Ungrateful woman!' over his shoulder, left in search of coffee.

In the kitchen he found not just Mrs Boyter, resplendent in a bright pink pinny purchased specially for the occasion, but Jaki at the kitchen table eating toast. She smiled at him a little uncertainly.

'Morning, darling!' Marcus said brightly, kissing her on the forehead. 'How's the headache?'

She took her tone from him. 'Oh, much better. I slept really well. It's so quiet, and the light didn't wake me so I didn't stir until after half past ten.'

'It's very dark with the curtains drawn,' he agreed. 'Mrs B, Miss Lascelles would love some coffee. There will probably be five or six of us, if you could bring through a pot.'

Mrs Boyter's face positively shone. 'Of course, Marcus. I've made some of my wee biscuits as well – she'll like those.'

'Thanks. I'm sure we all will.' He turned to Jaki. 'Are you finished? Or are you on a toast jag?'

'I've been on a toast jag.' She got up. 'I've bribed Mrs Boyter not to tell anyone how many pieces I had.' She grinned impishly at the older woman, who shook her head at her.

'Oh, you're a wee terror for toast, right enough,' she said indulgently.

As Marcus shut the kitchen door, he said teasingly, 'Mrs B has clearly decided TV stars are almost as good as film stars. I, of course, don't count because she knew me as a wee boy scrumping apples.'

They were in the long below-stairs passage leading to the front hall. Jaki stopped. 'Marcus, I don't know quite how to say this, but I don't think—'

He turned, reading what she was going to say in her face. 'No,' he agreed. 'I don't think, either. I'm sorry.'

Jaki's relief was obvious. 'I'm sorry too. We had fun, didn't we?'

Marcus stooped to kiss her cheek. 'Oh, we had fun. You're a terrific girl, love. It's just—'

'No,' she said firmly. 'Hold it right there – I'm not into angst and analysis. No agonizing, no regrets. I'll get them to find somewhere for me to doss down and move my gear.'

He didn't reply immediately. Then he said, 'Would you mind very much staying on here? There'll be so much gossip and whispering – better if we could drift apart discreetly back in Glasgow.'

She didn't want to do that. She was open by nature and she didn't fancy having to act off-stage as well as on – and she was desperate to get out of this place too. But he was right enough about the gossip.

After a moment she said, unconvincingly, 'No, of course I don't mind. I see where you're coming from – the conversations that stop just as you come into the room, the fake sympathy . . .'

'And the "never thought it would last" remarks. Well, I don't suppose we did either, really. But we've been good friends as well as lovers, haven't we, and I'd like to think I wouldn't lose the friendship part.'

'I'd like that too. You could come out clubbing sometimes.'

She was very attractive, smiling up at him like that, and for a second he felt a pang. But he only winced elaborately and, hearing Mrs Boyter opening the kitchen door, they went to join the others.

At half past two, DI Fleming straightened her aching back, thoughtlessly rubbing her hand down her face. She put the papers back carefully in order so that she could find them next time.

She'd had only the most cursory run through to familiarize herself with the background. The hard part would come with the analysis of procedures followed and actions taken, and interviewing Donald about the gaps.

She could pinpoint some already. Despite there being no suicide note and no direct evidence that the woman had thrown herself into the sea, the assumption of suicide had bedevilled the early investigation. There had been no proper search for signs of a struggle on the headland from which, given its proximity and the currents, the body had been pushed into the sea. No casts had been taken of tyre marks, to check against cars known to be in use by the keepers. The questioning of the lighthouse residents had been perfunctory, and she could find no record of interviews with people Ailsa might have talked to when she had been at home in the two months before her death, and only brief and unilluminating statements from colleagues she had worked with as a secretary to a firm of exporters in Glasgow. Worst of all, despite Jean Grant's accusation, Marcus Lazansky/ Lindsay had never been directly interviewed.

The investigation was riddled with flaws. She certainly was not going to be able to pat Bailey on the head and tell him it was fine.

Lacking evidence of anyone else's involvement, apart from the phone call Ailsa had allegedly received, there had been follow-up only on Robert Grant, though with his alibi from his wife and son, there wasn't much they could do. Experts nowadays compare the friction burns with the rope found around the farm – and track phone calls – but at that time they had nothing to go on.

Fleming couldn't discover any details about that phone call. Of course, you didn't record every informal conversation unless something useful emerged from it, which might well explain it.

Her notebook was full of queries and follow-ups to be done, many of them awkward and time-consuming. Of the four officers most directly involved, only Bailey was readily available: one was dead; one had retired and, she thought she remembered, gone to live in Spain; the other had left the Force and could be anywhere. The lighthouse keepers would be hard to trace too, with the lighthouse having been automated in 1988, and Ailsa's secretarial colleagues of twenty years ago were unlikely still to be there – even if the firm of exporters was – and more than likely would have married and changed their names.

That would all take time, possibly a lot of time, and Fleming wanted to move quickly. When you lifted a stone, dark creatures, safely hidden before, panicked in the light of day: when the investigation became common knowledge, someone out there would become desperate to stop her finding out the truth, and desperation breeds danger. She had to move fast.

Where to start? If the Grants were farmers, they'd probably still be at Balnakenny – farms rarely changed hands. Marcus Lindsay was definitely around. They might find some locals, too, who had been friends with Ailsa; the pull of Galloway was strong and even if young folks left, a surprising number came back later. It would also be interesting to find out what local wisdom had made of the case. Fleming had a profound respect for the intelligence system which operated in rural areas.

She needed to get to the Mull of Galloway this afternoon, and if Tam MacNee was in the building, she'd take him along, though she'd better wash her face and hands first.

DS MacNee was indeed in the building. He too had been at a desk all day, complaining to anyone who would stand still long enough that this wasn't what he'd signed up for.

When the phone rang and DI Fleming's voice said, 'Tam? Oh good. I've been working on this cold case all morning—' it rekindled his grievance.

'Aye, I know that. I've been at my desk all morning too, doing what you'd have been doing if you weren't. The Super said it was all to be diverted to me to keep your desk clear and give you time to do it.'

Fleming's voice sharpened. 'He can't do that! What are you working on, Tam? Not budgets, or manpower requirements or—'

'I wish! I could've put in for another couple of lads for the CID and a raise for overtime.'

'At least I've been spared that! The Super must be mad – I'll have a word with him. There's nothing that can't wait.'

'You know your problem?' he began.

'Yes. I'm a control freak. I like it that way. Now, stop playing with my reports. I want you to come out to the Mull of Galloway with me, to do some interviews. I'll fill you in on the details on the way down.'

MacNee rose with alacrity. 'This stuff's all yours. I'm sending it on to you now – or at least, I will be when I find someone to tell me what button to press.'

'Just one other thing – a report's come in about an assault with a knife. Can you get the background from Jock Naismith? That sort of thing's contagious – we need to get on top of that before it spreads and we've a serious problem on our hands.'

'How's it going, boys?' Diane Hodge, wearing a DKNY tracksuit in a challenging shade of yellow, with wet hair and a white towel round her neck, jogged across from the swimming pool. It was under a glass dome, covering a tropical jungle of green plants which struck a bizarrely exotic note on this bright, cold spring day.

The four men plastering the walls of a brick construction on one side of the sprawling house glanced up, but only one stopped work. He was much older than the others, with longish greying hair, and a weather-beaten face – a bit rough, admittedly, but the lean, mean type who might be quite good-looking if he wasn't always so gloomy.

'Hey, Stefan! Cracking the whip, then?' Diane always tried to raise a smile; she hadn't managed yet, but she wasn't a quitter.

'We are on schedule to meet your target next week.'

'That's brilliant!'

Still he didn't smile. Looking for a new audience, Diane walked over to admire the work, and noticed that one of them, Kasper, was sporting a bandage on his left arm.

'Hey, what happened?'

Kasper was a serious hunk, with those dark, smouldering looks. Occasionally he smiled at her in a way that made her feel quite kittenish, but today he only directed a look towards Stefan, who said, 'He had an accident with a tool, Mrs Hodge.'

She wagged a playful finger at Kasper. 'Need to be a lot more careful in future, won't you? But anyway, you're all doing a terrific job – keep up the good work!'

Kasper went back to his plastering and the others hadn't looked up.

Defeated, Diane turned away. She crossed the extensive garden, landscaped into total submission, and entered the house through the large conservatory, where her husband, in one of the rattan peacock chairs, was leafing through a yachting magazine.

Gavin Hodge did not look up. Relations had been strained since their row in the car coming back from Tulach.

Diane gave him a wary glance. She was by nature unreflective, but the atmosphere was beginning to get her down. Trying to ignore it, she said, 'I try really hard to be friendly to these men, just to show I don't mind them being immigrants, but Stefan just won't lighten up. And how the others manage here I don't know – they don't understand a word I say.'

'Don't bet on it – I reckon it suits them to play dumb. They've work to do, so leave them alone. And Stefan probably thinks you're coming on to him and he's terrified.'

Diane gave Gavin a look of dislike. 'You really do have a nasty tongue. For God's sake, just because last night I mentioned something that happened years ago, you don't have to act like this.'

'You deliberately humiliated me. And you exaggerated and made out that little prick Lazansky was some sort of hero.'

Diane sighed. 'I didn't humiliate you deliberately, and I didn't exaggerate. If anything, I underplayed it. It was funny, that's all, and after all these years you might have a sense of humour about it.

'And if we're talking about how people behave, slavering over a girl in her twenties is pretty disgusting. She thought you were a dirty old man, quite obviously.'

Gavin Hodge's face turned an alarming shade of puce. He dropped the magazine and stood up.

'Women have been hit for less than that. I'm leaving before you're one of them. And I'm going out. Don't wait lunch.'

Diane looked after him as he stormed out. She bit her lip, then, with a shrug and a small, angry laugh, went off to have a shower.

In the car, Fleming briefed MacNee, with professional succinctness, on the facts of the case. Wanting to see what he would make of it, she tried not to give it a subjective slant.

'Reaction, Tam? Take your time – it's a long, long drive down the Mull.'

MacNee glanced about him. 'It's a rare day for it, anyway.'

They had turned off the A75 and were driving now past Sandhead, looking out to Luce Bay. It was, indeed, a fine day for early April, clear and windy, the sea a dark blue flecked with white caps. The tide was out: miles of wave-scoured sand fringed the bay, punctuated by long lines of black rocks, draped in bladderwrack. To the landward side, great clumps of gorse were just coming into flower and behind these stunted trees leaned away from the prevailing wind.

'I like the countryside fine,' MacNee observed, 'but just to look at, mind, not live in. Too quiet.'

Fleming smiled. MacNee was still a townie at heart, even if he had compromised on the douce charms of Kirkluce to keep his adored wife Bunty happy. Somewhere inside, though, he was still hungering for the raucous, edgy atmosphere of his native Glasgow.

He began thinking aloud. 'The father – I'd be taking a good shufti at him. He'd got motive, means, opportunity – and what have we got instead? Someone phoning her up to arrange to kill her? Sounds kind of far-fetched to me. What does he do – rolls up to collect her, ties her wrists, bangs her on the head then tips her off the cliff, all within half a mile of her home? Surely there'd be better ways.'

Fleming agreed. 'It was the risk that struck me. He couldn't be sure she wouldn't tell someone who she was meeting.'

'She didn't tell anyone who the father was. But even so ...'

'I want to see what the parents and the brother have to say now. It'll be useful to compare with the original statements.'

'Have to consider the brother as well, of course. You never know what goes on in these country places,' MacNee said darkly.

'Not, of course, in Glasgow? But I agree, that needs consideration – which it certainly didn't get last time round.

'The other visit this afternoon is to Marcus Lazansky – or Lindsay, I suppose he likes being called now. Based in Glasgow, but he's here filming *Playfair's Patch* this week, Cat tells me. She has dreams of stardom once she's spotted during her twenty seconds of glory as an extra.

'It sounds as if he'd a solid alibi not only for the murder but also the time of the child's conception, but as far as I can tell he's never been questioned. If we do that now, pushing a bit to see if it checks out, we can maybe eliminate him. I thought we'd go there first and hope to catch him at Tulach House.'

MacNee grunted. 'You don't watch that rubbish, do you?'

'Never managed to watch an episode right through. The kids and Bill like it and they send me out of the room because I keep groaning. I can see why he's popular, though.'

'Oho – fancy him, do you?'

'Tam, don't leer. It's not a pretty sight. No, not really. I prefer the rugged type that make me feel small and feminine.' She gave him a warning glance. 'And snorts of derision constitute insubordination.

'And by the way, what did Jock have to say about the knifing?'

MacNee pulled a face. 'Not a lot. Bad feeling between the Poles and the neds, he reckons, and I'd put good money on it that our old friend Kevin Docherty's at the bottom of it. But they stonewalled the nurse at the medical centre when she asked.'

'I'm edgy about this. They all begin carrying knives for protection and that's a recipe for disaster. I'll get someone out there tomorrow to see what we can do. Getting Docherty back behind bars would be a good start.

'Oh, that's the turn for Ardhill. Not far now.'

The wind took them as they climbed out of the car outside Tulach House. MacNee staggered and swore.

'What a godforsaken place! If you'd money to build a big grand house like this, what would you put it here for?'

'Look at the view, Tam!' Fleming gestured towards the Irish Sea on one side, Luce Bay on the other. 'It's amazing!'

'Oh, it's that, right enough.' Muttering something only marginally appropriate about 'chill November's icy blast', MacNee gave a disparaging look round, pulling up the zip on his black leather jacket and heading for the shelter of the pillared porch.

A thick shrubbery encroached on the side of the house, and what had once been a lawn looked more like a hayfield.

The flowerbeds were overgrown, and the paintwork of the house too showed the signs of neglect. It was sad, Fleming thought, given the elegance of the original building – like a grand lady reduced by circumstances to a down-and-out.

There were several cars parked on the weedy gravel in front of the house. As MacNee rang the bell, Fleming glanced at them, noticing that one had a disabled sticker.

It wasn't Marcus Lindsay who opened the door. This was a short, plump little man who greeted them cheerfully when they explained who they were.

It wasn't often their unexpected arrival met with such enthusiasm. 'Oooh, how splendid! I'm Barrie Craig, but I expect you really want our First AD – Assistant Director. He takes care of liaison with the police – actually, if I'm honest, takes care of just about everything. I promise you, he'll see that none of the locals are upset.

'But do come and meet Marcus first – he'll be so tickled to meet you!'

'Yes, it was him we were hoping to speak to,' Fleming said.

'My goodness, fans – in the Force! I'm thrilled skinny!'

MacNee opened his mouth but at a look from Fleming shut it again, and they followed Craig through an airy hallway floored with black and white marble tiles and with a curved wrought-iron staircase sweeping up in front of a long arched window. From an open door came the sound of animated conversation.

There were five people sitting around, but Fleming's eyes went immediately to the woman in the wheelchair, pulled up close to the log fire. She wasn't speaking, just watching with a slight smile on her face, but even in her silence her presence dominated the room. There was a much younger woman, whom Fleming recognized from the series, perched on the arm of a sofa talking to a man with a clipboard.

Beside him was another man with a bag full of technical-looking stuff at his feet. There was some sort of argument going on.

'OK, I can do that,' Jaki was saying, 'but you really can't expect—'

Craig bustled in. 'Marcus! Someone you simply have to meet!'

Fleming hadn't noticed him initially. He was behind the woman in the chair, a little in shadow. She recognized him too, naturally, but he was much less striking in real life – a quiet, attractive-looking man with none of the swagger of his TV persona. Then he smiled and stepped forward, and it was as if he had suddenly taken the spotlight. Out of the wings, on to the stage, Fleming found herself thinking.

'Superintendent Playfair, meet DI Fleming!' Craig declaimed. 'And – er – and her sergeant.'

As Fleming moved forward to shake his hand, she realized MacNee hadn't moved. He was staring at the woman in the wheelchair, who had noticed this, and as Lindsay disclaimed entitlement to such an introduction, directed a smile at MacNee which had him moving forward with a silly smile on his own face.

'Miss – Miss Lascelles!' he stammered, taking the hand she held out to him and holding on as if he wasn't quite sure what to do with it now.

Sylvia Lascelles detached herself with the grace of experience. 'Goodness, you are clever to recognize me! I must have changed a bit since last you saw me.'

'Couldn't forget,' MacNee said, a little hoarsely. '*For Ever* – my – my wife's favourite film.'

It wasn't kind of Fleming to say, 'Oh come, Sergeant MacNee, I'm sure you enjoyed it too,' but she did enjoy the unusual spectacle of Tam MacNee blushing. She went on,

'We really wanted to have a word with you, Mr Lindsay, if you don't mind.'

Barrie Craig interrupted. 'He doesn't know a thing about it. The person you want is Tony here, our First AD.' He indicated the man with the clipboard. 'Show the officers the arrangements, Tony.'

'That's all right,' Fleming said quickly. 'There may be questions from the local uniformed branch, but it's not really our business.' She turned, making a gesture towards the door. 'If there's somewhere we could talk, Mr Lindsay . . .?'

He was looking politely puzzled. 'Yes, of course – this way.'

'Oooh, they've caught up with you, Marcus!' the irrepressible Craig was saying as they left, and Fleming heard Sylvia's voice asking, 'What on earth was that about?'

The room he took them into was a book-lined study. It had an air of decay; motes of dust danced in the sunlight and the backs of the old volumes, untouched for centuries, were dry and faded. There were leather chairs and a chesterfield, cracked and splitting; the tapestry curtains were heavy with the grime of ages and at one end had fallen off the curtain rail. Above the mantelpiece was a striking portrait sketch of a very good-looking man in the traditional pilot's pose – flying jacket, white silk scarf. Laddie Lazansky, presumably: he was clearly still a presence in the house.

The room was very cold. Apologizing, Lindsay switched on a small electric fire, incongruous in the impressive fireplace. 'Sorry – I'm afraid I don't use much of the house. Things got neglected latterly and I'm hardly here myself. Now, what can I do for you?'

He took the chair nearest the inadequate fire and MacNee, in a swift outflanking move, secured the one on the other side,

leaving the chesterfield and the draught from the window for
Fleming.

'This is going back a long way, Mr Lindsay,' she began.
'You may remember that in October 1985 a young woman
was found dead in the sea at the Mull of Galloway – Ailsa
Grant.'

'Ailsa Grant!' he said slowly. 'Yes – yes, of course I remember.
A tragedy – I used to know her when we were young.'

Was that a guarded reply? 'A murder enquiry followed,
but no one was ever charged. It is policy to review cases of
this sort, and I am in charge of a fresh investigation.'

MacNee, too, was watching the man closely. He leaned
forward. 'You see, however long ago it was, it's still our job to
see she gets justice.'

Lindsay seemed quite relaxed – but then, Fleming
reminded herself, he was an actor. 'Glad to hear it,' he said
gravely. 'If there's anything I can tell you, I'm happy to do it.'

A wholly appropriate response – almost too perfect, as if
someone had given him his lines. Fleming went on, 'Did you
have a relationship with Ailsa Grant?'

'Relationship? Oh – I don't know that I'd call it that. I
took her out a few times when we were – what, seventeen,
eighteen? It didn't amount to anything except a few kisses in
the back of my mother's car.'

She pressed him. 'No more than that?'

'Yes, inspector, no more than that.' Lindsay was firm.
'Teenagers weren't always shagging the way they do nowadays
and down here we've always been behind the times anyway.
And, as I said, it didn't last long.'

'And afterwards, when you were in Glasgow? She was
working there too.'

'I heard she was in Glasgow, but I never saw her. She
didn't follow me there, if that's what you're suggesting. It

was a couple of years later, I think, and I'd started acting by then – bit parts, with bar work to pay the rent – so I hadn't the time to chase up old acquaintances.'

'So the relationship had finished? Was she unhappy about that?'

Fleming thought she sensed tension, but he said easily enough, 'Perhaps, but we all move on. I got caught up with the theatre crowd and didn't come home much. No doubt she had her own friends.'

That sounded defensive. Good. You always got more out of people who felt defensive. Fleming went on, 'Her friends – who would they have been?'

'Don't know, really. As teenagers we hung out in cafés mostly – the pubs were a bit strict round here. The café in Sandhead was popular, I remember. But there were kids I didn't know.'

'I'd be grateful for any names – addresses would be helpful too, if you have them.'

'The only two I can produce are Gavin and Diane Hodge – their house is Miramar, in Sandhead. They stayed around here longer than I did, then went to Glasgow – her father had a building company there – so they could probably tell you more. I'll warn them to expect you.' Lindsay sat forward in his chair, assuming this was the end of the interview. 'Anything else?'

With a glance at Fleming, MacNee took over. 'When Ailsa died, your parents claimed you were in America.'

Lindsay bristled. '*Claimed*, sergeant? I *was* in America.'

'You see,' MacNee went on, 'no one checked. Maybe you were, but even in those days there were such things as planes. And it could have been worth a trip over if, let's say, you found you'd got a girl pregnant—'

Lindsay stared at him, astonished. 'I don't believe I'm hearing this! Is this some sort of accusation of *murder*? I thought the series had some improbable plot lines, but this is something else.'

Fleming said soothingly, 'No, no, sir, it's not an accusation. Sergeant MacNee was just thinking aloud.'

Lindsay's smile was unamused. 'I'd really rather he didn't.'

'The thing is, Mr Lindsay, at the time you were actually accused of murder. Did you know that?'

'Accused of murder?' His shock was clearly genuine. 'But – who by?'

'I'm afraid we're not at liberty to tell you. But it would be a great help if we knew your movements at that time, say between March and November 1985.' She nodded to MacNee, who got out his notebook.

Lindsay seemed more irritated than uneasy at the questioning. 'At this distance in time? I was in New York, I suppose – waiting and bar work again. I'd blagged a green card – my father had contacts from the war – and the actors' unions weren't as tough then as they are now, so I got some off-Broadway stuff, doubling as stage manager – that sort of thing. Then I was lucky enough to get a season in Connecticut doing summer stock. Great experience – got me touring dates afterwards and then TV work when I came home.'

'So you were out of the country all that time? No visits back?'

'Couldn't have afforded it. Starvation wages, they paid.'

He had relaxed again, and indeed the flat statement left nothing to follow up. Yet Fleming couldn't quite let it go.

'I know it's a lot to ask, but it would be most helpful to get corroboration – friends and colleagues at the time, for instance—'

Lindsay was shaking his head. 'I haven't really kept in touch. I was more or less nomadic for years and there wasn't text or email, of course. But hey – hang on! I think I can do better than that.'

He got up with a triumphant air, went to the back of the room and stooped to lift a big album from the bottom shelf. He brought it over carefully and laid it on a round rosewood table in the window, blew dust off it, then opened it as Fleming and MacNee came to join him.

It was a scrapbook, crammed with yellowing cuttings and photographs. 'My pa kept this, bless him,' he said. 'Right from when I was in school plays. I'd to send everything to him, though he censored the bad reviews.'

Lindsay pointed to one faded cutting. 'This one was borderline. "Lindsay took on the role of the young Englishman and beat it into submission." ' He laughed, and turned the page.

'Here we are!' he said triumphantly. 'The programmes. This one's February – that run didn't last long. Then March – *The Importance*. I was the butler with the cucumber sandwiches, look. We'd a good long run, right to the end of April, as far as I remember. Oh yes, here's the closing notice – May 2. And here are the programmes for the summer stock, half a dozen plays, going into rehearsal at the end of May. Here's *The Chalk Garden* – that transferred to Boston in September and we toured after that. Chicago, Indiana, even Illinois, for God's sake!'

It was a convincing record. Lindsay was enjoying himself, talking about old times. It was quite hard for the officers, assuring him they were satisfied, to get away.

'Thank God! They didn't arrest you!' Barrie Craig greeted Lindsay with a dramatic clutch at his heart. 'Tony was having kittens.'

Tony Laidlaw, a thin, dark man with the expression of one who has heard everything and believed very little of it, said acidly that he had managed somehow to contain his panic.

'What did they want, Marcus?' Jaki asked. 'CID – has there been a burglary?'

'Probably, but they don't bother to investigate unless they think the householder's duffed up the burglar,' he said with uncharacteristic bitterness. The others exchanged surprised glances.

'That's not like you, darling,' Sylvia said. 'You usually have a rather romantic view of our boys in blue.'

'Black,' Craig corrected automatically. *Playfair's Patch* prided itself on accuracy.

'Let me guess – they've caught up with your unpaid parking fines,' Laidlaw suggested.

'No, no. Nothing like that. They're reopening a cold case from twenty years ago – wanted to know if I was here then, but I was in the States so I wasn't much help.'

'Lucky, that! Could have been expensive if you were dragged off in irons,' Craig giggled. 'Might have done wonders for the show's publicity, though.'

'Without Marcus there wouldn't be any show,' Jaki said with asperity. 'You're not as funny as you think you are, Barrie.'

Sylvia directed an anxious glance at Marcus before saying brightly, 'Tony, have you tomorrow's call sheet for me? I like to know where I'm going to have to be when, well in advance.'

He found the sheet on his clipboard. 'Nine a.m. Just some shots of you in your car. We've found a wonderful old banger, falling apart. Then it's the neds sequence, with them throwing stones as you drive past in the village, only of course you won't be in it. Dave here's going to run the gauntlet, wearing an old straw hat Frocks has found for you.

'Hope the school sends us some decently scruffy kids. Say ten of them – OK, Barrie?'

The professional talk started again, but Marcus Lindsay didn't join in. He stood looking out through the French windows to the neglected garden beyond. He didn't look as if his thoughts were happy ones.

Back at the main road again, Fleming checked her watch. 'Oh, for goodness' sake! Is that the time? I don't know what's happened to today – an hour seems to go past every five minutes.

'I don't think we can go on down to the Mull. It'll take half an hour to get there, then interviews with the three Grants, the best part of an hour back to Kirkluce – could be eight o'clock by then, and I should touch base with the Super before he goes home. I'm supposed to phone the Fiscal as well.'

'Sounds like fun.'

'Yes, if your idea of fun is taking a sharp stick and repeatedly poking yourself in the eye. But the Grants can wait. Won't be pleasant for them anyway, stirring it all up again.'

Fleming gave a slight shiver as she spoke and MacNee looked at her. 'Are you cold? Why don't you put up the heater?'

'No, no,' she said. 'Just a goose walking over my grave.'

'This is a late call, inspector. I had expected to hear from you sooner.' The acting Procurator Fiscal's voice was chilly.

'I'm glad I caught you before you left,' Fleming said. 'There have been a lot of demands on my time today.'

'And on mine, which is why I'm still here. So – what is the situation?'

'There's very little to report as yet. I'm mainly familiarizing myself with the facts, but I did interview one of the people named, Marcus Lazansky – now known as Marcus Lindsay.'

There was a silence at the other end of the phone, then an indrawn breath. 'Marcus Lindsay – the actor?'

Fleming was surprised. 'Yes – do you know him?'

'He's very well known, isn't he?' Milne didn't answer the question. 'What had he to do with it, anyway?'

'The girl's mother accused him of her murder. They'd had some sort of relationship two or three years before, and Jean Grant seems just to have assumed that Lindsay was the father of the baby. Lindsay was actually in the US at the relevant time – showed us theatre programmes corroborating his story.'

'So he's eliminated from enquiries?'

Milne couldn't be sounding relieved, could she? 'Not quite,' Fleming said perversely. 'It's always possible he might have flown home in between plays, though unlikely.'

'Inspector, you must have more to do than entertain unlikely scenarios. For a start, I need a clear summary of the facts of the case and such concrete evidence as you do have, so that we can shape your investigation in the most effective way.'

'I'll have that for you tomorrow,' Fleming said, putting the phone down before she could say something she would most definitely regret.

Her other phone call, to Donald Bailey, wasn't easy either. He too expected a report, but she couldn't let herself be drawn. In the case she was reviewing, he was suspected of running an ineffective investigation and no more entitled to know what she was doing than any other suspect would be.

She stalled him politely, but in a way which made it clear what the position was. It was obvious he was upset, and even a little alarmed.

'I see. Doing it by the book, Marjory? Well, I suppose that's fair enough.' Then he said, 'Just like your father – except that one time. You'll have seen what happened by now.'

'I'd like to talk to you about that, but for the moment I'm only clearing the ground. Oh, and don't worry about my paperwork. I've got it under control and I hate to think what Tam MacNee might do if he was let loose on it.'

'Fine, Marjory, if you're sure. The thing is, I just think it's absolutely essential that this thing doesn't hang on too long.'

His voice sounded as if he felt the thing hanging might easily be the sword of Damocles.

Jaki Johnston tiptoed up the stairs. She'd gone out with the team to the local pub – not strong on atmosphere, but the beer wasn't bad, the company was good and she'd had a great laugh. Maybe the jokes weren't as funny as all that, but when you'd spent two days hearing amusing tales of old Hollywood, you really appreciated them.

Marcus and Barrie had stayed with Sylvia, but they obviously hadn't gone on late into the night. As she came in the only sound she could hear was – well, probably Hollywood legends didn't snore, but certainly heavy breathing, from behind the door of Sylvia's downstairs bedroom.

In her own room, she switched on the light beside the bed, then went to close the curtains before undressing. Light was spilling out from the guest room next door; Marcus must still be awake, but if he'd heard her come in he had obviously not wanted to see her any more than she wanted to see him.

As the light from both windows lit up the garden below, Jaki suddenly remembered what she'd seen the night before. She could settle the mystery now.

It had been raining all evening, quite heavily, and she peered through the gloom to where she had seen the shadowy shape. It was still there – a bush, just as she had told herself it must be. Was she ever glad she hadn't rushed off to Marcus with her tale of alarm!

6

'*Wcześnie dzisiaj wstałeś*. You're up early today,' Stefan Pavany said.

It wasn't quite seven o'clock, and a dull morning with drizzling rain. The run-down kitchenette in the rented house had only a small window, covered by a dirty net curtain, but Kasper Franzik hadn't put on the light. At the other man's entrance he spun round so suddenly that water from the kettle he was holding splashed on the floor instead of on to the instant coffee in his mug. He dodged it and swore.

'Not like you.' There was an edge to Stefan's voice. 'Usually I'm turning you out of bed to get on site for eight. What's going on?'

He advanced on the meagre floor space so that Kasper was forced into the angle formed by the units and the chipped enamel sink.

'It's – it's just—' he stammered, his prominent Adam's apple bobbing up and down.

'What were you and Jozef talking about last night? I could tell you were plotting something. I don't like plots.' Stefan's dark blue eyes were fixed on the younger man.

Kasper somehow could not look away. 'It's just . . . well, I was going to tell you before I left. I'm taking the rest of the week off.'

There was a brief silence, then Stefan's face lit with rage. 'What?' he yelled. 'Oh no, you're not!' He explained, in obscene detail, precisely what he would do to stop him, then went on, 'We've a contract, remember? A great bonus if we finish next week, and we lose another job the week after if we don't. Do you think I run this for your benefit?

'Still, good that you're up early. I'll take you to the house now and you can start while I go back and fetch the others.'

Kasper was taller and broader than the older man but even so he had to screw up his courage. 'I won't go. These people pay double what you pay me. It's four days. That's all.'

He had been prepared for argument, prepared even to have to pay some share of his windfall into the gang's kitty. He was not prepared for immediate violence, and Stefan's punch caught him squarely on his cheekbone.

Shock came first, then dismay. He was no stranger to street fights, yet for the second time recently he was trapped. He couldn't dodge the rain of blows and kicks and with his injured arm, both his defence and attack were feeble.

The noise had brought the other two occupants of the house bleary-eyed from their beds to stare, stupefied, at what was going on. At last one of them, Jozef, pulled Stefan off but not before a final vicious kick left Kasper doubled over in pain.

Stefan had not escaped unscathed either: his lip was bleeding and there was a bloody bruise on his temple, but his adversary was in a much worse state. His nose was pouring blood, one of his eyes was half-shut and his jaw was swelling visibly. He turned to the sink and spat out blood and a chip off a tooth. He grabbed a dish towel and put it to his nose.

Still breathing heavily, Stefan shook himself free of restraint. 'Just a little misunderstanding. Kasper thought he would dump us and lose us the bonus, but he's changed his mind.'

He walked back into the living room. Kasper, his face black with rage and humiliation, limped out of the kitchen past him. He turned at the doorway in stubborn defiance.

'You heard what I said. I'm going. You've beaten me up – you can't kill me, or I'm no use to you. I can come back next week and work overtime, or I walk out and you're a man short. You choose.'

'The circus come to town, has it?' The old man, a bemused look on his face, looked up and down Ardhill's main street.

There were trucks everywhere, almost constituting a small village on their own. A Winnebago stood in the pub car park and a catering truck opposite was producing a fine smell of frying bacon. A queue of people was lining up at the hatch for breakfast.

Across the road, a generator with cables snaking from it was running and nearby a woman with a clipboard was in earnest conversation with a man who had headphones draped round his neck. The early rain had stopped, but the sky was grey and threatening, and clearly a source of concern.

A uniformed policeman, there to reconcile production demands with the needs of the motorist, was eating a sausage butty and there were faces at the windows of the houses. A small crowd had gathered and a party atmosphere was rapidly developing.

A minibus appeared and disgorged a self-conscious group of schoolchildren, among them Catriona Fleming and her friend Anna. They had been up since six this morning, getting ready and having intense phone consultations about such important matters as shades of lip-gloss. The result, in each case, was impressive: two pretty girls, one fair, one dark, dressed similarly in jeans and tops from Gap (one blue t-shirt, one green smock).

Cat and Anna had checked out the competition and were now feeling distinctly complacent. 'None of the others have even bothered,' Anna whispered. 'Some of them look a right mess.'

They were directed to the breakfast truck, but Cat and Anna hung back. The bacon smell was tempting and they both had healthy adolescent appetites, but having taken so much trouble with the lip-gloss – renewed on the bus – it would be a shame to eat it off before the director got the full effect. Cat waved to Karolina, serving at the hatch, but she was looking harassed and gave her only a brief smile.

'Look,' Anna said, nudging her friend, 'someone's coming over.' They both produced nervous grins.

There were two men, one small, plump and cheerful-looking and the other dark and unsmiling.

'You're the kids from the school, right?' the dark one said. 'If you wait all together over there, I'll come and explain.'

The youngsters gathered slowly, clutching bacon rolls and croissants, and in one case a bowl of cereal. When they were assembled, the dark man looked round them with a professional eye.

'Hi. I'm Tony. Can't use you all, I'm afraid, but thanks for coming anyway. The storyline calls for a bunch of kids throwing stones at a car. Who fancies stone-throwing? Legal vandalism – could be fun.'

All the hands went up, Cat and Anna looking at each other uncertainly. It wasn't what they had expected and both were getting a sinking feeling that all their efforts might have been wasted.

'OK.' Tony's eyes scanned them again. 'I need five. You, you, you, you and you.

'The rest of you – sorry. Thanks again for turning up. Feel free to wander around, have some more breakfast, watch for a bit if you like. I warn you, though, it'll be slow. Watching paint dry's a thrill a minute by comparison. If you're heading back to school, the bus is there to take you whenever you want to go.'

Cat bit her lip. Anna gave a small, miserable sniff as they turned away with the other rejects. One of the scruffiest boys went past them sniggering.

'Being smart's not always as smart as not being smart,' he said, leaving them, as he would have said if he'd thought of it, smarting.

Karolina had been looking forward to today, and now it had been ruined by anxiety. Oh, the cooking wasn't difficult and the kitchen crew had been friendly – at least until Kasper's arrival.

The Glasgow friend who had got her the job in the first place had phoned on Saturday to say another person was needed locally to fill in. She'd mentioned it to some Polish friends after Mass on Sunday, among them Kasper who got in first when she said what it paid. She hadn't been altogether happy – and she certainly hadn't told Rafael – but at least she'd been able to say she'd found someone.

When Kasper appeared, it was clear he had been fighting. With his height, his dark colouring and his usual intense expression, he tended to look forbidding. Today, with the gashes on his face and a black eye, he looked positively alarming.

Chef, a plump and peaceable man, looked at him askance. 'You all right? What happened to you, then?'

'Had problem. OK now. What you want I do?'

He was set to peeling vegetables. Karolina, pink with embarrassment, came over and hissed at him, '*Co to jest? What is this? Why have you come looking like this? You have let me down.'

Kasper was aggrieved. 'You think I wanted this? My gang boss didn't like me taking days off. Went for me like a crazy man.'

'I can see that. Why did you take this, if you had a job already?'

'Because it paid more. Why do you think?'

'You are too fond of money, Kasper. You haven't learned—'

He interrupted her. 'I don't need a lecture. This man is a slave-driver – takes most of the money for himself, then charges us rent to live in a pigsty house.'

He set down his knife and took her by the wrist. 'Karolina, I don't know if it is safe to go back. He is dangerous – you can see. If the others hadn't pulled him off me, he might have killed me.

'Can I stay with you and Rafael, just for a while? We're old friends, you have a house, we are Poles who must stick together—'

'No!' She wrenched her hand away. 'It's a small house, we have Janek – you must find somewhere else. Or go back to your job now and say sorry. I will explain here—' She would be glad to, with the curious looks she was getting.

He turned to stare at her fiercely. 'I will never apologize. He must apologize to me.'

'That's one way of looking at it,' Karolina said wearily. 'Anyway, I've got work to do and so have you.'

Chef looked at her enquiringly as she turned away.

'It's all right,' she said. 'He had a row with one of his housemates. He'll be fine. These things – they make up again, I guess.'

And how Karolina hoped that what she said was true!

Jaki Johnston came downstairs yawning at ten o'clock. Reaching the foot of the stairs, she heard Marcus's voice from the drawing room and stuck her head in. He was on his mobile, but waved and mouthed, 'Won't be long!'

He said into the phone, 'For goodness' sake! I can't see it coming up in general conversation, anyway. Surely anything more would be most unwise? I'm sorry, I just won't go down that road.'

There was a lengthy response, then he said, 'Easiest if you just keep them off my back, really.' He laughed. 'Then I won't be tempted to confess.'

Even Jaki could hear the agitated squawking at the other end of the phone.

'OK, OK, calm down. That was a joke, all right? Yes. Yes, fine. See you sometime.'

Marcus switched the phone off, pulling a face. 'Idiot woman! Thinks I'm going to cause her trouble and wants me to lie to the police. I hate people trying to manipulate me – sends me in the opposite direction.'

Jaki looked at him quizzically, but he only said, 'Looking for breakfast? Mrs Boyter's out shopping – an excuse to see what's happening in the village, I reckon – but we can find you some toast, at least.'

'It must be up that lane there, look,' DS Andy Macdonald said to DC Ewan Campbell, dodging the chaos in Ardhill's main street, avoiding cameras mounted on dollies, trolleys of equipment and people who seemed oblivious to anything except what they themselves were doing. 'I hope we can manage to get through – and get back out again!'

'Just as long as we don't get ourselves blocked in,' Campbell said.

Macdonald looked at him in surprise. Campbell, who came from Oban, was famous for his linguistic economy. This almost came under the heading of small-talk.

'Why does it matter?' Macdonald asked, and saw Campbell's pale skin go pink under the freckles.

'It's Mairi. She's due today and I might get a call any time.'

It was the most personal observation Macdonald had ever heard him make. He knew Campbell was married, but he couldn't have been sure of his wife's name and had no idea the arrival of a small Campbell was imminent.

'Well – congratulations,' he said, a little lamely. 'My sisters tell me first babies are always late, anyway.'

'Aye, maybe. But if she's needing me they'll have to get their cameras out the road right away.'

He spoke ferociously and Macdonald looked at him, astonished. Maybe that was the Campbell blood coming out, and as a Macdonald he'd better watch his step.

'Er – yes,' he said, then with some relief, 'Here we are – that looks like the house.'

The address was the one given to the medical centre by the young man with the knife wound. It was a run-down area at the back of Ardhill, in sharp contrast to the smartly painted main street. The house was an ugly semi-detached bungalow, built of concrete slabs coated with beige pebble-dash. The garden gate was off its hinges and in the garden itself rubbish had accumulated – a rusted engine, some old enamel pails and buckets, a bicycle chassis with no wheels. Dirty net curtains hung at the window, one with a jagged tear in it.

'How many of them do you suppose are living there?' Macdonald wondered, not really expecting an answer. Campbell followed him up the path in silence as he went on, 'Can't be paying much rent for a place like this, though of course they won't be earning much. They work for about half of what the locals charge.'

They walked up the path to a front door which had once been blue but was now blistered and peeling. There was no bell, so Campbell knocked, then knocked again.

'Out at work, probably,' Macdonald said. 'Not the best time to catch them in, really, when you think about it.'

He stepped back, looking at the front of the house, then, noticing the rip in the curtain, walked over to the window and peered through it, shading his eyes. 'It's messy enough for a lot of men, anyway. Dirty dishes everywhere – just like home.'

'Someone's watching us next door,' Campbell said suddenly. 'Curtain moved.'

The adjoining garden was similarly untidy, though this time the litter was mainly plastic toys, their colour bleached by sun and rain. The doorbell played a silly tune when Campbell pressed it.

After a pause, the door opened a fraction and a young woman in a grubby T-shirt, tracksuit bottoms and bare feet appeared, holding an even grubbier infant clad only in a plastic nappy.

She eyed them suspiciously round the door, the tall young man with a dark buzz-cut and the shorter one with red hair, one wearing a raincoat and the other a brown zipped jacket. 'You're polis, aren't you? What are you wanting? He's not here, anyway.'

She had realized what they were remarkably quickly. Who, Macdonald wondered, was 'he'? And if they went through the back, would they find someone they'd a warrant out on? From the woman's anxious looks over her shoulder, he reckoned they would, but the rules were so strict now that it seemed as if you couldn't pick anyone up without phoning first to ask if it would be OK to come round.

Anyway, it wasn't their business today. Macdonald said, 'We're not looking for anyone here. Just wanted to ask about the people next door.'

The front door opened a little further. 'The Poles, you mean?'

'That's our information.'

'Wouldn't know. They all talk funny, anyway. They'll be out working – always away before we're out our beds. There was a real stramash this morning – woke the baby. Some folks are just ignorant – no consideration.'

'Where do they work, do you know?'

'Someone said they're at some big posh house over in Sandhead.'

'You didn't hear whose house, I suppose?'

'No.' The baby, an unprepossessing child with a runny nose, had started crying, a dreary, grizzling sound. 'Oh, shut it,' she said, jiggling it without effect. 'That's all I ken about them.'

The door was closing again. Macdonald said hastily, 'How many of them live there?'

'Four or five maybe. No point speaking to them – wouldn't understand a word I said. They've no right, coming here taking the jobs—' The child was yelling hard now, snot mixing with its tears. Its mother went back inside and shut the door, still muttering.

The piercing screams followed them down the path. 'That's what you've got to look forward to,' Macdonald pointed out unkindly, and Campbell gave him a hunted look.

'Not all like that, are they?'

'Going by my nieces and nephews, pretty much. Mercifully it doesn't seem to be so disgusting when it's your own.

'Now, how do we find this big posh house in Sandhead? Go and ask around, I suppose. There can't be too many having work done at the moment. Mind you, I don't know why we should be doing this instead of the uniforms. Big Marge seems to have her knickers in a bit of a twist about racist gang warfare in Kirkluce.'

The great white bulk of the Stevenson lighthouse was shrouded in rain and mist as DI Fleming, pulling on a hooded oilskin jacket, stepped out of the car. She was on her own today: there had been a break-in at a solicitors' office in Stranraer and she'd had to despatch MacNee and Kerr to deal with it, since Macdonald and Campbell were detailed to question the Poles, and she wasn't prepared to postpone that. They were short-staffed at the moment, with one detective away on leave and another off with flu.

What a shame the weather was so bad, with the views over to England and Ireland blotted out completely! It must look fantastic in sunshine – and even today, the place looked dazzlingly well maintained, the walls round about painted white like the lighthouse itself, but with a band of bright yellow on the coping-stones. The whitewashed cottages for keepers, long since departed, had windows and chimneys painted the same cheerful colour.

Fleming set off to walk round the lighthouse to the farther side, bracing herself as she came out of its shelter into the wind from the sea, then stopped as she reached the point where she could see to the north-west.

Visibility was poor, but she could make out the line of cliffs stretching up the Irish Sea coast, sandy-coloured with a black high-water mark of seaweed round the base. And there, a few hundred yards away, was a sharp spur of rock jutting out of the sea with a low, almost level platform connecting it to the cliff. Judging by the seaweed line, this would be submerged at high tide, but at the moment it was just above the water-level, with the stronger waves washing over it. It had been well described: Fleming could almost see Ailsa Grant's wave-battered body lying on it.

Today the sea was metallic grey, with a heavy, oily swell, and making a low, threatening moaning. That was the only sound: even the gulls flying about under leaden skies weren't screeching. It was so cold, so bleak! Fleming shivered and turned to walk out along the headland.

The turf was springy underfoot, and all around were great wet swathes of dead bracken, brown after the winter frosts. It would have grown and spread after all these years, and the points where there was easy access to the cliff edge would have changed. And you would need that, on a wild night, impeded either by a struggling woman or her dead body.

There was, Fleming noticed, one area right at the cliff edge where rocky outcrops on either side had stopped the bracken from encroaching, and she went, rather gingerly, to peer over.

It was a dizzying drop. Here the land fell sharply away straight into the water hundreds of feet below, whereas to left and right the cliffs seemed to slope outward more, so that a body falling would strike rocks before it reached the sea. Ailsa's body had shown none of the mutilations that a fall on to rocks would produce, so it seemed quite likely that Fleming was standing now where the murderer had stood.

She walked back towards the lighthouse, trying to think herself into his mind. He could have driven the car as far as the edge of the shorter grass here below the walls where the car would have been invisible from the lighthouse, and certainly he could have gambled on no one being about on a night like that. She paced the distance to the edge – thirty yards.

Had he been carrying her body – staggering under the dead weight, buffeted by the storm? Or was she still alive, being coerced with an iron grip across the rough ground, her hands tied, her screams torn away on the wind?

Surely she must have been dead by that stage? No woman would have consented to go with her lover to a place of such danger with a tempest raging. And yet—

There is something intensely romantic about Nature's power unleashed. Could he have lured her there with the promise of the ultimate in passionate proposals, wild, storm-tossed . . . Heathcliff and Catherine?

Unlikely. But even so, should Fleming perhaps have it in mind to look for someone with a strong romantic streak – someone, say, like an actor? Marcus Lindsay's alibi seemed solid enough, and surely Mrs Grant must have been told this. Why, in that case, had she been so certain of his guilt?

Her father would have stood here once, just about where she was standing now, looking down at the drowned woman, his inbuilt prejudices blinding him to any evidence of murder. Procedure, he would have been the first to tell you, existed to prevent too personal judgements, and yet on this occasion he had thrown away the rule book.

Ailsa's father had at the very least been a strong suspect. What else had happened back at the house, when Ailsa's hair had been combed? What other evidence had been removed, which might have pointed to him? She'd find it hard to have to put in her report that her father's action had assisted a cover-up.

Still, there was a job to do. Balnakenny Farm was her next port of call, but before she returned to the car park, she looked back once more.

The wind blowing today, though strong enough, wasn't gale force. She had been hesitant about going near the edge; Ailsa's killer must have been a brave man to take the risk of finding himself going over with the body. Brave – or desperate. And how would he feel now, when he heard questions were being asked all over again?

It didn't take Macdonald and Campbell long to find the house they were looking for. The Hodges' Miramar was a source of fascination locally and the woman they stopped to ask was delighted to give them all details.

'Oh, it's a right knacker's midden! Started off like one of thae ranch houses, ken, but I don't know what you'd call it now, with all the bits they've added on.

'That's where you'll find the Polish lads, right enough. At least, I suppose that's what they are. Foreign, anyway. Keep themselves to themselves.'

'So there hasn't been any trouble here?'

The woman's eyes lit up. 'Not that I've heard. Here! What've they been up to?'

'Nothing at all,' Macdonald said hastily. 'I wasn't meaning that. Just we heard some of the boys around here had been making things difficult.'

'Oh, there's some right young limmers about,' the woman acknowledged, but went away disappointed. Bad behaviour by the local neds wouldn't be news to anyone.

Miramar stood on its own in an extensive garden up behind the village looking out to Luce Bay. It was, as described, a complete jumble, as if someone had got first one idea for the house's layout, then another and another, without any attempt at reconciling them.

Macdonald put up the collar of his coat against the rain and stared at it. 'Can't imagine how they got planning permission for this. Must know the right people.

'Pity it's raining, though – the men'll have packed it in, with weather like this.'

He was wrong, though. Walking towards the front door, they could see a building in the later stages of construction and three men working as if the sun was shining.

There was no one else around. They crossed the lawn towards the builders, Macdonald taking out his warrant card. As always, it had an effect: all three men stopped working and one, older than the others, stepped forward. He was wearing a beige sweat-shirt darkened by rain and his grizzled hair was plastered to his head.

They could almost see his hackles rising. 'What do you want with us?' he said, his battered face stony.

Macdonald eyed the bruises and the split lip. 'Been in a fight, then, have you?'

He didn't waver. 'An accident.'

'Funny kind of accident. Look, we're here to help you. One of you got a knife wound and we don't want something worse happening.'

'That was an accident too.'

'You seem to have a lot of accidents,' Macdonald said crisply. He turned to the silent men. 'Which of you is Kasper Franzik?'

Again, it was the older man who answered. 'He is not here. And you cannot speak to them, since they do not understand. It is only me who can speak good English.'

He could, too – heavily accented, but perfectly clear. Macdonald found himself nonplussed. You couldn't get far if the only English-speaker refused to acknowledge there was a problem. He had one more try.

'We're concerned that there's ill-feeling between you and some of the local lads. Have you had any trouble of that sort?'

He caught a look pass between the two younger men, but they said nothing and their boss replied flatly, 'No. None.'

'Then we'll have to take you at your word. Can you tell me where I could find Mr Franzik?'

'He is gone. I don't know where.'

The man went back to his plastering. At a gesture from him, the others too resumed work and Macdonald and Campbell had no option but to leave them to it.

'Scary kind of bloke, isn't he?' Macdonald said as they went back to the car. 'My bet is you should see what he did to the other fellow.

'Anyway, we've ticked the box. Write up the report and file it and then we can forget about it.'

7

The Grants weren't good farmers. With her practised eye, Marjory Fleming could tell that immediately.

For a start, the cattle grazing on either side of the single-track road between cattle grids were a ragbag assortment of Old Galloway, Aberdeen-Friesian crosses, a few Simmental and a lone Charollais, obviously picked up cheaply at cattle sales when the chance arose. The beasts looked dirty and their pasture wasn't well managed either; Fleming could see docks and even dangerous ragwort growing.

A rusting tractor stood in one corner of the farmyard, minus its tyres, and the yard itself hadn't been hosed clean of mud and dung. In the barn, machinery and tools had been crammed in higgledy-piggledy over the years, so that finding what you needed must be a frustrating business.

There were hens, too, in a chicken-wire enclosure long since pecked clear of vegetation where the miserable creatures, feathers bunched against the rain, still scavenged listlessly in the unproductive mud. It wasn't as if grassy areas were in short supply; the enclosure would only need to be moved regularly to give them a richer environment. Thinking of her own chookies' enjoyment of the grass and grubs in the orchard, Fleming conceived an anticipatory dislike of their owners.

The farmhouse looked neat enough, but it had a forbidding aspect, built of stone so dark that it was almost black, with dark maroon paintwork. Fleming parked and went through the gate to the small garden at the front. This was well kept too, though there were no flowers, just rows of fruit bushes and earth turned over for spring planting. The brass knocker on the front door was very shiny.

The woman who opened it looked as dour and unwelcoming as the house itself. She was tall, gaunt and angular, with iron-grey hair pulled into a bun at the back. She had a beaky nose and a prominent chin and her face was innocent of make-up, taut and shiny from soap and water. Her grey eyes had a stony, hostile stare.

She was an ugly old woman, and her daughter had been a bonny enough girl, yet Fleming could see a strong resemblance. Had Jean Grant in her day, too, been bonny enough, she found herself thinking as the woman snapped, 'Yes? What are you wanting?'

Fleming introduced herself. 'Mrs Grant? I've come to see you and your husband and son. I was hoping for a word with you all.'

'You're seeing me now. My son's away and you'll have a job seeing my husband, unless you dig him up first. He's been dead these seven years.'

The callous response shed a light on the relationship. 'I'm so sorry,' Fleming said, but as that received no acknowledgement, went on, 'May I come in?' She took the customary step forward which made it harder to refuse.

'If you have to.'

Jean walked away down the narrow hall, leaving her visitor to follow and shut the front door. Fleming expected to be taken to the farmhouse kitchen where, as she had reason to know, most social interaction on farms took place, but instead Jean opened the door into what would once have been called the front parlour.

There were antimacassars on the backs of all the chairs. Fleming hadn't seen one since she was a child, and the cut-moquette, wooden-framed suite didn't look as if it merited such protection. The room was otherwise sparsely furnished with only a couple of side-tables and a display cabinet full of glasses. On the mantelpiece an orange china vase held dry grasses and in front of the empty grate was a fan of pleated paper. It was all spotlessly clean but the room felt dank, as if it had been unheated and unused for years. Half-drawn blinds made it dark and no pictures brightened the beige wallpaper.

The only personal touch was some formal photographs on a side-table. Fleming had seen the one of Ailsa, but there was also a somewhat faded wedding photo, presumably the Grants' own, and two or three others, including the kind you order through the school: one of a boy with red hair and a dark-haired girl – Ailsa, presumably, before she went blonde.

Apart from that, the room gave nothing away, any more than did the face of the woman who had sat down in a chair with its back to the light.

Uninvited, the inspector chose the chair nearest to the photographs. An opportunity to study them might present itself.

'I'm sorry to be raising again what must be a very painful subject, but a decision has been made to reopen the case of your daughter's murder.'

She could see no flicker of emotion on the other woman's face, but then it was in shadow.

'Oh aye?' was all she said.

'I need to go over the events leading up to Ailsa's death, and ask you what you can remember.'

'What for? They asked enough questions at the time, and wrote down what we said.'

This degree of hostility was unexpected. Feeling slightly defensive, Fleming said, 'I've read the reports, but other questions have occurred to me that you may be able to answer. I'm sure you're even more anxious than I am to get justice for your daughter.'

At last she got a genuine response. 'Didn't get justice last time, did she?' Jean said savagely. 'All these years, he's gone on living his decadent life, spending his money, strutting about. And I told them – I told them. And they did nothing. Why should I go through it all again – for nothing to happen?'

Fleming leaned forward. She had a low, attractive voice, now at its most persuasive. 'I know you mean Marcus Lazansky, and if you believe he killed Ailsa I can understand your bitterness. I have a daughter myself.

'But you will know he was in America at the time. I need to hear exactly why you blame him. You can tell me anything, however trivial, that gave you reason to believe that.'

Jean had raised her head and was looking at her. Her eyes were still cold and watchful, but it was progress.

'They had a relationship when they were quite young, didn't they?' Fleming prompted.

'Oh aye, he did. And then dropped her. I saw how my bairn suffered – though dear knows she'd had warnings enough about him. And there were plenty others wanting her – you can see how bonny she was,' she said, gesturing towards the large photo, 'but she couldn't see past him.

'I told her till I was sick telling her, that she'd to have nothing to do with him. He was –' she spat the word, 'poison! But I could tell she wasn't listening.

'Oh, she'd say, "Yes, Mum, got the message." That was her great phrase, but I knew what was in her heart. We were close, me and Ailsa.'

'The relationship they had as teenagers – was it sexual?'

For a moment Fleming wondered if the woman would rise and strike her. 'Sexual? Certainly not! She was only sixteen and I'd warned her well about what men were like.'

'Of course. But—'

'Oh, I know what you're at! By then she was away from her mother, lonely in a big city, homesick most likely, and he took advantage of that.'

'Mrs Grant, I can appreciate your point. But is there a possibility that there was someone else in Glasgow? Marcus Lindsay can prove he was out of the country most of the time. How could you be sure that being lonely she didn't take up with another man?'

Tears welled up and Jean blinked them away. 'Out of the country? Wouldn't be telling you if he'd come back sometimes, would he? And how did I know? I'll tell you. She denied it was him, but she wouldn't name the father, even to me, and we were close, like I said. The only reason she wouldn't tell me was because I'd told her she'd not to see him.'

Was this really all – a mother's stubborn belief that her daughter tells her everything? Fleming, with clear and shaming memories of her own youth, cherished no such illusions, but she could hardly say that.

Jean had produced a handkerchief, blown her nose fiercely, and lapsed into stony impassivity. Fleming changed the subject.

'She had a phone call that afternoon. You didn't know who it was from or hear what was said?'

'The phone's in the hall there. I was busy in the kitchen and she answered, and by the time I came through to see, she'd finished and was running up the stairs. I asked her who it was but she never said.'

'How was she looking? Upset? Happy?'

'I didn't see. She was a bit quiet at her tea, but it wasn't unusual. She and her father weren't speaking.'

And that was something Fleming needed to know about too, but she wasn't going to interrupt.

'She went to her room, after, and then I heard her come back downstairs and she was all made up. I hadn't seen her like that since she came home. I said, "Where are you going?" and she said she was meeting someone.

' "On a night like this?" I said, and she said, "Don't stop me. He's there, waiting for me – I have to go to him."

'That's what she said.'

Jean's voice was thick with tears, but Fleming had to ask a question that hadn't been asked twenty years ago. 'Did you hear a car? Did she take anything with her? Clothes, money, a suitcase?'

Jean stared at her. 'I – I don't know. How could I possibly remember, after all these years? She went, that's all, and I had to let her go.' She was agitated; she got up. 'Excuse me – I've something to do for a minute.'

Filled with pity, Fleming heard her hurrying up the stairs. A woman as private as Jean Grant would not weep in public.

So it looked as if Marcus Lazansky/Lindsay could be scored off the list of suspects. Jean had held a grudge against the young man who had caused her beloved daughter heartache, and it all followed from that.

And yet, and yet . . . Jean Grant did not strike her as an irrational woman, and this was irrational to a degree. Fleming had a bristling sense of something not quite right. She wished that Tam MacNee had been with her, either to confirm this or to mock her 'intuition'.

In accusing Marcus, could Jean be protecting someone? – and suspicion, in the past, had rested on Robert Grant, despite a sturdy alibi. Was it possible the marriage was closer than it had sounded from Jean's unfeeling remark about digging him up?

The wedding photograph was on the side-table at her elbow. Fleming picked it up.

She wouldn't have recognized Jean, if she hadn't looked like a darker version of her daughter. She was very young; her face still had softly rounded contours with dark curls framing it. She was wearing a soft, pretty chiffon dress, holding the arm of a burly red-haired man with a ruddy complexion who did, indeed, look like a farmer. He wore an uneasy grin; she looked solemnly towards the camera, as if even then she did not smile readily.

Life, for Jean, was a serious business. It had been, for them – or had it, until tragedy struck, been good enough? It wasn't uncommon for marriages to go sour when these things happened. Fleming was trying to frame tactful questions as she heard Jean coming down the stairs again.

Sylvia was visibly weary when she returned to Tulach House. Marcus saw her hands shaking as she propelled herself along the hall. He went to kiss her, feeling concerned and responsible, even.

'Darling, what have they been doing to you? I shall have to set about them. You look exhausted!'

Sylvia summoned up the famous smile. 'No, no, of course you mustn't! They've been clucking round me like mother hens. And your make-up girl has a magic touch. I'm thinking of putting her on a retainer – it was only when I took the stuff off that I started looking my age!'

'Nonsense, not a day over fifty-nine,' he said robustly, though wondering whether he had pitched it low enough to be flattering, without being so low as to be blatantly insincere.

Sylvia gave her throaty laugh. 'You're a liar, and I love you for it. But oh, God! It's a sad day when being told I look sixty is a compliment. Still, take what you can get, say I!'

'Sylvia, most women of thirty can't even dream of looking as good as you do now. Now, what can I get you? Mrs Boyter's still around if you haven't lunched – she'd love to whip you up an omelette.'

'Heaven forbid! They were practically force-feeding me. I had to shut my mouth like a toddler when I'd had enough, and even then I was afraid they'd start making aeroplane noises and try to buzz in the next mouthful. But darling, if you did happen to have a tiny bottle of champagne – I know, I shouldn't, but it's such a wonderful pick-me-up.'

Marcus sketched a bow. 'Your wish is my command. Now, go into the drawing room and keep warm, and I'll fetch champagne and a couple of glasses. I'm not scheduled today, so we can have a lovely relaxing afternoon.'

He had left the door behind her open and she did not hear him return. She was stooped over, as if sitting upright was an effort, and she was clumsily shaking what were probably painkillers out of a bottle into her twisted hand. His throat constricted as he looked at her, remembering her great beauty and glamour.

Sylvia dropped one of the pills, and swore. He came forward. 'Let me help you,' he said, and she jumped.

'I didn't know you were there. Damn! I hate being seen taking pills – so old-making!' She had straightened up, but with a betraying wince.

Marcus released the cork with a gentle sigh of vapour. 'Swallow them down with this and you'll feel better. Was it a tough morning?'

'My stupid old legs, darling – just couldn't get into the old banger they found, without pushers like they have on

Japanese trains. Not quite the image we're looking for, so they'd stuff to rework. Lots of retakes.

'But let's not talk about my boring problems. I've been longing for a proper chat. Tell me about you and darling Jaki – what a sweet, talented girl!'

Marcus smiled at her. 'You're always so generous – but yes, she is. I think she's definitely working herself into a permanent slot in *Playfair*.'

She gave him a stern look. 'Not what I meant, and you know it. How are things between you?'

'Sylvia, you're worse than a mother!' he protested, but without heat. 'We're calling it a day, but keeping up appearances at the moment – you know what the gossip's like. We're still friends, but that's all. I should have known she was too young for me, but somehow—' He shrugged.

'Oh, put it all behind you! The mid-life crisis – it does terrible things to your judgement. You should be looking for a nice girl with a bit of money who'll love the house and have lots of beautiful little boys just like you.'

'Sylvia, for heaven's sake—' he said with amused exasperation.

Sylvia reached out to take his hand. 'But darling, much more important – tell me all about this business with the police. What was that about? You seemed quite stressed.'

Marcus really didn't want to talk about that, but he couldn't snub her. He said as lightly as he could, 'It was a sad thing that happened twenty years ago. A pregnant girl was murdered, then dumped in the sea, but they never got the man who did it. They're reopening the case, and they're asking questions. That's all. I couldn't really help them.'

She wasn't to be deflected. 'But why you? You were with them a long time.'

He sighed. 'We had a brief romance as teenagers. We broke up before I went to Glasgow, and I never saw her again. When she died, and indeed at the time she got pregnant, I was in the States. I told them, and showed them Papa's old scrapbook with the programmes in it. End of story.'

Sylvia frowned. 'I still don't understand why they'd come to you now, not having seen the girl for years. Surely—'

There was no alternative. 'Someone accused me of her murder – her mother's my guess. She probably had a grudge against me because I dumped Ailsa, or something. All right?'

'*All right!*' Sylvia began working herself into a state. 'It's terrible! You can never trust the police! Look at all these miscarriages of justice.' She embarked on a long story about a friend whom she claimed they had fitted up, although to Marcus it sounded as if his activities had been, at the very least, deeply suspect.

At last he snapped, 'Sylvia, leave it. It's a damned un-pleasant thing, being accused of murder, and I'd rather not dwell on it.' He saw the wounded look come into her violet-grey eyes which any of her fans would immediately have recognized from *For Ever*, and weakened.

'Sorry, I didn't mean to sound short with you. I know you're just concerned for me.'

'Concerned for you? My sweet, now Laddie's gone you're the one important thing in my life. You're too trusting, too honest. It takes an old cynic like me to see things clearly.'

Marcus groaned. 'Perhaps you're right. It's a nasty habit you've always had. But if the police have it in for me, there's not a lot I can do about it, is there?'

Jean Grant did not sit down again when she came back. 'Will that be all? There's nothing else to tell you.'

Tact took time and she didn't have it. Fleming said bluntly, 'I expect you know your husband was suspected of your daughter's murder.'

No trace of emotion showed. 'He was here all that evening.'

'Yes, I know you and your son said that. Will he be in shortly?'

'No. He's away at the cattle sales in Carlisle.'

That was disappointing: she'd hoped she might get more out of him than she had from Jean.

'Suspicion arose about your husband because there was a report of family rows. You said yourself that they weren't on speaking terms.'

Jean gave a grim smile. 'Oh, there were rows, right enough. I'd been angry with her myself, for holding herself so cheap, and I told him if she wouldn't tell me, she wouldn't tell him because he yelled at her, but he always knew best.'

Without much hope, Fleming pressed on. 'You see, since your daughter was dead, you and your son might have protected your husband, feeling it would only bring further disaster to your family.'

Jean looked at her with contempt. 'You think that if he'd murdered my daughter, I'd have protected him?'

It was meant as a rhetorical question, but Fleming answered it. 'I don't know, Mrs Grant. From the way you spoke of your husband, I got the impression that relations between you weren't good, but that may only have happened after Ailsa's death. Was your marriage happy before that?'

Temper flared in the woman's face. 'I've listened long enough. I don't care if you're police, you're an impudent besom, asking questions like that. I've had enough.'

She held the door open and Fleming had no alternative but to leave.

★   ★   ★

'A right waste of time, that was,' Tam MacNee grumbled as he and Tansy Kerr came into the canteen, looking for a late lunch.

A golf competition was showing on the TV in the corner, and two uniforms on their break were sitting watching it. One looked round as MacNee spoke.

'Story of our lives,' he said cynically. 'You should be used to it by now.'

MacNee ignored that. 'Drove all the way to Stranraer and the guy had been picked up already.'

'Pointless,' Kerr chimed in, sounding thoroughly fed up. 'Drive for hours, then drive back. What a way to spend your life, pretending we're detectives when they've left behind a bag with their address on it. Brain dead, like most of the poor sods we're after.'

'Lucky they are, or we'd never get them,' said the cynic on the sofa.

'Speak for yourself!' MacNee returned to his grievance. 'But then we'd to be polite to the solicitors whose office he'd done over. Went against the grain, that.'

'Now, Tam, we're all servants of the majesty of the law,' Kerr said sententiously, then spoiled it by adding, 'allegedly.'

MacNee was surveying what there was on the counter without enthusiasm. 'No bridies, and nothing but cheese and pickle sandwiches left. Why do they make them, when no one likes them?' he demanded of the long-suffering woman serving.

'Don't ask me, pet. It's just what we're sent. But there's a lettuce and tomato as well, look.'

'*Lettuce!*' There was horror in MacNee's tone. 'Do I look like a rabbit?'

'Don't answer that, Maisie,' Kerr advised. 'I'll have that, and a cup of coffee.'

MacNee, settling grudgingly for cheese and pickle, drifted over to the TV.

'Daft game, that,' he said conversationally. 'Can't think what you see in it. The ball's standing still, for God's sake! Now, if you had it coming at you at an angle from a header—'

'MacNee, we're watching this,' the other uniform said. 'Why don't you go and talk football somewhere else?'

'All right, all right, if you're not up to the intellectual challenge. Anyone seen Big Marge?'

'She was in looking for you a while back. Go and annoy her instead of us.'

'I'll do just that,' MacNee said with alacrity, stuffing in the last of his sandwich and heading for the door. 'Tansy, you'll get that written up, OK?' he said indistinctly.

Kerr pulled a face at his retreating back. 'You can have enough of this job, you know that?'

It was late when Marjory Fleming left her office to drive back to Mains of Craigie, but she'd cleared her desk. She'd arranged for MacNee to check that Stuart Grant would be in if they drove down to Balnakenny tomorrow; she was keen to keep up the momentum, but it would be a long way to drive only to find him out.

Reaching the farm, she remembered that this was the day of Cat's screen debut, and she smiled. Bill, like Stuart Grant, was away overnight at the Carlisle sales, buying stock to fatten over the summer, but her mother's car was in the yard, and that was good, since she felt that Janet needed company. Cat would doubtless have told her grandmother about her day already but she'd probably be happy enough to go through it again.

But when she reached the kitchen Janet was sitting in the sagging armchair by the Aga, alone except for the collie Meg, who on seeing her mistress leaped from her basket to greet her, her tail wagging in circles of delight. Meg was always bereft when her master was away.

'Where's everybody?' Marjory asked, patting Meg, then going to kiss her mother. 'Early for them to be upstairs, surely?'

'Oh dear!' Janet got up and started to fuss with pots and pans. 'Cammie's through watching TV, but Cat – she's fair upset, poor wee soul.

'They weren't wanting nice, decent girls like her and Anna. It was just to be a clamjamfry of ill-faured bairns throwing stones at a car, if you can credit it! Small wonder there's all the problems today.' She was almost bursting with indignation.

Marjory began to laugh. 'You've lost me there. I gathered you weren't impressed with the type of child they chose, but *clamjamfry*?'

'Think shame to yourself, Marjory Laird!' In moments of emotion, her mother tended to revert to her daughter's maiden name. 'Do you not know your own language? You could say bad-mannered rabble, I suppose – but that's a poor, pathetic phrase by comparison.'

Marjory could only agree meekly, and Janet went on, 'I'm that sorry for Cat, her looking so pretty in her nice clothes! She went up a wee while ago. She was going to phone Anna and then go to her bed, so you'll need to away up and see her.'

'I'll leave her to lick her wounds meantime. Anyway, I'm starving, and something smells good.'

Janet looked pleased. 'Och, I knew Bill was away and you'd likely be late, so I came up to be here for the bairns when they got back from the school. And I'd time on my hands so I made broth and stovies – they were always a favourite with you.'

'Indeed they are, but you're an awful woman! Here's me trying to get you to take things easy, and you go looking for work.'

'Oh, away you go! I enjoy doing it fine.'

As Marjory ate, they talked about domestic concerns, but afterwards she broached the subject on her mind.

'Mum, you know we were talking the other night about Marcus Lindsay and his father?'

'Laddie Lazansky – oh yes. Quite took me back.'

'Do you remember a murdered girl they found in the sea down at the Mull of Galloway, about twenty years ago?'

'I mind it fine! Your father was first there after the helicopter brought her in. She was in trouble, you know, poor lassie, but he would always have it they'd made a big fuss about nothing.'

How much, Marjory wondered, had he ever told Janet about his position? Delicately, she asked, 'Were there problems about that? Him not agreeing with them, I mean?'

Janet smiled. 'You knew your father! Didn't matter what they said, he always just went his own way. They were used to him.'

It would be like Angus to be too proud to mention the blot on his record. If he hadn't, it wasn't her place to tell Janet now. 'The thing is,' she went on, 'no one was ever charged and I've been asked to take another look. I wondered if there was anything you could remember that might be helpful.'

'Dearie me! It's a long time back, and my memory's not what it was once.' Janet started a little hesitantly. 'You'll maybe mind your father and I both grew up in the South Rhins? Your father was a bitty older than me and Robert Grant was in his class at the school.

'They didn't have Balnakenny then. Robert's father was the postie – it was Jean's family were farmers, so it would have been from that side they'd get the farm. But we never saw him after we came to Kirkluce, and I never knew Jean – she was a good bit younger.'

'What was Robert like?'

'Like? Och, I don't know. He was only a laddie at the time.' Janet looked uncomfortable: it was not in her nature to be unkind.

'You didn't like him, did you? Be honest – I'm not asking from idle curiosity,' Marjory said, and Janet sighed.

'Oh well – he was always kind of sullen, and a bully too, sometimes. He and your father were quite pally at the time, though, but they never kept up.'

Was that why Angus Laird behaved so uncharacteristically in letting Ailsa Grant's body be taken home – out of loyalty to a long ago friendship? She admired loyalty – and perhaps, with suspicion centring on Robert, it explained too why Angus had wanted to believe the young woman had chosen to die.

'Do you remember hearing Jean Grant had accused Marcus Lazansky of killing Ailsa?' Marjory went on.

Janet frowned for a moment, then said, 'It's all coming back to me now! Yes, there was talk, with the Lazanskys being who they were, and Flora being from a county family.

'But it was all just haivers – the laddie was in America the whole time, your father said. But it'll not be very nice for him if you've to stir it all up again.'

'No,' Marjory agreed, 'it isn't. Not very nice for the Grants either, I'm afraid, but it has to be done.'

'If the poor lassie's to rest in peace, I hope you find out this time who it was,' Janet said heavily. Then she added, 'Even if he's dead.'

8

The Cross Keys in Ardhill was packed to the doors this evening. Norrie the barman was under siege, not only from the production team of *Playfair's Patch*, but from young locals who planned either to chat up the glamorous strangers or to ensure that the glamorous strangers remained strictly off limits to anyone already spoken for.

Marcus Lindsay recoiled as he and Jaki Johnston pushed open the door, not without difficulty. Condensation was running down windows and walls, there was a sweaty fug and the noise was deafening.

'It's as bad as a nightclub,' he bellowed to Jaki, hesitating on the threshold. 'Would you prefer—'

She wouldn't consider retreat. 'At least you're spared the music. Come on!' She grabbed his hand and plunged into the sea of bodies, heading for the corner where she could see Barrie Craig and Tony Laidlaw had installed themselves next to the bar.

There were cries of welcome and Barrie, who had pressed a lavish tip into Norrie's hand earlier, procured a vodka and tonic for Jaki and a pint for Marcus with impressive speed.

The arrival of the stars of the show had produced a buzz and even created a little space around them to make it easier to get a proper look at the exhibits and pass comment without being heard – almost. It came through that there was general agreement on him being shorter than you'd think and her being tiny, and Jaki plunged herself into conversation so she wouldn't hear the next bit which would doubtless be that she didn't look nearly as good off screen.

The men started discussing the best way to rejig the timings after overrunning today, while Jaki turned to look for the other members of the cast. They were in a cheerful group at the other end of the bar and she was just contemplating working her way over there when a voice spoke in her ear.

'Hey, sexy!'

Jaki turned. The specimen of manhood in front of her, flanked by two sniggering friends, was not appealing. He was very skinny, with a shaven head, and round his neck, exposed by a purple V-neck in shiny lycra, was tattooed a dotted line. He looked as if he might well have 'love' and 'hate' on his knuckles, and he had very bad teeth. Jaki involuntarily took a step back from the blast of beer and bad breath.

'I'm Kevin Docherty,' he was saying. 'Kev to my friends – like you're going to be.' A wink and a nudge to one of his pals produced a fresh burst of sniggering.

She swept him from head to foot with a contemptuous glance, then said, 'No, I don't think so,' and turned her back.

His hand shot out and grabbed her shoulder, spinning her round. 'Don't do that. I don't like it.'

His eyes had narrowed to malevolent slits, and she felt a lurch of fear. Then he was smiling again. 'Come on, doll – you be nice to me and I'll be nice to you. Very nice, later. Norrie!' He snapped his fingers. 'A drink for the lady!'

In Jaki's neighbourhood you got feisty or you got scared, and she'd never fancied scared. Anyway, they were in a crowded bar.

She struck his hand away. 'Keep your hands to yourself,' she said fiercely. 'Now get lost.'

'Oh, too posh, are we?' Suddenly he flared into violent rage. He began a tirade and Jaki, accustomed to casual swearing among colleagues, found herself shocked at the force of the same words used in malice.

Marcus, who had had his back to this, heard the raised voice and turned. 'What's going on? Is there a problem, Jaki?' He put his arm round her, and Barrie and Tony too moved forward to her side.

She managed to sound angry, not scared. 'This pond-scum seemed to think I might want to talk to him. I've explained I don't, and he's going to leave me alone now.' She turned her back.

Marcus said quietly, 'So that's it, right? We don't want any trouble.'

'You think?' Kevin sneered. He pushed Marcus hard, catching him off balance, and then laughed. 'Oh, you're not on sodding *Playfair's Patch* now. This is *my* patch.'

Marcus's face turned dark and Jaki saw that he was struggling not to gratify Kevin by reacting to his provocation. The other drinkers were beginning to notice and behind the bar Norrie turned pale and went to the telephone.

'We like trouble, don't we, lads?' Kevin went on, to growls of agreement from the grinning youths beside him. 'Outside, though – not much space in here for what we're planning to do.'

The drinkers nearby were moving back to be out of range while still ensuring a ringside seat, but Tony Laidlaw, dark and saturnine, came forward. 'Cool it, OK? No one's fighting anyone. And if they were, you'd get stuffed.' He looked past Kevin and nodded. 'Deal with him, guys.'

Before Kevin could move, two of the production team appeared, one on either side, separating him from his friends and neatly penning him up against the bar. They were both big men, and by now others from the cast and crew had joined them.

Outnumbered, Kevin could only deliver another volley of obscene abuse, directed at Marcus. Then he turned away, as if it were he who had seen them off, and shouted, 'Nip and a chaser, Norrie!' at the sweating barman.

A collective sigh ran through the company, either of relief or disappointment, and the noise rose again, louder than ever.

A few minutes later, the landlord appeared in the doorway. He was a large man, with considerable presence, and he had thrown the door open with force. A hush fell as he shouldered his way through the crowd to where Kevin and his mates stood in an uneasy grouping.

'You'd better get out of here, Docherty. I've called the police. And don't come back, any of you. You're banned.'

He listened impassively to the vituperative response, then said, 'You're still banned. Get out.'

For a moment, no one moved. Then Kevin, his face black with anger, walked out with his acolytes, a path opening before them through the crowd, and slammed the door hard.

'Good riddance,' the landlord said. 'Nasty character, Docherty – should have banned him years ago. Sorry about that. Now, what can I get you, sir? I'm a great fan of *Playfair's Patch*.'

Marcus shook his head. 'That's kind, but I'll take a rain check if I may – we've an early start tomorrow. What about you, Jaki?'

She was more shaken than she cared to admit. 'Yes, I'm coming back too.'

'But aren't you going to wait for the police?' the landlord protested. 'It'll take them a wee while to get here, but—'

'Much as I would like to nail the little bastard, I don't want to make matters worse,' Marcus said. 'Let's just say he'd had a bit too much to drink and you've dealt with it already.'

'If you're sure. But he's only out of prison now on condition he behaves himself, and it might be a good thing if he went back there.'

Marcus was dismayed. 'Oh, that's all we need! Look – it's bad enough that he's banned from his local. I don't want a knife in my back next time I come down here for the weekend.'

A lugubrious man, sitting on a bar-stool which had been a good vantage point, chipped in. 'You'd better watch it, then – that's what he was in for in the first place.'

With this comforting information, Jaki and Marcus left. The rain was pelting down and it was very dark, with only one feeble street-light nearby illuminating little more than the pavement in front of the pub. Marcus had parked at the end of the car park, beyond the dark bulk of the Winnebago, and they both peered anxiously into the shadows as they dashed for the safety of the car.

It was almost nine o'clock when Rafael Cizek got back from his work on the farm, looking depressed and very wet. One of the sheep had fallen sick and the vet had been unable to save it.

'I failed, that's the thing,' he said miserably.

'But Rafael, Bill will understand! I've heard him say sheep die deliberately, just to be a nuisance.'

'I know, but with Bill away it was my responsibility. I feel bad about it – I will hate to tell him.'

That was Rafael all over, taking his responsibilities almost too seriously. It might make him foolishly sensitive about Karolina working, but it made him a good husband and father as well as a good worker, and she loved him for it.

As she heated up Rafael's supper, there was a knock on the door. Rafael frowned. 'It must be someone from the house – not another problem, I hope,' he was saying as he went to the door, then, in blank astonishment, 'Kasper! What are you doing here?'

Rafael had been wet; Kasper was soaked to the skin. He had no raincoat and his short navy wool jacket was sodden. His teeth were chattering.

'Can I – can I come in?' he said.

'Of course, of course! Come in out of the rain. But – what has happened to you? You have been fighting again?'

With his thick dark hair plastered to his white face, the blackened bruising stood out luridly and his eye was a rainbow of murky colour.

'I was attacked this morning.' Pathetic as a half-drowned cat, he looked from one to the other.

'Well, don't stand there dripping on my clean floor,' Karolina snapped. 'Take your boots off and I'll put down some newspaper.'

Rafael stared in astonishment at his sweet-natured wife. He picked up the towel which had been drying by the fire, and handed it to Kasper.

'Here, dry yourself off a bit. I'll get something to warm you up. I'd say sit down, but—' He glanced apologetically towards Karolina, fussing crossly with newspapers to put under Kasper's wet stockinged feet.

She caught the look, which said that she was behaving very strangely, and that hospitality was hospitality, after all. She was too angry at being manipulated to care.

'How did you get here?' Rafael asked, pouring vodka into two shot glasses. Karolina had refused a drink and was now standing with her arms folded.

'I walked. Then I caught a bus, and then walked again. For

hours.' Kasper downed the vodka with a practised flick of the wrist. Rafael, still holding the bottle, filled it again.

'Walked? In that rain? Where from?'

'Ardhill. I was living in a house there, with a building gang. It was the boss who attacked me—'

'Tell him why,' Karolina said acidly, then before he could speak, went on, with a contemptuous gesture at Kasper, 'He walked out to take a job in the film canteen because it paid better. Let the others down. Small wonder the boss was angry!'

'The canteen – where you are working?' Rafael said slowly.

'Er – yes.' In her indignation, Karolina had forgotten where this would lead. 'He heard me talking about it after Mass – and then turned up looking like this! I had said he was respectable, and he made me look a fool – or dishonest, which is worse.'

For a moment Rafael had looked suspicious, but his wife's uncharacteristic hostility was reassuring. He asked Kasper, 'So, what happened then?'

'After work, I went to the house, but he locked me out. The others did nothing, but when Jozef went into his bedroom I knocked on the window.

'I told him the man is mad, me today, him tomorrow, but he – wasn't helpful. I said, "He's not one of us, he exploits us – he is a monster! We must fight him together!" But Jozef is a coward, only interested in the money he gets.'

'So unlike you!' Karolina sniped. 'And when the film people leave, what will you do then?'

'I don't know! I need help, that is why I've come to you, my old friends.'

'I told you—' she began, but Rafael interrupted her sternly.

'Karolina, he is our guest. Kasper, I have clothes you can wear. They will perhaps be a little short, but they will be dry.

'Come with me. Karolina will make you something to eat, then we can talk.' He gave his wife a meaning look.

There were always eggs in the house, courtesy of Marjory's hens, and Karolina broke them into a bowl for an omelette, but with a bad grace. She was slicing one of her own loaves when Rafael came back with Kasper's wet clothes.

'He's having a shower,' he said.

'He'd better not wake Janek, that's all.' Karolina took the bundle from him and dumped it on the table while she let down the pulley.

'I know you're angry with him,' Rafael said tentatively. 'But you know we can't turn him out on a night like this.'

She picked up a pair of trousers and hung them up. 'He planned this,' she said fiercely. 'He said, could he stay here and I told him he couldn't. Twice. So he just put us into a position where we couldn't refuse. That's why I'm angry.' She wrung out a sock in a way which suggested there was something else she would happily wring instead.

Rafael grimaced. 'He was no friend of mine, even before he took up with you. He was never entirely honest. But it is hard here, where we are all strangers together. We have to—'

'Rafael,' she said, in a strange voice, 'Look.'

In one hand she held the navy jacket, in the other a razor-edged knife with a horn handle with brass studs.

Sylvia Lascelles heard them returning from the pub and glanced at the travel clock on the table beside her. Only half past ten! It couldn't have been a very good evening.

She had said she was going to bed, but preparations took painful effort and she had been too tired even to try. She had dozed in her wheelchair, and now she was looking out into the rainy darkness.

The sound of the steady downpour was soothing. She had loved to listen to the rain long, long ago as she lay awake in the big bedroom upstairs, with Laddie asleep at her side, indulging the fantasy that she was mistress of Flora's beautiful house as well as her husband.

Laddie would never discuss divorce and Sylvia knew that the house, not his wife, was her rival. If Flora could just have died quietly, and painlessly of course – Sylvia was a compassionate woman – it would have solved everything.

But Laddie had died first, a prisoner latterly in this very room. The time for discretion had passed; Sylvia had begged Flora to let her see him, and in a two-minute phone call had been scornfully refused. She had heard the delight in power in the other woman's voice, and knew herself for once powerless. It was a bitter blow for someone accustomed – even, perhaps, addicted – to the ruthless exercise of charm in imposing her will.

Tears came to her eyes thinking of Laddie, old and wretched, alone with this cold, dreary woman. Admittedly, Flora had provided his creature comforts: this was a pleasant room, better heated than anywhere else, with its own little bathroom adapted for the infirm. He would have hated that necessity, as she did.

It was a wonder his bored, unhappy ghost didn't linger still, but it didn't. She couldn't sense him here at all. Elsewhere, in the conservatory in particular, his presence was so real she almost thought if she turned she would see him – not old, but young again, and with that extraordinary aura which the World War II pilots seemed to retain, as if winning their duel with death in the air had left them with more of the life force than earthbound mortals.

Marcus was like Laddie in many ways, but set in a lower key. Laddie could be an utter bastard, completely without shame; Marcus didn't have that ruthless streak. A darling boy, Marcus.

Though he denied it, Sylvia suspected that pity had prompted Marcus to get her the offer of the part. She knew he believed she'd been tempted by the promise of a last, brief flicker of the candle of fame – as if she didn't understand that her bright day was done and she was for the dark! She was a curiosity, a live fossil, and extravagant admiration for the woman she had long ceased to be left her merely impatient ('Homage, Miss Lascelles' – silly little man!).

It was Laddie who had brought her back here, still drawing her from beyond the grave to the house he had loved. And she had found him here; she could even hear his voice in the gallant, teasing things Marcus said.

She saw so little of Marcus these days! He was busy and successful, and when he came to London it was for professional reasons and the most she could expect was a brief visit or even just a phone call. Sylvia wondered jealously how often he had come to see Flora.

In her fantasy, she would have lived in this house and Marcus would have been her son. But theirs was only a bond of love, not duty, and the house—

She hated the thought of him selling it. She hadn't money to give him herself; she'd been flush at one stage, but the cruel onset of her illness had brought an end to high earnings just when older women – Judi Dench, Maggie Smith – seemed to be more in demand than ever. She'd been more famous than either of them, once, but all she could hope was that she would die before the money for carers ran out.

Marcus must marry money – that was the only answer. Laddie had done it and had never let it cramp his style. With Marcus's charm, it shouldn't be difficult.

At least Jaki – 'Jaki', for heaven's sake! – was history now. He must become more serious, and find some suitable young woman. If it wasn't a love match, they could come to the sort of arrangement Flora and Laddie had; being 'understanding' would be the price she had to pay to keep Marcus – and Marcus could charm any woman he chose.

Then, as if a cold hand had touched her, she remembered the visit from the police. She wasn't a fool: the police didn't turn up after twenty years to question someone who'd had a teenage romance long before the girl had died. Marcus had said it was routine, unimportant – but why, then, had he been so defensive and edgy?

Why would it have mattered if he'd fathered her child? He couldn't be forced to marry her and Laddie, who doted on Marcus, would have found the money to pay her off. There would be no need to kill her, and knowing Marcus she would stake her life on it that he hadn't – or bet her dwindling bank account, a gamble she would be much less ready to take.

Sylvia could see that quite clearly, but would the police? The magicians on *Playfair's Patch*, delivering justice within the hour every week, bore no resemblance to their real-life counterparts.

A sudden, savage twinge reminded her she must take her medication and once it had taken effect begin the ordeal of putting herself to bed. She swallowed the tablets and sat staring out a little longer.

She was feeling melancholy now. After this, what had she to look forward to? A quiet life was preferable perhaps to having allowances made for her by pitying colleagues – she, Sylvia Lascelles, who had been famed for her utter professionalism! But she would be alone with her rage against the dying of the light as twilight gathered.

★   ★   ★

'The police came today.' Jean Grant put down a plate with greyish chops, dried out from the oven, boiled potatoes and damp cabbage in front of her son.

Stuart went still. 'What were they wanting?'

'Just one of them. A woman. Asking questions about Ailsa all over again.'

'Ailsa – opening up the case?'

'Yes. Won't bring her back, though, will it? And they're going to ignore what I told them just like the last lot did.'

He began to eat. 'So – doesn't make any difference, then.'

'They'll be wanting to talk to you.'

'They can if they like. Talking's cheap.'

'You'll need to watch what you say.' Jean's eyes were fixed on her son but, chewing methodically, he wouldn't look at her. 'I told her Ailsa had problems with your father – they knew that already anyway.'

His temper was as fiery as his hair. 'Problems? That's what you call it? Between you, you made her life hell. Oh, you always say you and she were close, but the way you treated her, she'd have said nothing just out of spite. You couldn't break her, even going on about her bringing another mouth to feed—'

The slap across his face took him completely by surprise, rattling his teeth in his head.

'Wash your mouth out, Stuart Grant! That's lies, all lies.' She swept the plate off the table and it smashed on the floor. 'Say one word of that to the police, and I sell the farm and give the money to charity. Not a day goes by – barely an hour – when I'm not thinking about her. I'd only her good at heart. She could have been decently married by now, and me with grandchildren to make up for a lazy, fushionless lump of a son.

'If you want justice for your sister, you'll not distract the police with a load of rubbish.'

Stuart was rubbing his cheek. He didn't speak, as if afraid that speaking would produce another onslaught.

His mother continued, 'You spoke to them before. You just tell them what you told them then, and wait for them to go away. After that we'll carry on the best we can.'

Again he said nothing, and Jean's voice sharpened. 'Cat got your tongue? Did you hear what I said?'

He stood up, a big, clumsy man, a bit overweight. 'I heard. I'm doing what you want, all right? Just don't push me.'

'Push you? My certes, if I could ever have pushed you to any effect, the farm wouldn't be in the state it's in now. You're feeble, like your father before you.'

Stuart walked to the door. 'And maybe it was you made us that way.'

He slammed it behind him as he left, leaving his mother to stare at it with just a hint of uncertainty in her expression.

9

When DI Fleming and DS MacNee reached Balnakenny, a man was dragging sacks of cattle feed out of one of the sheds – a tall, bulky man with bright red hair. Seeing the car, he stopped and came over to them.

His expression was sullen, his eyes hostile. 'What are you wanting?' he demanded.

They showed their warrant cards and Fleming introduced them.

'Stuart Grant? Your mother perhaps mentioned I'd spoken to her yesterday about reviewing the investigation into your sister's murder. We'd like a word with you too.'

'If it doesn't take long. I've a couple of new beasts to settle in.'

Fleming followed his glance to a pen in the byre beyond, where two dejected-looking Friesian crosses stood in a deep layer of straw and muck. She looked away hastily. It wasn't a real case of cruelty so it wasn't her business, but she hated seeing the poor creatures so badly cared for.

'Perhaps we could go inside?' she suggested.

'Better out here.' He stood his ground, looking uncomfortable.

MacNee cleared his throat, jerking his head in the direction of the house. The front door was open and Jean Grant was on the doorstep watching them, hands on hips.

It wasn't actually raining, but it was cold and windy. Stuart obviously didn't want his mother present at their interview, but Fleming had no intention of staying out here quietly freezing to death.

'It would be more satisfactory inside,' she said firmly. 'Your mother will understand that our business is with you.'

Stuart snorted, with what might almost have been a sardonic smile. 'You explain, then.'

He led them round to the back of the house, kicked off his Caterpillar boots without undoing the laces – just the way Bill did with his, Fleming thought, amused – then ushered them into the kitchen.

Unlike the archetypal farm kitchen, it was austere and clinically tidy. There was a meagre fireplace and no range, only a gas cooker and a run of outdated kitchen units topped by red Formica, chipped here and there, with a big wooden table, scrubbed white, in the centre of the room. A dresser stored piles of crockery, with no attempt at artistic arrangement.

There was one incongruous object: a small, highly polished table in one corner with the familiar photo of Ailsa Grant, framed and with a candle placed on either side. Almost like a shrine, Fleming thought.

'You'd better sit down,' Stuart said grudgingly, seating himself at the table.

The door from the hall opened and Jean Grant appeared, face flushed with temper. Glaring at the officers, she said to her son, 'What are they in here for? The front room's the place for visitors. Through here.' She held open the door.

No one moved. Fleming said pleasantly, 'Thank you, Mrs Grant, but we're fine here. We'll talk to your son and then you can have your kitchen back.'

Her mouth pleated in a straight, angry line, Jean marched over and pulled out a chair.

'I'm sorry.' Fleming's voice was steelier this time. 'We want to talk to your son alone.'

MacNee went over to the door and held it open, just as Jean had done.

The woman didn't move. 'But—' she protested.

'He's a big boy now,' MacNee said. 'He's not needing you to hold his hand.'

'It's not that,' she snapped. 'It's—'

Fleming let the pause develop, then prompted, 'It's—?'

'Oh, what's the use?' With a final, vengeful glare at Stuart, Jean stormed out, leaving MacNee to shut the door, with ironic delicacy, behind her. It was a good, thick door: she wouldn't hear much from the other side.

Fleming sat down. 'Now, Mr Grant – Stuart, if you don't mind?'

He grunted. 'Whatever you like. Makes no odds to me.'

He was unattractive, with pale skin weather-beaten and marked with freckles, and a down-turned mouth. His eyes were dark, fringed by pale lashes.

'Before we get to the night your sister died,' Fleming began, 'I'm trying to form a picture of what happened before that. You know your mother claimed Marcus Lazansky was the father of Ailsa's baby, and that he murdered her?'

Stuart's face darkened. 'Aye, I know.'

'They had been romantically involved as teenagers?'

'Aye. Though she'd been well warned about him.'

'Why was that?'

'My parents didn't like it. Well, he was a different kind from us – and they were right enough, the way it turned out.'

'Different?' MacNee put in. 'Posh, you mean?'

'Aye. The way he spoke – could have been English, even, the way he spoke.' He sounded virulent.

'Was your sister older or younger than you?' Fleming asked.
'Older.'

'How did you get on together? Were you good friends?'

'Good enough.'

'It sounds as if you didn't like Marcus. Why is that?'

Stuart shrugged. 'Didn't dislike him.'

Was he being deliberately unhelpful, Fleming wondered. She thought he was tensing up, which interested her. As a younger brother, he could have useful light to shed on the relationship. She pressed him. 'You didn't dislike him? You sounded as if you did.'

He showed definite signs of unease and for a moment she thought he wasn't going to reply, then unexpectedly he burst out, 'She cried a lot. After he dumped her.'

Fleming felt the stirrings of sympathy. 'You were very fond of your sister, weren't you?'

There was a pause. 'Aye.'

MacNee leaned forward. 'Were you upset when she went away to Glasgow? Must have been rough here, a young lad, no company but your parents.'

Stuart shrugged again, with what Fleming interpreted as apathetic resignation.

MacNee was going on, 'Was she having a good time in Glasgow? Did you ever go to stay with her?'

'No. She came back a few times, like Christmas and Easter, before – before she came back the last time.'

'Did she talk to you about friends in Glasgow? Boyfriends?'

He shook his head. 'Mentioned some girls that worked with her. No boyfriends. But—'

He stopped as if he was afraid of saying too much. 'But—?' Fleming prompted very gently.

'I – I could tell there was someone, when she came back the time before she came home for good. She didn't say anything, but she was happy, like she hadn't been for a long time.'

Stuart was beginning to talk now, almost as if finding his voice after a long silence. 'There was a phone call one day – she'd been hanging around the hall half the afternoon, and she was mad when I asked her why, but it was like she was expecting it.'

This was new. Fleming, almost afraid to interrupt him, said, 'Did you hear any of it?'

'No. It was only short, but she was giggling and laughing. My mother asked her who it was and she said it was one of her girlfriends. But I didn't think so. I thought it was him.'

'Him – Marcus?'

Stuart nodded.

'Did she ever tell you he was the father?'

'No. It was like she was scared – she said once that if she said anything it would be the end. But—'

This time Fleming didn't prompt him. She was sitting opposite, in an attitude of close attention, her hazel eyes warm. It seemed to draw him on.

'She thought something good was going to happen, though. That's how I knew she hadn't killed herself. She could take whatever they threw at her, because of that. It didn't matter. She despised them.'

'Them?' Jean Grant had implied the relationship was close and affectionate. 'Not just your father?'

'He was the worst.' Stuart was becoming visibly upset. 'Called her every bad word you could think of. But she was raging as well, because Ailsa wouldn't admit it was Marcus.'

'Ailsa denied it?'

'Oh aye. But then she'd said it would be the end if she did, so . . .' He shrugged.

Fleming was pretty sure he knew nothing more. She glanced at MacNee. Time to move on, and for a change of pace.

'The night it happened,' MacNee said, 'you were all here, in the farmhouse, right?'

'Aye. We said.' The surly expression had returned.

'Did you see Ailsa before she went out?'

'Not after we had our tea. She went away up to her room – she was mostly in her room then. I hardly saw her except mealtimes. The roof of one of the sheds round the back was leaking and the tarpaulin we'd put over was lifting so I'd to go out to sort it before it blew away.'

'You were out?' MacNee said sharply.

'Oh aye. I got all the dirty jobs. He always said he'd done them for years and now it was my turn.'

Stuart had clearly misunderstood the thrust of the question, and MacNee wasn't about to enlighten him. 'On a terrible night like that! How long did it take you?'

'Hard to say, now. An hour – maybe longer.'

'Then what did you do?'

'Went in. They were watching the telly, so I watched for a bit, then went up to my bed.'

'And nothing was said about Ailsa having gone out?'

'I thought she'd gone to bed earlier.'

So Robert Grant's solid alibi was now only from his wife – was this why she had wanted to be present while her son was questioned? Presumably Donald Bailey had not insisted on separate statements. And while Fleming was sure Stuart would not have lied to protect the father he clearly hated, she could readily believe Jean Grant might have her own dark purposes.

There was one last area to cover and she was almost reluctant to do it.

'When your sister's body was recovered, you and your father went down to the lighthouse?'

Fleming could read in the sudden hunching of his body, as if against a blow, that this still hurt even today.

'You identified her?'

'Aye.'

'And the officer who was there – he said you could bring her back here?'

'That's right! I'd forgotten. I mind him fine, though. Thought she'd killed herself, and it was only to be expected, that she was just a wee hoor. A hard-faced bastard.'

It was surprising how much that unexpected comment stung, but Fleming said steadily, 'Yet he allowed you to take her body home instead of leaving it where it was?'

'Aye. I was surprised at that.' He sounded surprised too, even now. 'She was lying there, for everyone to look at . . .' Stuart chewed his lip, and it was a moment before he went on. 'I asked, could we not just take her home? Oh, he gave us this big lecture about what was supposed to happen, but then he let us take her anyway.'

Why had Angus done that? Fleming only realized that she was puzzling over that, instead of putting the next question, when MacNee asked, after a curious glance at her, 'And it was definitely you, not your father, who asked?'

'Him? He wouldn't care.' Stuart spoke with great bitterness.

Fleming recovered. 'And what happened when you got her back here?'

'My father just went away out. My mother was going daft – got a comb and stuff, fussing round, washing Ailsa's face and that.'

'Can you remember what exactly she did?'

His defences swung into place. This was, it seemed, simply too painful to talk about. He erupted into rage. 'No, I bloody can't. You're talking about my sister, lying dead. I didn't notice much – I was probably crying. All right?' He put his head in his hands.

'Yes, of course.' With a swift movement, Fleming stood up. 'You've had more than enough, Stuart, and you've been very helpful. We'll leave you now to get back to your beasts.'

As the car drove off Jean Grant came into the kitchen like an avenging fury. 'What did you tell them?'

Stuart was at the back door, pulling on his boots. 'Nothing.' He didn't look at her.

'What did you tell them?' she repeated. 'It was a long time, to have told them nothing.'

He stood up. 'Oh, I can tell folk nothing for far longer than that,' he said over his shoulder, and walked out.

Gavin Hodge, his hands in the pockets of his Diesel jeans and his Ralph Lauren jerkin zipped up against the cold wind, stood assessing the progress of the steam room.

'I thought you said you'd be putting on the roof before the end of the week?' he said aggressively to the silent man in front of him. 'You haven't even got the frame up.'

Stefan Pavany's face was stony. 'I am trying to find a roofer.'

'Trying to find one?' Hodge's voice rose. 'I understood you had the men to do the whole job. There's no way I'd have given you the contract if I'd known we'd be waiting while you "found" a roofer. I feel I've been conned, and no one does that to Gavin Hodge.

'Looks like that's your bonus for an early finish gone. And if you're late on completion, I'm going to dock your payment for every day it overruns.'

Hodge didn't stop to hear Pavany's reply. He wouldn't have understood it anyway, delivered as it was in a furious undertone and a foreign language.

The other two builders had paused to watch. Pavany swore at them too, then snarled, '*Zabieraj się do roboty*. Get on with your work. No breaks. I have something to do.'

He went to the battered white van parked on the gravel sweep and drove off.

'One down, one to go on the alibi,' MacNee said as they left the farm. 'I always had her old man fingered for it.'

'That's what they reckoned last time, too,' Fleming pointed out, 'but they'd no proof. And if they hadn't then, what chance have we got now?

'But don't forget Jean Grant. She told me she and Ailsa were close, which doesn't square with what Stuart said just now.'

'In it together, maybe?'

Fleming pulled a face. 'Maybe. I'm fairly sure they didn't have a good marriage.'

'With that ill-natured besom, who could? At least she's safe from hellfire – "*The de'il could ne'er abide her!*" But maybe they agreed the girl was bringing shame on the family. Or say he killed her, and she realized after. But by then Ailsa was dead anyway, and if he got the jail for it, who'd run the farm? Stuart would be too young. Or look at it the other way – here, see me? Just full of ideas this morning! Say she lost her temper, killed Ailsa herself, then made Robert lie for her. I like this – Jean Grant would knock you over the head as soon as look at you.'

MacNee was taken with his latest theory, but Fleming sighed, then shook her head.

'I know what I said. But somehow, when you spell it out, I just can't buy it. I wish you'd heard her yesterday. I believed she truly cared about her daughter – and yes, of course I believe Stuart too, that she was raging with her. Believe me, for a mother these emotions are not mutually exclusive.

'But there was something else there, Tam – something I can't put my finger on. She made an excuse to leave the room at one point and I thought it was because she wouldn't let me see her cry, but now I wonder if it was to get a breathing space.'

'What were you asking her at the time?'

Fleming shrugged. 'Nothing much. Something about whether Ailsa had taken anything with her, I think – it probably wasn't about that at all. I keep trying to pin down what struck the wrong note, but I'm not getting anywhere.'

'Park it and forget it,' MacNee advised. 'Anyway, I thought we got pretty straight answers from Stuart.'

'Yes. And I certainly think the brother–sister relationship was perfectly normal – bit of hero worship perhaps, for his older sister. And it was pretty obvious he resented Marcus, whatever he said.'

'Why not just admit it? Marcus seems to have been a right little sod. Still is, likely.'

'Speaking of which,' Fleming said, signalling a left turn off the main road, 'I just want to drop in again at Tulach. I'd one of my cosy girls' chats with Sheila Milne last night and she said she'd had a complaint about harassment from Marcus Lindsay. I thought I'd better go and apologize.'

MacNee turned to stare at her. '*Apologize?* For asking a few simple questions? Have you gone clean daft?'

'Apologizing shows a magnanimous spirit,' Fleming said sententiously. 'And it's a good excuse for going. I want to know why he should be so sensitive about those few simple questions. And why he should have complained to the Procurator Fiscal, when I'd be willing to bet he's one of about three people in Scotland, outside the legal professions, who would know she was in charge of investigations like this.'

It was Mrs Boyter, resplendent in her pink pinny and an air of importance, who opened the door. 'Oh, I'm afraid Mr Marcus isn't here. Miss Lascelles –' she lingered lovingly on the name – 'is in the conservatory and if you wish to speak to her, I can see if madam is at home this morning. The other two are filming down in the village. But you can give me a message and I will see he receives it on his return.'

'Thank you, but we'll try to catch Mr Lindsay there,' Fleming said.

They left Mrs Boyter looking crestfallen. 'Delusions of grandeur,' MacNee snorted. 'Thinks she's butler to the stars now. Doesn't take much to turn some folks' heads.'

The road through the village was an obstacle course of vehicles – vans, a bus, cars, and even cameras on mechanized trolleys. Weaving her way through it, Fleming was waved to a standstill by a uniformed officer. When he realized who it was, he saluted and came over to the car. She opened the window.

'Sorry, ma'am – they're going for a take. They'll be calling Action in a moment.' He used the technical terms with some pride. 'So unless it's urgent—'

'No problem,' Fleming said, not immune to the fascination of watching the cameras in action herself. She found a space to park, then she and MacNee strolled over to join the small crowd of onlookers, standing in impressive silence watching the process.

The cameras were set up to give different angles, their focus a man standing on the edge of the further pavement, with a woman fussing over his hair with a comb.

Fleming didn't recognize Marcus Lindsay immediately. His hair had been covered by a shaggy grey wig and he was wearing a thick navy fleece with a torn pocket over shabby blue jeans and dirty trainers. His personal style was neat, almost dapper, but now he looked what Janet Laird would have called 'a right shauchle'.

'Working under cover then, is he?' MacNee said in a hoarse whisper, earning a stern 'Shush!' from the formidable matron to his left. He subsided.

Someone stepped forward, snapped a clapperboard shut and called, 'Action!' Lindsay stepped off the pavement, walking like a man exhausted by heavy physical work, crossed the street, stepped up to the baker's shop in front of him, and had put his hand on the door handle when another voice shouted, 'Cut! Thank you. Very nice.'

A buzz of talk broke out as everyone stood by, waiting for the verdict on the shot. Fleming turned to MacNee.

'You don't quite believe they really do that – you know, the clapperboard-action-cut bit. It's such a cliché, you'd think it was probably rubbish – you know, like us saying, " 'Ello, 'ello, 'ello." ' Tam looked blank, and she went hastily on, 'Anyway, he didn't do very much, did he? It must take a hell of a time to film a whole episode, if it's in tiny pieces like that.'

'Took the best part of an hour just to get that,' MacNee's neighbour put in. 'Rehearsals and all. And then they all go and have a coffee. Oh look, there's that Jaki Johnston, coming out of the caravan. I like her – she's good.'

'Carrying on with him, is what I heard.' A woman on Fleming's other side leaned forward and the two began a lively discussion across the officers.

A voice called, 'That's a take!' and the scene of suspended animation burst into activity as cameras moved off and a woman hurried forward to take the wig Lindsay had pulled off to run his hands through his hair. He had taken the jacket off too and looked round. 'Where's Frocks? I don't want to wear this – I'll be in the Winnebago when you want me for the next shot.'

A young man came hurrying up and took it from him, and Jaki Johnston came over and slipped her arm through his. 'Well done!' she said, and Fleming heard Lindsay say ironically, 'Oh, absolutely. Move over, Ken Branagh!'

They walked off, Lindsay once again looking smart and fit, despite the cheap checked flannel shirt and baggy jeans. It had been a convincing piece of acting.

With MacNee following in her wake, Fleming excuse-me'd her way through the crowd. There were curious looks from the team as they walked up to the Winnebago and tapped on the open door.

Lindsay was sitting on a cream leather couch at one end of the van and Jaki was operating a coffee machine in a neat kitchen area at the other end. He looked surprised to see them, then got up.

'Inspector! This is an unexpected pleasure. What can I do for you?' The words and smile were amiable, but Fleming, as she tended to do, looked at eyes not mouth, and the telltale wrinkles which denote a genuine smile were missing.

'May we come in?' Fleming said, equally pleasantly. 'We're both intrigued to see where the stars hang out.'

'Of course! Jaki, can you find another couple of mugs?'

'No, no, not for us,' Fleming said without consulting MacNee, who gave her a dirty look. 'It really won't take a moment. I gather you made a complaint to the acting Procurator Fiscal about police harassment after our visit yesterday, and we're here to apologize.'

Lindsay looked stunned. 'Complaint? I don't know what you're talking about.' His bewilderment appeared entirely genuine.

'I had a conversation with Ms Milne yesterday and I understood from her that you had complained about the interview we did with you. It had seemed to me we were only making legitimate enquiries, but—'

'Yes, of course! A complaint would have been ridiculous!' Lindsay was seriously put out. 'I don't know what Sheila Milne is thinking about – oh, hang on, I made a joke about it during a personal conversation. I can't believe she took it seriously. This is a waste of your time – I do apologize, inspector.'

He seemed very anxious not to upset the police. That was interesting, and it was interesting too that Milne had not declared a friendship – had, indeed, all but denied it. 'You know her, then?' Fleming asked.

She wondered if she was imagining his hesitation, but then she saw MacNee was giving him a sharp look too. Lindsay said, 'Yes, I knew her in Glasgow.'

Despite an inviting pause, he didn't expand on that. Fleming asked, smiling, 'An old girlfriend?'

'No, no, nothing like that.' He smiled too, an amused smile that would have been convincing if she hadn't noticed, yet again, that the tiny muscles round the eyes hadn't moved.

There was a tap on the door, and a woman stuck her head in. 'Can you go across to make-up, Marcus? They're getting ready for rehearsals.'

Lindsay got up with alacrity. 'Sorry, inspector, sergeant. I have to go. But please don't hesitate to come back if there's anything more I can help you with.'

Jaki, who had been listening silently, held up a mug. 'You can still have coffee if you like,' she offered with a smile. A genuine one, this time.

'Thanks, but we'd better get on,' Fleming said, again to MacNee's disappointment.

'What did you say that for?' he grumbled as they left. 'I could just go a cup of coffee. And she was a nice lassie too.'

'Your star-struck behaviour with Sylvia Lascelles is bad enough. You're not needing another screen idol,' Fleming said as they passed the catering truck.

A voice said shyly, 'Hello, Marjory,' and she looked up to see Karolina leaning out of the open hatch.

'Oh – Karolina! I'd forgotten you were working here! How's it going?'

'It is very good,' she said. 'Everyone is very kind, and they like my cooking.'

'What's not to like? I'm glad it's going so well. How much longer will they be here?'

'Three days, maybe four. They decide when they see how the filming goes.'

'For God's sake, look where you're going! See what you've done, you young idiot! I'm in costume, and we're filming in ten minutes!'

Turning at the sound of the furious voice, Fleming saw that a tall, dark young man, who had come hurrying down the steps from the catering truck carrying a washing-up bowl full of wet, earthy vegetable peelings across to the compost bin, had rounded the corner of the truck at speed and cannoned into Marcus Lindsay, who was standing in conversation with one of the technicians.

Lindsay began brushing off the clinging debris, but the jeans were wet and dirty. With a cry of dismay, a woman from one of the other trucks came rushing across, and also started to berate the culprit.

He was standing with his head bowed. He muttered, 'Sorry,' but Lindsay only said angrily, 'The best thing you can do is just get out of the way,' and turned away, asking the agitated woman what could be done. They went off towards the truck she had come from, still in anxious discussion.

The chef, viewing this from inside the truck, hurried down the steps. 'You're pushing your luck, sunshine. You've been about as much use as a chocolate frying pan, and now this. I'm warning you, three strikes and you're out.'

The young man said nothing but scowlingly gathered up the peelings and continued on his errand. But Fleming was concerned to see that as he went, he directed a look of purest hatred at the unconscious Lindsay's back. Certainly, Lindsay had been angry, but this was an extreme reaction – and he looked, too, as if he'd been in a fight, with bruises on his face, a shiner and a bandaged arm. A violent young man, it seemed. She saw that Karolina had noticed both what had happened and her own reaction, and the girl's face flushed.

'That – that is someone I am to know from Poland. Kasper. He was being with us last night at the farm – this is all right?' Her agitation showed in the breakdown of her usual fluency.

Fleming was disconcerted, but said immediately, 'Yes, of course. It's your house, Karolina. You don't need to ask me if you want to have guests.'

Karolina looked as if she was about to say something, then thought the better of it. 'You are very kind.'

'Nonsense! We'd better get on, anyway. See you later.'

MacNee too had observed the small drama. 'Wouldn't like to meet him up a dark close on a Saturday night,' he remarked, but added plaintively, 'Are we in some kind of hurry? I'm sure we could have got our lunch if you'd asked. They're frying onions – I'm starving!'

Fleming was unsympathetic. 'You'll get something back at the canteen.'

'Oh aye, cheese and pickle, when we're late like we always are,' he said with some bitterness.

'Better for you than fried onions. Oh look, they must have sorted out the clothes problem – there's Marcus back in costume. You have to say he's convincing.'

MacNee followed her gaze and saw a man with his back to them, in a navy fleece with longish grey hair, apparently asking something of one of the crew, who pointed towards the catering truck. When he turned, they saw it wasn't Lindsay, but an actual workman of some description, his jeans and trainers white with dust.

He strode past them but before he reached the truck Kasper reappeared with the empty bowl. Seeing him, he stopped, but the older man came up and seized his arm, half-twisting it in what looked like a painful grip. He started speaking in some foreign language, then shouting as Kasper dropped the bowl and turned with bunched fists, replying with what seemed to be defiance.

Fleming and MacNee both spun round and MacNee stepped forward. 'OK, OK, that's it. Break it up, right now!' he said roughly.

Neither man heard. Kasper broke the grip on his arm and aimed a blow, which was parried effortlessly. Then the shouting began again as they circled each other.

A crowd was gathering. Lindsay had emerged from a truck, a plastic cape round his shoulders; he stood on the steps, staring.

MacNee grabbed the older man, yanking his arm up in a half-nelson, and Fleming seized Kasper by the shoulders from behind, spinning him away. Neither struggled, but breathing heavily stood glaring at each other.

'Do you speak English?' MacNee demanded, and as neither seemed anxious to reply, Fleming called, 'Karolina!'

The girl came from the truck reluctantly, her face aflame with embarrassment. A chef in a white apron came along behind her.

'Perhaps you can translate,' Fleming suggested, but before Karolina could say anything, the chef said, 'No need. He'll understand what I'm saying, all right.'

He walked over to Kasper. 'You're fired,' he said. 'Now get out. OK?'

The young man's dark eyes shot fury, but his adversary gave a short, harsh laugh. 'Good!' he said in English. 'Now you can come back. Right away.'

'Able to speak English after all, are we?' MacNee said. 'Have you and your pal quite finished? I'm letting you go, but next time you're on a charge.' He was still holding the man's arm; he released it now, though Fleming suspected he had given it an unnecessary extra twist as he did so. The man rubbed at it, but made no complaint.

In the silence that followed, Karolina stepped forward. She had a short, angry conversation with Kasper, and at the end of it he made what sounded like a plea.

'*Nie!*' she said, then turned and walked back to the truck.

Fleming once more saw rage flare in Kasper's face and tensed, ready to grab him again, but instead he said something savagely to the older man and then, as the other walked off, followed him.

'Well!' said the chef blankly, 'what was all that about?'

'Search me,' MacNee said. 'But I tell you something – if it was me, I wouldn't be turning my back on that one. Not without body armour – and maybe not even then.'

10

With some reluctance, DI Fleming dialled Superintendent Bailey's number. 'Donald?'

'Marjory!' It sounded as if he'd jumped when he heard her voice. 'I – I was hoping for a word with you today.'

Now came the hard part. 'I'm in my office all afternoon. When would it be convenient to come and see me?'

She was holding her breath. Her normal practice was to go to her superior's office; she wanted to make the point that this time it was different. He needed to realize right from the start that she was in charge.

In the silence, she could hear him realizing. Then he said, 'Of course, that will be easier since you have all the papers there. In ten minutes?'

She allowed him this fig leaf to cover his embarrassment. 'Thanks, Donald. Ten minutes is fine.'

He wasn't the only one who was nervous. Fleming squared the papers on her desk, made sure her list of queries was on top, and switched on a kettle on a tray in the corner of the room.

When his knock came the kettle was boiling. 'Coffee, Donald?' she asked as he came in.

'Very kind,' he said gruffly, going to sit down.

Fleming hadn't thought of the political implications of being out of her seat behind the desk, the seat of power, and briefly wondered if he would take it to reassert his authority.

But he sat down meekly enough on the visitor's side, while she brought over the mugs.

He was looking round him. 'It's not often I've been here, since I had your job. Always enjoyed the view up here on the fourth floor.'

'Yes. I like looking out into treetops. They're coming into bud now – spring's well on its way. It would be good if the March winds would drop, though, now we're into April.'

She was starting to babble. It wouldn't get any easier; she had to take a grip, now. 'The investigation,' she said.

'The investigation,' Bailey echoed heavily. 'Yes.'

'Let me brief you first on what I've been doing.' She outlined her sifting of the evidence, and told him she had seen the Grants and Marcus Lazansky/Lindsay.

'My first question for you relates to initial interviews with Jean and Robert Grant, while you still believed Ailsa had killed herself. You stated there was no suicide note. What searches were made?'

He shifted uncomfortably in his seat. 'I'm afraid we took her mother's word for it. It looked straightforward enough, and it seemed intrusive to do a search at the time.'

'But later, then – did you establish whether she had taken anything with her – clothes, a wallet, a bag?'

'Not – not that I recall. But I couldn't say for certain – it's a long time ago.'

'You see, if she'd been planning to meet someone—'

'Yes, I don't need it spelled out.' Bailey's interruption was tetchy.

'Sorry. Of course not.' Fleming looked down at her notes. 'The site was the next thing. I couldn't find any report on that. Was there an investigation of tyre-marks, say?'

'Marjory, we were talking about days later! There'd been heavy rain, a dozen cars coming and going at the site. There wouldn't have been the slightest point.' He was becoming very defensive.

That was his problem, and he'd just have to deal with it. She went on, 'I went there myself to have a look. There was a gap on the cliff edge that looked a plausible place for the body to have fallen from, but after all this time the configuration may have changed.'

'Ah! There I can help you.' He looked pleased with himself. 'The lighthouse keepers agreed that for the body to finish up where it did, it must have gone over on the west side, and there were muddy marks around the place. Nothing useful, of course, given the torrential rain that night.'

But you didn't log that anywhere, Fleming could have said, but there was no point at the moment. 'You saw no signs of a struggle?' she asked.

Bailey frowned. 'Not – not that I remember. I probably checked it, automatically, at the time, but it's hard to be absolutely sure, looking back without records.' He didn't sound convincing. 'But of course, then we just thought she'd thrown herself off – and the keepers and the helicopter crew had been moving around the area, churning it up. There wouldn't have been any point,' he said again.

Had all policing at that time been so incompetent? Fleming had a sinking feeling that perhaps it was a particular rather than a general problem. All she could do was move on.

'There's no record of searching the farm for rope that might have been used to bind her wrists. Was that done?'

'Ah, now that I do recall. There was any amount of it lying around, anything from cables to clothes-line. But you must remember, Marjory, that in those days pathology didn't have the resources to give chapter and verse from a fibre or a fragment of tissue.'

'I was going to ask you about the pathologist. His report wasn't very helpful. Do you remember what he was like?'

Bailey snorted. 'If you thought the report wasn't helpful, you should have met the man himself. Ought to have been retired years before, but they were closing down the mortuary and transferring everything to either Dumfries or Glasgow. His practices were rooted in the Fifties not the Eighties, but there wasn't much we could do about it. Died not long afterwards, actually.'

'So you don't think he would have retained specimens, say, of the foetal tissue?' She'd been pinning her hopes on that.

'Unlikely, I'm afraid, given how useless the man was. Still, you could try the present labs. They may have archive material.' Bailey was looking more cheerful now they were discussing other people's shortcomings rather than his own.

He wouldn't be happy about her next question. 'Moving on to the Lazansky accusations – you didn't at any stage speak to Marcus himself.' She hadn't meant it to, but it came out like an accusation and she saw him turn red.

'My dear girl, the man was in America! His parents had spoken to him on the telephone the day before all this took place.'

She didn't like being called his dear girl, and she didn't like having wasted her time leaning on Marcus Lindsay to test for weaknesses in his alibi. 'That isn't in your report,' Fleming said icily.

She had never spoken to him in that tone of voice, and she saw shock register on his face, along with consciousness of the tone he had used himself. 'I'm – I'm sorry if I sounded offensive. It was unintentional.'

Fleming didn't say anything, and he went on, 'I don't remember precisely what I noted down. The thing was that young Lazansky was so firmly ruled out that it didn't seem important. Sorry.'

There was no point in humiliating him further. Their future working relationship was going to be awkward enough, and whatever she might feel at the moment, damage limitation was called for.

'That's the end of my list at present, Donald. Thanks – that's been helpful. Just one more thing I'd like to ask – personal, not professional.

'Do you know why my father agreed to let Ailsa Grant's body be taken home? It was so unlike him, not to do everything by the book.'

'I wish I could tell you, Marjory. I asked him, naturally; he was a good officer, in his old-fashioned way, and if he could have produced some proper reason . . . but all he would say was that he'd made the decision, and why did it matter, anyway, and he stuck to that.'

'That was my father!' Fleming smiled wryly. 'Don't suppose I'll ever know. Anyway . . .'

Bailey got up. 'Finished? That's good. I've a couple of meetings this afternoon. Thanks, Marjory.'

He was out of the room before she could even say goodbye. Not a happy bunny.

She should never have agreed to doing this. Their professional relationship had worked well because he was fundamentally lazy. He was, though, a competent administrator and in general a decent and fair-minded boss. Fleming considered him a better superintendent than he had been DI though she had never expressed her opinion, even to Tam – who probably knew anyway, and agreed. But she didn't want that opinion forced upon Donald.

Had he really thought she'd perform a cosmetic exercise? If so, how little he knew her! Perhaps that was her fault. His patronizing 'my dear girl' had made her hackles rise, and he had seen a side of her he'd never seen before. But then, she'd played the deference game – even, with quiet amusement, pandering to his subconscious conviction that he was entitled to it by gender rather than rank.

That wasn't altogether a comfortable thought. Women were often accused of being manipulative, and Fleming didn't like to think she was. On the other hand, wasn't 'manipulative' one of these gender-specific adjectives – 'she is manipulative, he is brilliantly diplomatic'?

Janet Laird had once told a teenage Marjory, deep in introspection, 'It won't do any good, pet. It's like peeling an onion – you take off the layers and when you reach the middle there's nothing there. And all it does is make you cry.'

It was sound advice. The Bailey problem certainly wasn't going to be solved by thinking about it, and it wasn't going to be solved any time soon. With a sigh she got up and collected the coffee mugs. Neither of them had been touched; they were cold now and there was a scummy film on the surface.

When Diane Hodge came into the conservatory, her husband was by the window watching progress on the building. He turned with a triumphant smile.

'See that? Always pays to turn nasty. If I hadn't beaten up on Stefan, they'd still be poncing around, marking time at my expense. But that's them started on the roof now – he seems to have conjured up a roofer from somewhere.'

Diane went over to look. 'That's Kasper,' she said, pointing to the man in a precarious position on top of the wall. 'I noticed he wasn't there yesterday or this morning. I hope he knows what he's doing – it doesn't seem very safe.'

'Ah, that's the advantage of a gang like this,' Gavin said complacently. 'You don't have any of the scaffolding nonsense the local brickies insist on – doubles the cost! A few ladders were good enough in the old days, and that's what you get from these boys – sound, old-fashioned workmanship.'

Then he noticed that his wife wasn't in her usual casual clothes. 'You're all tarted up. Where are you off to?'

He seemed to have forgotten his festering grievance. Diane, who had planned to announce coldly that she'd had enough of his tantrums and was going away for a couple of days, changed her mind and said, 'I just decided to pop up to Glasgow for the night. I'll be staying with Hayley – we've promised ourselves some retail therapy.'

'Good idea. You could stock up at M&S food too, and I'll give you a list for the wine merchant.'

He sounded quite enthusiastic about her proposed absence. Was that a calculated insult? She considered a sharp response, then decided there was no point in resurrecting the quarrel. She was looking forward to a break from him, so it wouldn't be unreasonable if he felt the same.

'I'll be leaving in half an hour, if you can have the list ready by then.'

'Fine, fine,' he said heartily. 'I'll just go now and see what we're low on.'

He hurried out, leaving her to reflect uneasily that he did seem very pleased to be rid of her. They'd had their share of ups and downs over the years, with family problems not to mention the rest, but they'd been on a more even keel since coming back to Sandhead. She hadn't thought there was anyone else in the frame at the moment. Perhaps she was wrong.

For once, Fleming was keen to phone Sheila Milne. This time, she would set the agenda.

She announced herself formally. 'DI Fleming, Ms Milne.' So ridiculous, for the Fiscal, when you worked together so closely! It had always been Christian names with her predecessor, but Milne had at once made it clear that any such intimacy would be unwelcome. Humble coppers should know in their place.

'Inspector. Good. Where are we with the Grant case?'

'Progress is steady but necessarily slow,' Fleming said smoothly. 'I was actually phoning because you had expressed concern about the complaint Marcus Lindsay made to you. I just wanted you to know I had gone and offered an apology.'

Fleming heard a tiny gasp, swiftly covered up by a cough. When Milne spoke, she sounded guarded. 'I trust it was accepted?'

'He was very relaxed about it. In fact, he claimed the complaint had been a misunderstanding in the course of a joking conversation with you. I hadn't realized you were old friends.'

'Was that what he said?' She sounded angry. 'That is a complete distortion! It is only the slightest of acquaintances – I ran into him on a couple of social occasions.

'It puts me in a position where very properly relaying what he had said could be thought to be doing a personal favour and I am most unhappy at being misrepresented in this way, most. I wish to deny it categorically.'

Admittedly, Fleming had made this call with the express intention of tweaking the acting Fiscal's tail, but she was totally unprepared for what sounded almost like panic. It prompted her to go on. 'I did wonder why he should mind so much about entirely routine questioning. Still, if it was an ill-judged joke—'

Milne seized on that. 'Yes, yes, of course. I'm sure he has nothing to hide. Have you – have you eliminated him from your enquiries?'

The truthful answer, after what Bailey had said, was yes, probably. Instead, Fleming said pompously, using a meaningless phrase she particularly disliked, 'We're not ruling anything in or anything out, at this stage.'

Milne's voice was definitely shaky. 'I – I see. Well, keep me informed, won't you?'

She rang off abruptly, leaving Fleming to stare at the phone in some astonishment.

Sheila Milne looked down at the pile of files on her desk, waiting to be marked 'pro' or 'no pro', indicating her decision on whether or not each case should proceed to prosecution. She wasn't seeing them.

Her stomach was churning and she felt dizzy with the shock. What was at stake was her job – or more than that. She looked down again at the papers on her desk; if a file detailing her activities landed on another fiscal's desk, would they be marked 'no pro'? She didn't think so.

It had seemed so trivial at the time, just a little favour for someone glamorous she was anxious to impress. No one would ever check on her decisions, unless suspicion arose. To make absolutely sure it didn't, she'd asked him to do that one simple little thing, and he hadn't done it – selfish bastard! Like all men.

She should have left well alone. Why should it have come out, even if he was questioned by the police on some totally unrelated matter? She'd brought this on herself, by her own neurotic stupidity. But then, that was only the latest in a series of idiotic mistakes. How could she have been such a fool as to contact him in the first place, and then to attract Fleming's attention?

Doing the favour hadn't got her anywhere with him in any case, and even if it had resulted in a brief romance with a glamorous actor, it would hardly be compensation for losing your job and ending up in jail. What could she do now, to stop this becoming a total disaster?

'I can't face the pub this evening, Jaki, but I'll take you down and fetch you back if you fancy it,' Marcus Lindsay said as they sat over coffee in the drawing room after Mrs Boyter's excellent supper.

Jaki shuddered. 'You're kidding! I'm staying put, and the doors had better be locked. Kevin could be hanging around out there, waiting for revenge. Freaks me out, just thinking about it.'

They were alone, Jaki huddled as close to the fire as she could get and wearing a chunky-knit sweater she'd bummed off one of the cast who was in a B&B with serious central heating. Sylvia, despite Mrs Boyter's anxious coaxing, had eaten little at supper, and retired exhausted to her room immediately after.

'How much longer do you reckon we'll need to be down here?' Jaki asked, trying to keep the desperation out of her tone and not quite succeeding.

'Mmm. A bit dire, isn't it?' Marcus replied to the tone before the question. 'I can see it running into next week, the way things are. And I haven't made it any better, marooning you with Sylvia and me here. Sorry, love.'

The smile he gave her, the smile which largely explained Superintendent Playfair's screen success, almost had her regretting they'd broken up. Almost. Not quite.

'It would have been worse if I was in Ardhill, after what happened last night,' she said truthfully. 'At least here we're out of it.'

She looked round the drawing room, which had been such a great setting for Sylvia's impoverished and reclusive character, at the decaying fabrics and the damp patch in one corner of the elaborately plastered ceiling and the threadbare oriental rugs. Then she said, 'Do you mind me asking what you're going to do with this place? It's like – well, cut off, you couldn't live here, and—'

'And I obviously can't afford to keep it up,' Marcus finished for her. 'I know. Of course, I should sell it, but somehow . . . well, my father really loved it.'

But he's dead, Marcus, she wanted to say, but her eyes followed his gesture to a photo on a side-table, and she wasn't sure that was quite true. She was beginning to have a weird feeling about Laddie Lazansky. He was like a ghostly presence in the house: Sylvia and Marcus always talking about him, so many photos around the place – three more in this room alone. She'd only seen one of Marcus's mother, a faded snap which suggested it was only there because it was so good of the huge black Labrador at her feet.

Marcus was saying now it had been his mother's house. 'They were pretty broke latterly and after Papa died she got frail herself and let things go. She seemed to lose all interest after he'd gone – funny, really, when you consider that in many ways they'd led very separate lives.

'I'm contemplating holiday flats, perhaps – go into partnership with a developer and save something from the wreck, but Sylvia sees it as sacrilege. She's determined that it should all be just as it was when she came down here with him. She was utterly destroyed too when he died. He was . . . quite a man.'

He had poured them both large malts to go with the coffee. Jaki had begun to appreciate them – that addictive flame as it hit your throat – but she wasn't accustomed to neat spirits. Perhaps it was the whisky talking when she asked, 'Didn't your mum mind about Sylvia?'

'If she knew, and I suspect she did, she never gave any indication. We weren't close. She didn't invite intimacy and to be honest, Sylvia was more of a mother to me than Ma ever was – very protective, fussed over me, all for my own good, of course. And I could understand just what my father felt. He was a very passionate man, very warm, very charismatic. It's years since he died, but I – I miss him still.'

Marcus looked down at the whisky in his glass and swirled it gently. 'You could forgive him anything, and I expect my mother did. Sylvia, in a curious way, almost had more to forgive. She undoubtedly had his heart, but divorce was out of the question. Once I'd met Sylvia, I was sure that would happen, even asked him once, wondering if he'd been putting it off until I'd grown up.

'He laughed – I think he thought that was genuinely funny. "Dear boy," he said, "we have a home, a most beautiful home. Why would I spoil that for us? Your mother is my wife, darling Sylvia is my mistress." It was as simple as that.'

Jaki just didn't know what to say. Affairs, one-night stands, even – OK. A wife and an official mistress – that stank of a sort of decadence she had never experienced.

Marcus saw her face and laughed. 'Oh, he was a selfish sod! I'm not trying to defend him.'

He said that, but he sounded loving, almost amused. For Marcus, his father could do no wrong. Jaki said, aware of sounding disapproving, 'Can't have been terrific for either of them.'

'You're right, of course. Sylvia probably suffered more. She had to accept that he wouldn't sacrifice all for love, but I would guess my mother could choose to be in denial, as long as he didn't actually leave her.'

'Maybe Sylvia was into that too,' Jaki suggested. 'The way she talks, it always sounds like compared to them Antony and Cleopatra just fancied each other a bit.'

Marcus laughed. 'That's Hollywood! But I can only say she gave me, as a gawky, uncertain teenager, more warmth than I ever had from Ma, and I owe her for that. Though whether swinging this part for her was my smartest move—' He grimaced.

'She's got real problems,' Jaki agreed. 'But she's having a ball being here with you and part of the scene, a big star again. Trotting out all the old stories.'

'You're probably right. Oh, I know she can be a bit of a bore, but it's all she has left.'

Feeling ashamed of herself, Jaki said hastily, 'No, it's been cool, honestly, hearing her talking about all the legends she knew – the ones you never quite believed were real people.

'Changing the subject, Marcus, unless we're filming at the weekend, I'll head back to Glasgow for that, OK? If – if you don't mind.'

'Of course you must do what you like.'

She refused to notice he was looking slightly bleak at the thought of having only Sylvia for company. 'Right – what shall we do with the rest of the evening?' she said brightly. 'Poker for penny points, maybe? And you can freshen my drink. I'm seriously getting into that stuff.'

Jaki cuddled down in bed, electric blanket full on, and picked up the Katie Fforde she was reading, a cheerful antidote to the general gloom. She hadn't had so many consecutive early nights since she was six years old; it was only just after ten o'clock. Poker had passed a couple of hours quite pleasantly, but it had its limitations. What were they going to do all the other nights until the local scenes for this wretched episode could be declared a wrap? Maybe Marcus would invite some of the guys up for supper tomorrow night, and then it would be the weekend, thank God. She might even pop home to her folks in Wishaw; after all this, she quite fancied a bit of noisy, chaotic, normal home life.

It was quarter past ten when she heard the doorbell ring. It was an actual bell, swinging on a spring in the hall, and she always thought it sounded as if it belonged in a horror movie.

That would be Barrie, no doubt, or Tony, or both, to discuss the revised schedule. She almost thought of getting up and dressing again, to go down for a chat. But she'd just got properly warm for the first time today, and Katie Fforde was very beguiling . . . Jaki snuggled down and went back to her book.

From outside the window, she heard a voice calling something. Listening, she frowned. She couldn't make it out, then a moment later there was a sort of strangled cry, a groan – something, she couldn't quite be sure what. She sat bolt upright and threw back the covers just as she heard the spine-chilling sound of a woman screaming and screaming.

11

Just the four of them, talking round the table at kitchen supper, with Meg contentedly asleep by the Aga – when she was old, Marjory Fleming thought, these family meals would be treasured memories. The kids were growing up so fast: in a couple of years Cat would go off to uni, then it would be Cammie . . . She'd stopped taking these occasions for granted, lately.

Tonight, with Cammie setting off tomorrow for a two-week school rugby tour in France, they were having a farewell supper of roast beef – his choice. Marjory's roasts tended to be hit-and-miss affairs, but tonight it was definitely a hit, with the beef just pink inside and even the roast potatoes, for once, crispy without being charred.

'Better make the most of this, lad,' Bill advised as he carved the sirloin. 'Frog's legs and snails tomorrow night, I shouldn't wonder.'

His children ignored this facetiousness. Cammie took his plateful and began piling on potatoes; Cat, who had spent three weeks with a French family the previous year, said, 'Oh, he'll like the food all right. The big problem is that I'm not sure he knows the French for "That's not enough. I'm still hungry." '

Cammie looked up, alarmed. 'They'll speak English, won't they? Some, at least.'

'Don't you believe it,' Cat said darkly. 'Even if they do, they won't.'

At the last parents' evening, Cammie's French teacher had pointed out that oral competence could only be achieved by actually saying something. Marjory looked at her boy, wondering how he would cope. He was looking forward to the trip, but he was clearly nervous too; he'd never before been away for so long, and he'd be moving around the different homes of his French counterparts – quite a challenge for her quiet, home-loving son. He'd been such an undemanding teenager and she'd never had the run-ins with him that she'd had with Cat; Cammie was still close, still affectionate, and she'd miss him. She could only hope he'd be too busy and happy to think of missing her – as long as they won their matches!

'The important thing,' Bill was saying now, 'is to understand what the ref is telling you, or you'll get yourself sent off.'

'The coach has taken care of that.' With a certain triumph, Cammie turned to his sister. 'Bet you don't know the French for offside, anyway. Or handling the ball in the scrum—'

The ringing of Marjory's work phone cut into what he was saying. He stopped, she said, 'Damn!' and went to pick it up, conscious of accusing looks on all three faces. They knew it wasn't her fault when a family evening was spoiled, but they still blamed her.

'Fleming. Yes?' She knew she sounded terse. But listening, she began to smile. 'That's great news, Ewan! Mairi's all right? And have you decided on a name?'

She listened for some time, said once, 'Yes, of course. That's fine,' and eventually rang off.

'That's Ewan Campbell's baby arrived. A little girl, to be called Eilidh Shona, after her two grannies. And Ewan said more in the last five minutes than he's said in all the time he's been with us. Just as well he's taking paternity leave – his mind certainly wouldn't be on the job.'

Marjory sat down and everyone relaxed. It was only after she had gone to bed, and was in that first, profound sleep, that the phone rang again.

Jaki flew to the bedroom window and peered out. Lights from the house flooded the terrace outside, and she went cold as she saw Marcus below lying motionless and crumpled on his side, his head against the step up to the French windows of the drawing room. He had been wearing a pale grey cashmere sweater and even from here she could see a great dark patch on his back. Blood! She gave a stifled scream.

She could hear Sylvia's tremulous voice from the room below, calling, 'Jaki! Jaki! Help! It's Marcus! Jaki, are you there?'

'On my way,' she shouted back. But even as she turned, her eyes went with sudden recollection to where the shape had been that she had convinced herself was a bush. The space was empty.

Jaki gulped, then pulled the chunky sweater she had been wearing over her pyjamas, shoved her feet into shoes and grabbed her mobile. She ran across the landing and down the stairs, hands shaking so much that it took her three goes to dial 999. She was gasping out the details as she crossed the hall.

The front door stood open. For a fraction of a second she hesitated – was Kevin lurking just outside, waiting for her to appear? A terrifying thought, but she didn't lack courage. Marcus could still be alive and she might be able to do something for him – but he had been so utterly still . . . inert – not dead! Oh please, not dead!

Outside, it was a clear, cold, moonless night, with a touch of ground frost. To the left, light from the drawing-room windows spilled out over the scruffy gravel in front of the house. No one was visible, but the trees and bushes of the shrubbery made great pools of shadow and it was not only the cold that made Jaki shiver. The police and ambulance were on their way – but who knew better than she did how long it took to reach this place? She mustn't cry. It would only weaken her. Plunging into the darkness, she rounded the corner of the house.

It was treacherous underfoot, with an icy slick on the green slime on the paving stones. She slid and had to steady herself against the wall, and looking down she saw marks which showed Marcus, too, had slipped – clearly, that was how he had hit his head.

He lay in the oblong of light from the drawing room. The lights from Jaki's room upstairs revealed an expanse of overgrown lawn beyond the terrace, and from Sylvia's bedroom immediately below an agitated shadow was cast on to the paving stones further along. Jaki saw Sylvia was vainly trying to lift the heavy sash. She was mouthing something but Jaki didn't wait to see what it was.

She knelt down by Marcus's side. His eyes were horribly half-open, showing the whites, and in the dim light his face looked almost grey. The bloody patch on his sweater was spreading, spreading . . .

Dead bodies don't bleed. She had been working long enough on a crime series to know that. So he was alive – but for how much longer? And what could she do? She wished she'd had her fictional counterpart's training as she groped for the scraps of information she retained from first-aid lectures at school.

You put pressure on a wound to stop it bleeding, didn't you? But what if that was the wrong thing to do – what if it made things worse? What if – oh why, for God's sake, did anyone live more than ten minutes from an A&E department?

She could hear his breathing now, shallow, but steady enough. With both hands, she found the site – a neat slit, just below his shoulder blade at the left-hand side – and pressed heavily. After a few interminable minutes, it seemed as if the blood flow was at least slowing. She raised her head.

Sylvia, her expression anguished, had her face pressed to the window pane. 'He's alive!' Jaki yelled, wondering if she would be able to hear through the glass, and saw her put a hand to her throat in relief. 'Blankets! Can you hear me? Blankets!' Sylvia nodded, and turned away.

Jaki was beginning to realize that the cold could be as deadly as any wound. The knife must have missed his heart, or he would surely be in a worse state, but she didn't know what internal bleeding there might be, and with the head injury too she dared not move him. Her own teeth were beginning to chatter and her hands were growing numb, making it hard to keep up the pressure.

It seemed an age before Sylvia in her wheelchair appeared at the French windows, opened them with difficulty and threw two blankets and a quilt down the step to where Jaki could reach them.

'How is he? How is he?' Sylvia seemed almost hysterical. 'I can't help, I can't do anything! Have you called the police – an ambulance?'

Jaki didn't need this. As she cautiously removed her hand to spread the quilt under Marcus as best she could, then pulled the blankets over both of them and restored the pressure, she was thinking desperately of something else useful the woman could do, before she lost it entirely.

'They're coming, Sylvia. But we need hot-water bottles. Boil up the kettle and see if you can find any. Do you think you could manage that?'

'Yes! Yes, of course I can!' Given a task, Sylvia visibly took a grip on her emotions, and the wheelchair hummed into action as she disappeared back into the room.

It was very, very silent after she left. The stars in the night sky were so numerous and so close, they almost seemed to be bearing down on Jaki as she lay pressed to Marcus's back to share her body heat, looking about her fearfully. The thought that Kevin Docherty, out of sight but close by, perhaps admiring his handiwork and its success as bait to lure her out, took possession of her mind, and every rustle of leaves in the light wind, every snap of a twig as some night creature went about its business, made her gasp and stiffen with terror.

The bleeding, she thought as she removed her hand and flexed it to get the feeling back, seemed to have stopped, which for a moment made her panic – was she trying fruitlessly to warm a corpse? When she put her hand to his throat, she could feel a pulse – but he was cold, so cold!

Hot-water bottles would help, but Jaki didn't have much confidence in Sylvia. She'd been away a long time now – was she just going to come back in an even worse state, saying she couldn't find them? The frustration, that Jaki couldn't go and search on her own swift feet, was mounting by the time the wheelchair came into view again.

She had done the older woman an injustice. 'That's two.' Sylvia, now much more composed, threw the bottles down to her. 'I found four – the kettle's just boiling for the other two.' She turned and went off again.

Jaki was tucking in the bottles beside Marcus's still body when she heard the blessed sound of sirens, and burst into tears.

Karolina Cisek had been on edge all evening. She'd told Rafael what had happened, of course. He'd been much less bothered than she was about the fight, but then men were like that. And, she suspected, he hadn't been as shocked as she had been last night to find that Kasper carried a knife. He'd mumbled something about needing protection, and made her put it back without saying anything.

She didn't trust Kasper. He had a temper and he'd been furious with the man he called Stefan. Money was everything to Kasper, and he was a – what was that English word she'd learned the other day? *Chancer*, that was it. You couldn't trust him. He always had his own agenda.

She couldn't settle to anything. Rafael, watching TV, said at last impatiently, 'What's the matter? He's not coming now. You made it pretty clear he wasn't welcome, anyway.'

'As if he'd care!' she said scornfully – but at least Rafael seemed finally convinced she wasn't still secretly looking back over her shoulder at Kasper. She'd been a foolish girl at that time, very young and dazzled by the money he could flash about, until she realized a smooth tongue wasn't the same as honesty and a good heart. Rafael had his faults – and who didn't? – but he would never let her down.

It worried her that Kasper had followed them here. Why should he do that? He had not been a friend of Rafael's, and he couldn't possibly think that now she had a husband and child she would so much as look at him. But then, being Kasper, with his arrogance, he just might. And he might have reckoned they could be useful, too.

Karolina sighed, unconsciously, then looked at her watch. Half past ten – surely he would have appeared by now if he was going to? And that was late, when you had a six o'clock start.

'Never mind the football,' she said, getting up. 'I can tell you – the Manchester United will win. It always does. Time we were in bed.'

★   ★   ★

Sylvia was waiting in the drawing room doing breathing exercises to try to control the whirling thoughts that were making her feel dizzy, as the paramedics did their work on Marcus, making professionally soothing noises. A woman constable had taken efficient control, sending her male colleague to make tea and bringing Jaki, wrapped in a blanket, shivering and tear-stained, back into the drawing room.

'Don't worry, dear,' she was saying. 'You did great. Are you all right?'

Jaki, shaking uncontrollably with reaction, looked down at her bloodied hands. 'If I could just wash—'

Sylvia went to her side. 'Darling, you were so brave!' she said, her mouth trembling. 'If – if Marcus pulls through, he'll owe his life to you.'

Jaki nodded, biting her lip, then trailed off wearily.

Sylvia sat back in her chair, fighting fatigue herself. Her face was grey with shock and there were purple shadows round her eyes, but she was determined to show nothing more than dignified distress, if it took the last of whatever remained of her acting skills. She despised public displays of raw emotion.

When the doorbell had gone – it seemed as if hours had passed since then! – she had been sitting in her chair, looking out at the night and thinking her melancholy thoughts, as had become her habit before she began the long and complicated process of putting herself to bed. She'd seen the attack, but if she told the police that now there would be questioning, official statements, hours and hours of it, when she wanted – *needed* – to be with Laddie's son, whom she so wished had been hers too. They'd stop her going with Marcus – and anyway, she was still too confused to sort out exactly what she'd seen.

With her most gracious manner, Sylvia turned to the constable. 'My dear, I shall want to go to hospital with Marcus, obviously. Can you arrange for them to take me in the ambulance, or must I drive myself?'

Doubt showed on the woman's face. 'Are you his mother?'

'Stepmother,' Sylvia said unblushingly.

'Oh, I see. But really, you could help him more by telling us anything you can about what happened. They'll take care of him, you know, and there's nothing else you could do for him.'

'Of course. But quite honestly, I couldn't tell you anything coherent. I'm feeling very muddled, and until I know about – Marcus, I can't even bring myself to think about anything else.' Her control had slipped for a moment here, but perhaps it was all to the good: even she could not have produced quite such an affecting sob deliberately.

It worked. 'Don't get upset, now,' the woman said hastily. 'I'll have a word with the crew – it's not regular, but I don't think you should be driving—'

She gave her a worried look and Sylvia seized on this. 'I would have to, for Marcus. To be there if – *when* he wakes up.'

'That's right, dear. He'll be fine, I'm sure.' The woman went out into the garden, where a stretcher on wheels was waiting for Marcus to be lifted on.

Sylvia closed her eyes with a sigh of relief. She'd promised Laddie she wouldn't leave his boy, as she struggled and swore in her clumsy search for the hot-water bottles that just might save him from dying of cold. And would she ever have thought of looking in the cupboard under the kitchen sink, if Laddie hadn't put the idea in her head?

She wished he could have helped her think clearly now, but close as she felt he had been to her, Laddie had remained silent on that point.

★   ★   ★

DI Fleming passed the ambulance on the road between Sandhead and the A75. She'd been told there had been a possibly fatal assault, but no more than that, so she noticed with interest that its lights were flashing but it wasn't in a tremendous hurry. That could be a good or a bad sign for the victim inside, but at least it meant there wasn't a corpse waiting for her at the other end.

When she reached Tulach House there were three badged cars outside, and a sergeant standing by the front door saluted. There was blue tape stretched across from the front of the house and she congratulated him on his efficiency.

He gave her a quick description of what seemed to have happened, then went on, 'There's only one lady here now. The other lady, Miss –' he squinted at his notebook – 'Lascelles – she's disabled, so they took her with them in the ambulance rather than let her drive to the hospital. She's the victim's stepmother.'

Fleming's brows rose. 'Stepmother? Is she, indeed?' That wasn't her information, but perhaps Sylvia Lascelles had elevated her status to that of common-law wife – an old Scottish tradition. 'So who is it that's here?'

'Miss Johnston – Jaki Johnston, her that's in the series, you know?'

'Right.' Fleming went in, following the voices to the room on her right. The French windows were open and there was police activity outside. The room was icy cold, and a young constable was standing by the fireplace looking hopelessly at the dying embers in the grate.

'Looking at it won't help. Find a box of firelighters and shove in three or four – that should get it going again,' Fleming instructed him with the voice of experience. 'And for goodness' sake shut that door. It's freezing in here.'

He shut the windows and went out, looking helpless. The prospect of a fire in the immediate future did not look promising.

Fleming turned to the forlorn-looking girl sitting on the sofa beside a woman officer, her hands wrapped round a mug of something hot. She was wearing pyjama trousers and a sweater and was swamped by an ill-fitting man's overcoat.

'Miss Johnston – Jaki? I'm DI Fleming. I came here the other day—'

'Yes. I remember.'

Jaki was alarmingly pale and still shivering spasmodically. Fleming could barely recognize her as the bright, pretty girl she had seen before. Was there any point in trying to question her at the moment? She was clearly in shock and a doctor would undoubtedly say she ought to be in bed, under sedation.

'Jaki, I don't want to push you if you don't feel up to it, but the sooner I know what you can tell us the sooner we can get things moving. Can you help us?'

The girl's response was unexpectedly fierce. 'Of course. The sooner you go and pick the bastard up, the better.'

Startled, Fleming said, 'You mean – you saw who did it?'

'No, I didn't actually see him. Sylvia might have. She's gone to the hospital with Marcus.'

'But—'

'I didn't need to see what happened. The doorbell rang – I thought it was the director, maybe, coming to talk about scheduling. Then a few minutes later there was a noise, a sort of cry outside my bedroom window, and then Sylvia started screaming.

'But I know who it was. Kevin someone. He was in the pub last night, and he came on to me and then picked a fight with Marcus.' There were two hectic spots of colour in Jaki's cheeks now. 'Nothing happened because there were all these guys from the film crew there and they moved in on him, but then he got banned from the pub and he was just spitting hatred. They told us afterwards he was out on probation or something for knifing someone else. So it's not rocket science, is it?'

'Kevin someone?' Fleming asked, and the constable said, 'That would be Docherty, ma'am. Comes from Ardhill, out on licence after early release.'

'Oh yes, Docherty. Do you know where he lives?'

'There's a lad outside – he's local, so he'll know.'

'Find out, and get someone there. Quietly – we don't want to tell him we're coming. Pick him up and bring him in.'

As the woman went out through the French windows, she turned back to Jaki. The animation the girl had shown had disappeared and Fleming thought she was even swaying slightly. 'Look, you should be in bed. Is there—?'

She had been about to ask if there was someone who would come to be with her, but Jaki cried, 'No, no! I couldn't stay here! I hate this place! Can I phone Tony? – he'll find somewhere in the village for me—' She began to cry, wrenching, frantic sobs.

'Yes, of course!' Fleming said hastily. 'We'll get that fixed, don't worry. Oh good, constable!' she said, as the woman came back in again. 'Jaki will give you the number of someone who'll come and take her away – she doesn't want to stay here. All right, Jaki?'

The girl was still crying, but suddenly she stopped on a gasp. It was hard to make out what she was saying, but what emerged was, 'There's – there's just – just something, something I've remembered. The thing is – it sort of doesn't fit.'

'Yes?' Fleming felt the prickle of nerves that told her this was significant, more significant, even, than what Jaki had said before.

With a visible effort, Jaki swallowed her sobs. 'The second night I was here, Sunday night, I looked out of the bedroom window. There's a shrubbery between the front of the house and the back, and I saw what looked like someone standing there, just watching the house. But I couldn't be sure, and it just, like, seemed so crazy I didn't tell anyone. It didn't move, and I thought it was probably a shrub with a funny shape. Anyway, I couldn't see why anyone would be doing that.

'And next night when I looked out it was still there, in exactly the same place, so I was thankful I hadn't made a fool of myself. But tonight—' She gulped, and stopped.

Fleming knew what she was about to say. 'It wasn't there.'

'No, it wasn't. I told you it would be Kevin, after what happened last night. But before then, he wouldn't have had any reason to be watching the house. And I've only just thought, if I'd told Marcus about it at the time, perhaps this would never have happened. If he dies, and it was because of that, I'll never forgive myself, never!'

12

There was no reason to countermand the order to pull in Kevin Docherty. From the sound of his activities, he was breaching the terms of his licence anyway, but having thought at first that this was an open-and-shut case, Fleming now had to consider there might be more to it than that.

Jaki Johnston had held herself together long enough to point out where she had seen the figure in the shrubbery and give more details and times – ten to ten-thirty on both occasions – but when Tony Laidlaw appeared, his face dark with concern, she stumbled into his arms and her legs gave way. He was a fit man and she was small and slight; he picked her up, said only, 'She needs to get out of here,' and vanished again. A man of action, obviously.

Ordering the cars in front of the house to direct headlights on to the shrubbery, Fleming went out into the garden. The ground was hard with the night frost, but even so she made a wide circuit to approach the site from the side furthest away from the house. Footprint technology was very advanced now, and even in these conditions they might get something from the area round about, though evidence from the terrace would be hopelessly compromised already by the activities of the paramedics and others.

She paused by the edge of the shrubbery, studying the space between a sprawling rhododendron and a holly bush.

For Jaki to have believed the figure was another bush, it must have been relatively bulky, and she had indicated that though lower than the others, it hadn't been particularly small in comparison. The rhododendron was a good eight or nine inches taller than Fleming's own five foot ten, and she reckoned whoever had stood there must be at least her height, or more.

And the ground might be hard tonight, but on Sunday and Monday, she remembered, there had been rain. The light from the cars' headlights was in part blocked by trees and shrubs, but even so Fleming thought she could make out indentations in the ground.

'Make sure this is completely cordoned off – right along from the house to the shrubbery,' she instructed the constable who had been failing to relight the fire, and whose main activity at the moment seemed to be watching what other people were doing. 'No! *Don't* walk on it first, for God's sake. Use your common sense – go right round, the way I did. Got it?'

Losing sleep never put her in the best of tempers, but then, as someone said, with stupidity the gods themselves struggle in vain. Perhaps she should have been less critical of procedures in Bailey's investigation.

As Fleming went back past the terrace, illuminated by the light from the windows, she noticed with interest the marks on the stone slabs. There, in the green lichen or whatever it was, were signs that someone had slipped: there was one skid mark at the corner coming from the front garden and one longer and deeper, finishing where Marcus Lindsay had been lying.

She tried to reconstruct it. He had answered the doorbell and then, for some reason, come round to the back of the house. Had no one been there when he opened the door and he had come round to investigate? Then slipped just as he came on to the terrace? Though perhaps his assailant had slipped, or even Jaki, afterwards. Something to check. Marcus had certainly lost his footing later, and fallen heavily against the step.

Had someone lured him outside and waited for him, hidden in the shadow of the house? Had Marcus slipped as a result of being stabbed, or had he slipped as he half-turned at some sound, causing the deadly blow to miss its target? A fortunate chance, perhaps, though reportedly the head injury had been giving the paramedics more concern than the stab wound.

Fleming gave instructions for the marks to be preserved until photographs could be taken in daylight. They hadn't found a weapon as yet, but there was little point in groping around in the dark. Satisfied that there was nothing more she could learn here at present, Fleming headed back to her car.

She looked at her watch, yawning. One o'clock – and they'd have to question Kevin within the six hours allowed before they had to release or charge him. She'd be lucky to see her bed before three.

The night shift CID team had been standing by, ready to be called down here if needed, but she'd prefer to have MacNee in on this from the start if it turned into a murder enquiry. He was always a late bird, but if he'd gone to bed and was in that heavy sleep that made you feel you were underwater, fighting drowning when roused – well, he'd know how she'd felt.

They wouldn't let Sylvia stay with Marcus as they assessed his injuries. She had to sit in the waiting room under the harsh lights, looking at rows of empty chairs and watching a small family, the mother with a white, worried face and a limp-looking small child on her knee, the harassed father shouting at an over-excited toddler running up and down the hallway. A police officer was having a low-voiced conversation with the desk receptionist.

Sylvia wheeled herself to the farthest corner and tried to sleep. She needed to rest: it wouldn't help if she fell apart on them. But behind her eyes, the images flashed: Marcus, slipping away even as they worked on him; a doctor in a white coat coming out saying, 'I'm sorry . . .'; Laddie's face, looking more anxious than she had ever seen him in life; Laddie, Laddie . . .

She must have dozed off. She came to with a start as someone touched her arm. She was stiff in every joint; stifling a gasp of pain, she said, 'Yes? Is he – is he—?'

The nurse standing beside her smiled. 'He's all right. A bit concussed, but he's come round now and as far as they can tell there's no real damage. They're stitching him up and we'll keep him under observation tonight, but he's had a lucky escape. He'll be a bit sore for a few days but it was only a deep flesh wound.'

Tears welled up in Sylvia's eyes and spilled over. Joy was always harder to master than sorrow, and she fumbled for a tissue.

'It's been a bad night, hasn't it?' the nurse said sympathetically. 'I can get someone to take you home, now you know he's all right—'

'No! I need to see him for myself.' Sylvia was fierce in her stubbornness. 'He'll want to see me too.'

'It could be a long time – you could come back tomorrow,' the nurse argued, then hesitated. 'You're Sylvia Lascelles, aren't you? I loved that film – what was it called?'

'*For Ever*,' Sylvia supplied wearily. It would be nice to be remembered, just occasionally, for something else.

'That's right! I cried buckets. And – and you're his mother?'

'Stepmother.'

'Well, we're quiet tonight. Maybe I could arrange a family room, so you could lie down at least.'

'That would be so, so kind!' From somewhere she produced the famous smile, and saw it bring, as always, a light to the nurse's face.

'I'll do my very best,' she promised.

They found Sylvia a room and some painkillers, promising she would be summoned whenever Marcus could see her. She lay down on the bed and drifted into sleep. Laddie was there again, smiling, this time.

MacNee reached headquarters before Fleming arrived and was talking to the desk sergeant when she appeared. He went to meet her looking offensively bright and chipper.

She gave him a jaundiced look. 'You weren't asleep, were you? I didn't think you were, from the way you spoke. I was, when they phoned me.' She yawned, hugely.

'Watching a late-night movie. It was terrible – glad to have an excuse to switch it off, really.

'Here – he's telling me they're bringing in Docherty! If it's murder, it'll keep him out of our hair for years, if we're lucky. Though mind you, with the pleas they accept he could probably claim he was peeling an apple and his knife slipped, then come straight out in recognition of time spent on remand.'

'You'll need a word with the Fiscal about that. I'd have liked to dig her out too, since she's so keen to take charge, but it'll be a junior depute on duty and there's no point disturbing them till we know what we're dealing with. The stabbing's not fatal anyway, according to the paramedics, and the head injury may be no more than concussion.'

'Then his brief really will talk it down to assault and Docherty'll just get a slap on the wrist,' MacNee said in disgust. 'Not that I'd actually want the guy to die, of course—'

'Sure?' Fleming murmured provocatively.

He ignored her. 'But with prison overcrowding, we'll have Kev back on the streets carving patterns on other people with a chib before you can say "punishment, retribution and rehabilitation".'

'What height is Docherty?' Fleming asked, with apparent irrelevance.

'Height? Five eight, five nine, maybe. About my height.' MacNee always considered himself justified in rounding up his five foot seven – well, five foot six and three-quarters, to be strictly accurate.

'Bulky with it?'

'If it was raining, he'd have to see and not get washed down the drain.' MacNee frowned. 'Here – what are you on about?'

Fleming outlined Jaki's reason for accusing Docherty, then explained the girl's second thoughts, and the shape in the shrubbery.

MacNee listened, dismayed. 'You mean we can't nail the slippery little sod? I had fingered him for the knife attack on the Polish lad – and we could have had him on race hate crime for that – but everyone denied it even happened.

'But here, listen – maybe whoever was in the shrubbery didn't do it. Maybe he was watching the house for some reason, and then scarpered when he saw what Docherty had done—'

'Someone else waiting to take a pop at Marcus Lindsay, perhaps?' Fleming said sarcastically. 'Maybe they agreed to form an orderly queue. You wouldn't think he'd be that unpopular – seems pretty inoffensive to me.'

'If it's not Docherty with a grudge, somebody doesn't like him,' MacNee was pointing out when they heard voices outside and the doors were flung open.

Fleming and MacNee spun round. Kevin Docherty appeared first, handcuffed between two uniforms and looking surly and befuddled. Behind him were two other youths similarly situated. All three were visibly drunk, and the police officers were grinning.

'Take them down and book them,' the sergeant said, then turned to Fleming. 'Ma'am. You're not going to believe what we found at Docherty's place.'

As Fleming said, 'Go on,' MacNee looked at him with a sour expression. The man wasn't about to say it was a knife with Marcus Lindsay's blood on the blade and Docherty's prints on the handle.

'Before we got the call to Ardhill, we'd been attending a break-in at an off-licence in Stranraer. When we hit on Docherty, he and his mates were well into their celebrations, with the cases of booze all round them. Just sat there gaping, and we'd the cuffs on before they knew what happened.'

'I see. Good result, but not quite what we'd hoped for initially.' Fleming thought for a moment. 'So, to be perfectly clear about this, do I take it that the timing of the break-in puts him in the clear for the assault?'

'The alarm went off at a quarter past ten,' the sergeant said. 'Sorry about that.'

'There were problems about it anyway,' she conceded. 'Just carry on then.'

As the sergeant departed, Fleming turned to MacNee. 'Whoever's on the night shift can deal with all this. You can suit yourself, but I'm going home to bed.'

'Darling!' Sylvia propelled herself into the side ward where Marcus, pale but smiling, was propped up in bed, wearing a strange-looking hospital robe. She wasn't as soignée as usual herself, without her normal *maquillage*, but she had done her hair and put on a brave slash of Dior Rouge lipstick.

'They said they'd wake me whenever you could see me, but they obviously didn't.' She was reproachful.

'I wouldn't let them. You've had more than enough to cope with already. Sorry to give you such a fright.' As she reached his bed, Marcus took her hand and kissed it.

Sylvia patted his cheek. 'How are you? They promised you were all right, but are you in much pain, my poor angel?'

'Doped to the eyeballs – can't feel a thing.' Marcus sounded determinedly upbeat. 'I've to be careful I don't open the wound up again, but fortunately I'm right-handed. Shouldn't even bugger up the schedule, if they leave my scenes till tomorrow. My wig would cover the lump.'

Sylvia looked incredulous. 'Marcus, someone almost killed you! I know the show must go on, but they won't let you do it.'

His air of cheerful confidence evaporated. 'I don't suppose they will, really,' he said tiredly. 'But I'm looking for distraction. It's a bit of a facer to know someone hates me enough to try to kill me.'

'Jaki said it was that young man in the pub. She was wonderful last night, Marcus – probably saved your life.'

'Did she? She's quite a girl! Didn't know anything about it. Sylvia, what happened?'

'Don't you know?'

'Not really. I remember the doorbell ringing – thought it was Barrie, or some of the guys looking for a free drink. After that—' He hunched his shoulders, incautiously. 'Aah! Mustn't do that.'

'I saw some of what happened from my window,' Sylvia said slowly. 'But I'm still very hazy. I'd like to go through it, darling, but not if you're too tired.'

'I'll be fine. I'm seeing the police later at home, and I hope Jaki's there so I can thank her. But let's try stream of consciousness stuff and see if you can jog my memory and I can sort yours out.'

DI Fleming had been in since before eight o'clock, after waving Cammie off on the coach full of over-excited lads. She'd set up an appointment to speak to Superintendent Bailey whenever he appeared and she'd posted a briefing meeting for nine-thirty. The morning report from the hospital was very reassuring, but a near fatal attack on a star of stage and screen would bring the press pack down on them, and she spent an hour preparing notes, yawning and drinking black coffee.

It was just before nine when Bailey summoned her. His manner was stiff at first, but it eased as they became absorbed in discussion of the problems.

'It's a grave pity it wasn't that young hooligan,' Bailey said. 'If we could have had it all done and dusted by the time the press got on to it, we'd have been saved a lot of hassle. The infuriating thing is that the break-in would have been a lead story in the local press and we'd have got terrific publicity for getting it wrapped up so promptly. Now we'll be lucky if it's a filler at the bottom of page eight.'

'Mmm.' Fleming wasn't certain they deserved credit for a stroke of blind luck, but then again, they got stick when the luck ran against them.

She glanced at her notes. 'Teams will talk to every known contact locally, and the *Playfair's Patch* people too, of course, and we'll put out an appeal for witnesses – though with the house being so isolated we can't expect much from that.

'I'll send Tansy Kerr to talk to Jaki Johnston, if the girl's well enough to talk – she was in a bad way last night. And Macdonald can oversee general questioning in Ardhill, and I'll go myself with Tam to Tulach to see what Marcus Lindsay and Sylvia Lascelles can tell us. He's being discharged sometime this morning.

'Oh, incidentally, we're another man short in CID today – Ewan Campbell's a proud father for the first time and he's taking paternity leave.'

'Pshaw!' Bailey snorted. 'Paternity leave! I don't know, Marjory. We left it to the women in my day – happy to, in fact – and I don't see my boys were any the worse for it.'

'I'm sure,' Fleming said pacifically, stifling a smile. She always felt she should try to record Bailey's 'Pshaw!' for posterity: 'pshaws' were high on the endangered list for words. 'Anyway, we'll manage.

'There's just one thing, with reference to Marcus's contacts. It's a bit delicate.'

At once Bailey looked guarded. 'And that is—?'

'I've notified the Fiscal's office, obviously, but I would normally report directly to Sheila Milne. The thing is, she was a friend of Marcus Lindsay's when she was in Glasgow. And what interests me is that she all but denied it to me at first.'

Bailey's ears almost visibly pricked up. 'Really?'

'Probably it's totally unrelated, but we need it tidied up – exactly what was the relationship, and why she is so defensive? Would you consider taking that on? She's so touchy about status, she'd probably take it very badly if a bog-standard DI tried to grill her.'

He beamed. 'Delighted, Marjory. Give me quite a lot of satisfaction, actually, putting her on the spot for a change. It's a while since I last did it, but I daresay it's like riding a bicycle – the skill doesn't desert you.'

The shadow of the cold case fell on the conversation and he went on hastily, 'Yes – well, delighted, as I say.' Then he said, 'Just a minute! Lindsay was involved in the Ailsa Grant murder, and you've been stirring things up, haven't you?'

He was, and she had been. It had occurred to Fleming, but she had hoped, at least, that the picture might have become clearer before Bailey made the connection. If this was in fact linked to his botched investigation, the press would hang him out to dry.

Cravenly, she looked at her watch and said, 'Goodness, is that the time? I'll have to get down for the briefing.' She got up. 'Of course we'll consider the Grant angle. But that was a long time ago and now other factors are involved.'

After she left, Bailey sat staring at the statistical report on his desk, without reading a single word of it.

The postwoman was late in reaching Balnakenny. Aggie MacCabe took her community duties seriously, and this morning her obligation to keep her far-flung customers abreast of events had played merry hell with her official schedule.

She bumped up the track and parked her van in the yard, then with due regard for the lumps of dried mud and worse went to the back door, a plump little woman with sharp black eyes and a mouth that seemed to have grown loose from talking. She'd only a couple of letters to deliver, bills from the looks of them – the Grants' post was always disappointing

– and the usual junk mail she was paid to dump on folk. Not that she'd get away with that here: Jean would sniff, then refuse to take it, and Aggie would need to find a bin on the way back.

Jean was, as usual, waiting in the doorway. She looked pointedly at her watch but said nothing.

'Morning, Jean!' Aggie said cheerfully, holding out the letters, then, at a look from Jean, taking back the fliers. 'Sorry I'm late. There's a lot of folk upset this morning.'

She was gratified to see the stand-offish Jean looking so interested. She even said, 'Upset?'

'About the *murder*!' Aggie delivered the news with relish. 'That Marcus Lindsay – him that's the TV star. Stabbed to death in his own house! They've arrested that Kevin Docherty. Just out of the jail, ken – a scandal, that's what it is!'

She scanned Jean's face greedily. Was that a flicker of surprise? But Jean only pursed her thin lips, said, 'Sort of man he is, he most likely asked for it,' then turned and shut the door on the disappointed Aggie.

But not before Aggie had seen her give a grim smile – which would make quite a good story for tomorrow's round.

The briefing had been straightforward, with no awkward issues raised and duties being routinely assigned: a couple of detectives to tie up the details of the break-in, the rest knocking doors in and around Ardhill, Tansy Kerr assigned to a preliminary interview with Jaki Johnston. The SOCOs were working at Tulach House and a footprints expert from Glasgow had been promised.

That was the straightforward bit. The big picture was rather different. Now, when she was supposed to be shifting paperwork at speed, Fleming sat tapping her front teeth with a fingernail.

So far, the only people she'd involved in the cold case were MacNee and a Force Civilian Assistant, detailed to track down witnesses and trace any forensic samples retained when the Kirkluce mortuary was closed down. There had been, as far as Fleming knew, no gossip in the corridors.

There was a clear, possible link with the attack on Marcus. It needed thorough investigation, but once that had been openly canvassed within the Force, how long would it be before the press found out? It was a great story.

Press interest – avid, most likely, in this case – could drive the investigation, and they would assume this was the only direction to look in. But when nasty games with knives started, there was an urgent need to put a stop to them before worse things happened. Her first duty was to protect the public, and if she had to waste time justifying an angle she was taking, it might mean a knife being used again to even more devastating effect.

But if the press somehow made the connection anyway, and ran a story that she was involved in some sort of cover-up, it would be serious trouble. It was a question of policy, which at any other time she would have talked through with Bailey – now obviously impossible.

She'd always discussed cases with MacNee; their brainstorming sessions were central to her method of working. Tam on policy, though? He was a tactics man, bored by strategy: he'd never wanted to rise above sergeant, because the broader issues didn't interest him.

His was, in a way, a more idealistic attitude. Or perhaps it was just an adult extension of childhood games of Cowboys and Indians – or more probably Protestants versus Catholics, given Tam's background. You went after the bad guys until you got them, and if it caused trouble on the way, tough, which wasn't really a message she could give her superiors. It should be, maybe, but it was also a reliable shortcut to your P45.

Even so, it might be useful to talk it through with Tam this afternoon before committing herself. Even if he brushed aside as irrelevant the worrying questions, arguing with him would clarify her own thinking.

But, she wondered suddenly, where was MacNee? He hadn't said much at the briefing and, now she came to think of it, hadn't volunteered information about his own plans.

He wasn't in the CID room and she called his mobile. From the background sounds, he was in the car.

'Tam! Where are you? You didn't say what you were doing today.'

'No. Everyone else was talking and anyway, I just thought I'd have a wee discreet nose around. Do you mind Marcus Lindsay mentioned he knew some Hodges who live in Sandhead? I thought I'd have a word, ask if they knew anyone with a grudge against him.'

'The Hodges? Mmm. And then you'll segue into questions about Ailsa Grant, maybe?' She could read him like a book: his money was obviously on a link between the cases. 'I wanted to discuss that with you, since I can't talk to the Super about it. I'm not sure we're ready to follow up that connection until the dust's settled a bit.'

'Trust me. It'll only come up in the way of conversation, kinda subtly, ken?'

'Your idea of subtlety, MacNee, is to kick someone in the backside instead of giving them a Glasgow kiss. You're on your own, aren't you? You'd be better heading over to Ardhill and teaming up with Andy Mac.'

'I'll see if I've time. Oh, I think I'm losing the signal.' The phone went dead.

'*The best-laid schemes* . . .' Trying to force MacNee into compliance with general policy left you feeling as helpless as the wee, sleekit, cowering, timorous beastie. And it was a bad day when Fleming started coming up with Burns quotations even when MacNee wasn't there.

13

Jaki Johnston looked as if she had the hangover from hell, DC Tansy Kerr thought sympathetically. Her creamy complexion had a greenish tinge and the shadows round her heavy eyes looked as if they were smeared on with kohl. She was at the table in the B & B's front room with a plate of cold scrambled egg in front of her, so it didn't look as if she'd taken full advantage of the second half of the deal. And the way she kept yawning, she didn't seem to have got much out of the first half either.

There was a three-bar electric fire burning and the small room was stiflingly hot. Kerr had removed her coat, then her sweater, and was now in a T-shirt, but even so was uncomfortable. The sun was shining in too, and she ventured to say, 'Isn't it a bit hot in here?' but Jaki, huddled in a thick jacket, looked at her with lacklustre eyes.

'First time I've been properly warm in days,' she said, and Kerr realized she'd just have to sweat it out, to coin a phrase. She only wished she'd asked the kindly owner to bring her iced water instead of coffee.

'Feeling pretty rough?' Kerr asked.

'You really don't want to know.' Jaki pushed her chair back from the table and held her hands out to the fire, as if she were still cold. They were shaking.

With her in this state, questioning could class as police brutality. 'Look, you don't have to talk to us now if you don't feel up to it. We can wait – you gave us enough to be going on with last night, and now we know Mr Lindsay's all right we can expect some of the answers from him.'

Jaki shook her head. 'I'd rather talk. I keep running it over and over inside my head anyway, and it's making me feel like I'm losing it completely.'

She took Kerr through last night's events, from the moment the doorbell rang to the arrival of the ambulance, in graphic detail. She mentioned she had slipped and almost fallen on the terrace in her haste to reach Marcus, which neatly answered one of Kerr's scheduled questions.

In fact, there was little of significance which Kerr hadn't already heard at the briefing that morning. She stopped Jaki only once, when she talked about Sylvia Lascelles screaming. 'Did Miss Lascelles see what happened?'

'She must have seen something, but it was chaos at the time, and then she went in the ambulance with Marcus.'

Big Marge had said she'd be talking to Sylvia and Lindsay later today, so that would be taken care of, and Jaki wasn't suddenly going to remember she'd seen whoever it was sticking the knife in Lindsay's back. The best Kerr could hope for now was background, something to suggest a new angle.

'You mentioned Kevin Docherty last night,' she said.

Jaki shuddered. 'Gives me the creeps, just thinking about him.'

'He's been charged with another offence he committed last night, nothing to do with this. Don't worry – he'll be off the streets for the next bit anyway.

'So someone else wanted Marcus Lindsay dead. Anyone got it in for him? In the cast, say – professional jealousy, maybe?'

Jaki shook her head. 'Everyone likes Marcus – he doesn't come over all grand like some stars do. He was brilliant to me when I was new to the cast and feeling awkward.'

'You're his girlfriend?'

'Well – was, to be honest. We've been putting on a front meantime – you can imagine the gossip, with everyone together like this – but we'd agreed it was over.'

The favour of the lead man could do quite a lot for an unknown actress's career. If he had changed his mind about her . . . Jaki seemed convincingly honest, but then she was an actress, and she had, after all, been found with Lindsay's blood all over her hands. The question had to be asked. 'Agreed?' Kerr said, as neutrally as she could.

'Oh yes.'

If the ready reply was acting, she was certainly good. And she was going on, 'It was only ever a bit of fun, really. I was crazy for him at the time, but I kind of knew he was too old for me – or else I was too young for him. We had good times, though – really clicked. And I made him laugh.

'It was being down here finished it.' Jaki pulled a rueful face. 'Though, if I'm honest, it was starting to cool off a bit before that. But here, when he was around Sylvia – I felt like I was twelve years old.' She hesitated. 'It was all kind of weird, him and Sylvia.'

'Weird?' Kerr asked gently.

It was all the prompting Jaki needed. Laddie Lazansky's wife, his mistress and the games of ignorance they had played, involving the young Marcus, all spilled out. 'Probably they'd call it sophisticated, but frankly it seems a bit sick to me.' Jaki wrinkled her nose in distaste. 'And what got to me was how Sylvia would go on like theirs was the romance of the century, but Marcus said his father would never leave his mother because he liked her house too much. And it's a spooky place – have you been there?'

'No, not yet.'

'Oh, it's probably beautiful and stuff. But everything creaked, even when no one was moving about, and the atmosphere – it's so freezing cold, I kept feeling as if something was standing behind me, breathing icy cold down my neck. And then they rabbited on and on about Marcus's father, and there were all these photos, till I began to feel it was probably him. He was like one of those old pin-ups, with sort of greasy, slicked-back hair. Creepy. But Sylvia thought he was George Clooney and Jude Law rolled into one. And she got a kick out of just being in his house, with his son if she couldn't have him. Weird, like I said.'

'Sounds it.' Fascinating as this sidelight was on Marcus Lindsay's home life, it wasn't getting them anywhere. 'But there's no one you can think of, no one Marcus has had a row with, say?'

Jaki thought for a moment. 'There was this guy came round for a drink one night with his wife. Gavin Hodge – they'd known each other way back, and I think Gavin really hated him. His stupid wife kept flirting with Marcus, and told this story about Gavin getting paralytic and Marcus being a hero pulling him out of the water when he fell in and could have drowned. Gavin totally flipped and I was like, "Whoa! This is going to turn nasty," because I could see Marcus getting stressed, but he changed the subject and it was OK, sort of.'

That was interesting. It sounded as if there might be a back story. 'Do you know why they didn't like each other?' Kerr asked, but Jaki could only say feelingly that Gavin Hodge was the type you took an instant dislike to because it saved time.

'That's helpful, though,' Kerr said encouragingly. 'Anyone else you can think of?'

Jaki shook her head. 'No. At least—'

'Go on.'

'It's nothing, probably. But there was this phone call – some woman wanting Marcus to lie to the police, and he was annoyed – said he wouldn't and he hated being manipulated.'

'And you don't know who, or why he was to lie to the police?'

Jaki shook her head again. 'That's all I remember. I can't think of anything else at all.' She sounded as if she'd had enough.

Kerr said hastily, 'That's brilliant – certainly enough for one morning,' and went, leaving the girl to huddle again over the fire, alone with her thoughts.

'You're very quiet today,' the chef in the catering truck said jovially to Karolina. 'Don't worry – they took the guy who did it away last night, you know.'

Karolina nodded. Her pink cheeks were still pale with shock, though. They'd said at first that Marcus Lindsay was dead, so what they said about the person who'd done it being arrested might not be true either. She could only hope that it was, because her first thought on hearing the news had been the look Kasper had directed at Marcus Lindsay after the chef warned him about his clumsiness, and the knife she had found in his pocket.

DS Macdonald, in charge of the teams working at Ardhill, had been having an unsatisfactory morning. They were going ahead with filming scenes involving minor characters for *Playfair's Patch*.

Tony Laidlaw had been blunt. 'You can make us pack it in, obviously. But if you let us go on filming, you'd be saving the taxpayer money for the dole. Marcus claims he'll be fit tomorrow, and if we get this done now, and Miss Lascelles can manage a scene this afternoon, we may just be able to keep it on the rails.'

With some reluctance, Macdonald had agreed. As a result, witnesses being questioned were distracted and interviews had to be conducted in snatches – not that they had anything to say, except about the ruckus in the bar a couple of nights ago. As far as Macdonald could tell, there were no budding stars nursing an obsessive grievance about Lindsay's success.

By the time DC Kerr arrived, Macdonald was thoroughly frustrated. 'I hope you've had more luck,' he greeted her. 'None of this lot have anything to offer, and all the door-to-doors are bringing in is stories about Kevin Docherty being a villain, which is hardly news. Nothing about anything suspicious last night.'

'I've got a lead,' she said smugly. 'Well, two, but I haven't much to go on with the second one.'

She told him about the Hodges, and Macdonald looked around the cluttered street. A couple of DCs were having coffee at the catering truck, and he said, 'I can leave them in charge and come with you, if you like.'

'Just because you're bored,' she taunted him. 'Say please nicely.'

'Please nicely. OK? Your car or mine?'

DS MacNee stood on the sweep of gravel in front of Miramar and looked about him. He'd heard it was her that had the money, and if so this certainly suggested that she'd more of that than she had sense.

Its latest ambition was something looking like a boil on its bum, a small extra room with builders still working on it. The roof timbers were being put in place and MacNee recognized the man on the roof as one half of the fight yesterday. The other half, the older man, was installing a window frame.

They both noticed him and he saw recognition on the face of the lad on the roof; the older man, though, looked at him with dead eyes and turned back to his work.

A man wearing ash-grey chinos and a pink polo shirt with a crocodile on it answered the door. MacNee eyed the logo with contempt: he couldn't understand why anyone over the age of six would want wee pictures on their clothes.

'Mr Hodge? DS MacNee. Could I have a word?'

'Police! Well, well – to what do I owe the honour?' Hodge said with heavy jocularity. 'Smash-and-grab raid on the souvenir shop in the village?'

It was overdone. The man was distinctly uneasy, MacNee noticed with sharpened interest. Marcus Lindsay had said he would warn the Hodges to expect a police visit about Ailsa Grant; had this unsettled him – or was there some darker reason?

'Not exactly, sir,' he said with elaborate patience. 'May I come in?'

'Come away, officer, come away!' He bowed, and with a sweeping gesture ushered MacNee into the house. A door stood open on to a large conservatory, and Hodge took him through there. They both sat down.

'What's the problem?' Hodge said.

'I wonder if you've heard the news, Mr Hodge?'

'News? No,' Hodge said flatly, then, 'I don't know what news you may be talking about.' It was a slightly odd thing to say.

'Marcus Lindsay was attacked last night.'

'Attacked? At Tulach House? Good lord! Burglary, was it? We're like Fort Knox here, but I don't suppose there's a single modern lock in that house.'

He hadn't asked if Lindsay was all right. It seemed a

phoney reaction, but then the whole set-up here was phoney. 'No, not a burglary. This was an attempt on Mr Lindsay's life.'

'Attempt?' Hodge said. He looked taken aback and there was a pause before he said, 'Er – well, it's come to something when you're not safe, even in a place like this!'

Again, MacNee was picking up strange vibes. 'On his life?' would be the natural question, not 'Attempt?' And surely 'Is he all right?' was next?

He didn't ask it, though MacNee gave him the chance before he said, 'We're gathering background information. You and Mr Lindsay – old pals, are you?'

'Known him a long time, yes.'

'Someone's got a grudge. Any idea who?'

Hodge had no suggestions. 'Anything that might have set someone off?' MacNee persisted. 'Even if it was a long time ago?'

Who said he couldn't do subtle? That brought it round nicely – but Hodge wasn't playing ball, shaking his head and again looking blank.

That could only be deliberate, MacNee thought, unless you'd a space where your brain should be – though in this case that was a distinct possibility. Now Hodge was spreading his hands in a pantomime of openness.

'Wouldn't have the first idea, to be honest with you. We went over for a drink the other night – the wife thought it would be neighbourly, with him there for a week – but I hadn't spoken to the man in years.'

'Perhaps your wife might have more idea?' MacNee suggested. 'Is she—'

'Staying with a friend in Glasgow.'

'All on your own here, then – or have you family living at home?' MacNee nodded towards a photograph on one of the side-tables – a young man, with a marked resemblance to Hodge himself, standing beside a yacht.

For some reason, this threw Hodge. He jumped, then stammered, 'Er – no, not at all. My son's away. New Zealand. On a farm working for a friend of mine.'

What on earth was that about? MacNee filed it away as he went on, 'So you were here on your own last night?'

The man visibly collected himself. 'Yes, that's right. Watched a bit of sport on Sky, had a few beers. Of course, that was after I went over to Tulach and sank a knife in Marcus!'

He laughed. MacNee didn't. 'How did you know he was stabbed, sir?' he said quietly.

'You'll like this place,' Macdonald promised Kerr as they neared Miramar. 'It's like the Scottish parliament – cost a fortune and none of the bits relate to each other.'

As they turned into the drive, Kerr gaped. 'See what you mean. That's – that's awesome. I like the novelty tarmac path there – meant to match the lawn, presumably, supposing the lawn was bright emerald. I can't wait to meet the owners if this is their dream, not a nightmare.'

She was doomed to disappointment. There was no answer when they rang the bell.

'There's workmen round the side there,' Macdonald said. 'We can ask if they know where the Hodges are.'

'Probably won't speak English,' Kerr pointed out. 'Nearly all the builders around here are Polish.'

'One of them does – I spoke to him before.'

They went round the side to the new building. The younger workmen looked up but went on working. The older man glanced round and came over.

They showed their cards. 'We're looking for the Hodges,'

Kerr said. 'Do you know where they are, or when they'll be back?'

'She?' He shrugged. 'She went away yesterday – I don't know. But he – I think you will know?'

He had a harsh, stern-looking face, but when he smiled he was quite good-looking, Kerr thought. She smiled back. 'Why should we know?'

'It is one of your own takes him away. A small man, a black leather jacket—'

Tam MacNee! The words 'jammy bugger' formed in a thought bubble over the detectives' heads.

'Er – took him away?' Kerr asked delicately.

'He is not happy. His face. Grey like his trousers.' He was still smiling. Mr Hodge clearly was not popular.

One of the men guffawed and another was grinning broadly, though Kerr noticed that the one on the roof – seriously fit, that guy – was still doggedly hammering.

As they returned to the car, Kerr demanded, 'How the hell did Tam get on to that? There wasn't a mention of the Hodges at the briefing.'

Macdonald had the answer. 'Sold his soul to the devil years ago. We'd better get back – there may be new instructions.'

' "Helping us with our enquiries" – I see. I'll be right down, Tam. Well done.'

Fleming put the phone down, shaking her head in wonder. MacNee's instinct was formidable. He'd cautioned not to expect too much, but she couldn't help hoping.

On her way to the interview room she bumped into Macdonald and Kerr, just back from Ardhill.

'Anything useful come up?' she asked in passing.

'Not at Ardhill, no,' Macdonald said.

Kerr chimed in, 'Boss, do you know if Tam MacNee's brought Gavin Hodge in? They said he'd been taken away – we went there hoping to interview him.'

'Did you, indeed? What put you on to him?'

'Jaki Johnston said Hodge hated Lindsay – she didn't know why, really.'

'Thanks – that could be useful. I'm going to talk to Hodge now – he's helping with enquiries.'

'There was one other thing,' Kerr said. 'I asked her if Lindsay had been having problems with anyone else, and she said some woman wanted him to lie to the police and he wouldn't.'

'Lie to the police?' Fleming was startled. 'Any indication who it was?'

'Sorry. That was all she knew.'

'We were wondering,' Macdonald put in, 'how Tam thought of Gavin Hodge? It wasn't mentioned at the briefing.'

Uncomfortably, Fleming said, 'Oh, you know Tam. Has his methods,' and hurried on. It looked as if they'd be going public with the cold case review sooner rather than later.

'Thank you for finding the time, Ms Milne,' Superintendent Bailey said, sitting down opposite the acting Procurator Fiscal in her office with its walls of box files, table with unstable piles of books and paper-cluttered desk. Bailey looked round disapprovingly. He liked a tidy desk himself – organized desk, organized mind.

'Glad to see you, Superintendent. I've felt for some time we should have a chat about your problems.'

Her condescending manner made him want to slap her, but she wasn't looking well. She looked tired, and the thick, glossy lipstick she always wore – another thing Bailey didn't like – was too vivid, accentuating the pallor of her face.

'I'm sure that would prove most enlightening. However, I'm afraid I have rather more urgent business than discussing your no doubt helpful suggestions.' Bailey could condescend with the best of them. 'The attack on Marcus Lindsay—'

He thought she coloured, but she said, 'I was appalled to hear about it. And one of my deputes gathered from an officer of yours in court that someone appeared recently at the medical centre with a knife wound, but there has been no follow-up.

'You seem to be presiding over an epidemic. What are you doing about it?'

Bailey's teeth ground together. She was an advocate, of course, trained to think on her feet, return any attack and give nothing away. He was up against it here, but by God, he'd give it his best shot!

'I'm not personally familiar with the first case, but any complaint will have been followed up and I shall have you informed of the outcome. And as you know, the attack on Mr Lindsay is under intensive investigation as we speak.'

'That's all very well, but since his injuries were, mercifully, minor, we can't expend excessive police time on it, unless you can produce solid evidence of attempted murder which, I have to say, seems extremely unlikely when the result has only been a precautionary night in hospital which was in any case largely because of an accidental head injury.

'No, the bigger picture of knife crime has to be our priority before we have more of our citizens attacked. What steps are you—?'

He cut across her ruthlessly. 'We are both busy people and I suggest you contact my secretary if you want to arrange a general discussion.

'I am here to ask you about your relationship with Marcus Lindsay.'

'Relationship? What is this?' Her slightly bulbous eyes bulged now with temper – or was it alarm? She had started fiddling with one of her shoulder-length dark blonde curls.

'This is an investigation into an attempted murder. We are talking to everyone in recent contact with Mr Lindsay, and your name is on that list. I know you would wish to give us every assistance.'

She was still glaring at him. 'Naturally, though I can't imagine what information you could think I might have. Our acquaintance, when I was in Glasgow, was of the slightest, and our only recent contact was a phone call in which he complained about police harassment. As you no doubt know, I passed that on to DI Fleming.'

That, in fact, had never reached his desk. Fleming had presumably taken care that it didn't, but he wasn't going to betray her. 'And why, I wonder,' he said, 'did he phone you instead of me? That would be a more normal course of action – unless, of course, it was on the basis of your friendship?'

Bailey was proud of that question; it caught her by surprise. 'He didn't – er – he probably didn't want to cause too much trouble – just a word in someone's ear.'

'I see. It's not long since you moved here. You keep in touch, then?'

'No, no, not really.'

He couldn't quite understand why, but he'd definitely touched a nerve. Doggedly, he persisted, 'So how did he know you were here, and phone you, if you didn't keep in touch?'

Milne was actually becoming flustered. 'Someone here must have mentioned it, I suppose.'

'But who is likely to have known he would know you?' Bailey was honestly puzzled.

'Perhaps friends in Glasgow . . .' she began, then stopped. 'Wait a moment. I've just remembered. I – I think, perhaps, I may have phoned him.'

Bailey looked astonished. 'Phoned him – to see if he had a complaint to make about police harassment? I confess, I would find that very strange behaviour, very strange indeed – something I would need to take up with the Chief Constable.'

'No, no! Of course not! I – I heard he was in the area, phoned to ask how he was, and he mentioned this complaint in passing. That's all. Stupid of me to have forgotten. I apologize if I unintentionally misled you.'

She was quite confident again, challenging him with her cold blue eyes, and he still didn't know what that had really been about. He was beginning to wish Fleming had taken it on herself.

'Right,' he said, trying to regain the initiative. 'Now – your friendship with Mr Lindsay. My information is that you all but denied to DI Fleming that you knew him.'

Milne tossed back her hair and laughed. 'Did she say that? How ridiculous – just because I am not someone who chooses to claim friendship with celebrities based on nothing more than a couple of chance encounters. Our "relationship", as you so picturesquely term it, was that we met at functions. That's all.

'And as you said, superintendent, we're busy people. So—?' She raised very thin, pencilled brows.

Procedure. You couldn't go wrong with procedure. 'Just a couple more routine questions. Do you know anyone who would have a grudge against Marcus Lindsay, from your Glasgow days?'

'I can't imagine who would. He was always very charming.' She was smiling faintly now.

She had got away from the sensitive area, and Bailey couldn't quite see how to get back to it.

'Perhaps you could give me an account of your movements last night?'

'Oh dear, superintendent, you may have to lock me up after all.' She was laughing at him. 'I haven't a soul who can bear witness that I was in all evening, doing a bit of work, then reading and listening to opera.'

She would be the opera type, Bailey thought bitterly. Wagner, probably – he could almost see her with one of those horned helmets on her head. He got up, thanking her formally for her help.

Just as he reached the door, she said, 'Oh, and I won't forget about an appointment to discuss what we need to do to make your work more effective. I have serious doubts about DI Fleming.'

Bailey mumbled something and left the battlefield to go back to Headquarters and lick his wounds.

14

DS MacNee was waiting for Fleming beside one of the interview rooms. 'He's in there,' he greeted her, and she looked through the little inset window.

Gavin Hodge was slumped in one of the bolted-down chairs in the stark room, legs stretched out and hands in the pockets of his chinos, looking both sullen and scared.

Fleming turned to MacNee. 'Any chance he's our man?'

'Could be. No alibi, alone all evening. Just not sure. He thinks I took him in because he knew Lindsay was stabbed without being told—'

'Sounds promising – apart from the fact that you've no one to corroborate.' Fleming showed her annoyance.

'Aye, well . . . didn't know he was going to say a daft thing like that, did I?' He grinned hopefully, then catching her eye hurried on, 'Anyway, gossip in the local store is how he knows, he says, and it's maybe right – not that it puts him in the clear even so.

'What I'm really wondering is why he was like a hen on a hot griddle when I arrived and why he tried to kid on he knew nothing about it. It's all round the place that Lindsay's dead, Jock Naismith says, and Hodge looked shocked when he heard he wasn't. So—' MacNee shrugged his shoulders.

'So either he'd heard the rumour, or else thought he'd killed him. Or possibly both, I suppose. Let's work him over.'

'What are we waiting for? Oh, just one other thing – got a son in New Zealand he didn't like me asking about.'

'Black sheep, maybe,' Fleming suggested. 'Presumably if he's in New Zealand he's nothing to do with this. Let's go.'

As MacNee went through the formalities for the recording, Fleming observed the man opposite, who was not meeting her eyes. He was unprepossessing, big and flabby, with thinning fair hair combed forward to disguise a rapidly expanding forehead. He had watery blue eyes with heavy bags underneath them and his jawline sagged into his bull-like neck. Age or self-indulgence – or possibly even both – had not dealt with him kindly.

MacNee joined them, and Fleming began. 'Thank you for coming in this morning, Mr Hodge. We appreciate your cooperation.'

'Cooperation!' the man said bitterly. 'That's one way of putting it.'

Fleming raised her eyebrows. 'Are you alleging an element of compulsion?'

'No, no – apart from your sergeant refusing to accept a perfectly innocent explanation and leave it at that. I hope you're going to show a bit more intelligence.'

'I understand that you showed special knowledge of the attack on Mr Lindsay.'

'Yes, but I can explain it – I did explain it. I heard it in the local store. You can check.'

'We certainly will. And I'm sure you will prove to be right.'

Hodge smirked in triumph at MacNee. 'Well, thank God for a woman with some sense. Never thought I'd live to hear myself say that! Can I go now?'

The look Fleming gave him would have frozen boiling water. 'It's hardly relevant. What I want to know is why you lied about it.'

The change in his expression was almost comical. 'Lied? I – I didn't lie—'

'Sorry, of course not. You didn't lie, you just pretended.' Her tone was icily scornful. 'When DS MacNee told you what had happened, you pretended you didn't know anything about the attack on Lindsay. Then you showed surprise on hearing he was alive. Did you leave him for dead on the terrace last night, Mr Hodge? You have no alibi.'

MacNee stifled a smile. He almost felt sorry for the poor bugger, but he'd walked into it with that remark about women.

'I didn't – I didn't! Of course I didn't! Why should I want to kill him?'

'My information is that there was considerable ill-feeling between you, dating back some years.'

That was news to MacNee. Oh, Big Marge was good, no doubt about that. He could just sit back and enjoy the show.

And she had visibly rocked Hodge with that one. The broken veins in his cheeks stood out against his sudden pallor. 'That's – that's rubbish. I don't say we were best mates, but like I said to your sergeant, until this week I hadn't set eyes on the man for years.'

'Let's go back to why you lied – sorry, *pretended* – to DS MacNee.'

The man put his hands to his head. 'Look, give me a moment. You're getting me confused.'

Never! How could that have happened? MacNee was tempted to say it aloud, but a slight gesture from Fleming stopped him.

Hodge began, 'When your sergeant said something about news, I didn't know what he was talking about, I swear it. Yes,

I'd heard about Marcus – but why would that be anything to do with me? Then it got difficult to stop him and say I knew. Seemed easier just to go along with it – I didn't think it mattered. And anyway, it was a bit undignified to admit I'd been listening to village gossip – a man in my position.'

'Which is—?' Fleming asked politely.

'Oh, well known locally, that sort of thing.'

'Rich, he means,' MacNee put in coarsely. 'But very sensitive to the social demands that makes on him.' He was beginning to enjoy himself. Fleming flashed him a warning glance; he smiled blandly. Why should she have all the fun?

Hodge ignored him, speaking directly to Fleming. 'So you can see, inspector, that this is merely a misunderstanding which your sergeant has inflated out of all proportion—'

'Funny you should be so edgy, then, when I came to the door,' MacNee put in.

'Edgy? I don't know what you mean. I was surprised to see you, that's all. You say I was edgy, I say I was surprised – it's a matter of opinion. I'd advise you to be on firmer ground before you start making allegations, sergeant.' Putting his own spin on the story had given him confidence and he was starting to bluster.

It was an unwise tactic to adopt with MacNee, who leaned back in his chair and drawled, 'Oh, right enough, that was just a wee suspicion I had. But that wasn't when you were surprised. You were surprised when I told you Lindsay wasn't dead. Like the boss said, did you leave him for dead on the terrace last night?'

'This – this is outrageous! I have already denied that allegation, most forcibly. And it seems based on my knowing he was stabbed – I've explained that. In any case, it's only your word against mine that I said it at all.'

His look of triumph turned to uncertainty as MacNee smiled. His smile affected a lot of people that way.

'Why do you think I didn't arrest you, Mr Hodge? Of course that wasn't evidence, and what you said about how you knew about the stabbing may be right enough – doesn't prove anything, either way.'

'But something I did want on tape, and with DI Fleming here, was what you'd got to say about something that may be a link.'

'Ailsa Grant.' Fleming picked up the cue, and was intrigued to see the man actually jump.

'For the record, note that the witness was visibly startled,' MacNee said, and shook his head reprovingly. 'There you go again – being surprised. Shocked, even – maybe you should see the doctor about your nerves? Did you not know we were reopening the case of Ailsa's murder?'

'I – I'm not sure.'

'Oh, come now, sir! You seem to be suffering from a lot of confusion about what you know and don't know.' Fleming's voice had a harsh edge to it. 'We understand Marcus Lindsay was going to tell you. Did you know or didn't you?'

Wretchedly, he stammered, 'My – my wife might have known. Marcus phoned her the other day and she said something about it.' It didn't sound convincing.

'Is that a yes?'

'I suppose so. Vaguely, you know.'

'That'll be right,' MacNee said sarcastically. 'So vaguely that you were worried when I turned up, you went deliberately blank when asked about enemies in Lindsay's past – and you knew fine about the accusations against him after Ailsa's murder, didn't you? And just now, when DI Fleming mentioned her name, you jumped as if she'd stuck a pin in your backside.

'So let's discuss what it is about Ailsa that gets to you, shall we, before we go on to your activities when you were all alone in the house last night – oh, except for when you went over to stab Marcus Lindsay, as you said yourself.'

'For God's sake, man! That was only a joke!' Hodge howled. 'You're confusing me!' He drew a deep, shaking breath, then, like a cornered rat, came out fighting. 'I came here today voluntarily to help you, but I haven't appreciated the way I have been treated. I can give you five minutes more of my time, then I'm leaving. If there's anything further to ask me you can do it in the presence of my solicitor.'

'Ailsa Grant was just someone my wife and I knew when we lived here, before moving to Glasgow. Hearing her name gave me a shock because I'd almost forgotten her, poor girl. Her father bumped her off, but you lot failed to nail him for it.'

'That's one opinion,' Fleming said dryly. 'So – what can you tell us about her?'

'Not a lot, to be honest. Diane – my wife – knew her better than I did. She was blonde, quite good-looking – that's about it.'

'And you didn't keep in touch with her in Glasgow?'

'I didn't, of course. Diane may have – you'd need to ask her.'

'But you never saw her in Glasgow?'

'No.' A flat, definite response.

'Or know who her friends were there?'

'No.' He was much more confident now. 'Like I said, I'd no contact with her after we left here.' He got up. 'That's all I can tell you. And that's your five minutes. I'm leaving.'

Neither officer made any move to stop him. MacNee got up to open the door and send him away with the constable on duty, then signed off the recording and came back to sit down again.

'Something's eating him. But what?'

Fleming considered. 'We got him on the raw with the questions about Lindsay. But apart from reacting when her name was first mentioned, he was pretty collected about Ailsa. Does that just mean he was taken aback at the idea of a link?'

'Or maybe he's been preparing his answers to those questions ever since he knew – or sort of knew – we would be asking them,' MacNee said more cynically. 'How did you know there was bad feeling between him and Lindsay anyway?'

'From Jaki Johnston via Tansy. She and Andy Mac were a bit put out that you'd stolen a march on them.'

MacNee grinned. 'I'll take her with me when I go back to see Mrs Hodge. She's away in Glasgow for a couple of days.'

'Mmm.' Fleming wasn't really listening. 'I'm going to have to clue them in about the possible connections. I'd hoped we could maybe find out a bit more about it first, because—'

'Makes sense to me.' MacNee didn't wait to hear the arguments for and against. 'Let's get on with it. Might be interesting to know how the Grants were occupying themselves last night.'

'It might indeed. But someone else can talk to them this time – I've seen as much of the road down to the Mull as I want to. Possibly slightly more than that.'

It was very quiet and very dark in the drawing room, with the curtains drawn. There was one lamp lit and the fire was flickering; Sylvia Lascelles had drawn her wheelchair as close to the blaze as she could. She was sitting in a hunched position, as if she was simply too weary to straighten up.

She was staring into the flames, and somewhere a clock was ticking, but that, with the occasional crackle from the fire, was the only sound. Then suddenly, behind her, she heard the French windows being cautiously opened. The curtain rings rattled, and she swivelled round in her chair.

A man was coming in – a dark, swarthy man, who when he saw her alone in the room, smiled. 'Well, well, well!' he said. 'All by yourself? That's good. That's *very* good.' He advanced towards her.

She looked back, her eyes wide in horror. Then she screamed.

'Cut!' The clack of the clapperboard broke the tension. 'Fantastic!'

Barrie Craig came hurrying over to Sylvia. 'You were absolutely amazing, darling. You hit it perfectly – if the technical stuff is OK, it's in the can.'

Sylvia laughed shakily. 'I talked myself into it. I could believe there was someone ready to kill me.'

'No wonder, sweetie, considering last night. And to go on today, after all – that's star quality.' He went to talk to Tony Laidlaw and the cameraman in the far corner and the other actor followed him to look at the clip running. Then Barrie turned, gave a thumbs-up and came over to take her hand. 'It's a wrap. I don't know how you do it, darling. And you look great on the screen, really wonderful.'

'Don't be a fool, Barrie, of course I don't.' Sylvia found Barrie's fulsomeness difficult at the best of times, and this wasn't the best of times. She disengaged her hand. 'I look a wreck, and you know it. The only reason it's been possible at all is that my persecuted character would be showing signs of strain and ancient frailty, and it's saved Maggie in Make-up a job. I'm too old to relish insincerity.'

Barrie looked crushed. 'But darling, I meant it – I'm your biggest fan! Of course you're not looking your fantastic best, but you look – you look like a crushed flower—'

Tony, seeing a dangerous look in Sylvia's eye, came over. 'Barrie, could you go and have a word about the rest of the schedule?' Then, turning to Sylvia, he said gruffly, 'You're exhausted. I'm taking you back to your room.'

She gave him her most ravishing smile. 'I do love a masterful man! It reminds me of my darling Laddie – though of course when he said he was taking me back to my room it was for a rather different reason.' She looked naughtily up at him under her lashes.

It surprised a laugh from Tony. 'Don't tempt me!' he said, and wheeled her out.

When he had gone, Sylvia sank back in her chair, her hand to her head. It was aching, but she couldn't risk any more painkillers yet. She was bone-weary, and she needed to lie down. She fetched her stick and stepped out of her chair, groaning a little at the pain; it was a relief to be alone, when she didn't feel she must stifle it.

There was a handle on the wall by the bed, put there for Laddie, which made getting in easier, and she lay down thankfully, trembling from the effort, and pulled a cashmere rug over herself. She should really have waited for Frocks to help her out of her costume, but as lovely Tony had noticed, she felt completely drained.

Sylvia closed her eyes. Thoughts swooped around in her mind like the great bats she and Laddie had seen in Tonga, staying at that idyllic hotel. The white sand, the palm trees . . . and then she was asleep.

Laddie was coming along the beach, towards where she was lying in the sun, and she sat up smiling, holding out her arms. But his face, as he came towards her, was dark and menacing, and he held a knife in his hand. She cried out, the sound strangled in her throat, trying to jump up and run away from this monster, but now her legs were old and twisted and powerless . . .

A tap on the door woke her and she sat up suddenly with a cry that was half relief, half pain. Mrs Boyter's voice said, 'Madam, are you awake?'

'Yes, yes. Come in.' She eased herself up to a sitting position, trying to clear her mind.

Mrs Boyter bustled in. 'There's police officers wanting to talk to you. But I told them I'd see if you were at home, and I could just say you're not, if you're feeling a bit peelie-wallie.'

It was incongruous to see someone in a bright pink pinny adopt the gravitas, if not the vocabulary, of Jeeves at his most sombre. 'Darling Mrs B, you're a treasure! But of course I must. If you could just slip another couple of pillows at my back, I shall receive them here, in bed, like *le Roi Soleil* having a levée.'

Uncomprehending but obedient, Mrs Boyter did as she was asked, then departed. Sylvia reached for the mirror which always lay beside her bed, looked at it, and grimaced. She looked like a pantomime witch, but there wasn't much she could do about it now except pat her hair into place and prepare to smile.

The room Mrs Boyter showed them into was big and spacious, with a heavily ornamented ceiling and a marble fireplace – once the dining room, Fleming guessed. There was no fire burning but alone of the rooms she had been into in this house it was adequately heated.

Sylvia Lascelles was propped up in bed. She greeted them with an apology for being found resting, with that same charming smile. If it hadn't been for that, Fleming wondered if she would have recognized her. The last time, Sylvia had been wearing something very soft in a hazy mauvy-grey which emphasized the colour of her eyes; today she was wearing a shabby lovat-green twinset and her make-up could only be described as garish.

MacNee, smiling back, didn't seem to have noticed, but Sylvia caught Fleming's glance and gave her throaty laugh. 'I haven't taken leave of my senses, Inspector Fleming. I just hadn't the energy to change after they'd finished with me this afternoon. Just imagine that it's only the stage make-up that's turned me into a raddled old hag.'

Fleming, embarrassed, made suitable protestations, while MacNee, enjoying his boss's discomfort, said gallantly that he didn't doubt it for a minute, and was rewarded with another smile and, 'You're a wicked flatterer, Sergeant MacNee!'

Realizing that MacNee was overcome by Sylvia remembering his name, Fleming took control. 'I know you must be very tired, Miss Lascelles, but you'll understand it's important for us to know exactly what happened last night.'

'Yes, of course. I felt so confused last night – shock, I suppose – but Marcus and I were talking it through this morning before he left hospital and I've got it much clearer now. Oh, do sit down, won't you?'

As she fetched a chair, Fleming quietly ground her teeth. The last thing you wanted was your two principal witnesses discussing their evidence. There was always a tendency to rationalize, to be influenced by what the other person believed they had seen, whereas discrepancies were often revealing. They'd just have to read between the lines when they compared the two statements.

'I was sitting, just looking out into the garden. The stars, the peace – I live in a tiny London flat, and Tulach is simply heaven. I heard Jaki saying goodnight to Marcus in the hall and I remember looking at the clock, because it seemed so early – before ten. But they've just broken up their relationship, you know, so I suppose the evening was dragging, rather. I could hear Marcus moving about, locking up, probably.

'Then a little later, the doorbell rang—'

'Did you notice the time?' MacNee had taken out his notebook.

'I'm afraid not, Sergeant MacNee. But I don't think it was that much later. I assumed it was one of the *Playfair* people – there were problems with the schedule, and I remember hoping they wouldn't keep darling Marcus up late. He leads such a hectic life; I hoped he would get a good rest while he was down here.'

She spoke with a mother's fondness, Fleming thought. Perhaps stepmother hadn't been such a false description after all.

Sylvia was going on, quite collectedly. 'The window looks out on to the terrace. My bedside light was on, but I was sitting in shadow to have a better view of the night sky. I didn't notice anything, until there was a sound, something—'

'What kind of sound?' Fleming interrupted.

Sylvia looked helpless. 'I – I don't really know. Just something. Then I thought I sensed a movement but even when I leaned forward I couldn't see properly. I can't see right along to the end of the house. Go and look – you'll see what I mean.'

MacNee and Fleming walked over to the two sash windows, side by side. From the right-hand one, looking to your right, you could see just beyond the French windows, but no further.

Fleming turned back into the room. 'Were the curtains drawn across the drawing-room window?'

'No, I could see the light from it on the terrace. Then I heard a scuffle, and I levered myself up to try to see what was happening. I heard Marcus cry out and there was a man right behind him. I saw Marcus fall—' She caught her breath.

'A man – did you see what he looked like?' Fleming asked gently.

'No. No, I couldn't, I couldn't!' She was obviously upset by this. 'He was muffled up, with a hood – I couldn't see clearly—'

'But definitely a man?'

Sylvia paused. 'I thought it was a man,' she said slowly, 'but I couldn't positively state that it wasn't a tall woman. I – I just don't know. I couldn't take in what was happening, make any sense of it. It was all so – so unreal!' Again, she showed signs of becoming upset.

'Don't distress yourself.' Fleming's voice was warm and sympathetic. 'If you can manage to tell us a few more things, we'll leave you to rest.'

'Yes, yes, of course I can!' Sylvia said fiercely. 'I must. Go on.'

'We haven't found the weapon. Did you see the man use it, or throw it away?'

'No. As Marcus fell, I screamed. He had bent over Marcus, but then he looked up and saw me, I think, and took off across the garden. He disappeared beyond the shrubbery – and that's all, really. Poor Jaki had to deal with everything. I could only bring blankets and hot bottles, thinking all the time Marcus was going to die—' She dabbed at her eyes with a handkerchief.

MacNee leaned forward from his chair and patted her hand. 'But he didn't, Miss Lascelles. And if you hadn't screamed, the man might have gone on to finish the job. You probably saved his life.'

'I'd like to think so. I feel so useless, nowadays.'

'People still want to see you on the screen,' MacNee assured her. 'It'll be a real treat to see you acting again.'

Fleming watched him give her the restrained version of his smile which he used when he didn't want to alarm the recipient. She cut in, 'Miss Lascelles, just one more thing. Can you see in the shrubbery there that there's a gap between those two bushes? Have you ever noticed that?'

Sylvia leaned forward. 'Yes, I can see where you mean. But I've never paid any attention to it before.'

'And the man didn't come from there, or you would have seen him cross the grass?'

She was alert now, intrigued. 'I would definitely have seen that. The movement would have been visible, even in the darkness. Why – do you think he might have been hiding there?'

'Oh, it was something that occurred to me. One last thing, then we'll leave you to rest. Could you guess at a height for the person you saw?'

Sylvia frowned. 'Not really. Tall, I think – taller than Marcus. But I couldn't be sure.'

'Thank you. I think that's all, as far as I'm concerned.' Fleming looked enquiringly at MacNee, but he was looking at Sylvia and didn't notice. 'Is there anything that you want to ask us?'

'Just one thing. What will happen to him, if you catch him?' Sylvia's voice was suddenly surprisingly fierce. 'If he's convicted, I mean.'

It was interesting how gentle, well-bred ladies were always the most savage when it came to criminal punishment.

Sylvia obviously wasn't going to be pleased with the answer Fleming would have to give her.

'Three, maybe four years.' And that was probably on the optimistic side.

'Yes, that's what I thought,' Sylvia said grimly. 'It's not really enough, is it?'

'Certainly isn't,' MacNee agreed heartily. 'And with early release, a lot less. Out on the streets again—'

'MacNee!' Fleming said warningly, and he stopped.

'Sorry,' he said. 'Don't want to alarm you.'

He had, though. There was a definite pause before Sylvia said bravely, 'We'll just have to see Marcus doesn't go out alone on dark nights. Or hope that prison is the deterrent it's meant to be.'

Not trusting herself to comment, Fleming said only, 'And there's nothing else that you can think of that might be helpful?'

Sylvia looked at her with those haunted violet eyes. Her voice throbbed with emotion. 'Oh, Inspector Fleming, would that there were!'

It was a stagey response. With slight impatience, Fleming said goodbye and went out. She heard MacNee say tenderly, 'Goodbye, Miss Lascelles. You be sure and take care of yourself, now.'

With the door shut, Fleming mimicked him softly. ' "Take care of yourself, now!" Tam, there's times when I think you're a fillet short of a full fish supper! You weren't there as a fan, you were there as a detective.'

MacNee, never one to take an insult lying down, retorted, 'And what did you want me to do? Twist her arm up behind her back till she confessed it was her? Come on!'

'Hardly. But she really hammed it up at the end, I thought.'

MacNee bristled. 'You wouldn't recognize it, of course, but that was sensitivity. Still, she's probably used to insults, and so am I. "*Such fate to suffering worth is giv'n!*" '

'No doubt,' Fleming said dryly. 'Should I give you a bit longer to recover from your star-struck state, or shall we go and find Marcus Lindsay? He may be able to give us the information we need to get this whole thing tied up tonight.'

If she had been genuinely optimistic, Fleming would have been very disappointed. Mr Marcus, they were informed by Mrs Boyter, was asleep and couldn't be disturbed. Fleming suggested he might want to be told that the police were here, but Mrs Boyter, growing into her role by the day, said dramatically that her duty was to her master and they could arrest her before she would let them near the poor, exhausted man.

With some irritation, Fleming disclaimed any wish to enforce her obedience and arranged that he should be told they would come at ten next morning. She followed MacNee out and round to the garden, where he wanted to have a look at the shrubbery.

It was pleasant in the weak sunshine, and spring bulbs had pushed up through the weeds: daffodils and a few straggly tulips in what had been flowerbeds, and celandines under the trees. There was a pretty little arbour with stone urns on either side of the door, depressingly full of rank grass. A yellow forsythia had grown into an untidy bush and made a splash of vivid colour against the warm stone. Fleming could imagine that the house in its glory days would have been seductive indeed.

The SOCOs were still taking measurements and dusting windows for fingerprints and checking tyre-marks in the drive but it was all routine stuff, and still no weapon had been found.

'Let's get back,' Fleming said. 'I've plenty to do, and all this can wait. It isn't actually a murder, after all.'

MacNee looked at her wryly. 'Not unless he comes back to finish the job,' he said.

15

Stuart Grant was mending the drystone dyke which separated the grazing ground from the farmyard without enthusiasm, slowly placing stones, surveying his work, then, as often as not, having to take them off to try others more suitable. The skill of dyking was not one he'd troubled to master; it might have its frustrations but it was just one more way to pass the long, tedious day.

The view, had he looked up, was stupendous: the robin's-egg-blue of the sky, the glittering white lighthouse with its clean yellow trims, the gulls wheeling and calling, the vivid green of the pasture where his cattle browsed. He didn't raise his eyes, looking round for the next stone.

He fantasized regularly about what he'd do when his mother died – though the old besom looked like living for ever, unless he took a hatchet to her. Balnakenny was in her name; Stuart, and his father before him, had been pretty much hired hands. Perhaps that was why the farm had never really prospered. Robert Grant hadn't come of farming stock like Jean – not that she did much around the place – and he had worked Balnakenny for a living, without real commitment.

Stuart hated it. Maybe his father had too; he wouldn't know. Robert Grant felt things, like anger, but he didn't discuss feelings with his son or anyone else. You weren't meant to have feelings. Or discussions.

But Ailsa had ignored the unwritten rules. She had a temper to match her father's. And she felt things. Oh yes, she felt things. She'd come in and cry, and tell Stuart – not everything, never everything, but she'd tell him how she felt.

He envied her, in a way. Her feelings made her miserable in a way he never had been, but it was as if she saw in colour, while he saw in black and white. Sometimes he caught glimpses from her of what it felt like to be ecstatically happy and it made his own life seem drab, days marching in an endless procession of boredom and pointlessness.

The terrible thing was that, supposing his mother died tomorrow, he didn't know what he'd do. Sell up, yes. But he wasn't a fool. What was it worth, a place like this? Not enough to buy him the sort of girls that featured in the magazines he hid from his mother, that was for sure. He wasn't a big drinker, and he was too canny to waste his money gambling – so what would he do if he didn't even have to get up in the morning?

It would have been different if Ailsa had lived. They'd have shared the money, and if she wouldn't have shared her life – he'd no illusions about that – maybe she'd have let him in on the fringes to see, at least, how people who weren't like him lived.

Would he have been better never to have known her? Better, if he'd assumed life was just getting through what had to be done day by day, and as long as there was food in your belly and a roof overhead, you simply went on like that until you died?

Ailsa hadn't accepted that. Ailsa had been hungry for life, greedy, even. He thought, sometimes, that he could have given his life for hers, if there was a deal to be made. He didn't really want it.

But at least now Lindsay was dead. He had paid, at last, for Ailsa's pain. Stuart couldn't understand that pain, but he could understand her humiliation – like when he'd asked a pretty girl to dance at a Young Farmers do, and she'd laughed and refused. Since he couldn't put his hands round her throat and squeeze until she dropped dead, he'd never asked another girl to dance. And he'd stopped going to Young Farmers years ago. Stopped going to anything, really.

Maybe time had stopped when Ailsa died. Maybe he was in some strange sort of afterlife, when things looked the same, but—

'Stuart! I've been bawling for five minutes. Do you want your tractor fixed or not?'

The man who was standing hollering from the yard certainly looked the same – he worked in the local garage.

Stuart set down the stone he was holding, and without reply came over to the tractor which had stopped suddenly in the yard this morning. He described the symptoms, and the mechanic sucked his teeth. 'Oooh, sounds nasty. You'd be better with a new one. This one went out with the dinosaurs.'

Taking off the engine cover, he chatted on. 'Fine stushie in Ardhill the day! Place swarming with polis. Someone tried to kill that Marcus Lindsay – him that's the big TV star.'

Stuart grunted. 'Got him, too, by what I heard.'

'They were saying that, but you know what this place is like. He's back home from the hospital, and the man they arrested didn't do it, seemingly. There's a manhunt, now. Here, pass me that spanner, will you? Stuart – you deaf, or just daft? Pass me the spanner.'

'I wanted to have a chance to brief you before tomorrow,' Fleming said.

MacNee, Kerr and Macdonald were assembled in her office. MacNee had perched on the edge of the table in one corner while the others took the chairs in front of her desk.

Fleming always noticed where her officers sat: they weren't here often enough to have established 'rights' to particular seats, but anyone who chose the table instead of another chair was usually signalling detachment. So MacNee was reckoning he knew it all and could relax? She wasn't having that.

'You asked me this morning how Tam knew to go to see Gavin Hodge. I've been asked to review a cold case from twenty years ago and that was as a result of the link we felt might exist between the two.'

Fleming sketched in the background. 'That's just the bare bones. I'm making the files available to the three of you this afternoon, along with notes I've made on interviews I did, and once you've read them I'd appreciate your input. The three of you,' she emphasized. 'Which, if you count, means Tam as well.'

MacNee looked appalled. His dislike of deskwork was well known. Tough.

She continued, 'But keep this to yourself meantime. The press will pick up on it and I'm not sure that would be helpful – no, to be honest, I'm sure it would be totally unhelpful, unless we're sure this link actually does exist. So, an open mind on everything else.

'There was another knifing recently, a young Pole injured. Kevin Docherty? Maybe. Or has a bit of a knife culture developed around here that Lindsay might somehow have got himself involved in? If that's it—' She grimaced.

'Everyone in Ardhill went on about the problem in the pub,' Macdonald offered. 'But that was Kevin and his mates, and all of them were otherwise occupied.'

Kerr was looking thoughtful. 'When Jaki was telling me what happened, I kept wondering why Lindsay would go and look for someone who'd rung the bell then disappeared.

Docherty was a serious threat, so why didn't he go back inside and lock the door instead of wandering out saying, "Fancy a go at me?" '

'Good point.' Fleming scribbled a note. 'Tam and I are to see him tomorrow. We saw Sylvia Lascelles this afternoon, but she couldn't add much. And I thought – though Tam probably disagrees—'

There was a tap on the door, and Superintendent Bailey put his head round it. 'Marjory. I was hoping—' Then he stopped. 'Sorry. Don't want to interrupt.'

Fleming got up. 'Come in, Donald. I'm just briefing on aspects of the Lindsay case.' And how she hoped he wouldn't accept the invitation!

'No, no,' he said hastily. 'Just a word with you later.'

'I won't be long. I'll come up to your office, shall I?'

'Fine, fine.' He withdrew.

'I'd better keep it short. Andy and Tansy – Balnakenny, talk to the Grants tomorrow, OK? Make it early – it's a long way. You're watching for reactions to what happened last night. Stuart Grant was devoted to his sister and if he believes his mother that Lindsay killed Ailsa, there's no saying what he might have done.'

'Or she might have done, presumably,' Kerr said pointedly. 'No need to assume women can't use knives.'

Fleming smiled. 'Attempted murder as a feminist issue? Fair enough. Anyway, check their movements last night, and the other nights this week, when Jaki Johnston saw someone in the garden.'

'I can tell you what they'll say,' MacNee put in. 'At home. Watching TV. Both of them. All evening. Every evening.'

Macdonald promised to mug up on the programmes so he could put them on the spot, then Fleming got up. 'I'd better go and see the Super. Tam, enjoy your reading. And

Tansy, if Tam asks you just to tell him what it's all about, the answer's no.'

'*Ta belka krzywo leży*. It's not sitting straight,' Stefan Pavany said.

Kasper Franzik, coming down the ladder from the roof of the Hodges' new building, glared at the foreman. He'd been in the black mood for days, days when the world went dark and a sideways glance from a passer-by was enough to fill him with dangerous rage. Direct confrontation took him to a murderous pitch.

He came down the ladder with aggravating slowness, then, ignoring Pavany, turned his back and surveyed his work.

'See – there.' Pavany pointed to the final beam; it was slightly, but visibly, out of true.

It was nearing the end of the day; Franzik knew his mind had not been on the work in hand and he had done a shoddy job. But he shrugged and said stubbornly, 'So? Put on the tiles and who will see?'

'You put it right. Bad workmanship is no good to me.'

Franzik exploded in a volley of obscenities. The other man stood unmoved until he finished with, 'OK, you don't like my work – you sack me!'

Then Pavany smiled. 'I sack you,' he said softly, 'then you forfeit your pay. You're docked two days anyway and you owe rent for this week. You don't pay it, I keep your passport and I lock the door. And where do you sleep tonight? Last time, you had to come crawling back.'

Franzik squared up to him, locking eyes. Behind them, the others stopped work, watching the confrontation warily but making no move to intervene.

Pavany, with that flicker of amused contempt around his mouth, didn't move. Franzik wanted to smash the smile through the back of his head, but tormenting thoughts raged in his mind: he had no money and nowhere to go – Karolina had bluntly refused to help. The sun had gone in now and he could feel already the chill that would deepen as darkness came.

For a long, pointless moment he held the stare, then abruptly turned and went up the ladder, seething with helpless rage. If Pavany laughed, he would drop the mallet on his head.

Pavany did not laugh, or speak, even, just went back to the door frame he had been working on. The others, too, resumed their tasks. Kasper's run-ins with Stefan were just another fact of life.

'Hey, guys, you've really got a move on while I was away!' Diane Hodge hailed them cheerfully as she got out of her Mini Cooper S. 'Roof finished next week, eh, Stefan?'

Pavany glanced over his shoulder and nodded, but if he said anything, it was drowned out by the noise of hammering from the roof.

'You're getting all your aggressions out there, anyway, Kasper!' Diane called up gaily, but getting no response from anyone, said lamely, 'Well – that's fine! Terrific! Hang in there,' and went back to the car. She felt put out: it was all very well doing the mean, moody and magnificent act, but Stefan could at least show he appreciated her taking an interest.

She took her overnight case and several glossy carrier bags out of the car and carried them across the gravel. Gavin's car was there, and if he was in he must have heard her arriving, but he didn't appear to greet her. Not that she'd expected it – the best she could hope for was that he'd had time to get over their quarrel, which had been the main purpose of her bolt up to Glasgow. He was downright nasty to live with when he was in one of his moods, and she would only have got drawn in and found herself saying things that made the situation worse. Thank God, they were off on a cruise in a couple of weeks, with people to talk to and things to do instead of hanging around here with too much time on their hands. Once the house was finished she didn't know what they'd do.

It was different when Russ was living at home, demanding attention and filling the house with his noisy friends – and, as always, she had a pang of sadness for her only son, so far away now and almost lost to them, she felt. But it was best for him, she knew that, best by a long way, and they were planning a trip to see him soon. But she missed her bad boy, and her mouth was drooping as she went into the house.

'Hello!' Diane called. Her voice echoed in the great empty space of the hall, but there was no reply. She set down her burdens and went anyway to look in the conservatory where Gavin usually sat, if he wasn't watching the huge plasma screen in the TV room.

She found him there, just sitting staring straight ahead of him, not looking at a magazine or playing games on his BlackBerry. He looked odd, somehow.

'Hi, Gavin – I'm home,' she said, a little uncertainly.

He turned his head. 'Evidently. Had a wild time?' His words dripped sarcasm.

Oh God, she'd hoped he'd let it go by now – perhaps she should have stayed away longer. She decided to respond to the words not the tone. 'Oh well, bit of shopping, lots of chat. You know how it is.'

'Fortunately, I don't. I'm happy to say I've been spared shopping trips with two gabbling women.'

She wasn't taking this. Hands on her hips, Diane said, 'Gavin, what the hell is wrong? I won't be spoken to like that! I've just about had enough. OK?'

It was as if he had deliberately provoked a combative response to give legitimacy to his own anger. '*You*'ve had enough! Would you care to hear what I've been through today?'

Something in his voice – it couldn't, surely, be fear? – stopped her replying in kind. 'Tell me what's happened, then,' she said, and sat down. There was a cold feeling in the pit of her stomach and her legs seemed weak.

'Your little friend, the wonderful, brilliant Marcus Lindsay, almost got himself bumped off last night. And because you were away, and I was on my own here, somehow I'm a suspect.'

Diane looked at his face, red with temper, and his furiously glaring eyes, and the question almost slipped out, 'And did you do it?' Instead, she said irritably, 'So somehow it's my fault? But Marcus – what happened? Is he all right?'

Gavin gave a short laugh. 'Oh, the devil looks after his own! But someone told the police we didn't get on, and they actually took me in to the police station. Can you believe it? And I can tell you, the tone they took wasn't what you'd expect towards someone paying the sort of taxes I do. I walked out, in the end. It was quite ridiculous.'

'If they let you walk out, they'd probably got all they wanted,' she said shrewdly. 'Tell me about Marcus, though.'

'I might have known you'd be more concerned about him than about your own husband. Someone took a knife to him, but apparently he's back home and recovering.'

'Thank God for that! But who would do it – what for?'

'For being a total prick, probably, and I wouldn't blame them. But now the police are going back to that Ailsa Grant business too.'

'Ailsa Grant?' Diane said blankly. 'Goodness, I haven't thought about the girl for years! What on earth is that about? Her father killed her for getting herself pregnant – they just couldn't prove it, that's all. Everyone knew that.'

'Everyone except the police, apparently.' Gavin got up restlessly and went over to stare out at the garden. 'I told them we hardly knew her, and we'd no contact with her after she went to Glasgow. It seemed the simplest thing. We don't want to get drawn in.'

'But Gavin—' she protested.

He swung round. 'No buts,' he said savagely. 'And they're coming to talk to you too, so we have to say the same thing.'

'I'm a rotten liar,' she protested. 'Always have been. I go red and look shifty. It's really stupid to lie to the police. I can't think why you did – you'll just have to say they confused you, you didn't understand what they meant.'

'No,' he said. 'Oh no. You listen to me – I've said that, and that's what you're going to say as well. You'd better. I mean it.'

Diane had been prepared for temper. She was used to that, but she wasn't used to her blustering husband speaking to her in a quiet, cold, menacing voice. She found she was actually afraid.

'I'll – I'll do my best,' she said, feeling sick.

'Ah, Marjory!'

Bailey sounded nervous as he half-rose to greet her, and as he sat down he leaned back, away from her – a classic indication that he would rather be elsewhere.

'How are the investigations going?' he asked, and she told him what little they had established.

'The press secretary tells me interest has faded since they heard Lindsay was making a speedy recovery, so that's good.

If they don't hear any fanciful theories about the Ailsa Grant case, they should lose interest completely.' Bailey looked pointedly at Fleming.

'Indeed. We're checking that as discreetly as possible,' she said, knowing it wasn't quite what he wanted to hear. Then, since she had to put the question sometime, she asked with a sense of foreboding, 'How did you get on with Ms Milne?'

'Oh, impossible creature!' he sputtered. 'You won't believe it, Marjory – she tried to turn it into a discussion of our investigation methods! Wants to go through it with me – and she's not very keen on you, I can tell you that!'

'That's not exactly a surprise.' Fleming's worst fears were realized; he had clearly got nowhere and she blamed herself now for sending him. 'What did she say about Lindsay, Donald?'

He was fidgeting nervously with his fingers. 'Oh, she really wasn't helpful. Claimed she hardly knew him and she hadn't mentioned the connection because she didn't like people who tried to claim friendship with celebrities when none existed.'

'Did she, indeed,' Fleming said grimly. 'So how come they were having a joking conversation in which the complaint about police harassment was made?'

'She was a bit vague, actually. I pinned her down, because I couldn't see how he could have got her number. Then she claimed she'd just remembered that it was she who phoned him.'

'Why, if she hardly knew him?'

Bailey looked awkward. 'It – it wasn't clear. Just saying hello, was the impression I got.'

'But—' Fleming bit her tongue. Labouring the point that he'd been there specifically to oblige her to be clear was futile: obviously Bailey had blown it.

'I did ask if she had an alibi for last night.' Bailey presented this as an achievement. 'And she was at home all evening, alone.'

'I'm not really at the stage of thinking she slipped down to Tulach and tried to take him out,' Fleming said, trying to keep the edge of annoyance out of her voice, 'but it's a loose end that it would have been nice to tie off.'

'I know, I know. And we simply haven't the resources to thrash out all the finer points of this, you know. She made it clear that since Lindsay only has minor injuries, we can't waste too much police time on it.'

Did she, indeed! Fleming was startled, but Bailey was going on, 'You simply have no idea how difficult the woman is to deal with. In her position she ought to realize how important it is to treat a police enquiry with suitable respect.'

Bailey sounded petulant now, but Fleming didn't feel inclined to spend time indulging him. 'She's difficult, certainly,' was the most she was prepared to concede, then made an excuse to leave.

She was angry with herself, more than with him. It had seemed diplomatic to send the senior officer but now there was no way she could go to Milne herself and put on the pressure Bailey had so clearly failed to apply, unless she had further evidence. And the Fiscal's attempt at calling off the dogs, while suspicious, certainly wasn't enough to justify that, especially since Fleming had to admit that what Milne had said was perfectly true.

When they got hold of Lindsay, of course, she could bring the subject up, but why, instead of sending Bailey into the lion's den to be chewed up and spat out, hadn't she just said to hell with diplomacy and gone along herself with Tam MacNee to put the woman through the mangle? She knew the uncomfortable answer to that one, though. She had cravenly ducked it to protect herself, and now she was reaping the coward's reward.

'What's wrong with you tonight?' Rafael Cisek said to his wife. 'You've been up and down every five minutes.'

Karolina's round face was very solemn. 'Rafael, I am worried. Whatever you say, I think I have to tell Marjory.'

He didn't ask, 'Tell her what?' He frowned. 'Why? Why should you do this?'

'I thought, today, that it was the man they were all talking about, the man from the pub, who had tried to kill Marcus Lindsay. But it is not him. It is someone else, and they don't know who. So I think I should tell Marjory.'

'You don't know anything,' Rafael argued. 'You have an idea – but everyone has ideas. You could do so much harm with your "ideas". To tell this to the police—'

'To Marjory!' Karolina insisted. 'She would know if this is important. And she is a good person – she would not be unfair.'

'The police are the police, wherever you are. And we are foreigners in this country, Karolina. Do not do this! I tell you, it would be wicked – wrong.'

Karolina frowned. 'Wicked? Do you think so?'

He was swift to seize his advantage. 'Wicked,' he insisted. Everyone deserves another chance.'

'Well—' She weakened. 'You are a good man to say this, because you don't even like him. And because you are a good man, you don't recognize a bad one. But I will wait a little. See what happens.'

16

'Why the hell did we need such an early start?' DC Kerr grumbled as DS Macdonald signalled the turn off the main A75 towards the Mull of Galloway. 'I'm shattered.'

'Your problem is you think you can go to bed at three and still function,' Macdonald said. 'You're not twenty any more.'

'Nor are you,' Kerr snapped.

'No, I'm in my thirties and I've got a job to do.'

'Pompous prat!'

There was a silence, then Kerr muttered, 'Sorry. I can't function without coffee, and I hadn't time. Can we stop somewhere?'

Macdonald glanced at his watch. 'Eight o'clock – won't be anything open. You'll just have to suffer.'

'A shop, then. Bar of chocolate – something.'

'We'll get something later, on the way back.'

Suddenly suspicious, Kerr eyed him. 'What's the rush? There's something else you want to do, isn't there?'

'Might be. Tansy, when you read the case files and notes yesterday, did anything strike you?'

'Plenty of things.' Kerr was automatically defensive. 'But if you mean, can I guess your weird thought processes – no, not being psychic.'

With considerable forbearance, Macdonald said mildly, 'Dearie me! You do have a nasty temper first thing in the morning, don't you?'

'Not when I've had my coffee. If I had a nice nine-to-five job I'd be sweetness and light.' She gave him a darkling look.

'Anyway,' he went on doggedly, 'I noticed the lighthouse people weren't properly questioned, just asked if they'd seen anything that night, which they hadn't. But they were near neighbours, might have known the background.'

'I recognized one of the names – she's a pal of my auntie's, married to one of the keepers, but she's a widow now and I got her address. She's living in Drummore, down near the Mull there, so I got my auntie to phone her and she's happy to have a wee chat with us.'

'Will she give us coffee?'

'God, you never let up, do you? Actually, I'd put money on it. And probably home bakes as well. All my auntie's chums are into cut-throat competitive tea parties.'

'Maybe we could go there first, then?' Kerr suggested hopefully. 'It certainly doesn't sound as if we'll be offered so much as a drink of water at the Grants'.'

'No, we can't. Deprivation will give you a ferocious edge. Hell hath no fury like Tansy without her caffeine fix.'

Kerr glowered at him but didn't reply, sinking down in her seat and pulling the hood of her grey sweatshirt over her head. 'I'm asleep,' she announced.

'Don't feel bad about leaving me without conversation, will you? With Ewan in the car, I'm used to it.'

Kerr only grunted. Macdonald left her to doze, rather enjoying the peace and the quiet coast road. The tide was out, and on the wave-rippled sand a flock of oyster-catchers strutted on their pink, stilt-like legs, while they probed the beach with long red-orange bills. Every so often one would startle and rise and the others would follow with their wild 'weep-weep' cries, to swirl around and then come back to settle again. It was a soft, greyish morning with a pale sun struggling through, but it looked uncertain weather. April showers, no doubt.

As they rumbled over a cattle-grid, Kerr woke up. She yawned, stretched, and shook her head to clear it. 'That was probably a mistake,' she said thickly. What I need is—'

'No, don't tell me. Let me guess. Coffee.'

'Cold water to splash my face,' she said with dignity. 'And a toothbrush. My mouth feels—'

'I'd really rather not go there. Look, that's the farm. Up there on the right.'

Kerr looked about her and shuddered. 'God, this is bleak! Nothing but the lighthouse on the point, and then the farm. And the house gives me the creeps anyway with that black stone – it looks like it's scowling.'

'So does its owner. We've been spotted.' Macdonald drove into the farmyard and a tall, raw-boned woman marched towards them, reaching them before the car had stopped moving.

'What do you want?' she demanded as Macdonald opened his window.

Kerr leaned across. 'Mrs Grant? We're police officers. Could we have a word?'

'Can I stop you?' Jean Grant asked bitterly. 'Come in if you must.'

She led them to the front door, through the small fenced-off garden. Kerr, last through the gate, turned to latch it and caught sight of a furtive movement. A man had come out of the house, and was heading towards a clapped-out Vauxhall.

'Mr Grant!' she called, and saw him jump and look round. Behind her, Jean Grant snarled, 'I said "this way". You'd better come right now.'

Kerr ignored her, going to meet the man now hovering uncertainly, looking towards them, then to the car, and back again.

'Trying to avoid us, Mr Grant?' She took malicious pleasure in his confusion.

'No – er, I just – er—' he stuttered. He was a big man, slightly shambling, with bright red hair. He looked helpless and bewildered.

'We need to ask you a few questions,' Kerr said.

'Oh, right. Fine.'

He followed her to where Jean stood on the doorstep, fuming. Macdonald waited impassively.

'My son doesn't have time to waste,' Jean snapped. 'I can answer your questions, pointless as they are.'

Kerr was in no mood to be pushed around. 'Since our time is valuable as well as your son's, perhaps we could just get on with it?'

Tight-lipped, Jean opened the front door and stalked in. Ushering Grant in in front of him, Macdonald turned to wink at Kerr. 'I take it I'm the good cop today, then?' he murmured as they went inside.

Fleming was engaged in speed-reading a government report before going to see Lindsay when a tentative tap on the door announced a timid-looking Force Civilian Assistant.

'Sorry, ma'am, I didn't want to interrupt you but they said to tell you at once.'

Fleming smiled at the young woman. 'That's all right. Take a seat.'

The FCA looked at the chair indicated as if it might have jaws that would snap shut round her if she sat down. 'Oh, no thank you, ma'am. It was just a message came from the path lab in Glasgow. They've found the specimens you wanted. Tissues from the body and the –' she gulped, 'foetus.'

'No!' It had seemed such a long shot. Fleming hadn't been sure the unimpressive pathologist would even have taken samples, and even less sure that, if any existed, they would have survived the local lab being shut down. 'That's excellent. Can you instruct them to DNA-test the foetus? Not the body as yet, but the other ASAP. Thanks.'

When the girl had gone, Fleming sat back, tapping one fingernail on her front teeth. Hard evidence at last! If Lindsay let them take DNA samples it could lay to rest any suspicion of his involvement, and finally get Mrs Grant off their backs. Hodge was definitely in the frame but she couldn't see him submitting to testing without a warrant and she couldn't see much chance of getting one. And, of course, there was nothing to say that some man in Glasgow, as yet unknown, hadn't been the father of the child. Still, given the extensive DNA data base, there was even the wild card chance that the sample might match someone on file for a totally irrelevant offence.

Today, too, the footprints expert would be at Tulach. He might produce hard evidence as well, and they could make much-needed progress. They still hadn't come up with anything definite on the motive for the assault, and anything motiveless raised the spectre of murderous attacks on other upright citizens.

She brought her fist down on the desk in frustration. They needed this one wrapped up, now. Then she could devote herself to the murder investigation, where the events of the past had started to cast long, intriguing shadows.

In the cold, bare front room, Jean Grant seated herself on a small sofa with wooden arms, indicating that her son should join her. He squeezed uncomfortably into the space left him.

What a cheerless place, Macdonald thought: a bare minimum of furniture, dried vegetation in an orange vase, no pictures or photographs. It reflected the personality of its owner, as rooms tend to do.

He had suggested separate interviews, but got a flat refusal from both.

'If your time's so *valuable*,' Jean lingered sarcastically on the word, 'this'll be quicker. And if it's about the attack at Tulach the night before last, we were here together all evening.'

'You heard about that, did you? What was your reaction, Mr Grant?'

His mother answered. 'Oh, ask away. But you'll not get an answer from either one of us.'

'Mr Grant?' Macdonald said again, fixing his brown eyes steadily on the man's bent head, and after a moment Stuart looked up.

'Got what was coming to him, probably. But it's nothing to do with me.'

Jean's hand gripped her son's arm, and Macdonald thought she was digging in her nails.

'It couldn't be. We told you – we were here all evening, weren't we, Stuart?'

'That's right,' Stuart mumbled.

'And what were you doing?' Macdonald asked. Kerr was taking notes.

'Had our supper. Then washed up – ooh, now I don't want to mislead you. I washed and he dried. Then we watched TV until we went to bed.'

'At?'

'Ten o'clock. That's when we always go.'

'So what did you watch on TV?' Macdonald asked with some eagerness, reckoning he could go on *Mastermind* with last night's TV schedules as his specialist subject.

'A video. *He* likes them. Load of rubbish, but it let me get on with my knitting.'

'What was it?' Macdonald was crestfallen. Easy to choose a film you'd seen before, possibly several times.

'*Terminator 2*,' Stuart offered sullenly. 'I like watching it.'

Kerr chipped in. 'So you were here together all evening, just like you were when Ailsa was killed? Only then you weren't really, were you? Mr Grant, you said in an interview that you were out half the evening, doing emergency repairs round the farm.'

Stuart's pale skin crimsoned. He looked apprehensively towards his mother. She didn't look at him.

'The man's a fool!' she snarled. 'He was out the house for ten minutes, maybe. He's forgotten – he gets mixed up about things sometimes. Don't you, Stuart?'

Again, Macdonald saw the grip tighten on his arm.

'Yes, maybe,' Stuart muttered. 'It was a long time ago.'

'There you are!' Jean's voice was triumphant. 'Right – got what you came for?'

'Not quite,' Kerr said coolly. 'We'd like to know what you were doing on the other nights this week. Starting with Sunday.'

Stuart seemed suddenly to find his knees of compelling interest, but Jean stared straight at her questioner, hard-eyed. 'Just the same as last night. It's what we always do.'

It was another chance for Macdonald to show off his knowledge and he brightened. 'What did you watch?'

'If you think anyone can remember what they watched days ago, with the rubbish they put out, you're daft. We usually see the news. *Emmerdale*, maybe. And *he* likes *EastEnders*. I do my knitting every night. Oh no – I tell a lie.' She waited for their interest, then went on, 'One night I did my ironing. I hope you're satisfied with that, for it's all you're getting.'

'Mr Grant?' Kerr persisted.

He did look up, but his expression was as stony as his mother's. 'It's like she said,' was the only response.

Goaded, Kerr said with deceptive sweetness, 'You see, one of the things we're anxious to do is establish whether there's any link between what happened to Marcus Lindsay and Ailsa's death. You made allegations at the time, Mrs Grant, and you were very resentful that they didn't produce the result you wanted. Even though you've been told that Mr Lindsay can prove he was in the US at the time.'

There was an electric silence. Stuart almost looked as if he had stopped breathing, and Jean gave a gasp, swiftly covered with a cough.

'How dare you!' she said shrilly. 'I've told you, we were here together all last night. That's all I need to say. And maybe it's time you let my daughter rest in peace.'

Further questions met only silence, and Macdonald and Kerr had to give up. As they drove away Kerr said acidly, 'Oh, I *am* glad we came. Tam told us yesterday what they'd say, and we could have saved ourselves a long, boring journey.'

Macdonald, in some exasperation, said, 'I don't know what's wrong with you, Tansy. Their reactions told us a lot.'

'Oh, I suppose so.' It was a grudging admission. 'Now, where's this lady who's going to make with the home-made goodies and coffee? I tell you, there'll be bloodshed if you've got that wrong.'

'How do you thank someone who's saved your life?'

Marcus Lindsay came across the library to hug Jaki Johnston, as best he could with his arm in a sling. Mrs Boyter, having shown her in, hovered with a sentimental smile and then withdrew.

'I'm not sure I did, actually, as it turned out.' Jaki gave a shaky laugh.

He held her away from him, looking at her upturned face with growing concern. 'Hey, hey! What's happened here? Are you all right?'

He led her to the chesterfield in front of the fire and sat down beside her.

'I should be asking you that,' Jaki said. 'But you're looking pretty good, apart from the sling and the plaster on your head. Does it hurt?'

'Like they say, only when I laugh. The stitches are pulling a bit but all I've needed today is paracetamol. But you – to be brutally honest, you're looking terrible. I'm worried about you. And you're shivering – I'll poke up the fire.'

Marcus went over to the fireplace, picking up a steel poker to coax the fire into a clearer blaze, then sat down again, chafing Jaki's hands.

'I – I just seem to be permanently cold,' she said pathetically. 'It's shock, apparently. Tony took me to the doctor yesterday and he gave me sleeping pills. I hate taking them, though – I feel all woozy today.'

'Will you be fit for your scenes this afternoon? I can tell them you're just not up to it.'

'Oh, the show must go on!' Jaki made an attempt at jauntiness. 'Provided Make-up can put on enough slap to cover up – and they're ace at that. But at least it's the weekend. Can't wait to get back to Mum.'

'Ah,' Marcus said. 'You haven't spoken to Barrie, then?'

Jaki's eyes, huge in her pinched face, filled. 'Oh, Marcus – no!'

' 'Fraid so. The word has come down from on high. They're paying weekend overtime to get finished up. But if you're not fit for it . . .'

Tears had welled up and were spilling down her cheeks. 'How can I say that, when you and Sylvia aren't falling apart? She's old and frail and was just as shocked as I was, and you're the one who's been injured—'

'I have the advantage that I can't remember a damn thing about it. Worse for you – you'll be reliving it, with flashbacks.'

She gave a shudder as he found a handkerchief and dabbed at her cheeks, then said, 'Now, a good blow!'

Jaki obliged, with a watery smile. Then, visibly trying to pull herself together, she said, 'Sorry. I'm fine, honestly – disappointed not to be getting home, that's all. But Marcus, can't you really remember anything?'

'I remember the doorbell ringing, and that when I opened the door there was no one there. Then I woke up in hospital. Sylvia and I talked for ages, trying to trigger my memory, but it didn't work. It's a complete bugger.'

'But why ever did you go out? I'd have reckoned it was Kevin Docherty and slammed the door.'

'I suppose that is the obvious question,' Marcus said slowly, as if he hadn't thought of it. 'I – I haven't a clue. It was mad, when you think about it. But I'd assumed it was Barrie or some of the lads, so I suppose I thought they were mucking about. That's the best I can come up with, anyway.'

'Shouldn't you move to a hotel, or something?' Jaki urged. 'He might come back – I'm scared here, even in daylight.'

He squeezed her hand. 'Don't be, sweetie. It's silly. Someone came and put in extra security this morning and I won't step over the threshold without half-a-dozen of the more solid members of the crew round me until I get back to Glasgow. Anyway, the place is alive with coppers. It's bound to have scared him off.'

'But Marcus, who could possibly have wanted to kill you?'

'Don't think I haven't asked myself that. Who have I offended, who have I upset?' His blue eyes looked troubled, but he went on lightly, 'Now, if I really had Playfair's skills, we could get this solved in the next hour. Any suggestions, sergeant?'

She was too concerned to play along. 'I've been trying to think if there was anything else I can remember—'

'Don't, darling. You're only going to get more upset. It's probably some nutter whose wife fancies Playfair, and he's jealous. He won't know where I live in Glasgow.'

He was obviously trying to cheer her up, and she couldn't tell how worried he actually was – he was an actor, after all. She said earnestly, 'You're so brave. If it was me I'd be going into hiding and asking for police protection.'

'I don't think you'd get it – not for this. Anyway . . .' He was suddenly serious too, and his eyes went to the portrait sketch of the man in a pilot's jacket and white silk scarf, hanging over the fireplace. He said softly, 'I'm Laddie Lazansky's son. He flew dozens of Spitfire missions, dodging flak, hunted by enemy planes every night, his life or theirs. He did what he had to do, without whimpering that he was scared. I've got to show at least a little of that sort of courage.'

Then he laughed and said lightly, 'Though it could be, of course, that I'm not panicking because I don't understand the situation.'

Heather Fairlie opened the door of her neat semi, beaming at Macdonald and Kerr. She was a plump little woman in her sixties, with iron-grey curls, and her brown eyes had smile crinkles at the corners.

To Kerr's joy, she could smell baking. Their hostess chattered away, asking about Macdonald's auntie, then left them in a sitting room looking on to a lawn that seemed to have been mown with an electric razor, surrounded by spring flowers in weedless beds.

'Nibble, don't scoff,' Macdonald adjured Kerr, sotto voce, as Heather returned bearing coffee and cheese scones. When they were served, she sat down with pleasurable anticipation.

'I hear you're taking another look at what happened to poor Ailsa. My John always felt an interest, you know, with him being the first to spot her lying there in the sea. What can I tell you?'

Heather liked to talk. She had seen the helicopter bring Ailsa in, standing with the other two keepers' wives and the three men, a silent onlooker as the Grants identified the body and took it away. She had an admirably clear memory: the injuries to Ailsa's face which she unflinchingly described tallied exactly with the file photographs.

'I'm going to take notes if you don't mind, Mrs Fairlie. Nothing formal, just to keep me straight,' Kerr said.

'Oh, call me Heather, dear. And write down anything you like. I'd be happy if I thought some good would come of it.'

Macdonald asked about the night of Ailsa's death, but she had nothing to add to the original statement.

'Terrible night, that! Wind howling, the sea roaring away – oh, we did get some gales down there on the Mull! Once John went on duty, about seven, probably, I just fastened the shutters and found a nice cheery programme on the telly. Now, what was it again? I can't exactly mind what it was.' This lapse of memory clearly annoyed her; she was frowning, trying to recollect.

Kerr said hastily, 'Don't worry, Heather. It doesn't matter. Could you tell us anything about how things were at Balnakenny beforehand?'

Heather brightened. 'Now, that I can do. The Grants came to the farm just before Ailsa was born. We were all glad of a young couple moving in – I'd bairns myself at the time. Jean Grant was quite like Ailsa when she was young, though you'd never think it now – bright, with ideas about everything. But him – well, I don't think I ever got a word out of him.

'They'd Stuart later, of course – a chip off the old block, him – nothing to say for himself. Funny, quiet wee fellow, never joining in with our lot at the lighthouse – half-a-dozen of them, a right load of tykes,' her voice was fond, 'but they'd a great time with all the freedom here. Robert was a hard man, stood no nonsense, getting Stuart labouring on the farm from the time he was able for the work, poor wee soul. I always thought it couldn't be good for him.'

Kerr, thinking back to the monosyllabic, awkward man they had seen, had to agree. 'What about Ailsa, though?' she prompted. 'Did she join in?'

'Oh, she was one of the gang, right enough. They weren't over fond of her – too much like her father, if you ask me, with quite a temper and determined to get her own way. But my Kirstie was ages with her and they were pals, sort of.

'Ailsa turned out bonny, though, and a clever girl too, but she'd always kind of an impudent way with her and she wasn't feart of anyone – and headstrong! Oh, there were some fine rows at Balnakenny – Kirstie would tell me about them.

'When she got older, we didn't see much of her. She'd be off to Drummore or Sandhead, got to know a fancier crowd.'

'Marcus Lindsay?' Macdonald suggested. 'Lazansky, he was then.'

'Oh, we only heard about that after, with Jean raving about him killing Ailsa. But I'll tell you this.'

She leaned forward confidentially. 'We'd heard Ailsa had come home in the family way, and that Jean and Robert were going their length. Folks heard shouting going on up at the house, him and her both, on at the girl – though Ailsa would be giving as good as she got, mind.

'Just the week before she died, I saw her down here. It was a good drying day, and I was hanging out the washing on the green outby, and she was by herself, taking a walk – needing to get out the house, I don't doubt. I don't know when the baby was due, but she was definitely showing.

'I was sorry for the poor lass, and I called to her, asked if she'd like a cuppa. She seemed pleased to be asked – probably the first time anyone had said a civil word to her in days.

'She asked about Kirstie, and I'd to tell her she was married with a wee one just a year old. I mind she pulled a face and said, "She was smart enough to do it in the right order." '

Kerr interrupted. 'Do you think she meant she would be getting married later on?'

'Definitely sounded like that to me. I asked if she'd any plans, but she just laughed and said, "Oh yes, I've plans, but I can't talk about them yet. Wait and see!" '

'Did she sound happy about it?'

Heather paused, considering. 'More sort of high, I think you'd say – nervous maybe. I asked her, did her parents know, and her face went all white and angry. "No. I tell them nothing. They hate me, I think." Those were her exact words – I could never forget how she spoke.

'I said, "Och no, they'll just be anxious" – you know the kind of thing you say, but to be honest I believed her. I asked if she'd be staying after the wean was born, but she said, "You're joking! I've no choice for now, but it would be my idea of hell on earth." Then she changed the subject.

'And when I heard Robert Grant had killed her, I wasn't even surprised. Should have been locked up, that man, and none of us would speak to him, or her, after. I'd be happy to see justice done, even now when he's beyond the law.' Her cheerful face was stern.

Macdonald said gently, 'Heather, there was no proof then and there still isn't. The new investigation's to try and sort out what really happened.'

'If you ask me,' she said fiercely, 'Robert lashed out at her in one of his rages, then had to get rid of the body. And the man who was to marry her – that Marcus Lindsay, maybe – kept quiet, not to get involved. And Jean's accusations – well, with Stuart still so young, who'd run the farm if Robert got the jail?'

'It sounds as if you don't think she cared much otherwise,' Kerr suggested.

Heather pursed her lips. 'You never know what goes on behind closed doors, but Jean got harder over the years, cut herself off from everyone, took no interest in the way she looked, with no make-up and her hair just dragged back.

'The lighthouse was decommissioned a few years after and I've never seen her since. But she wasn't a happy woman then, and I doubt she's any happier now.'

There was little more Heather could tell them. As the officers drove away, replete with scones and information, Macdonald said thoughtfully, 'You know something? She's the only one who wants justice for poor Ailsa. Her mother and her brother are doing their best to block us – why are they doing that?'

'Good question,' Kerr acknowledged. 'But how high do you rate the chances of getting an answer?'

17

DS MacNee looked with disfavour at Marcus Lindsay, sitting in a leather wing chair by the study fire. With his sling and the head wound he looked as though he was playing someone in a war movie – suffering but too brave to show it, stiff upper lip, chaps, and all that. Though perhaps MacNee had only thought of that because of the portrait of his father the War Hero above the fireplace.

That got up MacNee's nose too – all glamour and slick hair. You didn't get sketches like that of the poor bloody infantry, did you? It was all about toffs showing off. And there were too many photos of the bugger as well, all round the house. It felt as if he was looking at you, and didn't think much of what he saw.

MacNee was disgruntled anyway because Lindsay could tell them so little. Hardly his fault, maybe, but MacNee couldn't help feeling if he'd not been such a wimp he'd have managed to remember somehow. His own experience of a much worse head injury hadn't made him blank it out, had it? Indeed, all too often he still – but he'd decided he wasn't going to let himself think about that.

Fleming was leading the questioning, asking why Lindsay hadn't gone back inside when he found there was no one at the door – how daft did you have to be to wander into the darkness when there was a man around with a chib and a grudge against you? 'Just thought it was the guys taking

the mick, probably'? What did Lindsay keep in his head for
brains?

Fleming was asking Lindsay now about the man in the
shrubbery, which did seem to twitch the upper lip. He was
startled.

'Jaki saw someone watching the house? Why, for heaven's
sake, didn't she tell me?'

'She thought it was nothing more than a bush and a lively
imagination, and seeing it in the same place next night
confirmed it,' Fleming explained. 'It was only after the attack,
when the "bush" wasn't there, that she realized.'

'The house was being watched? Someone planning
a break-in? It did occur to me that it might have been a
housebreaker, though ringing the bell seems a curious
method to choose.'

'Unlikely, I agree. You may have seen the footprints expert
here today?'

Lindsay nodded. 'Yes. He was telling me about his findings.
Interesting guy.'

'We're hoping he'll be able to produce something useful to
follow up. But can you think of anyone, anyone at all, who
has a problem with you – a quarrel, a grievance, resentment
maybe – just to give us a starting point?'

He sighed. 'I'd like to think I have no enemies, though I
suppose it would be naïve to think everyone likes me,' he
said with a smile MacNee considered smarmy, but it got an
answering smile from Fleming.

'Even police inspectors have been known to have delusions
like that, sir,' she said.

If she was going to start being winsome, MacNee would
definitely throw up. 'Delusion's right,' he said. 'So, if we cut
out fantasy, what're we left with? Mrs Grant's top of the list
– you know that.'

He got a look of annoyance from his boss, but if Big Marge didn't want him butting in, she should stop playing mental footsie and get on with the job.

'Jean Grant,' Lindsay said slowly. 'You think it could have been a woman?'

'Do *you* think it could've been a woman? You were there, I wasn't.'

'Unfortunately, sergeant, I might as well not have been. Can't help you, I'm afraid.'

Back to square one. MacNee subsided, and Fleming took over. 'On a different tack completely, could I ask about your relationship with Sheila Milne?'

MacNee gaped. Where the hell was Big Marge coming from on this one?

Lindsay gaped too. 'You're not suggesting she's somehow involved in this?'

'Of course not,' Fleming said smoothly. 'A different matter completely.'

'Er – well, we knew each other in Glasgow.'

MacNee noted Lindsay's discomfort with considerable interest. A casual friendship, eh? He wasn't acting casual now.

'I can't remember where we first met – at a party, probably. I was appearing at the Citizens' Theatre, and she was one of the Friends. Very supportive – came to all the social events for the stage-door johnnies and jennies.'

MacNee had a happy vision of the Procurator Fiscal staking out the stage door in her fake fur coat, holding out – what would you use to attract a male star? Hardly a bunch of flowers – bottle of single malt, perhaps.

Fleming was pressuring Lindsay. 'So you saw her quite regularly?'

'Oh well, you know . . .'

'And you've kept in touch?'

'No, no! Hadn't spoken to her for years. Not since I started *Playfair*, anyway.'

'Did you have a relationship with her?'

'Look, I can't see what this is about. So we knew each other – she knew a lot of people at the theatre. Why are you asking this?'

MacNee wanted to hear the answer to this too, but Fleming said only, 'Tying up some loose ends, that's all.

'Now, something else totally unrelated. Would you object to giving us a sample of your DNA?'

This, at least, MacNee knew about – Fleming had told him on the way here – but it certainly threw Lindsay.

'My DNA? May I ask why?'

'To eliminate you completely from the Ailsa Grant enquiry, since we're now in a position to establish the father of her child. The sample would be destroyed immediately afterwards, of course.'

MacNee thought he caught a flicker pass over his face, but Lindsay said quite steadily, 'A DNA test? It seems unnecessary, I have to say. I think I've already done all I need to do to prove I had nothing to do with it. Unless there's a more compelling reason for wanting it, this appears to me an unreasonable request.'

'You're entitled to refuse, of course.' Fleming looked disappointed. 'But I'm sorry you feel like that.'

Lindsay put a hand up to rub his temple. 'Is this going to take much longer? I'm beginning to feel very tired.'

To be fair, the guy didn't look great. It was surprising that Fleming had pushed him quite so hard.

But she immediately said, 'Of course,' and got up. As she and MacNee reached the door, she turned. 'Just one thing more, if you can bear it.'

Uh-oh! That old tactic! MacNee waited, with real interest, for what was coming next.

'You'd a phone call from someone asking you to lie to the police. Who was that?'

Lindsay jerked round, winced, and swore. 'Where the hell did that come from?' Then he gave a short laugh. 'Oh, of course! Jaki. It was a joking conversation, that's all, and as Jaki no doubt also told you, I said I wouldn't.'

Fleming went very still, like a cat who has suddenly seen a mouse poke its nose out of its hole. 'A joking conversation,' she said slowly. 'Oddly enough, that was just how you described your conversation with Sheila Milne. Mr Lindsay, did Ms Milne ask you to lie to the police?'

He was visibly shaken. 'No, of course not,' he tried to say, but stumbled on the words.

'I think that's exactly what you're doing now. And I wonder why? Could it have anything to do with some sort of favour she did you – to do with some charge against you? My guess would be for speeding.'

He was ashen now, but she went on mercilessly, 'Because you see, Mr Lindsay, I can order checks to be made. But a confession's always better.'

'I – I can't . . .' Lindsay stammered.

'My, you're a gallus fellow!' MacNee said in mock admiration. 'Brave enough to risk a charge of delaying the ends of justice! You can get the jail for that.'

'Can I remind you again – it will be on record.' Fleming piled on the pressure.

MacNee whipped out his notebook expectantly as Lindsay groaned.

'Oh, God! Very well then. I'd nine points on my licence, and I got zapped again. I mentioned it to her – hoping, I suppose, for advice – and she promised she'd try and find some reason to drop it.' He put his head in his hands.

'Better out than in,' MacNee said cheerily.

'Will – will I be charged?'

'Not on this basis,' Fleming said. 'We'd have cautioned you if you were anything other than a witness. Could I ask you why Ms Milne should have done this?'

Lindsay looked up at that. 'Why do you think! The bloody woman fancied me!'

'Take it out in trade, did she?' MacNee said coarsely, and got a look of loathing in response.

'No, sergeant. I do have my standards.'

For a terrible moment, MacNee thought Fleming was going to laugh.

As they went out into the garden, Fleming said, 'Well, what did you make of that?'

'I don't know,' MacNee said honestly. 'You tell me. But if you've got the Fiscal on your list of suspects now, all I can say is, *Welcome to your gory bed!*'

The footprints expert was a small, quiet man in a black sweatshirt and black jeans. He was on hands and knees on the grass beside the shrubbery, spraying a footprint impression with what, bizarrely, appeared to be hairspray, then pouring in some sort of thick mixture. Behind him, a platform of planks had been laid over the terrace, and there was a camera on the ground beside it. Fleming waited until he had finished the delicate operation before she spoke.

'Dr Madsen?'

He stood up. His hands were covered with white powder; he wiped them on the back of his jeans, clearly not for the first time, then looked at them ruefully. 'Better not shake your hand,' he said.

Fleming smiled and agreed, then jerked her head towards the footprints. 'Anything for us yet?'

Madsen was a man of few words and he had the scientist's usual reluctance to offer untested theories. He stalled, but eventually indicated that footprints had been made on more than one occasion.

'One set – ground dry, so very shallow. There's others, overlapping sometimes, deeper, when the ground was wet. Can't tell you yet how many occasions there were.'

'Kind of shoes?' Fleming asked.

'Boots, not shoes. Give you a size and make later.'

'Guess as to height?' Brevity seemed to be catching.

'Have to do some calculations. Not small, anyway.'

MacNee had drifted across to the patio. 'Wouldn't get much from here, I suppose,' he said.

Madsen followed him over. 'You'd be surprised. Don't need mud, these days. See the slime there?' He pointed to the green growth on the patio slabs. 'Came up well on the camera, enlarged. Can tell you about three people. One small, woman probably – she slipped. Someone with a bigger foot slipped too – finished up against the doorstep there. The victim?'

Fleming was listening, fascinated. 'That's right – concussed himself.'

'Now here,' he pointed to the area around the French windows, 'can't make any sense of this. Too many people back and forth. Your lot, I guess.'

'Ambulance crew too,' Fleming said regretfully. 'Tried to keep them off once I got here, but it was too late. Pity. Might have got something useful.'

'Not finished yet.' He led them to the edge of the patio nearest the house and pointed, with a smug expression. 'This is the interesting bit. The third set. See there? Someone stood just at the corner. Turned, moved quickly following the victim – his prints overlapped. Then beyond,' he indicated, 'the prints are closer. Running then, you see, then swerved off into the grass.'

'Our friend in the boots,' Fleming said, nodding.

Madsen shook his head. 'Someone in trainers. And smaller feet.'

'What? The person who was standing watching didn't make the attack?'

'Couldn't have. Different size of feet altogether.'

Completely taken aback, Fleming stared at the patio, then back to the shrubbery. After a moment, MacNee said jauntily, 'Queuing up, then, like I said, remember? And this is the guy who thinks everyone likes him!'

Jean Grant was cooking mince, prodding the greyish sludge of boiling meat and carrots without interest. There were doughballs, gluey and soggy, waiting to be put on top but it was still too early. Stuart had his dinner at midday.

So she was surprised at seeing him come across the yard towards the house. There was no way he'd get his dinner at half past eleven – he should know that by now.

To her greater surprise, she saw him going towards the car, parked at the back door. She hurried out.

'Where do you think you're away to? Your dinner'll be ready in half an hour and you've work to do before you get it.'

Stuart gave her a cold, sullen look. 'Never you mind,' he said, got in, and drove away before she could stop him.

'Someone must have deep pockets,' Fleming said, looking round with some amazement as she and MacNee arrived at Miramar and got out of the car. A grey-haired workman glanced round briefly, then went back to installing a window frame. He looked faintly familiar, though Fleming couldn't think why.

'It's her that's got the money, apparently. Quite a lot of it, by what I've heard.'

'You've spoken to her husband. Do you want to take the lead on this?'

MacNee rang the doorbell. 'Och no. You just carry on – I'll interrupt when I feel like it.'

'You always do,' Fleming was saying tartly as the door opened to reveal a matronly blonde in a bright yellow top and Diesel jeans that were a little too tight. 'Mrs Hodge? DI Fleming and DS MacNee. Can we have a word?'

She looked at them, dismayed. 'Oh! But – but my husband isn't here.' She gestured wildly towards the drive. 'He went to Stranraer to see his lawyer. I don't know when he'll be back, so—'

'That's all right, Mrs Hodge. It's you we want to see. May we come in?'

As Fleming moved confidently forward, the woman fell back, still murmuring, 'But – but—' in a helpless sort of way.

'Through here, I suppose.' Diane took them to the conservatory. She plumped down on one of the wicker chairs with a peacock-tail back, but sat forward on the edge of the orange cushion.

Sitting down herself, Fleming puzzled over the woman's reaction. She didn't look the nervy type: you'd put her down as bouncy, confident, a bit loud, perhaps. She certainly wasn't confident now.

Leaning forward, Fleming said, smiling, 'We won't bite, you know.' She spoke in the low, pleasant voice she used like an instrument, and Diane relaxed a little in the warmth of her smile.

'No, of course not! It's – it's just I'd have liked my husband here.'

'No need. It's the simplest of background questions we want to ask. You were away last night?'

'Yes. It was a pity, because I could have confirmed my husband was here all last night. He phoned me from here at – at about ten.'

'Did he tell you to say that?' MacNee shot at her.

Diane's eyes widened. 'Of course not!' she said unconvincingly.

Fleming didn't mention phone records – there seemed little point. 'Marcus Lindsay was an old friend of yours, wasn't he, Mrs Hodge?'

'Just Diane. Sounds more friendly, doesn't it?' She smiled hopefully at the less alarming detective. 'Yes, we knew Marcus way back. Before he was famous.'

'What was he like then? Was there a good teenage scene around here?' Fleming was trying to get her talking. Diane looked the chatty type and she didn't want her scared; she looked meaningfully at MacNee but he only looked back at her in the bland, infuriating way he had.

'Oh, he was lovely! Very good-looking, of course, and a bit sophisticated. We all fancied him like mad.' She gave a girlish giggle. 'His parents were very posh, but he wasn't stuck up or anything.'

'Were you one of his girlfriends?'

Another giggle. 'No, not really. Well, sort of – he once paid me into the cinema, but there was a gang of us going so I suppose . . .' She sighed. 'But then he started dating Ailsa Grant—' She broke off, as if the name had slipped out and she could have bitten her tongue off. Her eyes were round with alarm.

So this was what was bugging her! Before MacNee could jump in with both feet, Fleming said casually, 'Oh yes, she was a friend of yours, wasn't she?'

Diane's hands writhed nervously in her lap. 'Yes, well – we were all friends.'

'You must have been very upset when she was murdered.'

Genuine tears came to her eyes. 'Oh yes, it was dreadful, dreadful! I couldn't believe it.'

'Did you know how she felt about getting pregnant?'

'No.' Diane shut her mouth firmly, as if to make sure nothing else slipped out.

'You knew her in Glasgow, though. Your husband told me that,' MacNee said brazenly.

'Did he?' She sounded both startled and confused, and Fleming directed a sharp glance at MacNee. But she didn't correct him, and Diane went on, 'Well, I suppose we did, a bit. She came to the house sometimes, or we'd maybe meet for a drink, though I didn't get out much because I'd a baby by then. Then I suppose she got friends of her own – I didn't see her much after that. I hadn't spoken to her for ages when I heard she was pregnant and had come back here. I sent her a wee note, but she never replied.'

That last revelation was, at the very least, suggestive. They had got what they came for, if by dubious means.

MacNee was asking now, 'Your husband never got on with Marcus, did he?'

This, again, was uncomfortable territory. 'Oh, it was all just a bit of banter. You know how it is with old friends.'

'You see,' MacNee pressed on, 'we've been told your husband hated him.'

It was a step too far. 'That's – that's nonsense,' she said, but wouldn't be drawn further.

As they got up to leave, MacNee stopped by the photograph he'd commented on before. 'Your son, is it? Nice-looking lad.'

Diane's face lit up. 'Yes, he is, isn't he? Then, in a similar reaction to her husband's, her eyes clouded and she said awkwardly, 'He's away in New Zealand now.'

'Funny, that,' MacNee said as they went back to the car. 'She's edgy about the son too.'

'Not as edgy as Hodge's going to be when he finds out you lied to his wife,' Fleming said pointedly.

MacNee was unrepentant. 'Wasn't under oath, was I? Anyway, the way he went on, Hodge as good as told me. And no doubt you're thinking the same as I am about what his reason was.'

'You what! I can't believe it! You stupid, stupid cow!' The raised voice from the conservatory echoed round the garden.

The workmen on the roof looked up and grinned at each other. '*On nie jest szczęśliwy*. He's not a happy man,' Jozef said to Kasper.

'Hasn't been happy, since the police yesterday.' Kasper listened appreciatively to the sounds of strife. 'Serves him right, mean bastard.'

'She did *what*? And we can get proof?' Superintendent Bailey's face registered unholy glee. 'Marjory, we've got her now!'

'We'll have to search the records. Shouldn't be difficult – Lindsay gave us dates. If she's done it once, it's probably not the only time. We can get Glasgow to trawl for cases she marked "no pro" and see how many were known to her. To be honest, given that cases are dropped on nothing more than one Fiscal's say-so, I've always been surprised that more of this doesn't go on.'

Bailey gave her a cynical look. 'You sure it doesn't? Anyway, Marjory, I'm pulling rank on this one – once we've proof, I want to confront her with it. After her impertinence, I can't wait to see her face.' Then, perhaps recalling his previous humiliation, he added, 'Though of course, you can come too.'

'Thanks,' Fleming said dryly. 'But I don't want to start that running just yet. Lindsay's been well warned to say nothing to her, and I believe he won't – Tam scared him and he saw the merits of distancing himself.'

Bailey looked like a child who has just been told his birthday party's been postponed. 'Once we get proof, what's the point of waiting? The sooner she's out of there, the better.'

'This is major stuff, Donald. It's a serious criminal offence. She was scared enough about it coming out to ask Lindsay to lie to the police. How do you suppose she felt when Lindsay refused?'

Bailey stared at her. 'You don't think—'

'I don't know. Ruthless enough, controlling enough, and she has the murderer's characteristic of solipsism.'

Bailey frowned. 'Er – remind me?'

Fleming smiled. 'Thinking the world exists for your benefit, and Milne's arrogant dismissiveness is characteristic.'

'Her speciality,' Bailey said with feeling.

'And, interestingly, it was her attempt at control that put us on to her – inventing a spurious complaint to prevent me from having any further contact with Marcus Lindsay. Bad mistake.'

'So where do we go from here?'

'Wait for footprint evidence and DNA results. Nothing till Monday at the earliest, and there won't be much doing over the weekend.'

'Oh yes. You're remembering I fly to Ireland first thing tomorrow for a long golfing weekend – I told you where I was going, didn't I? There's this amazing hole on one of the courses—'

Fleming smiled. 'Yes, Donald, you told me. I hope you have a lovely time.'

'I'm looking forward to it, I must say. And you'll report to the Deputy Chief Constable if necessary, of course.'

'Of course.'

As she got up, Bailey cleared his throat. 'Er – before you go, Marjory, on the other case – any progress?'

She had hoped he wouldn't press her. She said awkwardly, 'Oh, this and that. Nothing very dramatic.'

He said, 'Of course,' but with obvious displeasure, and Fleming left feeling irritable. He'd put her in charge of the review and now resented the inevitable consequences. She wished he'd called in another Force to deal with it instead.

But did she? Ailsa's case had really gripped her imagination, and she'd hate to give it up now. When she reached her office, she went back to the box which held the photos of Ailsa Grant and took out the portrait shot and one of the post-mortem shots of her face and laid them side by side on the desk. The eyes of the living girl looked out with all the shining confidence of youth; the glassy stare of the dead one cruelly mocked all those hopes and dreams.

But at least one thing had fallen into place. It all added up: Hodge's violent reaction to questions about Ailsa; Diane's artless disclosures which had revealed his lies . . . Fleming knew, as surely as if she actually had the DNA evidence in front of her, that Gavin Hodge was the father of Ailsa's child. If she could find anything approaching proof that the bastard had done this as well, she was going to hound him until a prison sentence would look like a preferable alternative.

On impulse, she phoned Tam to see if he fancied a drink after work – like she had to ask! She needed a sounding-board, and nowadays Cat tended to drift in when she and Bill were talking over a dram – and she stayed up later than they did. It was like having a chaperone monitor all your conversations, since any meaningful bedroom discussion suffered from Bill's habit of falling asleep slightly before his head hit the pillow.

They went to the Cutty Sark, Tam's local, rather than the Salutation opposite the Kirkluce headquarters which was the Force's favoured watering-hole. It was bigger, with more space between the tables, and in the early evening comparatively quiet. MacNee hailed a few of his cronies, then found a table away from the bar while Fleming got in the drinks.

'TGIF!' MacNee said, raising his glass. 'And a weekend off. Dumfries were looking for extra manpower – they're at full stretch with a nasty rape they're investigating but they're reluctant to put their hand in their pocket.'

'I heard about that. Their DI is tearing his hair out – he's desperate for a breakthrough, but as always the budget's tight.'

'Have you anything planned?'

'I've a ticket for the match tomorrow – can't think why, really. Ayr United's not exactly the Rangers. What about you?'

'Might do paperwork at home, but I'm not coming in. Plenty to do in the house.'

'How's "*the hardy son of rustic toil*" these days? Need to get him in for a pint some night.'

'Do that – he'd like it. But never mind that. Look, we both know I'm going to have to open up about the cold case. After what Diane Hodge said this afternoon . . .'

'Never saw Ailsa in Glasgow, Hodge claims. Diane didn't get out much because she'd a baby, she writes to Ailsa when she hears she's up the spout and gets no reply – Might as well be a signed confession.'

Fleming took it on. 'Absolutely. And did he kill her as well, in case his wealthy wife divorced him? And did he think Marcus knew something, and had a go at him too?'

'What are the chances of getting a swab from Hodge? None, or less than that?'

'Less than that. Even innocent people get stroppy about giving their DNA,' Fleming pointed out. 'Lindsay refused, and I simply don't believe he elaborately sneaked home, once to impregnate the wretched girl and once to murder her.'

'Yeah. But I've a feeling he's not being completely frank with us.'

'You know someone who's completely frank with us? We must move in different circles.'

'And what about our Sheila? When can I let the rest of the lads in on the joke?'

Fleming pulled a face. 'Not yet. Have to check absolutely everything first. If we go off half-cocked and she wriggles out, we're dead in the water. Right enough, she had quite a solid motive to kill him, but be honest, Tam – can you actually picture her skulking around in the dark with a knife?'

MacNee looked at her for a moment, then smiled. 'Do you know, I think I can.'

The European Commission's agricultural policies were seldom popular with farmers, but the set-aside land at the foot of a grazing hill was one of Marjory Fleming's favourite places. There was a curved rock which provided a sheltered seat with a view out over the valley to the farmhouse and the cottage which, built as they were of the local stone, looked almost like rock formations themselves.

It was, for once, a glorious Saturday morning and she couldn't bear to waste it on admin. That could wait. She'd scrubbed out the henhouse, then gone for a five-mile hike, and glowing now from virtuous exercise, was sitting among the spring flowers which spangled the rough meadow – buttercups, a few clumps of primroses, bluebells over by the dyke. The gorse was in bloom now too, great banks of golden colour, and she could smell the faint coconut scent.

Karolina was in the cottage garden, watching Janek pedalling frantically round on a small trike, and Marjory watched them, smiling. A small, mean part of her still hoped Karolina's cooking venture wouldn't be so successful that she lost the help that had transformed her life. If it wasn't for Karolina, she'd be inside now, muttering under her breath while she did the ironing.

She'd left Bill struggling with accounts. She'd asked him if he wanted to come out with her, but he'd only growled like a bear and she'd left him to his misery.

Marjory leaned back in her stone chair, tipping her face to the sun. She'd done a lot of thinking on the walk and her plan of action was clearer.

Sheila Milne – essential to get that one right. The Fiscal would be fighting for her professional life, and their case when they confronted her would have to be as meticulously prepared as if it were to be presented in court – as indeed, it might well have to be. And was it possible that Milne could have been responsible, too, for the attack on Lindsay? Certainly Tam thought she could, and his instincts were remarkably sound. If so, the struggle would get even dirtier. Milne was a dangerous enemy.

Then there was Gavin Hodge. She'd need to set Tam on him again, since he'd got under the man's skin to a very useful extent. When the DNA result came through, if they chose their sheriff with care sweet-talking might get them a warrant for a swab, though of course that would only determine parentage. The murder was a lot more problematical.

Marcus Lindsay kept intruding on her thoughts. Marjory still couldn't make him out. Tam claimed he was keeping things back, and perhaps he was. Everyone has secrets, and from the start of this investigation she had sensed them all about her, thick and dark. As an actor, Lindsay would presumably be adept at concealing areas of sensitivity, though he'd certainly failed when it came to talking about Sheila Milne.

There was something about that house . . . It almost seemed as if this elegant white elephant was a sort of shrine to Laddie Lazansky, as if Marcus was more his father's son than his own man, and Marjory reckoned Tam's friend Sylvia had a lot to do with that. She was powerfully charming; perhaps Marcus would only win his freedom from the Laddie cult once she too was dead. Not a very strong character, perhaps?

And then, Ailsa Grant . . . Would they ever be able to prove who had killed her? Or find the answer to the question that still niggled at Marjory – why had her father not followed procedure, as he famously always did? He had to have had a reason.

You would think you would know your own father well enough to understand how his mind worked. She'd even been living at home at the time all this happened – but had she ever really known her father? Known him as a man capable of impulsive, irrational decisions, rather than as a harsh, rigid paternal figure who was always so right that even when you were quite old enough to know that he wasn't, you felt guilty for not falling into line? Did anyone ever truly know a parent?

Janet, of course—

'Marjory! Marjory!'

She had been gazing into space; Bill's urgent shouting brought her to with a jerk. He was standing in the yard, signalling frantically, and she jumped to her feet, waved in acknowledgement and hurried on down, her heart racing. There must be some new development – though why hadn't they phoned the mobile she always carried with her? Some problem with reception, perhaps.

She was breathless when she reached Bill, then stopped dead when she saw his ashen face.

'It's Cammie. He's been badly hurt in a game. They're – they're worried about him. Marjory, we need to go. Cat's trying to find us a flight.'

'*Jestes szalony!* You're crazy! Kasper, for God's sake—' Jozef leaped up and launched himself across the room to grab him in a smother-tackle. The blade of the knife in Kasper's upraised hand glinted in the light from the naked bulb overhead.

Stefan Pavany, trapped in a corner of the living room by Kasper's sudden, bull-like charge, had for once lost his composure, but as Jozef intervened he snatched the knife and shouldered himself free.

Kasper was still struggling. The fourth man of the crew, Henryk, joined in, frogmarching Kasper to the dilapidated sofa and forcing him on to it. They sat down on either side, still pinioning his arms.

Stefan slipped the knife into his jacket pocket and loomed over Kasper, sneering. 'What a fool! That's it – finish! You're lucky I don't hand you over to the police.'

'You daren't!' Kasper snarled. 'They'd look at how you treat us, your papers, everything. There's a law here, and you're breaking it.'

Stefan laughed. 'And you aren't, maybe? Be grateful I'll let you go. Get out – find another job. Or go back to Poland.'

Kasper's shoulders sagged, the fight going out of him. 'Give me my money, then, and I'll leave.'

'I told you – no money now. Money when we finish the job, when we have the bonus. Only maybe we'll lose it, thanks to you. So you haven't a claim.'

'Henryk, Jozef!' Kasper appealed to the silent men beside him. 'You'll let him do this? He's screwing us all, you know that. There are three of us – we should stick together, my friends, my brothers!'

Jozef hung his head, but Henryk said, 'We don't want trouble. You're a madman, Kasper – you'd have killed him, and then what? Do like he says – go away, forget about it, find another job. Maybe with the film people, like you did before?'

Kasper stood up in a sudden violent movement, shaking them off. Stefan retreated watchfully, but no further attack came.

'I will get my stuff – you will be so gracious as to allow me?' The ironic courtesy did not conceal his simmering rage.

He went through to his shared bedroom and the others sat down uneasily. Stefan switched on the television on mute and they sat in silence, watching faces contorted in unheard laughter in some incomprehensible quiz show. When Kasper reappeared, Stefan got up warily.

Kasper looked past Stefan to the men he had called his brothers. 'I am ashamed of you. You are a disgrace to Poland. And you—' He stared at Stefan with burning eyes. 'Not worth words.'

He spat in his face, then left, slamming the door behind him so that the flimsy house shook.

Stefan took out a handkerchief and wiped his face. 'So – we need a roofer now, eh? You ask in the pub tonight. I have to go and see one or two people. I never thought that scum would last. Good riddance!'

It was getting late when at last Barrie Craig pronounced himself satisfied and with a collective sigh of relief the crew began to pack up. He put his arm round Jaki Johnston's shoulders. 'Brilliant, sweetie – rose to the occasion like a trooper.'

Jaki's laugh was shaky. 'Phew! I'm half-dead now. But today was a lot better than yesterday.'

'Come to the hotel in Sandhead with us tonight. Tony says it does an almost bearable dinner, and we all need a change of scene – I certainly do! My nerves are shot, absolutely shot.'

'Sounds good to me. Pick me up at seven, say? Great.'

Tiredly, she went to the Winnebago and slumped down on one of the cream leather bench seats. Marcus was at the other end of the wagon, pouring boiling water into a mug.

'Dunk a tea-bag for me, would you?' Jaki said. 'Not sure I could stagger far enough to get it for myself.'

'Sure.' Marcus brought over their tea and sat down opposite her, then picked up the sling lying on the table. 'I suppose I'd better replace this. They told me I was to wear it for a couple of days, but I could hardly ask for it to be written into the script.'

'Does it hurt still?' Jaki asked, seeing him wincing as he put it on.

'It does a bit. All right if I keep still, but if I did anything violent I'd know all about it – burst my stitches, probably.'

It was unlike him to admit it, so he must be suffering. 'You're looking better today, though,' she said reassuringly.

'So are you. You must have slept all right last night.'

'Took a pill. I was a bit woozy first thing, but the fog's lifting now. I keep hoping it'll clear enough for me to remember something to help the police, but—' She grimaced.

'I wish my mind would clear! But there's no point in beating ourselves up – it never works. Anyway, what are your plans for tonight? Do I gather an invitation to Tulach would be unwelcome?'

Her polite denial lacked conviction and he laughed. 'It's OK, I wasn't planning to put you on the spot. You had a really bad experience and you don't need reminding of it.'

'Barrie and Tony are taking me to Sandhead for a meal. What about you? And Sylvia, of course,' she added hastily.

Marcus shook his head. 'After doing her scene this morning she was wiped out, and she needs an early night. I couldn't leave her alone in the house.'

With a tiny shudder, Jaki agreed. 'I'd flip, being there alone.'

Marcus smiled at her. 'Look, the police are working flat out and we have to trust them or else we'll all go mad. Sylvia and I will have all the doors and windows locked and the shutters fastened, anyway. We just need to be calm and sensible until we get away from here or they manage to pick someone up for it.'

'Can't wait,' Jaki said with feeling.

'Cheer up!' Marcus leaned over to flick her nose, then kissed her. 'Have a good evening, and sleep well. I'm off.'

Jaki sat on, sipping her tea. She didn't mean to go on and on, picking over that night, but somehow it kept coming into her head. There was something – something that had puzzled her at the time, but however hard she tried she couldn't remember what it was.

Sheila Milne had gone to a concert in Dumfries. It had seemed a good idea not to sit at home, with everything going round and round in her head, but even the demands made by the Beethoven late quartet couldn't banish her anxieties from her mind.

She had seen Bailey off all right – fool of a man! – but his inspector was a different matter. She had no doubt that Fleming would take a vicious satisfaction in engineering her downfall: the animosity between them was personal.

Everything she could do had been done, but still her restless mind searched and searched, like an animal trying to find its way out of a cage-trap, going back and back to the same places again and again, hoping to find a weakness.

She still hadn't found it when the applause at the end of the piece broke into her wretched thoughts.

'Wonderful! Wonderful!' the woman next to her exclaimed.

'Wonderful,' Sheila echoed hollowly.

'Are you sure you're all right, sleeping down here?' Marcus Lindsay said anxiously to Sylvia Lascelles. 'I could help you upstairs—'

'Darling, you've bolted the shutters for me. I'll be fine.' She smiled up at him, and he bent to kiss her.

'If you're sure—'

'Of course. And everything will be all right. Promise to put it out of your mind.'

'I'll try.' He looked very tired and stressed, though, with dark shadows under his eyes. 'It's just – difficult, that's all.'

'It's easier to be brave, Laddie always used to say. Allow yourself to feel afraid, and it's much harder.' She patted his cheek. 'Go to bed, and take some of those pills they gave you. You'll feel much better in the morning.'

'I suppose so. What about you?'

'I'll sleep when I need to,' she said. 'Goodnight, my darling.'

Marcus left her. Sylvia looked at the shutters, longing to open them and do her thinking, as she always had, looking out at the night sky. But it would be folly; instead, she picked up her stick, got herself out of her chair and limped the few agonizing steps across to the bed.

She lowered herself on to it, biting her lip against the pain, then looked at the photograph of Laddie Lazansky which always stood on the table beside her bed.

'Oh, Laddie, Laddie! Where are you, when I need you?' she murmured and her violet-grey eyes filled with tears.

Karolina couldn't sleep. It was partly because Janek had a cold and now he kept having bouts of coughing in his sleep. It didn't seem to be bothering him, but every time she dropped off, it started up again and she woke up.

She kept thinking about the poor, poor Flemings – they wouldn't be getting much sleep in that house tonight. If it was Janek – she couldn't bear even to frame the thought.

But she had other worries too. While she had been out in the garden with Janek this afternoon, the phone had rung. She heard Rafael answer in English, then switch to Polish. He didn't sound very pleased, but after a few minutes he said, 'All right, all right. I can't lend you much, and I'll need it back soon, OK?' Then, 'Yes, I'll come down tonight. But this is the last favour – you hear?'

With a sinking heart, Karolina guessed who was at the other end. She expected Rafael to come out and tell her about it, but he didn't, and when she wandered casually in a few minutes later, asking who had phoned, he said, 'Oh, just one of the boys. A few of us are going for a drink, but I won't be late.'

She should have told him immediately that she had overheard instead of pretending she hadn't, but challenging him would have led to a row in front of Janek, who had come running in at that moment to demand something to eat.

Karolina had tried again when he came back from the pub. 'Who was there?'

'Oh, the usual crowd.' He was looking everywhere but straight at her. 'Are we just going to bed? I'd better rake out the fire.'

'Was Kasper there?'

'Kasper? Oh, I think so. I wasn't really speaking to him.'

The unnecessary vigour with which he was riddling the fire betrayed him. Karolina said gently, 'I think you have something on your mind, Rafael. What is it?'

He looked startled, then muttered something about a problem with settling in the new stirks, which might be the truth but certainly wasn't the whole truth. He went straight upstairs and certainly appeared to be asleep by the time she had finished up downstairs and joined him.

She was angry he should have done this without consulting her. They had few enough savings, and it wasn't his money, it was theirs. If Rafael had lent money to Kasper, he was a fool. They both knew he wasn't to be trusted.

But Rafael still felt more of an alien in their new country than she did. He believed that Poles had a duty to look after one another, and he knew that she would have said no. Kasper didn't deserve looking after: he just needed to work harder and keep his temper.

Rafael had all but ordered her not to tell Marjory what she knew about Kasper's past, but she hadn't promised. If there was any more trouble, that was exactly what she was going to do.

It was the worst night of Marjory Fleming's life. The first flight they could get was the following afternoon, and Bill had wanted to set off immediately by car instead. It had been hard to convince him that in their distraught state this would be madness: neither of them had driven on the continent before, and they wouldn't even get there sooner. He knew

that, really, but he had a desperate need to do something –
anything!

She had never seen Bill like this before, her calm, wise
Bill, always a rock of common sense in any crisis. Now
he was so frantic in his anxiety for his son that he was
unable to keep still, hardly able to speak. Cat, though
white-faced, had been more collected, and it was she who
had spoken directly to the French doctor, understanding
enough to relay that Cammie was in intensive care and
deeply unconscious.

It had been the rugby coach who had phoned, distraught
himself, to tell Bill that a tackle which had caught Cammie
awkwardly had broken his leg, but this was a minor problem
compared to an injury to his neck which had occurred in the
ensuing ruck.

Marjory, who found herself calm with the cold numbness
of shock, had spoken to the man an hour later and could
almost hear him wringing his hands over the line. There was
no change, and Cat's phone call confirmed that there would
be no more news tonight, unless . . .

They could all fill in the blank. She didn't know how they
had got through the evening. She had put food on the table
and she and Cat had pretended to eat, but Bill wouldn't even
pick up his knife and fork, just sat staring straight ahead,
his face working. At last he burst out, 'I shouldn't have
encouraged him in his rugby – it's such a dangerous game!
But I urged him on, to practise, to train—'

'We all encouraged him,' Marjory said firmly. 'And anyway,
he didn't need encouragement. It's what he wanted to do
himself, more than anything. You couldn't have stopped him
if you'd wanted to. And this could have happened crossing
the road.'

'He'll be in good hands, Dad,' Cat urged. 'The French

health service is great – years ahead of us. And Cammie's tough – he'll be OK.'

Bill looked at them blindly. Then he said, 'I can't just sit here. I'm going out.' He got up. 'Meg!'

The collie, scenting distress, had been curled miserably in her basket. She leaped out and followed him, close at her master's heels.

Marjory watched them go and felt her eyes at last fill with tears. 'Oh, Cat, how are we going to get through this?'

Cat's lip was trembling too, but she said stoutly, 'Hang in there. Believe he's going to be all right. Pray. That always helps.'

'I've been praying already,' her mother admitted, 'though I haven't been very good at doing it when everything's all right.'

'I guess God's used to that. We should get Gran on to the job – she's got a better record.'

'We'll wait till the morning. I don't want her worrying all night. She's getting old – she doesn't need the strain.'

'I think she'd want to know. Gran's lived through a lot and I think she'd like to be here for you. And – and I'd like her to be here as well. It'd make me feel better.' Cat sniffed.

'I know, love – me too. But we can't be selfish, always making demands. It's our turn to look after her.'

'I think you're wrong about Gran,' Cat persisted. 'You keep trying to stop her doing things, and I think that makes her sad. She likes us needing her.'

'We can show her that without making use of her. I don't want her wearing herself out.'

'I don't think she would,' Cat said stubbornly, but Marjory just shook her head.

'I'm not going to upset her till we know a bit more.' Lurking at the back of her mind was an unacknowledged fear that if Janet, like Bill, was too distressed to comfort her daughter, Marjory wouldn't know how to find the strength to be comforter in her turn.

At last Bill came back and the long, silent evening dragged on and on until they could all go to bed. Marjory lay on her back in the darkness with her eyes open, while Bill, who always fell asleep instantly, tossed and turned. But at last his breathing thickened, grew regular, and he was asleep.

It was she who was restless now. Taking care not to wake him, she slipped out of bed and went through, heading for Cammie's room. There was still a light under Cat's door, but she didn't go in.

Cammie had never been a tidy child, and his packing had typically been done at the last minute. He had insisted on doing it himself, and the bed and floor were strewn with untidy clothes. Automatically, Marjory bent to pick them up, fold them and put them away, trying not to look at the rugby posters on the walls. There was a rugby ball in the corner, and team photos on his noticeboard; his weights and a chest-expander were thrown down in one corner. Rugby had been everything to her boy.

However often Karolina cleaned, the room always had that faint scent of boy – something to do with sweaty trainers and sports kit, probably. The clothes he had been wearing the day before were lying crumpled in the general vicinity of the laundry basket and she picked them up, burying her face in his sweater for a moment.

She was tired, so tired! She lay down on the badly made bed, the sweater still clutched to her like a comforter. It might be better if she could cry, but the tears just wouldn't come. Her mind kept going round and round the terrible 'what-ifs' – coma, death, coma, paralysis, coma, brain damage . . .

She must have fallen asleep. She heard the phone ring, and was out of bed to answer it before she realized it had been in her dream. The house was silent, apart from the pounding of her heart, so loud that she almost felt it would wake the others.

She looked at her watch. One o'clock – still hours and hours of terrible night until morning – and who knew what that would bring?

The car park of the Cross Keys at Ardhill was the recycling centre for the village, with huge bins for glass, paper and unwanted clothing. The bins hadn't been cleared for almost a fortnight; they were full, and impatient depositors had simply dumped what wouldn't go in around the base.

Beside the sticky, smelly bottles and over-filled plastic bags was what might almost have been a heap of old clothes, if it hadn't been for the hand which protruded from the sleeve of a dark jacket.

18

Rafael got out of bed before six. He'd moved quietly, but Karolina woke up.

'Go back to sleep,' he whispered. 'I want to tell Bill that everything's in hand before they leave. I can get my own breakfast.'

'I'm awake now. But don't wake Janek.'

The sun was streaming into the living room when she came downstairs. Rafael went to sit down at the table while Karolina made breakfast. He had a lot on his mind today; perhaps this wasn't the moment to tell him what had been bothering her last night. But it was bad to let things fester between husband and wife . . . yes, she would. She turned to face him.

'I need to tell you this. I heard you speaking on the phone yesterday, and I think you said you would lend Kasper money. Is that right?'

Rafael's face turned a dark red. 'You were listening?'

'I heard. That's different.'

'So – perhaps I did,' he said defensively. 'I know what you think of Kasper, so I didn't mention it. He's in trouble – the bastard foreman has cheated him—'

Karolina struggled to keep her temper. 'With Kasper, it's always someone else's fault, and he won't learn, if people like you say, "We are Poles, we must stick together against everyone else." How much did you give him?'

'Only a little. Twenty pounds – he'll pay it back next week.'

'Pay it back? Kasper? You think so?' She laughed. 'Suddenly we have twenty pounds to make presents to people who aren't even our friends? We need our money, Rafael, you know we do – especially now.'

Rafael got up. 'I did it, so that's that,' he said, and went out.

'Your breakfast—' she called, but he didn't come back.

Eyes stinging, Karolina looked after him. She knew hatred was wrong – you should forgive people, seventy times seven times, and then more – but when she saw what Kasper had done to her happy, contented marriage, she hated him, all right.

Then she sighed. At confession next week, she knew what the priest would say.

Marjory woke with a start. She sat up, her eyes thick and sticky from unrefreshing sleep, and for a confused moment didn't know where she was. Rugby posters – Cammie's room – oh, God!

She put her head in her hands for a moment, then got up slowly, limbs stiff from tension, and went to the bathroom where she splashed her face. She needed a shower, but that might wake the others. Judging from the light, it wasn't yet six, but a perfect sunny morning with a clear sky of a tender blue. There was painful irony there.

She tiptoed through to the shadowed bedroom where Bill still lay in exhausted slumber. They'd been told there was no point in phoning the hospital before nine, and though France was an hour ahead, the longer Bill and Cat could sleep the better.

Grabbing jeans and a sweater, she dressed in the bathroom, then went downstairs. She'd have liked to seek the soothing company of her hens, but whenever she let them out the rooster would start his morning challenge to all comers, and no one could sleep through that.

She made a cup of tea instead and sat down at the table, sipping it bleakly. Meg, puzzled by her master's absence, had greeted Marjory politely, then gone back to her basket, keeping a wary eye on the kitchen door. Rafael would come in soon to take her with him on his sheep rounds; Meg would stay with him while the Flemings were away.

The first available flight was at three. With the journey and security they'd need to be on their way shortly after ten – not a bad thing. At least they'd be doing something.

Marjory found a notepad and started a list. Passports, flight confirmation, credit card, mobile phone . . . In her present state, she could leave her head behind if it wasn't attached. Phone her mother – but she'd wait till they'd spoken to the hospital first.

And phone Headquarters. She should really have done it yesterday, but she hadn't felt strong enough for what, with Bailey away, would be a difficult and complicated business. The Chief Constable, for whom she had considerable respect, was still away at a conference, and she had a low opinion of his DCC, Paula Donald, a woman more versed in management-speak than in down-to-earth policing.

There had been, too, a tiny, stubborn spark of hope that perhaps if there was good news Cammie could fly home with them tomorrow or the next day and she'd be back before absence was a major issue.

This morning that optimism seemed to have vanished. Cammie had got through the night, thank God, but at the thought of the phone call Cat would be making at eight o'clock, Marjory could only feel sick and despairing.

★ ★ ★

It was early, for a Saturday, when the landlord of the Cutty Sark let himself into the pub. There was stock-taking to do, and he went through last night's beery fug – no stale-smoke smell now, at least – and headed for the small office off the kitchen. There were crates of empty bottles still lying on the floor, and a smelly bag of rubbish too.

He wrinkled his nose in disgust. Norrie really was a glaikit lump – so dopey you might as well talk to a blank wall. If he'd told him once he'd told him a hundred times: empties and all rubbish out to the bins, last thing.

They weren't going to walk out there by themselves. Swearing, he opened the back door, grabbed two crates and carried them to the bin area in the car park. He set them down and was turning to fetch the rest when something caught his eye.

'What the—' He bent, recognizing the man as the older one of the Polish builders and wondering if he'd got drunk last night and was sleeping it off. Then he saw the knife sticking out of his back.

'Oh, my God!'

Recoiling, he stood, running his hand down his face. Police. 999. That was all he could do.

By five to eight, the Flemings were assembled at the kitchen table, staring at the phone which Cat was holding, along with the paper with the hospital's number. She had black circles under her eyes, but Marjory could see a sudden maturity in the way she was steeling herself. A good girl, her Cat.

Bill was calmer this morning, more like her steady, stoical husband, but his hand shook as he drank his tea. She was glad she'd finished her own before they came down: her own hands weren't steady, but she didn't want it to show. If the news was bad, she might have to be strong for them all – no tears, no breakdown, however she might feel.

At last the hands of the clock inched round and Cat dialled the number. There was the agonizing wait while connections went through and the appropriate person was found, then Cat, in her careful French, was asking how Cameron Fleming was, and listening with painful attention to the answer.

Her face lit up. She forgot her French. 'Oh, is he? That's wonderful, just wonderful!' Putting her thumbs up to her parents, she tried to collect herself. '*Ah, je m'excuse! Merci bien, madame – c'est magnifique!*'

After a few more minutes, Cat put the phone down. 'He's sitting up, eating breakfast. He came round in the early hours, and he can move everything, apart from his leg. It's quite a bad break, but he'll be OK.'

A huge grin spread over Bill's face. Cat got up and did a jubilant little dance. And Marjory, at last, burst into tears.

After breakfast, when they had all found that after all they were hungry, Marjory went upstairs to finish packing. It was years and years since she had been to France and now, she thought guiltily, it almost felt like sneaking a holiday. Oh, poor Cammie would be having a hard time with his injuries, but they'd managed to have a word with him and, though wobbly, he was clearly all right. The broken bones would mend.

Immediately afterwards she had phoned her mother and got what was, coming from Janet, an ear-bashing.

'He's not just your son, he's my grandson. If there's something wrong with him, I don't want you keeping it from me.'

'I just wanted to spare you a sleepless night,' Marjory had pleaded. 'There was no point—'

'At my age, I think I've learned to cope with sleepless nights. But of course if I can't be a help, I'd rather not be a nuisance.'

The hurt in her mother's voice made her feel dreadful. 'Of course you're not a nuisance! Cat wanted me to tell you, felt you would be a help—'

'Then I wish you had. But never mind that now. The important thing is, the laddie's going to be fine. And I can look up to the house after you've gone, if you like, get things ready for you coming back—'

'Honestly, there's no need. Karolina's all ready to take care of it.' Having hurt her mother's feelings, Marjory wasn't going to compound her own feelings of guilt at her misjudgement by making use of her. 'But the minute we land at Glasgow I'll phone you, so you can be here to see him for yourself whenever he's back.'

She'd have to phone Tam too and tell him the good news. She'd asked him last night to cover for her, and now she could say that she'd definitely be back on Monday sometime, depending on flights. She was just zipping up her case to take it downstairs when her mobile, lying on the dressing table, rang. She picked it up, glancing at Caller ID. That was handy!

'Tam! I was just going to phone you. Great news . . .'

Marjory told him about the report on Cammie, but though he said the right things, his response seemed muted. Sharply she said, 'Is something wrong?'

'Sorry, boss, I hate to do this to you but I need your instructions. We've had another knifing – fatal, this time.'

Lack of sleep had left her a little light-headed. She sat down heavily on the end of the bed as MacNee gave her such basic details as were available so far. He finished, then said, 'What are you wanting me to do? Phone the DCC?'

'Hold off on that for a moment. I need to think. Call you back.'

Marjory covered her face with her hands. What was she to do? Paula Donald had no CID experience and Tam, though brilliant on the ground, had no sense of strategic planning. There was only one other Senior Investigating Officer in Galloway, and he was away on a course; she couldn't look to the Dumfries Force for cover either. They had their own priorities, trying to pull in a violent rapist before he struck again.

Her every instinct was screaming that she must go to Cammie. He would be feeling vulnerable, suffering and scared in a strange place, still young enough to want the comfort of his mother's presence. And she wanted to be with him too, to see her precious boy for herself; there was some part of her that wouldn't quite believe she hadn't lost him for ever until she could take him in her arms. But, but. . . . Cammie could be home in twenty-four hours' time, safe in the care of his father and his sister.

She had other responsibilities. Two stabbings, a death. No one competent to set up the structure that would capitalize on the early evidence available in the golden twenty-four hours after a murder, after which your chances of success diminished rapidly.

What should she do? Damned if she went, damned if she didn't. Guilt, guilt – the lot of the working mother.

It would have been different if Cammie had still been in danger – apart from anything else, she wouldn't have been able to think straight. But now, she could be importantly useful here, doing her duty as a professional. If she was the boy's father, not his mother, what would the decision be? Emotionally, this was tough; looked at rationally, there was no contest. With leaden feet, she went downstairs to find Bill.

He was beaming still. 'Got your bag packed?' he said, then his face changed as Marjory told him.

'Marjory, you're the boy's mother! He's had a nasty accident. He needs you.'

She bit her lip. 'Don't think I don't understand how he will be feeling. But Bill, he doesn't *need* me, he only *wants* me. You're going out to bring him home, tomorrow, with luck, and there's nothing I could do there that you and Cat can't.

'But I'm actually needed here. An attempted murder, and a successful one. We're short-staffed as it is, and Bailey's away. Suppose I go and he kills again?'

'Suppose you stay, and he kills again?' Bill said dryly.

'At least I'd have done everything in my power to prevent it. I wouldn't have turned my back to go to the bedside of my son who, thank God, is only suffering from a broken leg.'

'I can't tell you how wrong I think you are,' Bill said grimly. 'You're suffering from the delusion that you're indispensable. Supposing Cammie was still in a coma – what then?'

'He isn't,' Marjory argued. 'That's the point. It's hard on me too, Bill – I'm as keen to see him as you are. But this does make sense.'

'You've made up your mind, and nothing I say is going to make any difference, is it? But tell me this – are you absolutely sure that your very logical decision hasn't something to do with being reluctant to miss all the action?'

Bill turned away, leaving Marjory looking after him with a lump in her throat and a nasty, uncomfortable feeling.

'Marjory! Rafael told me – this is such good news!'

'It's a huge relief, I must say. It was a terrible night, but he was amazingly bright when we spoke to him this morning.'

'I am so glad. You would like me to go into the house today, to tidy up after you go? I have a call saying there is to be no filming.'

'No, I don't suppose there will be. Actually, Bill and Cat are going to have to go to France without me. A man's body has been found in the car park of the inn at Ardhill.'

'Oh no! What happened?'

Marjory grimaced. 'Another stabbing, only fatal this time. We seem to have a real problem with knife crime.'

Karolina's head began to swim. She put up her hand to it and saw Marjory looking at her anxiously.

'Are you all right?'

'Yes, yes,' she said, taking a deep breath. 'Do you – do you know who it is?'

Marjory hesitatcd. 'We're not really saying anything at the moment, but . . .' Seeing Karolina's anxious face, she went on, 'They think he's the foreman of a group of Polish builders.'

This time, Karolina's knees buckled. Marjory grabbed her just in time and thrust her into the open car to sit on the driver's seat with her head down. After a moment Karolina sat up. 'Sorry, sorry – I'm all right. It was just the shock.'

'I'm sorry too – that was incredibly stupid! I should have guessed you'd know him.'

'It's not that.' Karolina moistened her lips. 'I – I think I know who most likely killed him.'

Marjory stared at her. 'What do you mean – you know?'

'I should have told you before. Kasper Franzik is someone I knew in Poland. Well, an old boyfriend, I suppose. He is very good-looking, very – romantic, is the word, I think. But he loves money, and he got with bad people – selling drugs. He was caught and he went to prison.

'I don't see him after that, till he comes here. He hears somehow where we live, and thought maybe he can use us, I guess – this is what he is like.' Her round face became very stern. 'I told you he stayed with us – not by our choosing – because his boss is angry with him. He is very bitter – though it was he who cheated Stefan, coming to work in the film canteen instead. Then he goes back, but last night there is another row and he is thrown out with no money. He borrowed from Rafael.

'And he has a knife, a hunting knife. I find it in his jacket, the night he stays. I want to tell you then, but Rafael says, he is another Pole, we must give him a chance.'

Marjory had listened, frowning. 'I see. Well, we'd be checking on him anyway, so don't feel you've shopped him. And young men now do carry knives, unfortunately, even if they're not planning to use them. Remember the attack on Marcus Lindsay – your friend wouldn't have had any reason for that.'

Karolina's expression was tragic. 'Oh, but he has! I see how he looks when he is told off for spilling dirty water on Mr Lindsay – he would like to kill him then, if he could.'

When they lifted the cover from the dead man's face, Fleming recognized him. He had been working at Miramar and had turned his head to look at them briefly – and, she now remembered, he'd been involved in the fracas on the film shoot. With Karolina's friend.

The photographs had been taken, the pathologist had completed his examination and was waiting for Fleming's arrival.

'Killed somewhere else, dumped here,' he told her. 'Time of death – hard to say, with the body being moved, but given the progress of rigor mortis I'll stick my neck out and say before midnight, possibly even well before. Injuries – a contusion at the base of the skull there –' he pointed, 'then the stab wound, pretty much straight to the heart, so not much bleeding. Purposeful weapon.' He held up the knife, encased in an evidence bag. 'We'll run the usual tests, of course, but I think that's the story.'

Fleming looked down at Stefan Pavany's face. He hadn't known what hit him: his face showed no sign of agitation or fear. He could be mid-sixties – more, even, though the sagging of muscles in death was aging – but he'd been a good-looking man, despite stubble that looked careless rather than designer, and a bad haircut. Good-looking but severe: there were seamed lines from his nose to his down-turned mouth. A harsh man: she remembered his bullying tirade at Kasper that day. She remembered, too, MacNee's remark about that young man – 'Wouldn't like to meet him up a dark close on a Saturday night.'

'There's just one slightly odd thing,' the pathologist was saying. 'No shoes.'

Fleming raised her eyebrows. 'Curious. Still, may have fallen off in the car bringing him here. Or perhaps he was killed indoors. See you later at the autopsy.'

MacNee, who had reached the scene an hour earlier, was waiting to speak to her. 'We've got two of the Polish lads at the lodgings they've been renting round in the back street.'

'Which two?'

Her tone was sharp and MacNee looked surprised. 'Jozef something and Henryk something else. The other one got thrown out last night.'

'That's the one I'm interested in. Kasper Franzik. He was the one in a barney with Pavany, remember?' She told him what Karolina had said.

He pursed his lips in a silent whistle. 'Lindsay got the death stare from him, right enough. Scary bugger, I thought.'

'He's done a runner, I'd guess. Karolina gave me a description – I'll get a call put out to all cars. Talk to his mates, Tam. An incident room's being set up in the church hall.'

'I'll need an interpreter. They barely speak a word of English.' His tone suggested he took this as a personal insult.

'There's one in Kirkluce – does work for the courts. Get someone to fetch him. Are Andy Mac and Tansy on site?'

'Andy was on duty – he's organizing door-to-door. Tansy's mobile's off – asleep, probably, knowing her.'

'Send someone to give her a rude awakening, then. We need all the help we can get.'

Jaki Johnston shut the lid of her case with a feeling of overwhelming relief. Oh, it was awful about the poor guy, of course, but when Tony had come in to say they were packing it in, she had flung her arms round him in joy and kissed him.

He'd turned a dark pink, then said gruffly, 'All fun and games till we see our pay-packet,' but she could tell he was chuffed.

Now she was going home to Mum and Dad, and she'd ring a couple of her mates and go clubbing in Glasgow tonight. She felt positively guilty at being so happy.

Jaki went downstairs to the front door. She could hear voices just outside in the street, but couldn't make out what they were saying, and when she opened it, two young men were passing talking in a foreign language – Polish, most likely.

Her brow furrowed. That rang a bell, somewhere—

'Jaki, love! You can't go without saying goodbye! Isn't this a *disaster*!' Barrie was coming along the pavement, his plump face a mask of woe.

In a fine piece of acting, she agreed with him.

The church hall was crawling like an anthill with lines of officers bringing in tables, chairs, computers and the rest of the equipment from a van outside, stepping over the tangle of cables already littering the floor.

DS Macdonald was in the middle of it all, talking to a couple of uniforms, when he saw Big Marge arriving and went to meet her with some relief. The news about her son had gone round, and he hadn't fancied getting a murder investigation under way without her there to direct.

'Great to see you, boss. Is your lad OK, then?'

'Doing fine. His father and sister are away out to hold his hand. What's come in?'

'Not a lot, frankly. These guys there found someone who heard a car going into the car park around two a.m. Lives next door, thought it was funny, but didn't get up to look. And of course Ardhill's deserted once the pub closes.'

'The SOCOs say there are so many tyre marks that there's small hope of useful evidence. Tam's rounded up two builders, but there's one missing. Can you arrange an APB for the cars? Kasper Franzik, six-two or thereabouts, dark hair, longish, and dark eyes.'

As she was speaking MacNee appeared, escorting two bewildered-looking, large young men. He commandeered a couple of chairs from a passing ant, pointed to them and said, 'Sit!'

They obeyed like well-trained labradors and Macdonald almost expected MacNee to add, 'Stay!' as he turned away.

'I've been thinking,' MacNee said as he reached them.

'Wondered what the funny noise was,' Macdonald said, but Fleming only groaned.

'I really hate it when you say that, Tam. What is it this time?'

'You know we've to wait for the interpreter? Suppose I pop across to the Hodges' for a wee blether meantime – they were employing him, after all, and they've maybe not heard.'

'Surely this knocks that angle on the head? You're not thinking this is connected, are you, Tam?'

MacNee obviously knew what she was talking about, even if Macdonald didn't.

'Och no,' he said. 'Just wanted an excuse to raise the other matter anyway and this looked a good one. If the interpreter arrives before I get back, Andy can start on these boys.'

There was limpid innocence in MacNee's face. At that moment, someone came up to Big Marge with a query, so Macdonald didn't hear her reaction, but he knew what he thought himself.

'What new scam is this? There's something we're not being told, isn't there? What don't I know, Tam?'

'Hardly know where to begin, laddie.'

'Very funny. Why do you want to go and leave me to question the plum witnesses? It's not like you.'

'I'm all heart, giving you a chance to shine.'

'Sure, sure. Come on, what's going on?'

MacNee winked. 'That's for me to know and you to guess,' he said, and strode cockily off, leaving Macdonald fuming, frustrated and none the wiser.

To describe MacNee's reception at Miramar as unenthusiastic would be like saying it was a touch dusty in the Sahara desert. Gavin Hodge's face turned purple with rage, and even Diane's voice was shrill with anger.

'I don't know how you have the nerve to show your face here, after lying to me like that yesterday.'

MacNee was unmoved. 'I've never been a shrinking violet. And your husband maybe didn't admit to his relationship with Ailsa Grant, but everything he did say told me loud and clear.'

Diane stared at MacNee. Hodge's mouth fell open.

'Relationship,' she said slowly. 'I don't know what you mean. What relationship?'

Hodge blustered, 'I don't know what the hell this is about. There was no "relationship". I didn't choose to mention we'd seen Ailsa in Glasgow because it had no relevance to her death. As Diane told you, we hadn't seen her for months before that but I know exactly what happens when you lot think you're on to something – you warp the facts to fit the theory. That's what you're doing now.'

He turned to Diane. 'Look, he's playing games, trying to set us against each other. It's all lies. You know how the police operate. And you know he lied to you before.'

That pressed the right button. 'Yes. Yes, of course I do. Sergeant, you're scum. Get out of here.'

MacNee ignored that. 'Maybe you don't know you're closely linked to a knife crime? Again. Only this time it's murder.'

Diane gave a little scream. '*Murder?* But who? Not – not Marcus—'

'An employee of yours. Stefan Pavany.'

'You can't think this was anything to do with us!' Diane was horrified. 'We hardly knew the poor man – he was just our builder.'

'These things can lead to disagreements. Did you fall out over payments, maybe? And we know you and Mr Lindsay had problems, didn't you, Gavin?'

Hodge had gone very still. 'What – what time did this happen?'

'Last night. His body was found dumped in the car park at the pub in Ardhill this morning.'

Hodge cleared his throat. 'Last night? We went out for a drink with friends.'

'At—?' MacNee prompted.

'I'm not sure.' He was prevaricating, but Diane, always ready to be helpful, offered, 'Seven o'clock. We came home around half past eight.'

'And then?'

Blithely she went on, 'We had supper. Then remember, Gavin, someone came to the door while I was having a bath—' She stopped short at the look on her husband's face.

'A visitor?' MacNee enquired with polite interest. 'Who was that?'

Hodge's calculation was all but audible. Then he said, 'Look, sergeant, I'll be honest with you.'

'Always the best policy,' MacNee said piously.

'Pavany came round last night to talk about the building work. I'd promised a bonus if they finished by next week but he'd had problems and wanted to renegotiate. Of course, I was having none of it, and frankly, it's lucky it's not my murder you're investigating. I thought for a moment he'd go for me.'

This was unexpected, but MacNee seized on it. 'Are you sure he didn't? This is when to tell me – he attacked you, you grabbed his knife in self-defence, panicked and decided to dispose of the body—'

'No, no, of course I didn't!' Hodge was certainly panicking now.

It was Diane who stepped in. 'Don't be bloody silly,' she said coldly. 'I had my bath and then he never left the house. So bugger off, with your nasty allegations.'

MacNee found he believed her. But even so, it had given him another card to play.

'The thing is, sir, there'll be DNA evidence after the autopsy, so if you were to agree to having a swab taken, that could put you in the clear.'

'You'd better do it then, Gav. Get him off your back,' Diane urged, but Hodge was suddenly looking at MacNee with narrowed eyes.

'I've got an alibi. Why should you want—?' he began, then stopped. He gave a short laugh. 'Oh, I see. Forget it, sergeant. And now, I'm shutting the door.'

MacNee returned to Ardhill in a very bad temper.

Sylvia Lascelles was feeling her age this morning. She'd been tired enough, God knows, when she'd gone to bed, but she'd slept badly and wakened in the grey, depressing light of early dawn. Her lips were blue and the bags under the famous violet-grey eyes could, she thought bitterly as she looked in the mirror, hold Joan Collins's wardrobe for a fortnight in Las Vegas.

But it wasn't very funny, really. Or actually, not funny at all. She had a performance to do today and she'd heard Barrie arriving, so she'd better see what could be done before she had to face the world. She laid out every cosmetic in her extensive armoury and set to work with the *Touche Éclat*, then took particular trouble with her hair, twisting the thinning grey rope into its upswept coil before loosening it to form soft waves around her face.

The stress was getting too much for her. She'd always believed spirit could overcome age and infirmity, but it was only true if you didn't push your luck. They were to film her big scene this morning, when she was to confront her attacker, and she was just afraid she wouldn't get through it.

She must, though! Finished with her *maquillage*, if not satisfied, she picked up the moonstone ring from the dressing table and forced it over the swollen knuckle of the ring finger on her left hand, then looked at it. Laddie's ring – her talisman. She must be brave. Not let the side down. On with the motley.

As she propelled herself across the hall, she was grateful that the drawing-room door was open – so humiliating, to have to struggle with the handle, or knock. Barrie spotted her and trotted over, his face tragic.

Marcus was standing by the fireplace looking sombre.

'Such awful news, darling!'

Her heart began to race. 'What's happened?'

'I don't know how to tell you. They're pulling the plug. And this was to be our showcase episode – the return of the legendary Sylvia Lascelles!'

Relief washed over her. Sylvia looked up at him with her luminous smile. 'How sad – and sad for all of you, after working so hard. But I've been a pro for long enough, heaven knows – that's just show business, isn't it?'

Barrie picked up her hand and raised it to his lips. 'I don't know what to say. Marcus, she's amazing, this lady. Takes a blow like this with so much understanding, such grace—'

'Why?' Her tone was a little sharper than she had meant it to be, but she couldn't stand gushing.

Marcus said, 'They've found a body. No, nothing to do with us – some brawl in the pub, probably. But the producer decided enough was enough.'

'A body? Oh, Marcus, how terrible. Do they know who it was?'

'A Polish labourer.' His voice was soothing. 'Like I said, some quarrel—'

'But he was stabbed, Marcus, stabbed – that's the thing!' Barrie, oblivious to Marcus's warning look, was revelling in sensation. 'You have to think—'

'Stabbed!' Sylvia put a hand to her throat. 'Marcus, that could have been you!'

Exasperated, Marcus said, 'Thank you, Barrie! That really wasn't helpful. Sylvia, it only means they'll pull out all the stops and get hold of this maniac.'

'But what if they don't?' she cried. 'What if—'

Barrie, abashed, tried to soothe her. 'He's right, Sylvia. Anyway, you can get straight back home to London now and be safe and sound.'

He got a withering glance. 'And leave Marcus here alone? I'm not afraid for myself – I'm too old to be afraid. But somehow, he's got across someone, and though I can't quite see myself leaping into action to protect him, I'm not going until he's safe in Glasgow.'

Marcus came across to kiss her cheek. 'Darling, you can't take much more of this. I don't mind you going back to London. I'll be leaving tomorrow or the next day.'

'I'd rather be here. Anyway,' she smiled at him, 'it may be the last time, you know, and in spite of everything it's felt good to be so near darling Laddie again. As long as you're around, I can feel I haven't quite lost him.' Her eyes misted over.

Barrie murmured, 'So romantic! I feel quite tearful myself.'

Sylvia was grateful to Marcus for saying bracingly, 'Well, Barrie, if there's nothing else, you probably have a dozen things to do.'

Snarling wouldn't really have suited her gracious image.

'One of them thinks he could recognize the knife. The other's not sure.'

MacNee had got back in time to question the two Poles, to Macdonald's annoyance, then returned to Kirkluce to brief his boss.

Fleming was looking rough, suffering, he guessed, from divided loyalties. Her son must be on her mind, and she'd had all the demanding formalities to deal with – informing the DCC and the Fiscal's office, putting out a press statement, starting her log of actions taken – and that was just for a start.

He went on, 'Both said there'd been quite a stramash. Franzik erupted and went for Pavany with a knife. They'd to grab him, then Pavany took it off him – put it in his pocket or maybe down on the table. Then Pavany threw him out.'

'Dangerous young man,' Fleming said. 'A temper and a powerful motive. What was the row about?'

'Pavany was cheating him over his wages – both lads agreed on that. Didn't like the man, but said Franzik was mucking him about as well.'

'Good solid stuff, if we can lay hands on him. They've got fingerprints off the knife – smudged, but quite clear. No doubt they'll get Franzik's prints by elimination if nothing else – off a toothbrush or something.

'I've got the autopsy later, then I'll come back, sift what's come in and set up for tomorrow. Briefing at eight-thirty – I'm calling everyone in. We're seriously stretched and Dumfries won't be able to help. Don't think we can press-gang Ewan, though – statutory paternity leave's tricky. Pity – he's got a real talent for cutting straight to the point. Anyway—' Fleming looked meaningly at her cluttered desk.

'Another thing,' MacNee said. 'My wee chat with the Hodges – that was quite interesting. Pavany turned up there last night wanting to discuss payment for the building work and it ended up being a bit of a barney. But Diane gave Hodge a solid alibi, so—' MacNee shrugged. 'I told him we knew about him and Ailsa—'

Fleming cut him short. 'Let's leave that meantime. Once this is over, I'll pick up the Grant case again, but we're stretched right now. Put in your reports ASAP, anyway.'

He tried again. 'Suppose I see if I can try to trace any stuff about Lindsay's speeding charge? Just quietly—'

'Tam, we have a murder to deal with. Suppose we concentrate on that?'

'Fine, fine.'

He left, disappointed. But she hadn't actually forbidden him to phone one of his pals in Glasgow. The Fiscal would be all over them like a rash with the new case and having something they could use to get her off their backs could be very handy – very handy indeed.

19

The incident room was full by 8.30 on Sunday morning with uniforms as well as CID. Some were enjoying the buzz, looking at the diagrams and photos stuck to the whiteboard; some, like Tansy Kerr, were disgruntled.

'I could still be asleep,' Kerr grumbled to Andy Macdonald. 'Dragged out of bed yesterday too. You can get sick of this bloody job.'

Macdonald eyed her thoughtfully. Tansy had been subdued since her ill-judged affair last year with a fellow-officer. She'd ditched her ferocious hair colours for more muted shades, but her enthusiasm seemed muted too. He was going to say something when Kerr exclaimed, 'Oh, look – our very own new dad! Didn't think they could pull you in off paternity leave, Ewan!'

'Didn't,' DC Campbell said with his usual brevity. 'Wanted to come.'

Macdonald and Kerr exchanged knowing looks. 'Baby a bit much, is she?' he asked.

'Baby's OK. It's the wife and her mother. I don't have the Gaelic and all they do is blether away. Sounds like breaking glass with their teeth. The only time they speak English is when they're telling me what to do. Better here.'

Before they could coax him into further loquacity, Big Marge appeared and the briefing began.

*　　*　　*

It had been good to announce Kasper Franzik had been arrested and charged, Fleming reflected in her office later. Slick operations boosted morale, and her Force would be more effective today as a result.

As usual, she'd kept it short, telling them Franzik had been arrested after a call from a householder alarmed by a prowler in his garage, and charged when his fingerprints matched some prints on the knife. She'd ordered door-to-door around the Stoneykirk area where they'd picked him up, and searches of bins and roadsides in between for the missing shoes – likely to be trainers, according to Pavany's workmates. She had mentioned, as if in passing, that no other knife had been found on Pavany's body, but since it was possible he had carried one it might have been thrown away.

Had anyone noticed how flimsy that sounded? She didn't want to make her real reason public – that there was one major flaw in the neat case against Franzik which she was still hoping to argue away. Her team – MacNee, Macdonald, Kerr and Campbell – should arrive any moment, and she could only hope they'd brought their brains with them.

Last night Franzik, through an interpreter, had denied guilt, then clammed up, his dark eyes flashing hatred of his interrogators. Dishevelled and dirty after sleeping rough for two nights, he still looked romantic, as Karolina had said, in a mad-bad-and-dangerous-to-know Byronic way.

He certainly had a dangerous temper. He had flared up during their persistent questioning, and she had no problem at all with accepting that he was capable of stabbing his cheating boss.

There was just that one thing . . .

Jean Grant parked the old Vauxhall by the farmhouse door and got out with a basket of shopping from Ardhill. Her son, forking muck on to a trailer, didn't turn his head as she slammed the car door.

She came across the yard. 'Someone else been stabbed, they were saying at the shop. Dead, this time.'

Stuart still didn't turn his head. 'Oh?'

'One of thae Poles. Do you know them?'

He turned to face her now. 'Listen to me, woman. I've been thinking. If the polis come back, I'm not keeping quiet.'

Jean stiffened. 'Oh yes you are! You'll keep your mouth shut, like I told you. And if you don't, that's it. You lose the farm.'

He moved closer. She was a tall woman but he was inches taller, broad and burly. 'The thing is,' he said, 'I got curious the other day, after the police were here. Something they said made me wonder and then I found a box under your bed, with a couple of interesting things in it.'

She took a step back, her face contorted. 'How dare you! That's – that's private!'

'Shouldn't have been, though, should it? You've been using me, lied to me, again and again. All my life, practically. I've got them now, in a safe place.'

'Give me them back!'

He smiled a sneer.

'I'll find them! And anyway—'

'You'll change your will? So what? I went to a lawyer yesterday, and he says whatever you say, I'll get the bairn's part – half the estate. That's the law in Scotland. And once you're dead, you were just a mad old biddy when you altered it anyway, weren't you? After the way I've worked the farm for you I'd have no trouble at all in getting it set aside.

'And if we're talking about the law . . .'

Jean's face changed. There was fear there now. 'You wouldn't do that, to your own mother!'

'After what you did to my sister, this muck heap's clean.' He turned his back on her and went back to his task. Perhaps it was an accident that a lump of dung landed on her shoe.

It was Kerr this time who chose to perch on the table in the corner, while MacNee and Macdonald took the seats across the desk and Campbell pulled another forward to join them. Fleming had been concerned about Tansy recently, and this physical detachment from the group confirmed a suspicion that her heart wasn't in it these days. She'd have to tackle that, even if today the last thing she needed was extra aggro.

She was pleased Campbell was back, though. What little he said was always sharply to the point.

'I didn't expect to see you, Ewan. That's good. How's the baby?'

'Kind of noisy.'

Fleming laughed. 'They tend to be. You get used to it, sort of.

'Anyway, something emerged from the autopsy and I want your thoughts. As I said in the briefing, Pavany was hit on the head, then from a gash on his temple they reckon he fell forward on to the corner of something and was stabbed as he lay there. No evidence of whether conscious or unconscious.'

Nothing new here. They nodded.

The knife Fleming had taken into the briefing in its evidence bag lay on the desk before her, a razor-sharp blade with a Polish maker's mark and a horn handle with brass studs. She held it up.

'The kicker is, this wasn't the knife that killed him.'

'*Wasn't?*' MacNee exclaimed. 'But—'

'Found in the wound, yes. But look,' Fleming indicated, 'this has a curved blade. The knife that actually killed Pavany was longer and thinner, with a triangular blade. It was pulled out and this one, for some reason, inserted, not even far enough to reach the heart. The handle had been wiped, but they found Franzik's prints on the blade.'

Again, MacNee was the first to speak. 'According to the other two builders, Pavany had taken that knife off Franzik in a fight earlier. And those boys had grudges against him too.'

Macdonald gave a puzzled rub to his buzz-cut. 'You're not saying someone tried to frame him?'

'I hope to God I'm not,' Fleming said, 'but obviously it has occurred to me.'

MacNee was thinking aloud. 'If Pavany had Franzik's knife in his pocket, one of them could have killed him with his own knife, then taken it out and replaced it with Franzik's. Job done.'

'But someone I spoke to definitely said those lads were in the pub all evening till closing time – midnight on Saturday,' Macdonald argued. 'Though I suppose they could have got him earlier – left him dead in the house, then dumped him at the pub once everything was quiet.'

MacNee shook his head. 'Doesn't work. Pavany was at Sandhead around eight, having a run-in with Gavin Hodge about payment.'

'Everybody's pal, Pavany,' Fleming said. 'Any other thoughts?' Throwing ideas around with everyone participating was a useful exercise. If everyone participated. She looked pointedly at Kerr, trying to draw her into the discussion, but again it was Macdonald who answered.

'Pavany had taken Franzik's knife off him. So Franzik used another one, but maybe he had felt humiliated – losing the knife made him look helpless, a loser or something. So when he found it in Pavany's pocket, he switched the knife he'd used. A revenge, sort of.' He grimaced. 'Just an idea.'

'Certainly lateral thinking,' Fleming acknowledged.

'But would it convince anyone, that sort of psychological guff?' MacNee was sceptical. 'I can see his brief having a field day with that.

'Any chance it was the knife that stabbed Lindsay? If we'd just had him on a slab, they could've compared the wounds – that would have been a help.'

'I really don't want to think you're sounding regretful, Tam,' Fleming said. 'Maybe the surgeon who stitched him up could tell us something. But leave Lindsay out of it for the moment. It's what happened last night that we need to focus on.'

'You'd think he'd have realized the knife would incriminate him,' Macdonald said.

Fleming sighed. 'Yes, but with his temper, does he think ahead? Didn't have much of an escape plan, did he?'

Campbell was frowning. 'Anyway, how did he get the man there?'

'Who where?' Kerr made her first contribution, but the others looked at Campbell with respect.

'Didn't have a car, did he?' MacNee said slowly. 'Could hardly have wandered through Ardhill with a body over his shoulder.'

'Might have nicked one and returned it,' Macdonald suggested. 'Half the time around here they leave them unlocked with the keys in.'

'That's certainly possible,' Fleming said. 'Any other thoughts? No? Thanks for the input, anyway. Mull it over, and if anything occurs to you come back to me. Now, assignments . . .'

As they were going out, she said, 'Oh, Tansy – a word, if you don't mind.'

Startled, Kerr turned. 'Oh – fine,' she said, and came to sit down, but it was with the sulky, slightly nervous air of a child who knows a discussion of unsatisfactory behaviour is on the agenda.

Fleming began mildly enough. 'You didn't seem to have a lot to contribute today, Tansy.'

A little shrug. 'Didn't think of anything someone hadn't said already.'

'You didn't seem to be thinking much at all.' There was a slight edge to her voice.

That was Kerr's cue to apologize, but she didn't pick it up. 'I was tired. I didn't expect to be on duty today. It's my weekend off.'

Fleming raised her eyebrows. 'How many years of service do you have? And you haven't understood yet that when there's an emergency we all get hauled in?'

'Doesn't mean I like it.'

Fleming was startled, then annoyed. She was on edge and exhausted herself, and she wasn't about to take that sort of impertinence. She said coldly, 'Constable, I think you have to rethink that response. Right now.'

Kerr flushed and sat up a little straighter in her chair. 'Sorry, ma'am. But it's just all a bit much for me at the moment.'

Perhaps the girl really did have problems. Fleming said more gently, 'I have missed the sort of enthusiasm you used to bring to the team, Tansy. What's wrong?'

After a brief hesitation Kerr said, 'Well, to be honest, I'm just getting tired of missing out on things. I'd plans for today, and they've all been ruined.'

Suddenly, Fleming saw red. 'It just might occur to you that the plans the victim probably had for today, and all the other days, and all the rest of his life, have been just slightly dented! For heaven's sake, Kerr, you're a grown woman, not a teenager, and until you're ready to behave like one, you're not much use to me on the team.'

For a long moment, Kerr said nothing. Then she got up. 'I think that does it. I've been wondering whether I should stay in the Force, and I suppose I should be grateful to you for making up my mind.

'Maybe I should have come to you sooner to talk about it, but I was scared you'd react just the way you have. I'll be putting in my resignation.'

'Tansy—' Fleming said, then as Kerr waited, went on wearily, 'Oh, nothing. You've clearly made up your mind. You'd better come off the team now, then – I can't see you giving the investigation your best shot. OK.'

As the door shut behind Kerr, Fleming slumped in her chair with a groan. She hadn't meant it to go like that. Tansy had been a valuable officer until quite recently, and if Fleming hadn't been so completely wrung out herself, she might have been able to coax her into a better frame of mind.

On the other hand, she'd seen it before with young officers, male and female: if the job stopped being the most important and interesting thing in your life, you started minding about the things you were missing out on.

Like a normal family life.

When Marjory arrived back at Mains of Craigie, late, tired, and desperate for food and a glass of wine, she saw, to her dismay, that Karolina had been watching for her.

She came hurrying over from the cottage and approached hesitantly. 'I don't want to be a nuisance, Marjory. I know it's late. Just, I wanted to know – have you found Kasper?'

Groaning inwardly, Marjory said, 'That's all right, Karolina. Yes, we found him, and I'm afraid he's been charged with murder.'

To her surprise, Karolina nodded approval. 'Good. He is a bad man.'

Marjory had never seen the sweet-natured Karolina look so savage. 'Er – yes, I suppose he is. And of course, it is very sad about Stefan Pavany. Did you know him too, in Poland?'

'No. He is not Polish, I think.'

'Not Polish? But I saw his passport today.'

'I heard him talking to Kasper, when he came to the filming that time. He speaks Polish like – you know, the way a foreigner speaks. The accent, I think that is the word. It is wrong. Probably, he has a false passport. You are surprised? They are not hard to get, you know.' She was very matter-of-fact.

'I – I see. Thanks, Karolina.' Shaking her head, Marjory went inside. It wasn't often Karolina made her feel unworldly and naïve.

The house felt very empty, without even Meg to welcome her. Bill had phoned earlier to say that they'd arrived safely and that Cammie, though badly shaken, was on the mend, and might even be cleared to fly home tomorrow. He'd spoken without warmth, though, and that had hurt.

She went straight to the phone now, and managed to speak to Cammie, but it didn't make her feel any better. Yes, he was feeling OK, yes, they were looking after him fine, yes, the food was good, and then at the end, a rather bleak, 'I thought you'd have come.'

The bloody job. Marjory was too tired to feel hungry at the moment; she poured herself a glass of wine and went through to the sitting room. The pleasant room, with the shabby chair covers and all the casual evidence of family life – books and magazines on the side tables, videos and CDs stashed below the television – seemed for once chilly and unwelcoming.

She flicked on the TV, then, after staring at it without seeing it for ten minutes, switched it off again. She'd made her choice to do what she thought was her duty, so she'd better go on and try to sort things out in her tired brain. It was preferable to thinking about the damage she'd done to her relationship with her son.

The suggestions Macdonald had made in the session this morning about the knife and the transport were ingenious explanations, but they were just that – ingenious. What she liked were straightforward explanations that clicked into place whenever you thought of them. And somehow, despite the hard evidence of fingerprints on the knife and the circumstantial evidence of Franzik's previous attack on Pavany – and, indeed, Franzik's resentment of Marcus Lindsay, if you threw that in as well – she was wretchedly unconvinced.

Shoes.

Fleming sat at her desk next morning looking at the report on the footprints round Tulach which Dr Madsen had emailed through.

They had to assume Franzik had assaulted Marcus Lindsay before killing Pavany. But the facts were there in front of her on the desk and, as Tam would have put it, *'facts are chiels that winna ding'* – you can't get away from them.

She had the size and make of the trainers Franzik wore in front of her. And she had the size and make of the trainers which had made the prints on the terrace – amazing what they could find out nowadays! – and they simply weren't the same.

This, along with the knife problem, meant that the charge against Franzik was looking distinctly shaky now. She'd have to phone the acting Procurator Fiscal, who would be asking for Franzik to be remanded when he appeared in court this morning, and share her misgivings.

When she got through, Sheila Milne was dismissive. 'As I understand it, the accused went for Pavany earlier that evening, and his prints were on the knife. You haven't come up with anything that could allow us to charge him with the minor assault on Lindsay, and frankly, inspector, it's irrelevant. Leave it alone. It's only going to muddy the waters.'

'But—' Fleming said, and was cut short.

'I'm due in court. Goodbye.'

Still trying to call the police off Lindsay, was she? The horse had bolted from that particular stable, though with all this going on, the checks on Milne would have to wait. But supposing . . . She'd more or less written Milne off the suspect list after Pavany's murder, but what if the two really were unconnected and this had given the Fiscal a godsent opportunity to drop a case in which she herself was guilty?

Hold on! MacNee had said something – what was it? 'She's had a big extension put on her house . . .' Coincidence, surely, and nothing to say she'd used Pavany's gang. They could check it out, but come on!

Perhaps she was losing it completely; she was beginning to wonder what size Milne's feet were. Fleming ran her fingers through her hair. She had more to do than indulge in wild speculation.

The other footprints, the ones in the shrubbery, were from well-worn Caterpillar boots. You could get them locally – Bill had boots like that. From their size, these might have been Franzik's, but the report was quite definite: the person who had stabbed Lindsay was wearing the smaller trainers, not the boots.

She had an idea about that, but she had to put it to one side; the press officer was tapping her foot, waiting for a statement.

Shoes! There were too many pairs of shoes in this case.

Then, on a sudden thought, she picked up the phone and dialled the mortuary number. If the answer they gave her to the question she was going to ask confirmed what she thought, it would open up a whole new angle on the case.

The Force Civilian Assistant hovered on the edge of the CID room, clutching a print-out to her like a breastplate and blinking around helplessly.

There were three detectives working at computer stations; DS MacNee, in the middle of writing up reports, looked up hopefully, and spotting a chance to leave his desk, got up.

'Looking for someone?'

'Well – I reported to DI Fleming before, but apparently she's not to be disturbed unless it's urgent.'

MacNee beamed at her, then tempered his smile when he noticed her alarm. 'No problem. I'll deal with it. What's it about?'

'It's a DNA test they did on Ailsa Grant's baby,' she said. They've found a sort of match.'

'Have they? The wee dancers!' Tam crowed. 'Thanks, hen.'

The FCA scuttled away. Savouring the moment, MacNee took it back and began to read.

'Well, well, well,' he said aloud, almost to himself. 'I did wonder about that.'

'What?' One of the other detectives looked up in mild irritation.

'Oh, nothing, nothing,' MacNee said, but he didn't go back to his report. He closed the file, seized his leather jacket from the back of the chair and went out.

Jaki Johnston woke slowly and gave a luxurious stretch. She was in her own wee room, warm and safe, with the huge teddy bear she'd had since she was six sitting in the kiddie chair she'd had since she was three, watching over her.

The house was silent. Mum and Dad and her brother must have tiptoed out to work so as not to wake her. She'd been completely wiped out when she got back and the planned clubbing hadn't materialized; after a few drinks she'd been out on her feet and yesterday she'd spent half the day sleeping and the other half trying to stop her mother shovelling food down her because she was looking peaky.

This morning she felt fine. No bad dreams last night, head clear this morning because she'd stopped taking the pills.

Jaki went to shower, luxuriating in one that worked properly. The ones in Tulach House were antiques and tended to turn icy cold without warning. The whole Tulach experience had been totally unreal, so random she could hardly believe it had actually happened.

Then suddenly, in the way of these things, what she had been struggling to recall came back to her. It wasn't very significant, after all. But probably, once she'd had breakfast – she was starving now – she'd better phone that nice inspector, just in case.

'You again,' Gavin Hodge said. He looked worried rather than angry.

His wife's car wasn't in the drive, and MacNee wondered if his previous anger had been staged for her benefit to show injured innocence.

'Can I come in?'

MacNee's grave, measured delivery successfully scared his victim. Hodge gave him a terrified look before taking him to the conservatory where they had talked before. MacNee, never averse to a little bit of theatre, had hoped he might do just that.

He didn't sit down, stopping instead, apparently casually, just beside the table where the photo of the Hodges' son stood.

'We now have the DNA results from the child Ailsa Grant was carrying.'

Hodge sat down heavily. There was a greyish tinge to his florid complexion, but he tried to sound indifferent. 'So? If you want a swab from me the answer's no, unless you've a warrant.'

'I don't,' MacNee said, and saw the man's tense shoulders relax. 'We don't really need one, except for confirmation,' and he took a malicious pleasure in seeing the tension return.

'Don't try playing silly games with me! Say what you mean and get out.'

'It's kind of a funny story.' MacNee picked up the photograph. 'You see, they've come up with quite a close match with one Russell Hodge, convicted of embezzlement three years ago. And the funny part of it is that according to our records, Russell would have been a baby himself at that time.'

'So it's pretty obvious, isn't it? You and your wife are ashamed that your son's got a criminal record, but he's as much reason to be ashamed of you. More, maybe, if that was only the start of the damage you did to that poor girl.'

MacNee watched with clinical satisfaction as Hodge fell apart before his eyes.

'I – I didn't kill her.' He put his head in his hands. 'Yes, all right, it was my child. But I swear to God, I didn't harm her.' He began to sob.

MacNee's lip curled. 'And why should I believe this, when you've told black lies about everything else?'

'It was – it was all for Diane,' Hodge snivelled. 'I didn't want to upset her. It happened so long ago, and she's been through a lot with Russell – misses him terribly, you know, but he needed to make a new life—'

'Spare me your son's problems,' MacNee said coldly. 'And spare me the crap about your wife. She's got the money, hasn't she? You've been terrified all along she might find out about Ailsa. If she'd found out at the time, you'd have been out on your ear.'

Hodge took out a handkerchief and blew his nose. 'I never meant it to happen. I didn't plan it, but Diane had the baby, you see, and not much time for me. I suppose I was lonely and Ailsa – well, she really came on to me and . . .'

MacNee didn't try to conceal his contempt. 'Oh, you're just your mammy's big tumphy! Next you'll be telling me a big boy did it and ran away. So cut the sob stuff. Did you tell Ailsa you'd divorce Diane and marry her?'

'Of course not!' He was protesting vehemently, but his eyes were shifty. 'Her getting pregnant was a mistake, that was all. There were no strings attached – Ailsa knew the score. We agreed she'd go home to her parents to have the baby, and I'd send money when I could. I was pretty broke – Diane's dad had the money then.'

'Why didn't she have an abortion?' MacNee asked bluntly. 'Nothing I've heard so far suggests to me that she fancied being a single mother.'

Hodge was almost writhing now. 'Maybe she was religious or something,' he mumbled. 'I don't know – we never talked about it.'

'Funny, that, do you not think? Talked about you giving her a bit of money now and then – discreetly, of course, so as not to cause any trouble with your wife's family – but you never discussed what she and that wee kid were to live on in between times? Listen, you little bastard—' MacNee's hands had curled into angry fists and he had to take a deep breath to stop himself using them. Childless himself, he was not entirely rational when it came to casual indifference to a child you had produced.

Hodge had shrunk away from him, back into his chair, and MacNee's voice was still ragged with anger when he went on, 'I tell you what it sounds like to me. It sounds a great motive for tipping the poor girl off a cliff. How did you persuade her to go with you that night? Say you were doing the decent thing, taking her away and planning the divorce later?'

'No! No!' Hodge cried. 'It wasn't like that. I never came near her. We'd a few phone calls, that was all, but I never came back here. I was in Glasgow when it happened. Can't remember what I was doing, and I don't suppose anyone else can, but you're looking in the wrong place, so help me God.'

Did that have the ring of truth? The man had told so many lies and so many half-truths it was hard to tell. MacNee didn't want to believe him, but there was no scrap of evidence to link this sordid man to Ailsa's death. Yet.

MacNee stood up. 'You'll have to come in and make a formal statement. But not immediately,' he added hastily, remembering Fleming's instructions. 'And no doubt you'll gladly give a DNA sample then.'

'Of course, of course. And – and can we keep this from my wife?' Hodge was wringing his hands. 'For her sake. It's all a long time ago, and there's nothing to be gained by distressing her.'

MacNee eyed him with disgust. 'They really don't come much lower than you, do they? Oh, I won't make a point of telling her, but I won't conceal it either. And of course if we end up charging you with murder it'll be a bit of a giveaway.'

Leaving Hodge staring after him in consternation, he left the house. He glanced at the building round the side, its roof half finished and some of the window frames still empty.

MacNee snorted. The man hardly needed a steam room; he was in enough hot water already.

Fleming set down the phone. Ideas were starting to whirl in her mind, chaotic as yet, but she could see a way to order them, if she just had time to think.

The phone rang, and she swore. This better be important—

It was Jaki Johnston. 'It's probably nothing,' she began, 'but I thought of this silly tiny thing, and I just thought I'd better tell you.

'The other day I went out into the street in Ardhill and I heard these men talking. I couldn't make out what they were saying, and then I realized it was because they were speaking a foreign language. Then, just today, I remembered that the night Marcus was attacked, I'd heard someone shout something in a foreign language too. That's all, really. I hope I haven't bothered you for nothing.'

'Of course not, Jaki. We need every scrap of evidence we can get. Was it the same language you heard the men speaking in the street?'

'I wouldn't have a clue. Just, it wasn't French or German or anything.'

'Right. Thanks, Jaki. And anything else you think of, don't hesitate to phone.'

A new piece for the jigsaw, but where did it fit? Indeed, did it fit at all? Fleming sat back to think.

To keep down costs, Henryk and Jozef were interviewed together, big, solid young men, one fair, one dark, wearing identical expressions of polite interest as DS Macdonald's questions were relayed through the interpreter. Neither seemed intimidated, even by DC Campbell's coolly analytical gaze: it clearly hadn't occurred to them that they could be suspects.

Yes, they agreed, they had been together all evening in the pub. It was, Henryk said, a good place now the boys with knives were banned.

'Did you carry knives?' Macdonald asked, and saw for the first time a certain shiftiness. No, no, they didn't; it was, Jozef explained virtuously, against the law.

From a side table Macdonald produced a plastic evidence bag with a large, wicked-looking Bowie knife in it, and put it down on the table in front of them. 'Do you recognize this?'

They glanced at each other, then Henryk said that Stefan had a knife like that. He had seen it in his room sometimes.

Since that was where the SOCOs had found it, this was hardly news to Macdonald and Campbell.

'Did he usually carry it?' Campbell asked.

They didn't think so; it was a bit too big to put in a pocket and he certainly didn't wear it. Macdonald put it away again; it was to go off to the labs for testing today.

Henryk and Jozef, it transpired, knew almost nothing about Stefan. They were friends, had wanted to come to Scotland to work, and saw an advertisement from Stefan in a Polish newspaper, as Kasper too had done.

But they knew Stefan was Czech, not Polish. They had no idea why he had a Polish passport, but seemed unsurprised.

They didn't know much more about Kasper, except that they guessed he'd been in prison, and that he'd been pleased to come to this area because he had friends here. He always carried a knife for protection; Jozef said, with marked disapproval, that he looked for trouble.

'Where was Kasper last Wednesday night?' Campbell asked, and Macdonald had shot him a warning look. Big

Marge had been explicit about focusing on the job in hand.

They looked blank for a moment, then Jozef turned to Henryk and said something; Henryk nodded.

Macdonald raised his eyebrows to the interpreter. They had remembered – with all the aggro in the Ardhill pub, Stefan had let them have the van to go to Sandhead. Kasper hadn't gone with them. They didn't know any more.

After they had gone, Macdonald turned to Campbell. 'So that still leaves Franzik in the frame for the attack on Lindsay. Hoping they'd hand you something incriminating?'

'Hoping they'd give him an alibi,' Campbell said. 'Then we could stop this bloody farce and drop the charges.'

Campbell, with his usual efficiency, had filed the report on the interview with the Poles by four o'clock. Fleming read it, then sat back in her chair, thinking through the implications. It confirmed what Karolina told her, but it had created, too, a sort of echo in her mind: something she'd heard before somewhere, in another context . . . but that remained tantalizingly vague.

The information from the mortuary told her that she had indeed been right in her guess. It hadn't translated into firm evidence – yet – but it could be a step forward.

The acting Fiscal believed – or said she believed, which might be two very different things – that Franzik was responsible for the attack on Lindsay, but unless he had crammed his feet into trainers that were way too small for him, he hadn't been there.

Terrific – she'd eliminated the chief suspect, but without having any obvious successor to fill the position. The trouble was that you could read the crimes as two separate incidents, just the unfortunate results of the epidemic of knife crime

which was becoming a serious problem nationally. Three
incidents, in fact, since there was Franzik's wound earlier to
take into consideration too, though that she was inclined to
ascribe to Kevin Docherty or one of his friends; she'd seen
a report from the Kirkluce patrol car about scuffles between
Poles and the local neds that night.

Knives. Three knives: the one found in the wound, the one
from Pavany's bedroom – again with a curved blade – and
the triangular one that had actually killed the man. She had
a feeling that if she could unlock that particular puzzle, she'd
have the answer to the whole thing.

She kept coming back to the elusive memory – what was it
that she knew, that related to all this? She couldn't get at it; it
was like an itch she couldn't scratch.

There had been so much background noise in this case
that it was hard to filter out the extraneous stuff. But her
guess, as far as it went, gave her at the very least a reasonable
basis for a hypothesis. Just supposing . . .

Fleming scribbled a mind map, with arrows, crossed off
names. Then she reinstated some of them, and started again.
It took a long time, but gradually a clearer picture started to
emerge.

And at last she tracked down the thing she had been trying
to remember, something her mother had told her – and
immediately the significance of Jaki's information became
plain.

That could be the connection. But what? Why? *Why?* She
still couldn't see where to go with it. Then suddenly, like a
flash of lightning illuminating a dark landscape, she saw the
answer as she remembered the mistake she had made in the
street at Ardhill.

One by one, the tumblers started falling into place.
Excitement fizzed through her. It was all making sense,

with exhilarating clarity. She felt the high, heady sense of excitement that kept her in thrall to the pressured job she did. It just might be addictive.

Fleming knew now why Marcus Lindsay had so foolishly gone out into the darkness; she knew why Pavany's trainers had been removed, and she knew exactly why Franzik's knife had been found in the wound. And that was just for a start.

There wasn't enough for a search warrant, quite. The sheriffs were very fussy about human rights these days, and she'd need something more solid than a deductive process to offer. She should probably wait until the labs had done their job on fibre samples from the dead man's clothes.

But tomorrow, Cammie was coming home. She had a gut feeling that despite the gaps in the evidence, despite the imaginative leaps she had had to take, she could get better than technical evidence if she went for it, right now. Then she could trust MacNee, Macdonald, Campbell and Kerr – not Kerr, of course, she thought with a pang – to dot the 'i's and cross the 't's, ready to hand it to Bailey with a big red bow when he got back from Ireland on Wednesday. She'd take compassionate leave and start trying to mend fences with her family.

She picked up the phone and dialled MacNee's mobile. 'Tam? I need you to come with me. And you just might need handcuffs.'

20

Power seldom passes without great bitterness, and the atmosphere at Balnakenny was toxic. Stuart Grant had carried on with his work in the yard, steadfastly ignoring his mother's white face and burning eyes as she watched from the kitchen window.

When he came in for his tea, there was no table laid, no food prepared. Jean was sitting by the fire, exuding malice.

Without comment, he went to the larder, coming back with a tray of eggs and a frying pan. He broke half-a-dozen into it, stirred them up with a fork, then set the pan on the heat while he fetched a loaf and butter. The eggs had stuck to the bottom when he came back, but he scraped the pan and decanted the half-cooked, half-burnt mess on to a plate and sat down at the table to eat.

Neither spoke. Stuart finished and got up. As he went to leave the room, he noticed the table where the shrine to his sister had been. It was bare. He looked over his shoulder at Jean with an unpleasant smile.

In the small back room where they watched television, Stuart sorted through the CDs. He'd mentioned *Terminator 2* to the police the other day, which had reminded him how much he enjoyed it. He switched it on and sat down.

He had been watching for about half an hour when Jean came in. With a return to her customary authority she went to the set and turned it off, then stood, arms folded, in front of it.

Her face was hard and angry. 'I want to talk.'

Stuart looked up at her from his seat, then rose, looming over her. He took her by the shoulders and moved her bodily out of the way, turned the TV back on and sat down again.

'I don't,' he said.

Jean was left staring helplessly at the son whose malleability she had in her heart despised. She was very much afraid.

MacNee glanced surreptitiously at his boss as she drove, rather too fast, down the narrow road towards Sandhead. He'd never seen her like this, so high on adrenalin. She'd worked it all out, she told him, but she wouldn't tell him anything more.

If she had, she'd every right to be pleased with herself. He still hadn't got it sorted out, whether the three cases they were dealing with were linked to one another or not.

If she was right. But it was exactly when you got carried away with the thrill of the chase that you got it wrong. He'd actually found himself urging caution – hardly his usual style!

Even when he enlisted Scotland's Bard, with dark warnings about passing Wisdom's door for glaikit Folly's portals, she only laughed.

'Bear with me, Tam! If a little drama is needed to get Pavany's killer locked up tonight – well, it works for Playfair!'

The drawing room looked at its best in the evening. With the curtains drawn and the great Chinese lamps lit, with the flames from the log fire dancing in its polished steel basket, the threadbare rugs and damp patches on the walls disappeared into shadow.

Sylvia Lascelles, sitting in the upright Jacobean chair by the fireplace, was uncomfortable with the shadows tonight. They seemed to be encroaching on the little island of light and warmth she and Marcus were sharing. Though it was a still, mild evening, there seemed to be an icy breath coming from the darkness of the room behind her, and she gave a little shiver.

Marcus, sitting opposite watching the flicker of the flames, looked across to her. 'Cold? Shall I fetch your wrap?'

'No, no, it's all right – just foolishness.' With an attempt at gaiety, she said, 'You know what I would love, darling? Just since it's our last night here?'

He played to her tone. 'Let me guess. Champagne?'

'Champagne,' she said, with a gurgle of laughter. 'Terribly, terribly wicked of me, with my pills, but I don't care. "*What though youth gave love and roses; age still leaves us friends and wine!*"'

He got up, smiling down at her. 'I could arrange for roses, from time to time.'

'Dearest boy, so kind! No need.'

But when she was alone, a melancholy French poem came into her head, *Nous n'irons plus au bois* . . . We will go to the woods no more; the laurels are all cut down . . . She turned Laddie's ring on her finger, looking towards his photograph on the table beside her. So handsome, such a lover – dust now, as she would be before too long.

Her last night here. Ever. She would love to see what Marcus would do with Laddie's beloved Tulach, but soon she would no longer be able to leave her flat, her prison, and photographs were the best she could hope for. The shadows were creeping closer.

Marcus came back and she heard the sigh of a cork being released. She took the glass from him, held it up to touch his. 'Music, maestro! Not something gloomy and proper – I know! *Chicago*. Do you have it? She sang the first line from *All That Jazz* in her throaty voice, gesturing a Charleston movement with her hands.

He was meant to laugh, but he didn't. He said very seriously, 'You're a great girl, Sylvia. The greatest. The best.'

And just then the doorbell rang, and Sylvia's heart fluttered, like wings beating beneath her breastbone.

He ushered the officers through to the drawing room, then stood back for a second – in the wings, he would almost have said. Marcus had felt sick and light-headed with stage nerves many a time, so this was no different. Deep, slow breath, slow exhalation . . . Entrance.

Sylvia was smiling her special smile at the short detective. She'd joked with Marcus about her latest conquest, but tonight the man didn't respond. He was unsmiling, his eyes not quite meeting hers.

The inspector didn't smile either. She was a tall woman, taller than Marcus himself, with an air of effortless confidence. Not good-looking, but there was something about the face, the eyes, perhaps . . . Yes, the eyes. Clear hazel, with a penetrating gaze. But he sensed something else tonight – an aura of controlled excitement. He tried to banish the image of a lioness, moving with infinite caution towards her prey.

Deliberately, he waved the officers to a low sofa. 'Yes, Inspector Fleming?' he said. 'Rather late for a social call.' He sounded respectful, but not entirely pleased, as any middle-class householder might.

'Yes.' She looked towards Sylvia. 'Miss Lascelles, our business is with Mr Lindsay. Mainly.'

Sylvia went into fluffy mode. 'So difficult. I'm such a helpless old fool, it's quite a performance to leave the room.' She gestured to the cane propped up beside her, and to Marcus's alarm he saw Fleming's eyes go to it thoughtfully.

Sylvia was going on, 'So darling, if you don't mind—'

She looked towards him and he collected himself. 'Of course not. As they say in all the best movies, we have no secrets from each other.'

'Speak for yourself!' The quick comeback, he noticed, got a smile from the sergeant. Less encouragingly, it was swiftly suppressed.

'Very well.' The inspector had not smiled.

Lindsay dragged forward a heavy wooden chair. The height, he felt, would give him a psychological advantage.

'I see you have recovered from your injury, Mr Lindsay. Your left side anyway, wasn't it? And you're right-handed?'

Had Fleming said that pointedly? 'Yes, I was lucky. I had to wear a sling for a few days. Any violent movement could have torn the stitches.'

She secmed unimpressed. 'But you weren't incapacitated? I see.' She went on, 'I gather your father was Czechoslovakian?'

'Yes.'

'Do you speak Czech yourself?'

'A little. I can understand more.' He couldn't see where this was leading.

'The murder victim was a Czech.'

Tone of polite interest. 'Really? Well, it's quite a big place.'

'You see, we were puzzled that you should have gone outside at all on the night you were attacked, given that one of the local neds had it in for you.'

He shook his head, holding out his hands in a pantomime of incomprehension. 'I've asked myself that, again and again, but—'

'You see, I think we now know exactly why.'

Cue enthusiasm. 'Really? That's wonderful! Are you closer to discovering my assailant, then?'

Sylvia leaned forward. 'That is just so clever! Was it this poor young man who has been charged with the murder of that other poor man?'

The inspector gave her a sideways glance; the sergeant, taking notes, didn't raise his head.

'No,' Fleming said. 'We can now say quite definitely that it wasn't. And I am fairly sure that the person who attacked you was the man calling himself Stefan Pavany.'

'Stefan Pavany – was that the name of the man who was killed?' He sounded interested, though puzzled. They wouldn't review this one, but it was possibly one of Marcus's finer performances.

'His assumed name. Mr Lindsay, we have evidence to suggest that after you opened the door and found there was no one there, someone called out something in a foreign language. It was after that you went round into the garden.'

'Really? Do you know what was said – or even what language?' It would be natural, wouldn't it, to let just a hint of annoyance creep in, given the way the woman said it?

'No.'

She didn't like admitting that. It was his first small victory. 'It would be helpful if you could find out,' he suggested. 'Might trigger something, you never know. It has to be in here somewhere.'

He tapped his head, smiling blandly. But just as he dared to think he might be winning, she moved the goalposts.

'Mr Lindsay, what were you doing on Friday night?'

He stalled a little, artistically. 'That's a very pointed question! Let me think – Friday? Ah! Of course.

'May I call on my principal witness, Miss Sylvia Lascelles?' Maybe, just maybe, it was going to come out all right after all. 'Miss Lascelles—?'

Sylvia had been looking shaky, but he could see her begin to enjoy herself. She took a sip of champagne from the glass at her side.

'Inspector, I can confirm that the defendant and I were here together all evening engaged in a killer game of Scrabble until half past ten. Then, for some reason, the defendant didn't think several hours more of losing at Scrabble would be amusing – though I disagreed – and he phoned the pub to rustle up some of the film crew to play poker instead. Though I'm afraid he didn't fare any better with that.'

Marcus saw the sergeant stifle a grin and was encouraged. 'I'm not at all sure what you're saying here, inspector. I don't suppose you're really suggesting that, having for some unknown reason murdered a Czech whom I didn't even know, we then called in colleagues to party round his body before dumping it in the pub car park?'

Fleming paused, then said coolly, 'I don't know how familiar you are with recent changes in the law, but when they're determining sentence it makes quite a difference to the tariff if you have cooperated with the police.

'We're still at an early stage in the investigation, with a lot of evidence waiting to come in. So, unusually, I'm going to tell you our thinking, because I think this is a very unusual case.'

He composed his face into an expression of polite interest, but that was when he knew, quite definitely, that it was all over. Somehow, she knew.

'Your father, a Czech, was married before he came to Britain during the war. Stefan Pavany was a Czech, but for some reason he was anxious to conceal this. I freely admit this is a wild guess – though of course it can be checked – but I thought it possible your father might have had a child, or children, there.'

Marcus felt his heart beginning to race. He looked at Sylvia; she never had a lot of colour, but she looked worryingly pale and she was breathing faster.

'I was at the film set when Stefan Pavany came to speak to Kasper Franzik. You had been in costume, acting an older man, and for a moment I thought he was you. Was Stefan Pavany your half-brother?' Fleming waited for a response, but he only looked back at her.

'You see, I think he tried to kill you. Revenge, inheritance – I don't know, but again, we can find out. Just as we can find out whether there are fibres from this room on the clothes Pavany was wearing.'

Sylvia gave a little gasp, almost a cough. Marcus saw the sergeant look at her anxiously.

'It was Pavany's shoes being missing, you know. It may have seemed clever to remove them, but it made me ask questions. You were the only person who had talked to Dr Madsen, who knew how much the footprint evidence could tell him, and you couldn't afford to have Pavany associated with the attack on you.

'And the knife that was in Pavany's back – you found it in his pocket, assumed it was his, wiped the handle and put it there after you'd killed him. You're familiar with forensic science; it's my guess that you thought we wouldn't know whose knife it was but would assume the same man was to blame for both crimes. But rigging evidence isn't as easy in real life as on television, you know. Pavany didn't take the knife we think he used on you to the meeting you agreed; he had one in his pocket anyway that he'd taken from Kasper Franzik.

'Did he fall against that fender there? We can match it up with the wound on his temple. Did you, even, strike him first with that?' Fleming's eyes were very bright and hard as she gestured towards the cane with its heavy silver handle which was propped by Sylvia's chair. 'If so, we can tell that too. All the evidence we need to convict you is right here in this room. We only need to look for it. You know that.

'So why did you do it, Marcus?'

There was a long, long silence. It was Sylvia who broke it, leaning forward in her seat, trembling with rage, and Marcus knew the play was over. They'd had the denouement; now they were only waiting for the curtain to fall.

'It's your fault!' she cried, her husky voice cracking with emotion. 'If you were going to throw away the key because he tried to kill Marcus, that would have been all right. But you wouldn't – you admitted it yourself. He'd have been in prison for a couple of years at most, and he'd have come back. He would always have come back, until he did what he meant to do last week. Marcus could never be safe. This was self-defence, that's all. Anyway, why should he have anything?'

'Sylvia,' Marcus said, but there was no stopping her.

Her lips had a blue tinge. 'Laddie was so proud of Marcus – his wonderful, beautiful son! His first wife trapped him into marriage because she got pregnant and he was young. She was a peasant, and her son was like his mother – coarse, not worthy of him, he said. That man had a peasant's greed – greed to the point where he would kill!'

She was gasping for breath. Alarmed, Marcus said, 'Sylvia, stop this. You'll make yourself ill—'

But she went on. 'I knew what Laddie would do. He was a man – he was—'

Then Sylvia's face changed. She jerked, knocking over the table beside her. The champagne glass fell to the floor and broke as her hand went to her chest. 'Oh, God! Oh, Laddie!' She spoke as if the two were one.

346ALINE TEMPLETON

It was the sergeant who moved first. He was on the phone, almost before Sylvia had slumped forward, shouting, 'Ambulance! Priority!'

The inspector moved fast, beginning resuscitation, but Marcus knew there was no point. With exquisite pain, he heard the last rasping breath of the woman who had meant more to him than his own mother. His adored nemesis.

'I know what forensic science is able to do,' Marcus Lindsay said, his voice flat and toneless. 'Few better, after all these years on *Playfair's Patch*. Every contact leaves a trace – you only have to know where to look . . .'

The man looked – extinguished, Fleming thought. But then, MacNee, with stubble growth on his cheeks, looked as if he'd slept in a ditch, and she was exhausted. She felt grubby too, grubby in soul as well as body. MacNee was barely speaking to her, and she didn't blame him. She had let her triumph at disentangling the web of confusion surrounding Pavany's death betray her into something worthy of *Playfair's Patch*, and this tragedy had been the result.

It was six in the morning. The drama and the formalities of Sylvia Lascelles' death had taken hours; they were only now in an interview room beginning the questioning under caution.

'There's no point in fighting it, in the endless lying,' Lindsay was going on. 'I'm too tired.'

'Do you want to make a formal confession, Mr Lindsay?' Fleming said. Everything was going to be straight by the book this time.

He didn't hesitate. 'Yes. Oh God, yes. The strain, waiting and waiting, expecting something to go wrong – worse than a first night.' He gave the ghost of a smile.

He had a very charming smile but, looking at him now, Fleming could see the lines of weakness clearly marked.

'I knew nothing about my half-brother, except that he existed. To my knowledge, my father never had any contact with them after the divorce. When there was no one at the door that night, I did think immediately of the wretched youth in the pub. I was going to shut it hastily when a voice shouted in Czech, "I am your brother Stefan. We need to talk about Vikova." '

'Vikova?'

'It was my father's old home. To be honest, I never believed his stories – what money there was in our family was my mother's and most of that's gone now – but the Czech government has started paying reparation. Sylvia talked about it, suggested finding out, but I wasn't ready for the legal fees and the hassle.

'But Stefan had done it, only to find the authorities knew I was the legal heir. I'm a young man – it would be unlikely that I had made a will and he was next-of-kin. So he came after me. Pretended to be Polish so there would be no connection made.

'Most of what I told you was true – I genuinely remember nothing after I went round the back of the house to meet him. I only found all this out on our – our second encounter.'

MacNee had been brooding and withdrawn. Now he said in the tone of one anxious to disbelieve, 'So how come you knew it was Pavany – or where to find him for what you like to call "your second encounter"? Or "his murder", as the rest of us would call it.'

'Sylvia saw him attacking me. He looked up as he ran away, and she said it was like a nightmare – she was looking at a distorted version of Laddie's face. And when she said that, I remembered the man who'd turned up at the filming. I'd looked at him, thought he was familiar, somehow, just as you did.

'It was Sylvia who wouldn't let me tell you. She didn't trust the system. She said Stefan would only get a token sentence, that he would never give up, that he'd shown already that he had our father's ruthlessness, even if I didn't. When he got out of prison he would come after me; I'd be forever looking over my shoulder and one day he'd get me.

'To be honest, I thought she was mad at first. I argued with her. In fact, I even put in a call to our legal expert on *Playfair*, pretending it had given me an idea for the series, to ask about a probable outcome, and he confirmed that unless there was major injury it would be all but impossible to get a conviction for attempted murder.

'So I had a choice. I could go around for the rest of my life, being afraid of the knife in my back, or I could do one terrifying, risky thing and live in peace. And she was utterly convinced we could stage it and get away with it, that all I needed was a little bit of courage – and I was Laddie Lazansky's son, after all. "Do you want to die because you're too much of a coward to defend yourself?" That was what she said.'

'Now I've heard bloody everything!' MacNee exploded. 'All her fault, is it – a gracious old lady that you've killed with what you've done?'

Lindsay's own grief was clear in his face. 'I killed her with what I *didn't* do,' he corrected. 'I didn't have the courage to stand up to her, and do the right thing.'

With a warning glance at MacNee, Fleming said, 'As your father, perhaps, would have done?'

Lindsay gave a short laugh. 'Laddie? He'd have knifed the man without a second thought. He was a total bastard, but I idolized him. He was pure magic as a father, glamorous, amusing, indulgent. Oh, I know just how much there was to disapprove of in his life – the way he treated my mother, for a start, having Sylvia as a *maîtresse-en-titre*. But when he died, the colour went out of my life too. Everyone else, apart from Sylvia, seems grey and boring. Including me – oh yes, particularly me. I look like a faded version of him, and I think I am.'

It was pitiable: this successful man, seeing himself always through the prism of a child's view of a charming, ruthless sod of a father. But MacNee clearly wasn't feeling sympathetic.

'We're not paid to listen to a plea in mitigation. Just get on with it.'

'Mr Lindsay, it's been quite a night for all of us,' Fleming said soothingly, earning a sullen look from MacNee. 'I'd like to finish this interview as soon as possible. What happened on the evening you killed Stefan – Stefan Lazansky, as I suppose we must call him now?'

'It was ridiculously easy. He'd put a card through my letter-box a few weeks ago, hoping to be employed on building work – to give him a better shot at me, I suppose – and I phoned him. I said I could call in the police, but I thought for both our sakes it would be smarter to talk business. He was very taken aback that I'd found him, but he agreed. I even hoped we might actually come to some sort of arrangement, but Sylvia told me I was being a naïve fool.

'She insisted on being there. It would reassure him, she said, if she was in the room – a sweet old lady like her. He came in and we talked about Vikova. He wanted it in a way I never had – he sounded like my father talking about Tulach – and I knew I could never trust him. He didn't want to sell it and split the money; he was just playing me along while he worked out the next step. And he was no actor – I could see murder in his eyes. Sylvia had been right. She usually was.

'She looked casually towards me and I gave a tiny nod. A little later, she dropped her handkerchief on the floor, and when he bent to pick it up, I took her cane and brought the knob of it down on the back of his head.'

MacNee looked down. Fleming could see him biting his lip.

'And then – yes, I killed him,' Lindsay said.

They had it on tape. Fleming gave a small sigh. 'Then – you phoned friends, for an alibi?'

'I took – the body,' he swallowed, clearly uncomfortable with the detail, 'through to the library, wrapped in a rug. You were right that I found the knife in his pocket. And you needn't look for the kitchen knife I used – it's in the sea now, along with his damned trainers. Then I washed my hands – again and again. Symbolic, I suppose.'

Encountering a hostile look from MacNee, he went on quickly. 'Sylvia was amazing – utterly calm, and when the others arrived she did all the talking until I had time to pull myself together.

'Later I drove down to the pub and – and left it. And that's it, really. We'd rehearsed beforehand, of course, rehearsed and rehearsed. I kept thinking that it would never actually happen, that this was just like acting in a play – that made it easier. Sylvia was sure we would never be suspected, but I was afraid. If once the connection was made, you would find out – I knew that.'

'Didn't want us testing your DNA, did you?' MacNee's tone was still aggressive. 'You had it worked out long before – callous bastard!'

Lindsay, bizarrely, began to laugh. It was genuine laughter but with a hysterical edge to it, and it took a moment for him to control himself long enough to say, 'You flatter me, sergeant. Though I flattered you – I thought you'd probably worked it out by now. I didn't want to give you my DNA because if you tested Ailsa Grant's child, you might get some rather curious results. My father told me, though I doubt if her mother ever told her.

'Ailsa was my half-sister.'

21

'I'm suspending you, Marjory,' Superintendent Bailey said on Wednesday morning, his face sombre. 'I'm afraid I have no alternative.'

He didn't. Even when everything has been done by the book, a death during police questioning is subject to an enquiry, and now the media was baying for blood and claiming that police brutality had caused the death of one of Britain's national treasures.

'I know,' Fleming said. 'It was an inexcusable misjudgement. I should have brought Lindsay in for questioning.'

'Indeed you should, instead of staging a drama which gave the woman a heart attack. I can't think what possessed you, Marjory – she was a frail, elderly woman, in a wheelchair, for God's sake! What could have been a triumph of police work has become a complete disaster.'

Fleming, her head bowed, said nothing, and Bailey sighed. 'Well, there's not a lot more to say. We'll have to wait and see whether Lindsay lodges a formal complaint, and take it from there.'

'Thanks, Donald. I can only say how deeply I regret this.'

The poor woman looked crushed. He had resented her attitude over the cold case, but he was not an ungenerous man. 'Marjory, as I've said before, you're the best officer I have. I'll move heaven and earth to get the CC on side to work for a positive result.'

She nodded, and left the room.

Bailey sat back in his chair and put his fingers together in a pyramid. The acting Procurator Fiscal had been on the phone demanding a meeting once the news broke this morning, and she was expecting him shortly.

The interview wasn't going to go quite as Milne was planning, though. Fleming had wanted him to hold off from investigating the records, but he hadn't actually agreed. So when Tam MacNee, working on the same basis, had come to him with evidence he'd got from Glasgow by the sort of devious route a superintendent didn't want to know about, he had not allowed himself to be troubled by scruples. And what he had to say to Milne now would, in MacNee's phrase, put her gas on a peep.

Marjory Fleming drove home to Mains of Craigie with unusual attention to the road. Exhausted and wretched, she might drive into the back of a ten-ton truck if she wasn't very careful. She shouldn't be driving at all, really, given the 'Tiredness kills' campaign, but one more breach of the rule book hardly seemed to matter.

She kept glancing in the mirror, but so far at least it seemed the press weren't on to her, though no doubt there would be that ordeal to come. She turned off up the track to the farmhouse, then parked the car and dragged herself into the house. Bill and the family would be hours yet, so at least she would be able to get the sleep she so desperately needed. Things would look better after that. Probably. Or 'perhaps' might be a better word.

She could hear the vacuum cleaner – Karolina at her work. Her heart sank at the thought of talk and enquiries, but pinning on a smile, she followed the sound to the sitting room.

To her surprise, it was Janet Laird hoovering, humming to herself above the noise of the motor. When Marjory appeared, she jumped.

'Oh, goodness me, pet, what a fright! I didn't expect you home just now.' She switched the machine off.

'What on earth are you doing, Mum?' Marjory demanded. 'You shouldn't be doing my cleaning! Where's Karolina?'

Janet smiled. 'Poor wee soul! She's expecting again, and she's feeling just terrible. I was out here yesterday evening, and she nearly fainted over the ironing. So I've told her she's to rest, and if I do the work for her, you can pay me and I'll give it to her – they'll be needing the money, with another mouth to feed.'

'But – but—' Marjory protested, 'I wouldn't cut her wages because she's not feeling well enough to work – you know that! There's no need for my elderly mother to be slaving away – I can do it myself.'

Janet's face was glowing with the exercise and – was it satisfaction? 'I'm having a fine time,' she said firmly. 'I was never one could sit still for long, you know, and I've been getting quite low with nothing to do and feeling useless. And then the other night, when you didn't tell me about Cammie – I know you mean to be kind, pet, but I'm not decrepit yet. And you're so busy—'

'Not any more,' Marjory said bitterly. 'Mum, I've been suspended.' And if her mother said, 'Oh, my lamb!' and put her arms round her, she'd burst into tears as if she was ten years old.

Janet didn't. She said, 'Dearie me, they're always getting things wrong. I'm going to make a cup of tea and you can tell me about it. And then you can get to your bed and catch up on some sleep – you're looking wabbit.'

Washed-out was exactly how she felt. Meekly, Marjory followed her mother through to the kitchen and embarked on the long and sorry tale.

'I'm delighted that you have suspended Fleming,' Sheila Milne said. 'As you know, I've been saying for some time that incompetent woman has no place in the police force. Presumably now her career is at an end.'

'Suspension is a temporary measure, pending enquiries.' Superintendent Bailey's voice was cold. 'DI Fleming is a most valuable officer and I have every hope that she will be reinstated at the end of this process.'

'I should inform you that I will vigorously oppose it, right up to the highest level.' Milne's full lips tightened in annoyance.

'I'm sure you will. However,' Bailey sat back with a little smile, his moment come at last, 'I have to tell you the police are instituting an enquiry of our own. Recently information has come to me which indicates that your marking decisions in certain cases in Glasgow were, shall we say, suspect.'

Milne's eyes, slightly protuberant anyway, bulged. 'I can't think what you mean!'

'Favours for friends, you might call it, though for all we know as yet money may have changed hands as well. Or just gifts to show appreciation, perhaps? We have information already which is concerning to say the least of it, and we also have a statement made by Marcus Lindsay—'

'I can't think the court will be impressed with the evidence of a *murderer*.' Milne sounded angry, but her thick, creamy skin had turned a chalky colour. 'Flimsy, I would have said, against my word.'

'You're forgetting the paper trail.' Bailey was enjoying himself now. 'And once we start tracking people down, I think you'll find your middle-class friends won't risk a charge of delaying the ends of justice, especially since the speeding cases that weren't raised against them then are time-barred by now.'

'It's – it's quite ridiculous.' She couldn't disguise the fear in her voice. 'I – I have nothing more to say to you. I shall be contacting my lawyer.'

'Yes, I should, if I were you.' Bailey got up. 'We shall be contacting the Lord Advocate, and I think you may well be joining DI Fleming on suspension any day now.'

Janet Laird had hardly spoken as her daughter told her what had happened. Now Marjory was pouring out a confession of thoughtlessness and self-loathing.

'I had no excuse. I'd seen Sylvia Lascelles resting after she'd been working one day and she didn't look at all well, so I should have considered that. I've seen a grown man faint under the stress of intensive questioning, for heaven's sake, and that was only for housebreaking. But she had such spirit, you just didn't think of her as being frail.'

'But you'd suggested she should leave,' Janet pointed out. 'It was her decision to stay. And from what you've told me, she got herself wrochit up with her nasty, spiteful raging about the poor souls her precious Laddie had abandoned. He left sore hearts there, and it's no wonder the boy turned out how he did.

'And anyway, I'm an old woman myself. If you told me all I had in front of me was living on my own in London, no family, crippled and in pain and getting worse with every week that passed – well, I'd say it was doing me a favour to let me get away before I knew what was happening.'

Marjory gave a wry smile. 'Good try. Certainly better than anything I've been able to come up with myself by way of justification, but I can't quite see it like that.'

'Then you should maybe consider that from the sound of it the poor man would never have thought of it if she hadn't goaded him to it,' Janet said with some asperity, 'and as far as I can tell, the woman would have stuck the knife in by herself if she'd been able. An evil besom, if you ask me.'

'Oh, I suppose she was. But oh, Mum, she had such charm! And she was still a beauty, even in old age. You remember her in that weepie, *For Ever*?'

Her mother sniffed. 'Never could be doing with that film. I said at the time she was ower sweet to be wholesome, like a frosted tattie.'

That surprised a laugh out of Marjory and satisfied, Janet went on, 'Now, my bairn, you're needing your bed. You'll want to be fresh for the family when they get back – around four, Bill thought.'

Marjory's face clouded over again. 'I'm – I'm not looking forward to that either. They're all angry with me. Did I do the right thing, Mum?'

Janet's eyes were loving, but troubled. 'That's one thing I can't tell you, my lamb. I've never had to think there might be anything I should put ahead of you and your father – I was lucky that way. It's harder for all you young women nowadays.

'But you just did what you believed was right, didn't you, and that's all any of us can do. Now, away you go!'

Marjory went slowly up the stairs. She didn't want to examine her conscience too closely, just at the moment.

'Lindsay's not making a complaint, sir, anyway,' Bailey said over the phone to Chief Constable Menzies. 'He says that Miss Lascelles had it suggested to her that she should leave and flatly refused.'

'That's always something,' Menzies said. 'I don't want Fleming hung out to dry. After all, she did an amazingly good job on a very complex case. Let's get this pushed through as quickly as possible.'

Bailey swallowed hard. 'There's – there's one other thing.'

'Bad news, from the sound of it.'

'Franzik's been released, of course, but he's filed a complaint of racism. Looking for enhanced compensation, of course, but . . .'

There was a heavy silence at the other end of the phone. Then Menzies said, 'Oh, God. Not racism. It's beyond ridiculous, but we have to be seen to take it seriously. You'd better put in for a temporary replacement meantime.'

Bailey put down the phone. He was sorry about Fleming, of course he was. She'd got a bit carried away, certainly, but she didn't deserve this.

But there was a small part of him breathing a gentle sigh of relief. Sheila Milne would be gone shortly and there would be no more pressure to investigate Ailsa Grant's murder. They all knew Robert Grant had done it anyway, and since he was dead it wasn't worth the time and the money. By the time Fleming came back to work, he could tell her to shelve it.

Marjory had been waiting in the kitchen for half an hour before she heard the car arrive, driving her mother mad by fiddling with the things on the table set for tea and doing aimless tidying, several times putting away something Janet was just about to use. Meg, brought back by Rafael earlier, began racing round and round with joyful barks.

'Mercy, between the pair of you I'll be driven clean gyte!' Janet exclaimed with uncharacteristic exasperation. 'Away you go out and see your wee lad, and take that daft animal with you.'

Meg dashed outside, confident of her welcome. Marjory followed more slowly.

Bill was helping Cammie out of the car; Cat was holding his crutches. He was in plaster beyond the knee and his face was pinched and pale. Her heart wrung, Marjory ran across. 'Oh, my darling, how are you?'

She put her arms round his neck. She had to reach up to do it; even stooped, he was taller than she was now, almost as tall as his father.

'Hi, Mum,' he said, and let her kiss him. It was obviously because of the crutches that he didn't even attempt to hug her back. 'I'll be fine – a bit tired, that's all.'

As Marjory hugged Bill and Cat, asking about the journey, Janet appeared at the back door. Cammie swung himself across to her, beaming. 'Hi, Gran!' he said, and this time, despite the crutches, he was able to put an affectionate arm round her.

Janet smiled at him, shaking her head. 'Dearie me! Let you out of our sight for two minutes and this is what you do! Still, I doubt if it's spoiled your appetite. I've just made girdle scones, and there's a chocolate cake.'

Bill bent to kiss her too. 'Oh, he's used to all this fancy French food now, Gran! He'll be wanting gâteau, at the every least.'

'He can wait for gâteau if he likes. I'll have Gran's chocolate cake meantime,' Cat said, laughing, and they all went in together, leaving Marjory to follow behind.

At the table, she heard the details about the accident, the hospital, the flight home – 'Took me up on a special lift, Gran – it was really cool!' – and Cammie did indeed do justice to his tea. But Marjory could see how tired he was, and when he'd refused a third slice of chocolate cake, she said, 'Cammie, you're out on your feet. Come on and I'll help you up to bed.'

'Yeah, I think I'll turn in.' He struggled to his feet. 'But Dad can give me a hand – he's had a bit of practice.' He didn't say it, but he hadn't met her eyes, and the words 'and you haven't' hung in the air.

'I'll come up too,' Cat said quickly. 'I want to unpack.'

They all went out together. Fleming's eyes prickled. She got up quickly and started clearing the table. Janet, in unhappy silence, did the same.

It was a few minutes later that Bill came downstairs. He gave Marjory a brief smile and said a little stiffly, 'So how are things down at the station?'

'Oh, great,' she said ironically. 'I've been suspended.'

Bill stared at her in astonishment. 'Suspended? What the hell for?'

'Read all about it in the papers tomorrow. I'm a monster who more or less murdered one of Britain's screen legends, and I'm a bad mother who puts her career before her child. I'm not surprised that no one wants to speak to me.'

Her eyes were too full of tears to see her mother quietly leave the room, or to see Bill come over to her. She was wiping them fiercely when she felt Bill's arms round her.

'Hey, come on! I'm sorry, I did think you made the wrong call, but actually you were right – Cammie didn't need you. His feelings are a bit hurt, that's all, and he'll get over it.

'Sit down, blow your nose, and tell me all about it.'

Feeding her hens the next morning, Marjory was feeling better. The sun was shining, it was the best sort of April day when you could almost see the grass growing and smell spring in the air. Bill had, as usual, talked her into a sense of proportion about it and he'd told the kids what had happened, which had made them both more sympathetic when she apologized to Cammie and tried to explain why she had felt she must stay.

Marjory still had work to do there, though. She and
Cammie had always had a happy relationship; now the job
had come directly between them, and she'd have to convince
him that this didn't mean he wasn't still one of the three
absolute priorities in her life.

Well, she'd have a week or two free to show him just how
much he did matter. She'd be on hand to look after him,
ferry him to and fro, have long conversations – though to be
realistic, long conversations had never much been Cammie's
style.

There was a good number of eggs this morning, and she
quite fancied a leisurely breakfast – there was nothing like
a new-laid boiled egg. She came back into the house in a
cheerful mood.

It was only later that the blow fell. When she had spoken
to Bailey, she put the phone down slowly. That wouldn't be
speedy reinstatement; that would be weeks at the very least.
And what would she do with all these empty days?

'Mum, you know there was a bit of a fuss about Dad and the
Ailsa Grant case?' Marjory had come in to see her mother
when she came back from Stranraer, where she'd been doing
her shopping. The press, after a couple of torrid days, had
lost interest, but she almost found sympathetic enquiries
from chance-met friends in Kirkluce harder to deal with.

'Och yes. They gave him a reprimand, but he never let it
bother him.'

So Angus had told Janet about it after all – Marjory had
wondered about that, and wrongly concluded that pride had
led him to keep quiet about it.

'It was because he allowed the Grants to take Ailsa's body
back home, instead of leaving it by the lighthouse to be taken
direct to the mortuary. Did you know that?'

Janet shook her head. 'No. He never told me much about the job. Sometimes I thought it would be better if he did, but—' She gave a little sigh. 'That was just Angus.'

'So there's no point in asking you why he ignored the rule book? It wasn't like him.'

Janet shook her head again. Then she said slowly, 'Mind you, I know a woman who lived at the lighthouse then. Heather Fairlie – she stays down near Drummore. She's a fair clatter-vengeance – her tongue never stops. You could ask her.'

'Goodness, I'd forgotten about Mrs Fairlie,' Marjory said. 'She gave a helpful interview to Tansy and Andy Mac. Thanks for reminding me. I was planning to take a drive down that way this afternoon anyway.'

Janet looked at her anxiously. 'You know your own business, but I'm just wondering if it's maybe wise to do that, with the way things are just now.'

'Oh, I just want to refresh my memory,' her daughter said airily. 'I've peace just now to think about the other case. I'm not planning to put my neck on the line – I'm not daft.'

It had been wet when Fleming left Mains of Craigie, but it was clearing up now. She switched off the wipers and as the sun appeared pulled down the visor, squinting into the sharp, watery light.

She didn't much enjoy the long, solitary drive. The worries about her own future were bad enough, but going over and over what had happened was worse.

The denouement in the country-house drawing room hadn't been about getting the job done. It hadn't been about justice, or even about retribution for the sake of the dead man, who had only by chance not been a murderer himself. It had been about demonstrating her cleverness in outwitting a clever killer – or two, rather, since Fleming had believed Sylvia Lascelles to be complicit at the very least, though she had underestimated that redoubtable woman's direct involvement.

It had been foolish to ignore procedure, but much more importantly, what she did had been lacking in humanity. No wonder Tam was disgusted. She was pretty disgusted herself.

As Janet had said, it probably wasn't wise to come down to Balnakenny today, but there was one loose end in the Lindsay/Pavansky enquiry which kept niggling away at her. It shouldn't cause trouble: the Grants could simply refuse to answer her question, and probably would.

The whole can of worms about Ailsa's parentage she would leave unopened. Fascinating though this was, it had nothing to do with Pavany's murder, and when – if! – she was reinstated, she would get back to the cold case and review it all then.

There was nothing to stop her thinking about it, though. If Robert Grant had a grudge against the bastard child his wife had brought to the marriage along with the rundown farm that was Lazansky's silence money, followed by years of disgust and resentment at having allowed himself to be bought, Ailsa's return pregnant might have induced the sort of simmering rage that could erupt into violence.

But there was Gavin Hodge too. The threat of losing his comfortable life and the promise of future wealth was a solid motive for killing an inconvenient girlfriend. Heather Fairlie had said Ailsa definitely believed she was to be married. He could be leaned on a bit more, but that was most definitely for another time. The Hodges would not be sympathetic to an unofficial enquiry.

But today, she would at least be able to ask Heather if by any chance she knew why Angus Laird had thrown away the rule book. Like father like daughter, she thought with a wry smile.

At last, she could see the lighthouse looming ahead, dominating the skyline. There was the track to Balnakenny now, and with just a whisper of misgiving about what she was doing, she turned up it.

A man was working with a roll of barbed wire, mending a fence by the track. He turned his head and when he straightened up at her approach, Fleming saw it was Stuart Grant. He didn't speak, but she could sense from the way he approached her that his attitude was less hostile than before.

She lowered the window. 'Mr Grant, could you spare me a minute of your time?'

For some reason, this seemed to amuse him. A sour smile came to his face. 'Oh aye, I reckon I could.'

'It's not official. I want to emphasize that. It's just something I want to know for my personal satisfaction.

'When I was last here, I noticed you wore Caterpillar boots like my husband's.' He was wearing them now, she noticed. 'Did you stand in the shrubbery at Tulach House and watch Marcus Lindsay?'

'Yes, I did.' He spoke with surprising vehemence. 'And I'll tell you why, too. That lying old bitch up there –' he jerked his head back towards the farmhouse – 'got me to do it. Wound me up and pointed me, and it's time you heard the truth. We'll do this inside.'

Totally taken aback, Fleming stammered, 'Mr Grant, this may not be appropriate. As I said, I'm not here in an official capacity.'

'Better, maybe,' was all he said, walking off towards the house.

★　　★　　★

There was no sign of Jean Grant. Stuart had taken Fleming, once more, into the front sitting room. Glancing round, Fleming noticed immediately that the photographs had gone, including the one of Jean as a bride with the husband this farm had bought her. Had she decided that some curve of the dress might give away her secret to suspicious eyes?

In contrast to his former reluctance to speak, Stuart barely waited for her to sit down before he began talking. 'I heard the news on the radio so I reckon you know now that I never touched the man. Never even spoke to him, in fact.

'My mother told me he got Ailsa pregnant and killed her, only no one could prove it. She wanted me to go and beat him up, to show him we hadn't forgotten. Last week was to be my chance. He was never there, usually.

'He had to know it was Ailsa's revenge – I was to tell him that. I think my mother probably reckoned I'd get angry, and kill him – I've a temper, you know.

'But, well – long time ago, wasn't it? I went and watched the house a couple of nights. But there was no point – I wasn't going to break in like a thief. I saw him at a window a couple of times and maybe if he'd come out, I'd have spoken to him, had a bit of a barney, but he didn't. Somehow, anyway . . .' He paused, then shrugged his shoulders. 'Like I said, it was a long time ago, whatever I might have felt at the time.

'Then two of your lot came to the farm, after Marcus got stabbed. They said he was in America all that year, and I got to thinking. Why was my mother telling me Marcus was the father, when she'd been told he definitely wasn't?'

'Yes,' Fleming said. 'That struck me too.'

'I had a bit of a look around. There were two things I found.' He put his hand into the inside pocket of the weatherproof jacket he was wearing and handed her the first of them.

It was the deeds to the farm, showing it had been bought by Ladislaw Lazansky, then gifted to Jean. 'Yes,' Fleming said. 'I knew about that.'

'I didn't. Ailsa wondered, sometimes, why she was so different. She didn't know. My mother never told her why she shouldn't have anything to do with Marcus, why he dumped her like that. I guess he was told?'

Fleming nodded.

'This is the other thing.' He handed her the paper he was holding in his hand.

Fleming looked at it, and gasped. 'Why . . .?'

'She can tell you herself. She's not getting out of this.' He got up and went out, leaving Fleming staring at the paper he had given her.

Jean Grant, when she came in, seemed smaller than Fleming remembered her, diminished by impotence, perhaps. Her expression was still hard, though, and she turned a rancorous look on her son as he pushed her, ungently, into a chair. She didn't look at the inspector.

'Mrs Grant,' Fleming said, 'why did you lie about this?' She held up the piece of paper.

Jean Grant looked at it. She did not cry; tears simply welled up, rolling down her cheeks unchecked. She seemed oblivious to them.

'Why should he have his son, when I lost my daughter?' she said. 'It was his son's fault – he broke my Ailsa's heart. She was bright, shining, the best thing in my life – not like this.' She cast a contemptuous glance at the man, silent now, sitting opposite her.

'She came back from Glasgow, destroyed. I knew he was in Glasgow – I knew it was him, when she didn't tell me the father, and by the time she came home it was too late anyway to get rid of that – that disgusting child. Not that I told her. There was no need for her to know my shame, and maybe it would have been . . . normal, anyway.

'Yes, she took her own life. But he killed her, as surely as if he'd pushed her himself. So I wanted him – and his father – to suffer. What's wrong with that? They ruined my life, twice over. Why should they escape?

'Oh, but he was clever – he fixed it so no one would ever know. You didn't catch him out, did you? It's only now he's getting what he deserves, and another man had to die first.'

'He wasn't the father, Mrs Grant.'

'If it wasn't him, why wouldn't she tell me? We were close, up till then.' Disbelieving, Jean glared at Fleming, demanding an answer she believed she wouldn't get.

'Because,' Fleming said gently, 'the man was married. She believed, I think, right up to the end, that if she kept quiet about it, when the moment came he would leave his wife and marry her.'

Jean's face went blank for a moment, her body rigid with shock.

Fleming went on, 'When he told her he wouldn't—'

Jean interrupted, eyes suddenly bright with anger. 'Who was it? I want to know, who killed my daughter?'

Before Fleming could answer, Stuart leaned forward. 'You did,' he said. 'You and my father. You made her life – look, she says here –' he snatched the paper back from Fleming and pointed, ' "a living hell". Once he'd let her down, what could she do?'

And Fleming suddenly understood. *You have left me with no alternative*, Ailsa had written in her tragic, tear-blistered letter. *My hands are tied.*

And she had tied them so that she wouldn't struggle and would die more quickly, poor, poor sad girl, betrayed on every side, hungry for a life with excitement and warmth and colour. Yet, when it had come to the moment, as she was in free fall flying through the tempest to the cruel sea below, she had fought to release herself – and succeeded. But she had changed her mind far, far too late, when her only destiny was Death, the lover she had spoken of in her last, haunting words to her mother – 'He's waiting for me now. I must go to him.'

Badly shaken, Fleming drove away from Balnakenny, but at the end of the track, paused. Her work here was done; perhaps Ailsa Grant's troubled spirit could find rest now the truth about her passing had been told.

She could turn left, go back to Kirkluce, where despite her suspension she would get a warm welcome from Donald Bailey. His reputation would be preserved when the case was quietly closed, and it might even do Fleming herself a considerable amount of good, given her discretion in handling it.

But somehow . . . She turned right, parked the car at the lighthouse and got out.

It was a beautiful afternoon now, with a clear sky and a soft breeze. In the far distance, she could see the other coasts – England, Ireland – and hear below her the sounds from the nurseries: the demanding brays of seagull chicks and the screaming of their parents as they filled the day with their domestic duties.

Fleming walked on along the headland, heading for the spot where Ailsa had most likely jumped to her death. Her father had been right all along in his stubborn refusal to accept the official view, and she had no need now to imagine dramatic scenarios, only the drama of a young woman who could see no future she cared to live for.

She looked down. She couldn't imagine the sort of despair that would drive you over the edge to the sea below, still foaming round the foot of the cliffs even on this calm and peaceful day. Poor, poor Ailsa.

At her feet, sea pinks were growing in tufts out of the springy turf, beautiful, surprisingly delicate, in this harsh, salt-sprayed environment. Marjory picked handfuls, collecting them from across the headland, then went back to the edge. She threw them into the offshore breeze.

So light, they were! But they drifted down, down, some falling on the edge, some blowing back into the cliff-face, and just a few reaching the waves below, though by that time, they were too far away for her to see.

Marjory wasn't really in the mood for the full array of scones, cakes and biscuits, but there they all were, laid out for her, so she had to do her best.

Heather Fairlie had greeted her warmly. 'I've heard such a lot about you! How's your mother? I was so sorry about your poor father, but Janet will cope – she always does. Never happy unless she's busy.'

'Oh yes, she's amazing,' Marjory agreed uncomfortably. She hadn't been exactly sensitive to her mother's need to be needed – not to mention other things.

'Anyway, my dear, how can I help you? Just start with some of that tea-loaf – the dried fruit gets boiled in tea first, and though I say it myself, it gives a lovely rich flavour.'

'Delicious,' Marjory said, though she would hardly have known if it had been boiled in washing-up liquid. This was her last chance to find out why her father had risked his professional reputation for a girl whose loose behaviour he would most definitely have deplored.

She took a deep breath. 'Heather, you know when Ailsa's

body was brought ashore, that my father agreed to let the Grants have her home until the ambulance arrived? It wasn't correct procedure. Do you have any idea why he did that?'

Heather hesitated. 'Well, yes, I do. It surprised me, I have to say, for you'd never have said your father was exactly a sympathetic man. You maybe won't like it, mind – I don't know.'

Fleming steeled herself.

'He said, "If that was my daughter, and this had happened to her, I wouldn't want her lying there. I'd want her at home." '

Marjory never knew how she had got out of there without breaking down. She had finished the tea, had a slice of coffee and walnut cake, then pleaded urgent business.

She drove from Drummore to a point where she could park by the shore, and then got out. It was classic April weather: the rain had come on again, glancing silvery showers. Bareheaded, she scrambled down on to the stretch of beach, with its view across Luce Bay.

The rain misted her hair and bloomed on her cheeks. She picked up a smooth stone and skimmed it across the water, but after three skips it puddled and sank.

Marjory's throat was tight with tears. Her relationship with her father had always been complicated. She had spent her life striving for his affection, his respect, and, she had always felt, failing because he demanded perfection, and on his terms. Yet, when Ailsa Grant, a 'fallen woman' to him, had been brought ashore and laid on the ground, Angus Laird had risked censure to spare her lifeless body indignity.

He and his daughter had both set aside rules and procedure. His punishment had been a black mark on an unblemished record; hers, she didn't yet know. He – rigid, uncompromising, puritanical in his daughter's eyes – had acquired his for too much humanity. While she . . .

As she gazed blindly out to sea, Marjory's shoulders drooped. Where did that leave her? She had always seen herself as compassionate both personally and professionally, but by her own standards, she had failed.

She threw another stone as hard and as far as she could, into the sea, then, sick at heart, went back to her car and drove away.